GAY HOLIDAY PACKAGE

Three Romantic Novels by

ANTHONY MCDONALD

Spring Sonata
The Paris Novel
The Van Gogh Window

Anchor Mill Publishing

Anchor Mill Publishing
4/04 Anchor Mill
Paisley PA1 1JR
SCOTLAND
anchormillpublishing@gmail.com

The cover illustration shows *Study of Bathing Boys* by
Henry Scott Tuke.

CONTENTS

SPRING SONATA

First published 2014

A quickie on Hampstead Heath. An invitation to play chamber music in the Dordogne. These two pole-star events will between them set the course of young theatre manager Robbie's future life. More than one grand passion lies in store for him during his next twenty-five years. Chris, Jeremy and Luke will all spend time with him in the countryside and elegant houses of southern France. But with whom will he find himself lying out under the stars when the beautiful music stops? Originally published as Gay Romance: Spring Sonata, 2014.

Dedicated to the memory of Antony Linford, and to Stephen Gee

ONE

This story began in 1981…

I just about knew that Luke had a place in the Dordogne. But then I only just about knew Luke. He lived across the road from my parents' house in Putney.

'Luke's taking some of his pupils down to the Dordogne for a holiday course at Easter,' my mum told me when I was round there one February Sunday for lunch.

'Sounds fun,' I said. I tried not to feel envious. Luke was professor at the Kensington College of Music. I had wanted to go to music college when I was younger but I didn't play well enough.

Saying that Luke was a professor makes him sound as old as God. Actually he was in his early thirties, just ten or so years older than me. Quite by chance I ran into him in the road later when I was on my way back to the tube station. We knew each other well enough to exchange a few words when our paths did cross. 'I hear you're giving a chamber music course in the Dordogne,' I said. The words just tumbled out somehow. I hadn't planned to say that; I wouldn't have dreamt of it.

'Yes,' he said. 'Care to join us?'

The words astonished me. The casual way he said them shocked me even more. It actually hurt. Because there was nothing I'd have liked to do better. Though I couldn't say that. I laughed and said, 'Don't wind me up.'

He turned a bit serious. 'Well, I said that lightly but … it wasn't a wind-up. I am actually looking for a spare pianist.'

I shook my head, more in surprise than anything else. 'I don't play,' I said.

His brows knitted for a second. 'Yes you do. I've heard you.'

I'd always been glad that Luke lived opposite my parents' house and not next door to it. I would have hated him to overhear my clumsy rampages with Beethoven and Chopin on their upright piano. I said, 'Oh God.'

Luke shrugged slightly. 'You sound all right from out in the road, he said. 'Though distance lends enchantment perhaps. When are you next here?'

'Probably next Sunday,' I said.

'Well if you want to drop in and play me something...' He shrugged again. 'I'd like to hear you play – just out of curiosity. Chamber music course or no chamber music course.'

'OK,' I said.

'Bring something you're comfy with,' he said, now sounding quite earnest. 'Nothing too difficult. Don't try to dazzle me, because you won't be able to. Know any Mozart?'

There was an upright piano in the foyer of the little fringe theatre where I worked. I used to play on it in my lunch breaks and in the gap before the audience arrived for the evening show. Now, I was on it every spare second I had. 'You're going at that like the clappers,' someone commented. 'You got an audition or something?'

'I don't know,' I said. 'It might be something like that.'

People say Mozart's piano sonatas are easy. They're only easy if you don't know how. They're full of little details, little difficulties, that occur only once and which you manage easily the first time you sight-read the piece, but which will trip you up the next time you attempt it

... and for ever after if you don't work like mad to get on top of them.

I decided not to give hostages to fortune by working up one of the more complex or fiddly sonatas. Or one of the ones with very fast finales. I chose the small, modest but beautifully proportioned sonata in B flat, K570. At least Luke would know I wasn't trying to dazzle him with that.

I didn't really know why I was doing this. Luke surely wasn't serious about wanting me to go on this chamber music course. Even if he was, it would be hideously expensive. A residential course – tuition, accommodation and food – and in France, right down in the south. There was no way I'd be able to afford all that. Plus, I'd never be able to get the time off work. But sometimes in life you find yourself just doing something, even if there can be no possible gain from it. You do it because you just feel you have to do it. Which is why I spent every moment of my free time during that week practising Mozart.

I'd never been inside Luke's house before. It was about the same size as my parents'. Nothing inside it looked particularly new. It wasn't the sort of place that a thirty-year-old lives in on his own unless both his parents have died and he's been left it, or else he's trapped where he is by the fact of owning a concert-size grand piano. Or both. I was pretty sure that in Luke's case it was both.

His piano was a Bechstein. Built before the First World War. You can tell by the legs. The legs of Luke's Bechstein were machine-turned, bulbous and elaborate. Later instruments have plain, straight legs.

Luke didn't offer me coffee, although it was eleven am. I was quite glad of that. I just wanted to get the thing done.

Old Bechsteins are difficult to play. The keys resist you strongly if you touch them lightly. You apply a bit more pressure ... and they go down with a bang. Like when cracking eggs into a bowl: it's difficult to apply exactly the right degree of force. It took me most of the first movement to get the measure of the instrument. It came out lumpy, and some soft notes didn't sound at all. I managed the slow movement better, willing myself to go on and not give up. Then somehow the last movement came out more or less all right.

'Well done,' Luke said when I'd finished. 'Would you like a drink?'

I said I would. Happily he didn't mean a coffee. We had a can of lager each.

'So, what about joining us on this chamber music course next month?' Luke said.

'I just can't,' I said. 'I couldn't possibly find the money. And even if I could, I'd be a fish out of water, among young professionals...'

'Hmm,' said Luke with a frown. Oddly enough, when he frowned he looked rather nice. 'Actually I need a bit of help with the course. Someone to do the admin stuff. You're an arts administrator – or so your mum told me once.'

'Well, up to a point,' I said. If ordering beer supplies, changing the roller-towels and doing the Friday payroll was arts administration – well, I did do that. 'I'm in a very junior post...'

'I wouldn't be asking you to do much,' Luke went on, suddenly sounding – to my astonishment – as though he needed me more than either of us had thought up to that point. 'Write a letter or two perhaps, beforehand. Helping Mrs Fox do the shopping when we're out there. Can you speak French? Keeping a record of money in and money out... That's all I'd want. In return you'd get your transport, food and accommodation free. You'd get to work on a Mozart trio with young professionals...' He smiled at me. 'You might even learn a bit.'

'Bloody hell,' I said. Then, 'Sorry, I didn't mean it to sound like that. I mean, I'd love to. It's just a bit of an overwhelming thought. I don't know if I could get the time off work.'

'You'd know if you asked,' Luke said, just throwing the words out casually. I warmed to him for the way he said that.

'I do speak a bit of French,' I said, remembering his earlier question, which he hadn't given me time to answer. 'At least, I've got an A level in it.'

'Good,' said Luke. 'Mrs Fox's French is non-existent.'

We had a visiting company at the theatre the next week. I helped with the get-in and fit-up on Monday morning. It was a way of making a bit of extra cash before my real job started in the afternoon, with ferrying the weekend's takings to the bank. A visiting company meant a visiting stage management team and a visiting light-and-sound guy too. Sometimes these temporary people got on well with our resident crew, sometimes they fought like cat and dog. Till the week was under way you didn't know which it would be. It was always a bit of a toss-up.

This week was a lucky one. The visiting team blended seamlessly with the resident one and we all went out for a beer together before the half-hour call on Monday evening. I found I was getting along very well with the visiting light-and-sound man. He was a couple of years older than me, I guessed. He wasn't especially handsome, but he had a nice physique hidden beneath his jeans and T-shirt, I thought, and an alert and smiling face. Also a soft furry moustache. His name was Chris. But the half-hour call put a punctual end to our conversation. The Half, which was actually called precisely thirty-five minutes before curtain-up, was the most sacred moment in the day's schedule and was observed religiously. Being Late for the Half was one of the few things – another was Being Drunk on Stage – for which you could be summarily dismissed.

After the show the bar stayed open a bit, just for the actors and the crew, with me dispensing the drinks. And then I turned the lights out and locked up. I went outside to unlock my push-bike, which was chained to the railings, and found that Chris was unlocking his own bicycle which was next to mine. He looked up when he saw me and said, 'Fine evening.'

'Yes,' I said. 'Yes it is.'

'Fancy going for a bit of a ride before heading home?' he said in an artless voice.

'Where to?' I asked. I felt amazingly calm, given the circumstances. Given my nervous disposition. I knew what was happening here. Even before he answered my question.

'Hampstead Heath'

It's all uphill to Hampstead Heath, whatever your starting point. We didn't have mountain bikes or anything sophisticated. Just a three-speed gear-box each. For large sections of the way we had to dismount and walk.

What did we talk about? Nothing important. Nothing suggestive was said. Nor did we touch each other. When we were walking we needed both hands for our bikes. We knew what we were up for. We didn't need to test the water or pre-empt events.

I knew when we'd arrived at the right part of Hampstead Heath, though the place – presumably familiar to Chris – was new to me. I could tell by the scattering of red cigarettes that shone like glow-worms in the dark, and brightened as the invisible smokers inhaled on them if we drew close.

But we weren't interested in those others. We'd come up here to be together, just Chris and me, and I became even more aware of this when I suddenly felt Chris's fingers feel for my fingers, and then clasp them, in the dark.

Chris evidently had a particular spot in mind. To me it was just like any other part of the Heath. But as we approached one particular tree he stopped, laid his bike down on the grass – an action I copied – then turned to face me. Then he slowly put his arms around my waist and drew me close in to him, so I could feel his tummy and his erection pressed against mine through jeans. The softness of his clothed tummy, the hardness of his cock, the warmth of both.

'You're shaking,' he said – in a way that I can only describe as *tenderly* – and added, 'Are you sure you're all right with this?'

My own next words surprised me. 'I've never been more all right with anything in my life.'

The next thing that happened: we undid each other's waist-studs and pulled down the zips. With our hands we weighed each other's cocks up. His felt lovely in my fingers. He said, 'My God, Robbie, you're massive.'

I had been told that before. But not often. I hadn't very often had sex.

'Shall we lie down?' Chris said.

We pulled each other to the ground as if in a modern dance, following the movement through with the graceful sliding of our jeans down to below our knees. It never gets totally dark in London. Not even on the Heath. I could see the dim ivory glow of Chris's thighs, lightly hair-sprinkled. And his upright cock between them. The sight was gorgeous.

I heard Chris's voice, now a whisper. 'I'd like you to fuck me. But with that monster of yours… I'm not sure

11

about it.' His tone was respectful, thoughtful. Not lewd or comic. 'Are you OK for me to fuck you instead?'

I said, 'Yes, I think so.' And then I realised that something was about to happen. I didn't want it to happen yet. But I couldn't do anything about it. I said, 'Oh God, I'm going to lose it.' And I did. In an agony of embarrassment. I had to use my own hand, desperately, to get it out of me comfortably, pouring it out across Chris's beautiful sturdy thighs in the dim light.

After that I froze rigid. 'Oh no,' I said. 'Chris, I'm sorry.' I knew at that moment that I couldn't stay. I couldn't let Chris fuck me now. I couldn't even help him get his rocks off with my hand or mouth. I just needed to get out of this place, whatever place this was, into which the promptings of my sex drive had brought me.

I got to my feet, unsteadily. 'Sorry. I can't do anything after I've come.' I felt my whole being reeling giddily. 'Sorry. I just have to go now.'

The awful thing was that no reply came from Chris. There was no, 'That's all right, my friend,' no final touch of his hand on my calf as I left. I just left him, with his trousers down and his prick erect and unfulfilled, lying alone and lonely on the grass, under a tree – at what was presumably his special spot – on Hampstead Heath.

I cycled back home, scarcely needing to pedal at all. From Hampstead Heath to Colville Terrace, just off the Portobello Road, was downhill all the way.

There was another awful thing, of course. I would have to meet Chris next day. When I came in to work.

Our paths crossed in the foyer the next afternoon. 'Hallo, Robbie,' Chris said. His tone was neutral, guarded. At least he spoke.

We were alone in the foyer – a rare event. I was minding the tiny box office: the chap who was on duty there had gone to take a leak. Whether I was glad we were alone or not I was uncertain. At least I had the opportunity to say what I said next. 'I'm sorry about last night.'

He smiled cautiously. 'Don't be. You're a bit less experienced than I thought you were, I guess. Anyway,' Chris looked quickly around the empty space before finishing, 'I got lucky shortly after you left.'

Talk about a rush of mixed emotions! Delighted that Chris hadn't gone unsatisfied, I was furious and churned up at the thought that he'd been satisfied by someone else. Someone other than me.

Though who was I – other than someone he'd gone on a bike ride with, had hugged briefly and who then had shot all over his legs? We hadn't even kissed.

The box office guy came out of the toilet at that moment. The door was right by where Chris and I were talking. 'Drink before the show?' Chris said casually, then, hardly waiting to hear my mumbled yes, walked off and climbed the stairs towards the lighting box above. Without a backward glance.

TWO

I got my afternoon's work finished early, whizzing through the book-keeping as quickly as I could and hoping for the best that it would all cross-add first time. For once it did. This gave me time to do some work on the Mozart trio on the piano in the foyer before I met Chris at the five o'clock break. It wasn't a big or difficult piano part, but I had to be on top of it in a couple of weeks. That's something the professionals routinely do; I had no experience of this.

I hadn't been at it many minutes, breaking off to pencil in my ideas for fingering – I was holding the pencil between my teeth while I played, the way I knew that real pros did – when I heard the sound of plimsolls coming silently down the stairs behind my head. The reason I could hear those silent plimsolls was because they belonged to Chris.

I didn't stop what I was doing. I waited for him to appear beside me or else speak. He did neither of those things. From behind my shoulder he blew gently into my ear. That made me stop. I turned quickly and he laughed at the surprise in my face.

'What are you playing?' he asked.

'It's Mozart,' I said. 'It sounds a bit odd without the violin and cello. It's a piano trio. I'm learning the piano bit.'

'It sounded beautiful,' Chris said. He hadn't said that lightly. I could tell by the expression on his face.

'I've hardly started work on it,' I said. 'It goes much faster than that.'

'Then maybe it's a quality of great music that it sounds wonderful even at the wrong speed.'

'You may be right about that,' I said. 'It is Mozart.'
But I had plucked from that compliment of his to Mozart

a kernel that I thought – or wanted to think – compliment to myself.

'Go on,' he said. 'Are you OK if I sit and liste

I nodded my head. I also noticed his sensi ..y in choosing a place to sit. Some people lean over your shoulder when you're playing, and peer at the score whether they can read music or not. You expect them at any moment to jab a finger at the page to let you know they've noticed that you've played a wrong note. Others position themselves directly behind you at some distance, so you don't know if they're still there or have crept silently out. Or they sit beside the keyboard and, from three feet away, grin encouragingly but off-puttingly into your face.

Chris did none of those things. He placed himself on one of the vinyl-covered benches that lined the bar alcove. About a dozen feet away from me. I could see him in my peripheral vision. Just the shape of him. I didn't have to be distracted by his face.

I sat and practised, absorbed in the task, for half an hour perhaps. Repeating and repeating sections of the first movement. Breaking off to re-finger a passage from time to time. But when he'd heard me reach the final cadence for the third or fourth time Chris got up and walked over to me. From behind me he wrapped his arms lightly round my shoulders. 'That's enough now,' he said quietly. 'Take a break.'

Nobody I'd previously had sex with had spoken to me like that. To my surprise I found I liked it a lot.

We part cycled, part walked, up Fitzjohn's Avenue to one of the pubs at the top, which was called The Holly Bush. Inside it looked like the kind of pub I fondly imagined my parents would have frequented before I was born. A fire in a grate. Hunting scenes on the walls. Leather armchairs and games of crib and shove-halfpenny. No food. Except crisps and pickled eggs.

I reached in my pocket quickly before Chris had time to reach in his. 'Pint of what?' I said.

He wrinkled up his face, which made his pert nose twitch. 'Not sure if I should be doing pints. Evening ahead in the lighting box...' He mugged a grin. 'Don't want to short the place out.'

'Glass of wine?' I suggested. I was determined to be in charge, for now at least. I would propose the drink, making one suggestion after another, until he fell in and accepted. Not until he'd got that down him would I feel I'd done enough to apologise for last night.

'Glass of wine would be nice,' he said.

'Let's have one each,' I said. 'Red or white?'

He gave me a look. His deep blue eyes were suddenly indescribably beautiful. 'Let's do white,' he said. 'Let's go the whole gay hog.'

We actually squeezed in a second glass before cycling down the hill terrifyingly fast. Overtaking buses that were pulling out of stops and accelerating; carving up the traffic at the Finchley Road lights. Some things require desperate measures. Love. War. Being Late for the Half.

Hugh, the box office chap, got to his feet behind his desk as soon as I walked in. 'Where've you been? The Rothschilds are querying the seat numbers we've given them. And there's no bar staff yet.'

I outranked Hugh in the staff hierarchy. Nevertheless he was ten years older than me. And six foot tall against my five feet eight. 'Bar staff should be here,' I said.

'They're not.'

'Caught in traffic like I was, I expect,' I said. 'Ivy'll be here any second, I'm sure. Meanwhile, if you can point me out the Rothschilds I'll go and sort them out.'

Which I did.

When the show was over, the audience had gone, and I was serving drinks to the cast and crew before closing up at eleven o'clock, I found a little routine going on between Chris and me. We were making a point of not standing close or of looking at each other too much; acting as though we hardly knew each other, let alone had a sexual contact. Yet we couldn't help looking over towards each other often and holding each other's gaze each time for a meaningful moment. Nobody could have guessed there was anything going on between us... A fond delusion. Anyone who was remotely observant would have seen it at once.

Then we were outside in the late night air, un-locking our chained bikes. 'Would you like to come back to my place?' I asked.

'Where do you live?'

'The other side of Kilburn. Off the Portobello. Fifteen minutes at most.'

'Yeah,' Chris said, with a deliberate nod that suggested firmness of purpose. 'I'd like that.'

We bumped our bikes down the steps beside the tube station. That was my short-cut down to the junction with Belsize Road. We cycled abreast up the winding little rise to Kilburn High Road, then down again, through derelict, boarded-up Walterton Road where the prostitutes stood around in hope. Past Westbourne Park station, then zigzagging the short-cuts towards Colville Terrace, a few yards short of the Portobello Road. Chris was the same height as me, though chunkier and more solid. His legs filled his jeans out and made them taut. Unlike mine, which were still at the skinny stage. I noticed the look of his legs particularly when he was on his bike. Especially when he occasionally got a foot or two in front.

We lifted our bikes up the front steps at Colville Terrace, I let us in and we chained them to the banisters in the uncarpeted hall. 'Take the lamps with us,' I said. 'I've lost one or two from here in the past.'

Up flights of stairs, then in through the huge front doorway of the flat I shared.

'God, it's like time travel,' Chris said, as we made our way round disorienting corridors that were narrow, because cluttered with tall furniture, and about nine feet high. He was right. The place might have looked much the same in the nineteen-twenties.

'Bloody hell! Where are you taking me?' he asked as we rounded the final corner and faced the last leg of the journey to my room. It lay down steps inside a glassed-in bridge. It gave the impression of a terraced greenhouse, with pot-plants ranged on the steps, and on shelves at waist height, down both sides.

'Nearly there,' I said. 'My room's at the bottom.'

At last we were inside. There was my iron-framed bed, my kitchen alcove, the familiar rush matting on the floor. My place was self-contained – except it lacked a private bathroom. I shared the communal one at the top end of the greenhouse bridge. With four other people who I hardly knew. Nobody thought anything of that back then.

I shut the door behind us. I turned and looked at Chris. He looked at me and smiled. 'Let's get undressed,' he said. 'We won't rush things. But if you come too soon again, don't worry. I won't run away if you won't.' His smile became an impish, moustache-framed grin. 'We've got all night if we want it. Plenty of time to have a second go.'

We took our own clothes off, then turned and appraised the result. I thought Chris looked lovely naked. His tapering cock stood proud in front of him. Like a figurehead at his prow, I thought. He said, 'You're dead gorgeous, Robbie. Thinner than you look when you're wearing clothes. You're like a skinned rabbit. Mmmm. You're just great.'

By the time he'd got to the end of his verdict he had already embraced me and was running his hands up and down my back and through my hair. The *Mmmm* was hummed into the side of my neck as he rested his lips there. The *You're just great* was whispered in my ear.

More cautiously I wrapped my arms around his back, then suddenly found I'd taken the initiative and kissed him boldly on the lips. Our noses pressed together like two thumbs. He kissed me back. Neither of us went any further with our tongues than each other's front teeth. As Chris had pointed out, we had all night. For the moment he disengaged his lips, though still kept holding me. 'Come on,' he said. 'There's a bed right handy here. Let's get you into it.'

It wasn't a bad idea. There was a small gas fire in the room, the gas supply controlled by a coin meter. Normally the first thing I did when I entered the room was to light it. Tonight I'd been otherwise occupied. I didn't even light it now.

'Don't touch my cock for a bit,' Chris said. 'I'll try not to touch yours. Just cuddle for a bit. OK?'

I nodded my reply, letting him feel the nod against his cheek. I saw the good sense in what he'd said. We stroked and fondled each other, arms, backs, heads and legs, allowing our calves to rub up and down each other like grasshoppers or crickets. But they were softer and warmer than the calves of crickets and rubbing them together was much more fun than grasshoppers dreamt of.

We might have agreed not to touch each other's cock, and we didn't touch them with our hands. But the cocks themselves had other ideas. They found each other constantly, either on purpose or by accident. Mine broad-headed, cut, and Chris's, slightly smaller, tapering and with an elegantly hooded, cone-shaped tip. They nuzzled each other at frequent intervals and gave each other wet kisses, and I was hugely pleased with myself for managing not to come precipitately and all over the shop.

'Would you mind lighting the gas fire?' Chris suddenly said.

'Light the fire?' I'd never got up to light the fire after I'd gone to bed.

'It's just that the sheets'll slip off if we do anything energetic and it'll be...' he chuckled, '...fucking freezing.'

I got out of bed and it was exactly as Chris had described it. Crouching naked and shivering in front of the fire I struck a match and lit it, acutely conscious of my hard-on jutting between my compressed thighs.

Turning back to the bed I found Chris had pulled the covers right back so that I had a full view of him, complete with wagging erection between his raised, spread knees. He was looking into my eyes. 'Why don't you just climb aboard and go for it,' he said.

'I thought you thought I'd be too big for you,' I said.

'I'm over that now,' he said. He raised his eyebrows for a second in a what-the-hell kind of way. 'Just use plenty of spit. On yourself and inside me.'

I followed his instructions to the letter. Knelt between his legs at first while I anointed both of us, then lowered myself – my rabbit haunches, rabbit elbows and rabbit chest – onto him, then pushed my far from rabbit-size penis up against the tight whorl of his sphincter. It didn't go in easily: I had to push hard. I could see that it was hurting Chris a bit. 'Do you want me to stop?' I asked.

'Go on,' he said. 'I'll be fine once you're right inside.'

I struggled and wriggled and pushed my way in with difficulty, like a cat burglar who's growing too big for his job. Twice I thought I would lose my load on the way in, but by pausing for a judicious moment each time and trying to think of other things (trying to remember the next morning's soft drinks order was sometimes a good one) I managed to get the whole way in. I stopped when I hit the buffers. At which point I felt Chris relax, and saw him smile fondly up at me. 'Now go for it,' he said. And I did.

Although I'd been on the receiving end a couple of times in my life, this was the first time I'd fucked another human being. I think I forgot to mention that.

Sometimes, half an hour after you've both come, you know that's the end of the experience and one of you gets up and, with no hard feelings on either side, gets dressed and goes home. But it wasn't like that for the two of us this night. Chris said, after we'd both rested and I'd come out of him, 'Is it OK if I stay the night with you?'

I said, 'I'd like that too.'

I'd come inside him and he had come over his tummy, with some help from my hand and, at the end, his own. Now he said, 'I need to get up, though, and use the loo.'

'Of course,' I said. I'd shown him where it was, at the top of the greenhouse bridge of steps. He went up there naked. I reckoned he was unlikely to bump into one of the other denizens of the place, as it was nearly two.

In the morning we were ravenously hungry. We hadn't had anything to eat the night before. 'What time are you in?' I asked him.

'Not till about lunchtime,' he said.

'Same as me, more or less,' I said. 'If you want to put the kettle on and get some coffee sorted, I'll nip out and get a loaf of crusty bread and something to put on it.'

When I came back a few minutes later Chris was still naked, drinking coffee in front of the gas fire, which he'd lit. 'I got kippers,' I told him. 'Is that OK? To eat with the bread?'

'Sounds perfect,' he said. Then while I heated the smoky kippers in butter on the stove he carefully removed the sweater and jeans I'd thrown on, with nothing underneath, in order to go out shopping. We ate our kippers and crusty new, buttered bread, naked at my small table, over our morning hard-ons – or hards-on: whichever it is.

'Cocks and kippers,' said Chris thoughtfully, between mouthfuls. 'Title of your future autobiography, perhaps?'

'Or yours,' I said with a laugh.

After breakfast we got back into bed again. 'You can borrow my razor and toothbrush before we go to work,' I told him, just so he'd know we still had nothing to hurry for. Then Chris laid me on my back and, in a role reversal of last night's action, gently and meditatively fucked me while we looked with a degree of wonder into each other's blue eyes.

THREE

'Your playing's changed since yesterday,' said Tanya. She was the designer who was working on the next show. She was walking through the foyer but stopped as she got up to the piano where I sat practising my Mozart.

'What do you mean?' I said, stopping and turning round. I heard myself giggle with embarrassment as I spoke.

'Is there a new man in your life?'

God, how women managed so often to hit the nail smack on the head. 'Could be,' I said. But I giggled again and, this time, felt myself starting to blush.

Tanya laughed, and a wonderful light came into her eyes. 'That makes two of you around the place this afternoon. Everyone's been listening to Chris whistling as he works in the lighting box.'

I didn't have a reply to that. Actually I did. It came in the form of a deepening of my blush. I felt the prickly hotness of it and could guess all too easily the vivid shade of fuchsia on my face. It told Tanya everything that she – and the rest of the theatre – needed to know. I could see that in her face.

But she confirmed it anyway. 'Well, I think that's lovely. For both of you. Just great.' She went on her way and I went back, with renewed energy, to Mozart.

'I'll need to get back to my place tonight,' Chris said, over our five-thirty drink at the Holly Bush. 'Get a change of kit.'

'Of course,' I said. I waited for him to say, *You come back with me of course,* but he did not. The pause grew embarrassingly extended. 'You going back straight after the show?' I asked. My voice had become small and timid. I was dreading the answer yes.

He said, 'We could go up to the Heath, I guess.'

'Yeah,' I said. 'Let's do that.'

He must have seen the anxiety on my face. Despite the fact that we were sitting on stools at a public bar and there were other people all around, he reached across and placed his hand on my knee. 'It's all right, Robbie.' The gentlest of smiles appeared through his moustache. 'It's all all right.'

Cycling back down Fitzjohn's Avenue, with the trees above us just starting to break bud, with the wind in our faces, not needing to pedal... It felt like flying. With the sight of Chris just half a bike-length ahead and beside me, his confident shoulders and his curly head, his sturdy thighs and rounded calves, his firm buttocks on the saddle – that bum of his into whose private space I'd last night inserted my cock... I doubted that heaven could be as good as this.

And even when, some hours later we struggled back up that very same hill, all the panting way to the Heath, a little way beyond the Holly Bush at the top, it still felt like paradise.

We found our way back to Chris's favourite spot, near the tree, but finding it already occupied by another pair of men, writhing, trousers down and shirts up, ivory-skinned in the moonlight, we moved a little way further on and tumbled each other to the ground on another grassy space.

'You go for it this time if you want,' I said. And this time, when we'd cuddled a bit, he pulled both our pairs of jeans down a little way – for obvious reasons mine needed to go down rather further than his – and took up a position behind me as we lay on our sides on the grass. Then he entered me smoothly and gently – very differently from the blunt-ended way I'd pushed myself into him last night – and we moved and rocked together, his hand grasping and pulling my dick, until we'd both come. He inside me. Me in a little outpouring on the grass.

After that we cuddled together for a bit. But not for long. The grass was night-damp. 'OK,' said Chris after a while, disentangling himself. 'Better get off.'

'Yep,' I said in a businesslike way as we both got up and, after brushing stray bits of leaf and grass from our naked middle sections, did our jeans back up. Then we wheeled our bikes to the edge of the Heath. To Whitestones Pond. At which point...

'Right. That's your way and this is mine,' he said, nodding in those two directions with his head. I knew he lived at Gospel Oak. That he'd naturally head down East Heath Road while I returned down Heath Street and through Hampstead Village to Fitzjohn's Avenue and the rest of my road home beyond that. My head knew that. But now I discovered that my heart did not. I'd had no idea of how much this moment was going to hurt. Even when he leaned over and gave me a bike-to-bike peck on the cheek it hurt. But then he said, 'See you in the morning – or afternoon. Maybe we can do your place tomorrow night.' That *maybe* didn't put everything all right. It didn't light my road home for me. But it was better than nothing. A little wavering match-flame, burning for a brief moment in the dark.

Why had he said, 'Better get off?' like that. Last night there had seemed no impediment to his staying for ever – except for the lack of a wash-bag and a wardrobe of clothes. I knew nothing about the place he lived, except its rough location. I supposed he shared a flat with mates or strangers, the way most of us at the theatre did, except for those older people who were already married or shacked up with the person of their choice. The possibility now ran shivering through my mind, as I cycled past the Walterton Road prostitutes, that Chris might be among that latter set.

I wondered what would have happened if I'd stayed the course on Monday night and not run off like a shocked kid. Would he have said, 'Better get off,' after he'd fucked me? Would I have been surprised, or hurt, if he had? I thought, probably not. What a difference there can be between a Monday night and a Wednesday night when there's been a Tuesday night in between.

But in the morning I felt better. It was daytime and the sun was shining, for a start. I cycled to the theatre around noon, though I didn't need to be there before two. And when Chris, who didn't need to be there till about three, turned up on his bike just a few minutes after I did my spirits flew upwards like a kite. We pottered in our different departments for a bit, catching up with fiddlesome unnecessary jobs just for the sake of it. To fill the time. To be near each other. The theatre building was tiny. People likened it to a shoe-box. The staircase in the foyer led to a small corridor above. Off the corridor led only three doors. The first opened into the office I shared with the theatre secretary, the second was the director's and manager's shared office. The third was the electricians' den – which in turn led to the lighting box. Pottering in our respective domains this morning Chris and I were never more than ten feet apart. And in the nature of things we often found ourselves needing to use the corridor to go to other places, and we ran into each other every time we did. Roughly every ten minutes.

We'd run out of things to do by one o'clock. We went across the road to the enormous Swiss-style pub that stood on the traffic island. Its interior was divided into a number of small bars which were very dark because of the blackly varnished Swiss pine interior. If the Holly Bush was all atmosphere and all Hampstead, this place was no atmosphere and no place. Each bar was exactly the same as the others. They even smelt all alike, Every time you went there. An unvarying sweet-sour smell of stale beer and furniture polish. We picked a dark bar at random and Chris bought us both a half pint.

'So, where is it next?' I asked when we'd sat down at a table in the otherwise empty little space. 'You told me but I forget.' I hadn't forgotten, of course.

'Stevenage next week, like I said,' he reminded me, 'Wolverhampton after that. Week after that, I can't remember. Somewhere in the south-west, I think. Southampton, or Basingstoke.'

They were hardly in the south-west, I thought. Still, they lay south-west of London. And everything was relative. Especially if your starting point was Gospel Oak.

'You'll forget about me,' I said. I wasn't using the words to manipulate his answer. It was what I believed at that moment to be the bleak truth.

'I'll never do that, my sweetheart,' he said. Then, without even looking round to see if anyone was noticing, he laid his hand over mine on the table top and said, 'Now look me in the eye and I'll say it again. My sweetheart, I'll never do that.' He looked gorgeous while he was saying it.

'I know you're not going to forget I existed,' I said. 'Nobody forgets a thing like that. What I meant was that you'll move on, meet other people who you'll get involved with...'

'Oh, don't say that...' He sounded very dismayed. For a moment our roles were reversed and he'd become the younger of the two of us.

I ignored his interjection. 'We're ships that pass in the night.'

'Hope not,' he said. Then his mood seemed to brighten and he looked quite positive again. 'But if we are, then let's make the most of the passing moment. We only met on Monday. We've got till Saturday night at the very least. And we've hardly made a start on Thursday yet.'

I had to laugh at that. 'You're right,' I said. 'We're at the halfway point.' But as a time-frame for whatever was happening between Chris and me, six days seemed miserably short.

That Thursday night we did my place again. This time we got a takeaway and a bottle of cheap plonk on the way back. And when we got in I lit the gas fire before we did anything else. And then we did everything else.

On Friday night we did the Heath again, sixty-nining each other on the grass. This was highly dangerous: I didn't need anyone to tell me that. Our ears and eyes were badly placed for keeping watch for trouble, and we were in the worst possibly position for dealing with trouble if trouble materialised. And yet we seemed to have got beyond caring about that.

Forewarned was forearmed when it came to the parting of our ways this second time at Whitestones Pond. We managed quite a protracted goodnight kiss astride our bikes, gripping the crossbars like cold hard dick-shafts between our thighs as, leaning towards each other, we tried not to overbalance. 'Tomorrow,' I said.

'Tomorrow,' he repeated. And then he said it. Quoting Horatio's last goodbye to Hamlet. 'Goodnight, sweet prince.' I had to make a big effort at that moment not to fall apart.

Tomorrow was Saturday, which meant there was a matinee. We had a very quick half in the Swiss pub beforehand, and then we went back there for a glass of wine and a sandwich between the shows. There wasn't time to get up to the Holly Bush and back. Not without Being Late for the Half.

But we weren't alone this time when we arrived in the Swiss pub. Half the crew were there, and half the actors. They were a touring company after all. A week in this place, a week in that. For them every Saturday night was a Last Night.

'And you two,' someone said cheekily as we sat down at the big table they were all occupying and at which they made space for us. 'What becomes of you two after tonight?'

'What becomes of any theatre romance after the set is struck on the last night?' said someone else. He did a mime of someone striking a match on the side of a box and then blowing it out. Then he looked intensely at me, first, and then at Chris. 'Poof,' he said.

Chris said to him robustly, 'I think we'll manage better than that.' And, hearing those words I felt a surge of warmth inside myself, as if cherry brandy had for a moment replaced the blood that raced through my heart.

After the show I couldn't escape from behind the bar. Usually, during this phase of the evening I mingled with the actors and the stage crew in the foyer, only popping through the flap to go behind the bar when someone wanted another drink. But tonight everyone wanted drinks constantly, without let-up. I found myself a full-time bar-tender during that last half hour before closing time at eleven o'clock.

But Chris didn't desert me. He leaned on the counter opposite me, looking at me with both wonder and affection in his eyes. He took no part in anyone else's conversation and none of the others bothered to try and include him in theirs. He had sat and watched me every afternoon for twenty minutes or so while I worked on the Mozart. Nobody had been there on those occasions to see the rapt attention he had paid me. Tonight they all saw and knew and understood.

'Time, ladies and gentlemen, please,' I called at eleven o'clock, and with kisses and hugs and see-yous the company thinned out and disappeared, like the dancers do in Schuman's Papillons when the clock strikes the final hour.

Chris stayed with me. Together we took the optics down and stacked them in a crate, as I did every night, and put them in the secure cupboard under the stairs. Together we chucked the contents of the bar till in a cloth money bag, and stowed that in the safe under the concrete floor. Together we checked the toilets, closed the windows. We checked that the backstage lock-up had been done correctly, threw the mains electricity switches and finally padlocked the two sets of front-of-house doors.

And then we were outside together in the chill dark air. Just the two of us and our padlocked bikes.

I'd been in charge of us during the last few minutes, when Chris had been helping me to do my job. But now he was back in command again. At least, I thought he was. For half a minute neither of us said anything. We just unlocked our bikes. At last I spoke. 'Umm?' I said.

'Hmm,' he said.

'Meaning?'

'I don't think we can tonight.'

'Oh no,' I said, in one second losing six years of poise and confidence and strength.

'We'll be together soon, baby.'

'How soon?' I said.

'I'll be back in London at the weekend,' he said. 'I know where to find you.' He gave me a very hurried peck on the cheek, not giving me time to return it, then got on his bike and pedalled away rapidly into the night. I stared after him till he disappeared from sight among the Finchley Road traffic, but he never once looked back.

A moment later I was pedalling out into the same eternal traffic... Chris knew where to find me... Surrounded by the whole of Saturday night London... I had no idea where to find him... Alone and desolate.

FOUR

The magic went out of the Mozart. Practising it became a slog. But I persevered. There was another week to go before I was due to play it through for Luke. I worked at it dutifully on the foyer piano during all my breaks. Slowed it right down. Worked on the dotted rhythms till they went like the cogs and escapements of a Swiss watch. Took care with the dynamics: the louds and softs, the crescendos and diminuendos that bridged them. I found little joy in this. When Tanya would walk past and catch my eye while I was playing I'd see an expression on her face that would be hard to describe, though it was easy enough to interpret. You poor thing, it said. The music wore my desolation on its sleeve for me, it seemed, and she registered that.

It wasn't Mozart I was playing. It was the shell and skeleton of Mozart. A house of beams and rafters that all dovetailed perfectly but that was lit by no light. 'Mozart by candle-light?' a great pianist of the past had once protested. 'Mozart is not for candle-light. Mozart is the sun.' But no sun blazed in my playing now. There weren't even candle flames. They'd all been snuffed out.

Sometimes I'd stop and turn round to look at the corner of the vinyl-covered bench across the bar alcove. Some trick of mind had told me that he'd come in unannounced and was quietly sitting there. My eyes would light only on an expanse of mustard-coloured vinyl that mocked my gaze and mocked my hopes. But my hopes were foolish childish fantasies. He couldn't possibly be here. He was working in Stevenage.

I delayed locking up that next Saturday night. I'd done the timings. Curtain down in Stevenage. London train. Tube from Kings Cross... He could have turned up, at least in theory. Just about. I finally abandoned this fantasy too, and cycled homeward at one o'clock.

In the morning I was going to play for Luke, then have lunch with my parents. I stuck a forlorn little note on the big front door under the portico in Colville Terrace. It told where I'd gone and when I'd be back. I used four separate bits of Selotape.

All kinds of communication that we take now for granted, back in those days didn't exist. There were no mobile phones, no email, no Facebook, no Grind'r, no Whatsapp. There were ordinary telephones and there was the post. Keeping in touch with someone in a touring theatre company, whose address changed every week, was a more difficult matter even than most.

OK, there were things I could have done, even so. I could have looked up the number of the stage door phone at Stevenage in the British Theatre Directory. There was a copy in my office. I could then have left a message, to go in his pigeon-hole, asking him to ring me back at my theatre at a certain time. I could have given him the number of the communal pay-phone in the hall of the Colville Terrace flat. He could have taken similar steps. But he hadn't, and he didn't, and neither did I, and that was that. I didn't even know his home address.

'Well,' said Luke when I'd finished playing to him, and there was a pained look on his face as he spoke, 'you've done a terrific amount of work, I can see that. But the first and last movements... Well, they were at half-tempo. You'll have to get them up to speed before the course. Over the next two weeks.'

'I did practise them faster,' I said. 'But I still dropped the odd wrong note along the way.'

'Hmm,' said Luke. 'Nothing that is worthwhile in life is without risk. Even the risk of a wrong note in a simple Mozart piece. Even in Mozart we have to just go for it. Mozart himself always did.'

'Would you like me to play it again?' I asked tail-waggingly. 'A bit faster...'

'No,' Luke said. 'I'd prefer to sit on the terrace and drink a beer with you, actually. I trust you to get the Mozart up to speed in the next fortnight. We can think about weeding out wrong notes during the course.'

Sitting in the sunshine, enjoying that can of lager with Luke, I thought – perhaps for the first time – that having a sexual adventure with someone doesn't prevent you noticing the attractiveness of other people. In fact, I decided now, it was very much the reverse.

Luke was quite unlike Chris physically, just as he was quite unlike myself. He was much taller than either of us. Over six foot, I guessed. He was slim, with narrow waist and hips, but with quite broad square shoulders. He wasn't spindly, though. His long legs looked firmly muscled as far as I could tell, peering at his trousers, and his arms looked powerful and masculine inside the sleeves of his shirt. I didn't want to be embraced by those arms, though. I wanted to be embraced only by Chris.

Luke's face was finely chiselled, his nose not a lump of putty like mine or Chris's, but very straight. Not long, not big. Just straight, and with not much of an indentation above the bridge. His hair was mouse-coloured. It was quite thick, and he wore it long enough to cover the top part of his ears, the way that most of us, at that time, did. He had quite long eyelashes too, and his eyes were big and hazel and bright. There was a twinkle in them that suggested a sense of humour and a readiness to laugh at the craziness of life...

'You seem a bit...' I heard him saying suddenly. 'I don't know... You seem a bit different. A bit deflated. Was it the way I criticised your Mozart? Because...'

'No,' I said. 'It's nothing to do with that.'

'Ah,' he said. And he must have read the tone of my voice pretty expertly because he scored a bulls-eye with his next remark. 'A downturn in your love life, maybe? Sorry, I'm only joking.' He'd seen from my unguarded facial reaction that he'd hit the spot. 'I'm not prying. It really was only a joke. Forget I said that.'

'It's OK,' I said. But I changed the subject pretty quickly at that point. 'I should have told you straight away I've got permission to take a holiday from work and come on the course.'

'I knew that'd be a piece of cake,' said Luke.

I had in fact broached the subject almost two weeks ago with my bosses. They'd see if they could get a stand-in to manage the Front of House for the fortnight of my absence, they said. And a day later they'd told me they'd found a woman to do it who had done my job for several years in the past, who was now semi-retired and a free-lance writer, and who was only too happy to step into my shoes temporarily and earn some cash. I'd told Chris this happy news at the time. I'd already told him about the chamber music course and about my doubt as to whether I'd be able to do it. He was delighted for me. That had been the day we'd ended up at Colville Terrace together for the first time and I'd fucked him – the first time I'd fucked anybody in my life. What a happy day that had been, I now thought in retrospect. A halcyon day. A long time ago, it now seemed, though. It seemed to belong in the memory of a different Robbie, in a different life.

The new working week began. There was a grimness and a greyness about the weather at the beginning of that week that echoed and mirrored the grimness and greyness in my own heart. Chris was in Wolverhampton, presumably, while I remained in London, doggedly ordering Coca-Cola supplies, ironing out box office muddles, and cashing up at the end of each night. And in my spare time doggedly practising Mozart. I even came into the theatre the following Sunday, letting myself into the empty building and working on the trio's piano part. Theatres are vibrant, active places. It is strange to find yourself in an empty one, alone, finding that at every pause in the music you are playing there is a silence around you so intense that you could hear a pin drop.

I was only partly surprised to get a phone call from Luke that evening. Could I, in my role as course administrator, draft a letter to all the participants, outlining final arrangements for the course? He had already mentioned that he might want me to do something like this. He more or less dictated the letter over the phone. I saw at once why he wanted me to do this. The letter included a mention of the course fee and the date by which it was payable. It's always easier to have a request for money signed by someone else.

I said that I would do that in the morning. I didn't tell Luke that I'd get Fiona, the theatre secretary I shared my office with and was good friends with, to actually type it out and have it photo-copied 'accidentally' among more legitimate theatre-business stuff. I said I'd let him have a copy and he asked me if it was OK if he paid me for the postage next time we met. I said, yes, of course.

'In which case,' he said, 'as I'd hate you be out of pocket by the cost of half a dozen stamps for too long, would you like to come over and have one last look at the piano part with me before the end of the week?'

'To Putney?' I asked. On a working day it would be a bit of a trek.

'What about my room in college?' he said. 'Half the distance for you.'

'That's fine,' I said. 'I can do that in a few minutes on my bike.'

We arranged a time on Thursday morning, and he told me how to find his room when I got to the college.

I arrived in good time and, after chaining my bike up outside, marched into the building. How easy buildings were to enter back then! No security, not even a reception desk. As I walked along the route that Luke had told me to take I passed a scene of surreal strangeness. A severe-looking man in a suit was trying to call a reluctant lift. As he stabbed at the call-button an unseen pianist began a fortissimo scale from the bottom to the top of the piano in some out-of-sight but not out-of-hearing practice room. By coincidence this happened twice – the impression being that the scale was conjured by the imperious button-stab – and it made me smile. By the time I reached Luke's room, and I'd passed the muffled sounds of Brahms and Holst and Prokofiev being practised in different rooms by different combinations of instruments, I was beginning to feel like a real music student myself.

I reached the heavy door to Luke's teaching room and raised my hand to knock on it. As I did so it swung quickly open and a young man came out through it so quickly that he almost walked into my fist. I only just managed not to give him an upper cut with it.

We both called out in surprise. A sort of shared noise of, 'Ooomp!' Then I said, 'Sorry mate,' and he said, 'Sorry mate,' and then we both laughed. Part of the surprise of the moment was that I thought the young man extremely beautiful. I stepped sideways and let him get out of the doorway and escape down the corridor, while Luke's voice from inside the room came in a tone of concern and curiosity, 'Everything all right out there?'

I was inside the room before I needed to answer that. 'I just bumped into one of your students, I think,' I said.

'That's Jeremy,' said Luke. 'He's coming on the course. Plays the cello. You'll get on, the two of you. At least I hope you will. He's very nice.'

I certainly hoped we would get on. I thought we'd got on like a house on fire already. The image of his face was indelibly etched on my memory, as if it had been illuminated by a lightning flash. He was my height and size and shape and about three years younger than I was, I'd guessed. I was suddenly looking forward to our next encounter like crazy. I didn't say all this to Luke, of course. But I couldn't stop myself from saying, 'He looked nice.' Which, if Luke's antennae were finely tuned to such nuances, was as big a giveaway as if I'd come out with all the rest.

Luke's college room was almost the Doppelganger of his music room in Putney. A Bechstein grand occupied the area under the window. This one, though, was a bit newer than the Putney one. It was shiny black, not glowing rosewood, and its legs were austerely square and straight. In another corner of the room metal music stands clustered as though gossiping among themselves. The walls were shelves – all the way to the ceiling – on which music scores stood upright. You couldn't count them. There were dozens of scores, scores of scores, hundreds of them. If you wanted to get an idea of the size of the string and chamber repertoire, built up over the centuries, you only had to walk in here and look.

I sat down at the Bechstein and played to Luke. To my astonishment the Mozart did what it hadn't done for the last fortnight. It sparkled; it laughed, it capered, it danced. I couldn't believe what was happening under my fingers. When I finished I turned round and looked at Luke. To my surprise he was grinning broadly at me, his handsome face slightly flushed.

'Well done,' he said. 'Very well done. I may not be dazzled, but I am impressed.' Then his grin turned adolescent and collusive. 'Love life looking up, perhaps?'

I was strangely shocked by that. 'I wouldn't go as far as to say that,' I said. Did I hear a hint of panic in my voice?'

When Chris and his touring company had been at my theatre I'd had daily contact with the person who looked after his company's day to day finance. Jenny. I would phone her every morning to give her the attendance figures for the previous night's performance. Numbers, and cash. In due course my theatre would hand over to her company the agreed sixty per-cent of the box office take. This week Chris and the show he was touring with were in Southampton. (I'd checked that in The Stage.) But Jenny's job kept her in London. I had her phone number. I now rang her up.

'Jenny,' I said. 'Robbie here. I need to ask you a big favour. Could you give me Chris David's home address.'

'Oh,' she said, and sounded a bit embarrassed as well as affronted. 'I don't think I know that.'

'Do you do payroll?' I asked.'

'Yes,' she said.

'So do I,' I said. 'His address will be in the wages book.'

I heard Jenny sigh, then try to cover it up. 'OK, Robbie, I wasn't being straight with you. I'm sorry, but you know I can't give you his address. If you do the wages for your lot you already know that's the case.'

'Oh Jenny, you're my only hope,' I said. 'Look. Does it make any difference if I say it's a matter of the heart?' I paused for a moment. Then I pulled up from the depths the most fragile word in the world, carefully, as if I was hauling in a soft-shelled shellfish. 'It's about love,' I said.

There was a slight pause at the other end. Then Jenny said, 'Robbie, I'll phone you back in ten minutes. But there's a condition attached to this. Please, never, ever, whatever happens between Chris and you or doesn't, tell anyone where you got the information from.'

'I swear on my grandmother's old tin bath,' I said.

On Saturday night I locked the theatre after the bar had empted of crew and actors around half-past eleven. But I locked up from the inside. I tidied up a few loose ends of paperwork in the office after that. After all, I was going to be away from the place for a whole fortnight. Then, around half past midnight I let myself out and re-locked. I cycled up Fitzjohn's Avenue, though not as far as the top. I cut along Lyndhurst Road – eerily quiet in the midnight dark – and on to Pond Street. Then along deserted Fleet Road and Mansfield Road until I arrived at the street where Chris lived, in Gospel Oak.

The address Jenny had given me turned out to be a basement flat. The lights were on down there. I crept down the steps, with the strangest feelings – and the most mixed feelings – going on inside me that I'd ever felt. I arrived at the bottom, outside the door to the small place. *Behold, I stand at the door and knock.* But at nearly one o'clock in the morning it takes a moment or two to screw your courage up before doing that.

I heard a voice. A young woman's voice. I couldn't hear the words. They were low and intimate. Then I heard the voice of the person the words were addressed to. A very little girl's voice. Saying something about being too excited to sleep. And then a man's voice spoke. 'Back to bed for now, my sweetheart. Games in the morning. Daddy'll still be here. All day tomorrow we've got.' The voice was so tender and loving that it broke my heart. The voice belonged to Chris, of course.

I crept up the steps as quietly as I'd come down them, if a bit more quickly. I got on my bike and cycled the long distance back to Colville Terrace in the midnight black.

FIVE

Luke had not only given me the cash for the stamps I'd sent his letters out with, he'd also given a me a cheque to cover my travel expenses. I had immediately put that in the bank.

The course was to start on Tuesday. Monday was for getting to the place. For travellers to the Dordogne in those days there were no cheap flights to Bergerac. Unless you had a car and were prepared to drive the long distance on your own, as a solitary traveller you had the choice between an expensive flight to Bordeaux or Limoges – both a long way from your destination – or ferry and train. That last option was the cheapest, but also the slowest. I got up, that Monday morning, at four o'clock and travelled down to Folkestone in the dark.

There was light in the sky by the time I boarded the ferry, and just before we docked the sun climbed blazing above the black cliffs ahead. The sea turned suddenly gold around me and I shed the crippling burden of disappointment that had weighed on me since I'd confirmed my suspicions about Chris. It wasn't that I was 'over' him or anything close to it. But my strength had come back to me. I was outbound on a new adventure. Whatever might lie ahead of me in the course of it … well, I was up for that.

At Folkestone I'd walked off the train at the harbour station and straight onto the ship. At Boulogne it was the same. I walked off the ship, through a short hallway in which were passport control and customs, and straight onto a train that waited at the other end of the hallway. Short, sweet and simple back then.

Arrived in Paris I took a bus from the Gare du Nord to the Gare d'Austerlitz. I'd only been to Paris once before and I didn't want to miss a second glimpse of it by taking the Métro, mole-like, beneath its streets.

I'd never been south of Paris. Not within France at any rate. My new adventure now took me deep into history as well as deep into France. Heading like a plumb-line down the map to Orléans – where Joan of Arc began to turn the tide against the English – then turning east, roaring round the long curve at Blois, to follow the Loire to Tours. The route of the Plantagenets between their strongholds of London and Bordeaux. Then Poitiers, glimpsed between tunnels, different parts of the stone-built town on beetling cliffs. Poitiers, famous in England for the battle where the Black Prince, at the age of sixteen, beat the French. Famous in France for an older, bigger victory, at which in the eighth century Charles Martel turned the invading Moors back.

Then Angoulême, centre of paper-making in Europe for half a millennium, and which briefly gave its name – as Nouvelle Angoulême – to the city now called New York.

And then the landscape changed. Became softer. Became southern. Slates no longer covered the roofs. Red Roman canal-tiles were there instead. Vineyards sprang up beside the track... I got out one stop before Bordeaux. At Libourne. The air that met me on the platform was spring scented and, in the late afternoon, pleasantly hot.

I had a little further to go. A few miles, and a few stops, on the single track branch line that runs right up the Dordogne to Sarlat. In a little brown train that looked like a mouse. First stop was St-Emilion – a name and a wine to conjure with. But my final destination lay a little further on, just beyond Castillon, at a tiny, sleepy, chocolate-box-charming village called Moncaret.

The station lay at the bottom of a steep scarp slope. Luke's Dordogne house stood halfway up. In the warm sunshine and brilliant colours of a Dordogne April evening I took a deep breath, picked up my suitcase (nobody had yet thought to attach wheels to them) and walked up. I was glad at that moment that I played the piano. I did not have to – as violinists and cellist have to – carry my instrument.

I hadn't given much thought to what Luke's 'place in the Dordogne' might be like. Or what anybody's place in the Dordogne might be like, come to that. I suppose I'd realised that, since Luke had invited half a dozen students there, it would need to be bigger than a teensy cottage. But when I turned onto the short track-way that led to it and saw it in front of me... Well, if I hadn't known better I'd have called it a château.

It was two storeys high, with seven or eight windows on each floor at the front. Built of honey-coloured stone it had a steeply pitched roof of old tiles the colour of chestnuts. Positioned asymmetrically – one on a corner, the other just short of the opposite end of the frontage – were two round towers. Their walls rose no more than a foot higher than the eaves, and their conical caps, like medieval ladies' hats, only out-topped the ridge-pole by a metre or so. But they were unmistakeably towers. And towers do tend to impress.

The front door stood open in the sunshine. I walked in without knocking and, in the empty hallway from which a staircase wound upwards like honeysuckle, called out, 'Hi,' and 'Anyone about?'

A door opened a little way in front of me and a youthful figure popped out. It was Jeremy. We stopped in our tracks when we saw each other. The last time Jeremy had opened a door in front of me I'd been standing rather nearer to it and had almost punched him in the face.

His surprise was greater than mine. Luke had told me Jeremy would be on the course. He probably hadn't seen Jeremy since, to tell him – even if he'd thought it worth mentioning – that I would also be on it. 'Oh hi,' Jeremy now said. 'I saw you – didn't I? – outside Luke's room at college?'

'And I nearly put my fist in your face,' I said. I felt myself grinning stupidly. 'I'm sorry about that. I'm Robbie.'

'I'm Jeremy,' he said. I didn't tell him I already knew that. I gave him my hand; he gave me his. 'You wrote the letter asking for money,' he said next.

I squirmed. 'Well…'

Jeremy laughed boyishly and shrugged. 'Somebody had to,' he said. Then, 'We're just having cups of tea in the garden out at the back. Those of us who're here already.' He glanced down at my suitcase on the white marble floor beside me. 'You can leave your stuff down here and join us. Unless…'

'No,' I said. 'I'll join you for tea in the garden. Sounds like what the doctor ordered. Lead on, Macduff.'

Jeremy was slender and small-boned, with petite features. His hair was thick, brown and wavy and he had nice full lips. His eyes were the main thing, though. They were big and blue and a little bit doll-like. Only a little bit though. You can have too much of a good thing, and too much 'doll-like' about a man's face reduces its appeal somewhat. But in Jeremy's case his maker had got the dose about right. Coming out of the house again, this time through French windows onto a wide sweep of lawn, and approaching a group of strangers – out of whose midst Luke rose from a garden chair to greet me – I found I was as happy to have Jeremy at my side as I would have been (this was a sudden and shocking thought) to have Chris.

I'd had first times in my life before. First day at school. First day at university. First anal sex. But this evening was a different kind of first. I was meeting a small crowd of people, all of whom knew each other: all of whom were looking hungrily at careers as performing musicians, where I was a mere dabbling amateur. It went on from there. My new colleagues – God, I would be playing the piano with two of them tomorrow; that made me quake in my plimsolls – were nineteen or twenty. I was three years older than that. At the age we all were, that made a hell of a difference. And then, I was in a Sleeping Beauty kind of château, for the first time in my life, in the southern half of France.

As on those other 'first' occasions the details became a bit of a blur, or montage of impressions. (If there was an odd one out among those, an exception that tested the rule, it would be anal sex.) I was unpacking my stuff in a big bedroom that looked out across the lawns towards thick woods in the valley. Beyond the woods and hidden by them the Dordogne river snaked. I'd barely seen it yet. Running in the same valley as the train tracks from Libourne it had kept its writhing course a tantalising mile or two beyond easy sight for the most part. I hoped there would be time to explore its banks while I was here. For a moment I allowed myself to imagine doing that with Jeremy, then put the idea away. It belonged in the fantasy box.

From another room came the sound of a violin suddenly. I recognised the music. It was a section of my Mozart trio that was being tried over. That meant it was Elfrieda I was listening to. I'd met Elfrieda over the mugs of tea on the lawn, and learnt that we would be working together on the Mozart. I'd also met a Marianne. I wouldn't be playing alongside her, though. She was playing the viola part in another of the pieces being studied: Schubert's vast C major String Quintet. Marianne and Elfrieda had travelled down with Jeremy, in Jeremy's car, sharing the driving. Two more students were expected, but they hadn't arrived yet.

An interesting smell began to waft up from the kitchen below. Something very French was being cooked, I thought. I looked forward to finding out what it was when dinner time arrived. I knew who was cooking it. A young French woman called Sandrine. I'd met her when I helped take the empty tea mugs back into the kitchen. She didn't speak English. Working alongside her was a much older woman: Luke's housekeeper Mrs Fox. Who spoke no French.

There was a knock on my door. I opened it carefully. Jeremy was outside. He took a half-step backwards instinctively and so did I. That made us both smile as we realised what both our bodies were remembering. Jeremy said, 'Want a beer before dinner?' We both went downstairs

'Elfrieda sounds very good,' I said as we walked.

'She is.'

'It's a bit scary,' I said. 'For me, I mean. I'm not a music student. I never have been. Just an amateur pianist who happens to know Luke.'

'He must rate your playing,' Jeremy said nonchalantly. 'Else he wouldn't have invited you along.'

That was a comforting thought. I said, 'Thanks, mate.'

Jeremy led the way into the kitchen and opened the fridge. Although he'd only been here an hour longer than I had he seemed to know his way around the place. Casually he took out two cans of beer. 'We can replace them tomorrow,' he said.

'I guess we should,' I said. 'I think I'm supposed to be the quartermaster round here. Or purser or something.'

Jeremy chuckled. 'What do you do?' he asked. 'I mean, apart from playing the piano.'

I started to tell him about my job as we walked out into the sunshine again and, ignoring the chairs that were set about the garden, sat down chummily together on the grass.

There was a starter at dinner. Except for in restaurants I wasn't used to that. It was very simple. Tomatoes sliced into a vinaigrette with a garnish of basil leaves. Simple it may have been but it seemed to me exotic and very French. And it tasted heavenly, of course.

By now the last two course participants had turned up. There was Tarquin, the other violinist. He had driven down all by himself and now looked a bit shell-shocked as a result. He'd made the drive a bit shorter by taking the overnight ferry to St-Malo. Even so, it had been a hell of a hike.

And there was Lisa, the other cellist. She was a 'mature student' – in her mid-thirties, I guessed. She had come by train but had sensibly got off a couple of stops before Moncaret, in the town Castillon, and got a taxi to bring her the last bit. She hadn't had to carry suitcase and cello up the hill.

'You should have phoned from Moncaret station,' Luke chided her. 'I'd have come and got you. You didn't have to fork out for a taxi.'

'I'm not good with phones in foreign countries,' Lisa said.

Jeremy leaned across to her. 'I'll give you a lesson on it tomorrow,' he said, and the others laughed.

Our main course was a stew of beans and tomatoes and pork sausage and pieces of duck. It was called cassoulet. Apparently it was a very famous dish from the south-west of France. I'd never heard of it. But I thought it tasted more wonderful than anything I'd eaten in my life.

I don't know how it was that I suddenly found myself sharing the hallway for a moment, after dinner, with Jeremy and nobody else. Perhaps I'd gone to the loo and just returned from it. It's a detail I don't remember.

What I do remember is that there Jeremy was. And what he said. 'Do you fancy going out for a walk?'

I said what any gay man of whatever age or nationality would have said if that question had been put to him by someone who looked like Jeremy. 'Yes.'

We went out through the front door. We weren't being secretive, trying to get out without anybody seeing us. It just so happened that nobody did. A hundred paces brought us to the end of the track. Then we were on the steep road I'd walked up. It was barely a road actually, more like a double-width lane. Two cars could pass easily enough but if you met a lorry you'd need to slow down and pull into the hedge.

We stopped. 'Up or down?' Jeremy asked.

'If we go down we'll have to walk back up,' I said.

'And uphill right after dinner...'

'After cassoulet...' We both laughed. 'OK,' I said. 'Over there.' I pointed with my head. Across the road, just twenty paces down the hill, was a very small lane that went neither up nor down, at least, not in the foreseeable distance. It seemed to hug the contour of the hillside, winding its way among vineyards on both sides. No fence or hedge separated the vines from the road: just a strip of grass and a drainage ditch. The lane looked appealing, enticing. We crossed the road and set off along it.

'Have you got a girlfriend?' Jeremy asked, a bit unexpectedly, at that point.

'Er – no,' I said. I thought, do I tell him? and almost immediately decided I would. 'I thought I had a boyfriend for the last few weeks,' I said. 'But apparently I didn't.'

'Oh,' he said. 'Do you want to tell me about it?' He looked into my face a bit shyly and very sweetly. 'Or is that off-limits?'

'It's not off-limits,' I said. 'Be nice to tell someone about it actually. If you're OK with that?' He was OK with it, he said. I told him the story of Chris.

Spring was a week or two more advanced down here in the Dordogne than it was in London. Distant trees were a golden green so brilliant in the evening sun that it almost hurt. A few rose bushes had been planted along the edge of the vineyard on one side of the lane – for some obscure agricultural reason no doubt – and some of them were already in crimson bud. By the time I'd finished the saga of Chris and me our lane was pitching downwards and a valley with a huddle of trees and roofs at the bottom of it came into sight. We carried on.

'That's a bummer,' Jeremy said. 'Really sorry to hear that. But there's always some that like it both ways.'

'What about you?' I asked and immediately exploded with a laugh that infected Jeremy at once. 'Sorry, sorry, sorry, I didn't mean that! I meant your first question. Have you got a girlfriend?'

'No,' he said, struggling to pack his laughter back in its box. 'Not at the moment. I've had one or two in the past. Nothing that recent.' Then, laughter packed away, he paused for several seconds, and something in his manner or his tone of voice made me think he had something else to add but wasn't quite sure how to say it. I wondered what was coming. I hardly dared hope it would be what I wanted it to be, but yes, it was. He said, 'I've done stuff with boys too.' He wouldn't have told me that if he'd found me sexually unattractive.

I wasn't sure how to answer that, so there was another few seconds' pause while I considered it. Then the perfect answer came to me. 'Good,' I said.

We walked on in silence a little longer, going down the gentle hill towards the farmstead at the bottom. I knew that something was going to happen shortly. I just didn't know which one of us would start it. I could feel myself hardening up.

'I think I need a piss,' Jeremy said.

'I think I do too,' I said. 'But the state I'm in I don't think I'd manage it.'

'You too?' he said. 'I'm also in that state.'

The next move was simultaneous. Neither of us initiated it. We turned to face each other, shirt-front almost touching shirt-front, and each reached for the other's dick. Jeremy guessed the wrong side and I felt him groping vainly around the place from which, many years ago, my appendix had been taken out. But his fingers wandered over the denim quickly enough and soon he was grasping my cock. I'd got his first time. It was lying centrally, right underneath the line of his fly-studs. Bolt upright.

He spoke then. 'Bloody hell, you're big.'

It still surprised me when anyone said that. It was the only cock I'd ever had. I was used to it.

'I mean, for your size, at any rate,' he added, which rather reduced the size of the compliment.

'Yours isn't exactly minute,' I said, just in case he had any kind of complex about it. 'It feels just right.' Which was true. I wasn't simply being nice.

Our heads moved together. I nuzzled my chin into his neck as if I were a violin. I don't know... We were on a chamber music course; it seemed somehow appropriate. And he leaned the side of his head inward till it rested against my cheek. His cheekbone and his temple felt both soft and hard at the same time. And wonderfully alive and hot. For an awful second I thought I would accidentally tell him I loved him. Mercifully I didn't. Didn't love him. Didn't tell him I did. Though I wanted him of course. 'Hmmm,' I said instead.

SIX

The drainage ditch was a fraction too wide for us to stride across it. We took a run at it from the opposite side of the road and jumped it. As the vines weren't yet in full leaf they weren't perfect for hiding in. We had to go quite a way before we felt the mesh of twigs was deep and dense enough to screen us. Then we pulled each other to the ground and pulled down each other's jeans.

I thought Jeremy's cock was beautiful. Of medium length and elegantly tapering, it reminded me of Chris's. As for mine, it seemed to have scored a major hit with Jeremy. 'Oh wow,' he kept saying as he stroked it.

There was no question of taking all our clothes off. We were on rough ground and the air was rapidly cooling as the sun set. So it was exposed loins and thighs and bellies only. Next time we did this, I thought, I'd want us to be naked. I couldn't get enough of Jeremy's body. Next time I wanted all of it.

I came first, casting my seed on the stony ground in front of Jeremy. I didn't get up and run away after that. I'd grown up a bit in the last month. I kept going at Jeremy's cock for another minute, at the end of which he followed my example.

Then we hugged each other for a while. And then Jeremy pulled away a bit. 'I now really must do what I said before. Have a piss.'

'Ditto,' I said. And lying where we were, on our sides and facing each other we watered the ground between us, watching each other's streams and giggling a bit. Then we helped each other to our feet and pulled our clothes back up, fastening studs and tucking in shirts. Another running jump took us back into the lane where the dusk already swam in front of us. The first bit of the walk back lay uphill, though we hardly noticed the fact.

By the time we got to the end of the lane it was really dark and we crossed the road and went up the track-way guided by the lights of Luke's fairytale house ahead of us.

We heard music as we approached the front door. It was the Schubert quintet. 'Oh bloody hell,' Jeremy said. Two cellos were involved in the piece. Jeremy was one of them. There was no possibility that he hadn't been missed.

'Better go in,' I said. 'Face the music.' Jeremy groaned and gave me a friendly shove.

Actually we didn't face the music at once. We heard Luke and Mrs Fox talking in the kitchen and went in there instead. Jeremy clearly believed that attack was the best form of defence. 'Can we borrow another beer off you?' he asked.

Luke laughed at his boldness and said, 'Yes, of course. Did you two have a nice walk?'

We told him and Mrs Fox exactly where we'd walked to, but not what we had done when we got there. It was interesting to compare the expressions on Mrs Fox's and Luke's faces as they listened. They told me that Luke guessed, or at least half guessed, what we'd been up to, while Mrs Fox did not.

Luke said to Jeremy, 'Don't worry about the rehearsal. It wasn't official. They just suddenly decided to crash through it. But we're starting with it in the morning. Leaving Robbie,' he looked at me, 'free to go to the shops with Mrs Fox. Mozart at the end of the morning, probably going on with it a bit after lunch. Then the Beethoven in the afternoon.' I made a mental map of how this would all work. Jeremy wasn't in the Beethoven, he'd told me that. Perhaps we'd be able to spend some time together while everyone else was working on that. Perhaps we could go for another walk. Or tiptoe up the stairs and simply go to bed... In the meantime we took our beers out onto the lawn. Enough light spilled from the house to prevent us bumping into trees and things, but even so it was pretty dark. After a while the music ended and a couple of the others came out and accidentally found us.

'We missed you,' said Tarquin.

'We didn't expect you to be rehearsing,' I told him. 'We went for a walk.'

'I see,' Tarquin said. Because of the darkness I couldn't guess from his face how much he did see and how much he did not.

I drove Luke's car, with Mrs Fox in the passenger seat. I'd never driven on the French side of the road before. I just swallowed my momentary anxiety and did it. We went into Castillon. Mrs Fox had the shopping list, which Sandrine had written for her. In French, of course. My job was to interpret it and to get us into the right shops. 'They spell carrots the wrong way here,' Mrs Fox observed, peering at the words on the paper. *Carottes*. At least she was able to work out what the word meant.

It was like a morning re-inhabiting an elementary school text-book. We went *chez le boucher,* then *chez l'épicier* and then to the *boulangerie*. I did the talking, in my halting and English-accented French in each case. My most recent studies in the language – already six years behind me – had involved reading Racine and André Gide. It hadn't included discussions about the uses of different cuts of meat. In Britain the shopkeepers simply sold you the stuff. If you told them you were going to make a six-hour stew from fillet steak they'd just let you get on with it. Here it was very different. We were interrogated and vetted carefully before we were allowed to buy anything. It wasn't until I explained that the shopping-list had been drawn up by a French woman and that a French woman would actually be doing the cooking that they would nod and smile with relief and allow us to take the wares they sold out of the shop.

We got back, nosing up the lane on the right hand side of the road, with just a few minutes to spare before the first Mozart session was due to start. The trio we were working on was the G major one, K453. Elfrieda was our violinist and Jeremy the cellist. They were already warmed up – to say the least. They had had a two-hour session on the Schubert C major quintet. Except for a few self-conscious minutes before breakfast this morning I hadn't touched a piano for two days. But then I'd never driven a car in Mainland Europe before this morning and that hadn't gone too badly. We took up our positions like boxers in the ring, me on the piano stool, checking I could make eye contact with the others first. I gave the tuning A, the other two checked their As and fifths, and we were off.

There was no chance in the opening moments of the piece that Elfrieda and Jeremy would be too busy with their own parts to listen to me playing mine. They had nothing but a couple of long-drawn-out Gs to play initially. I was the one with the notes. Finely chiselled little phrases that Mozart had written with exquisite attention to detail and balance. They demanded something exquisite from the pianist when it came to performance. I did my best.

Elfrieda and Jeremy might be listening to me closely but I was also listening to them. Especially to Jeremy. It was just a long slow G, moving from octave to octave – first up, then down again. But the deep rich hum of his instrument filled the room. It was the first sound I'd heard him make on the cello. At that moment it was the most beautiful sound on earth. When we came to bar eight Jeremy and Elfrieda both had three beats' rest. Then something wonderful happened. They both turned and looked at me with smiles of pleasant surprise and encouragement. I felt the sun come out in my playing at that moment. Especially because in Jeremy's smile I saw not only pleasant surprise and encouragement but also something else.

We played through to the end of the first movement without interruption from Luke. It went pretty well, I thought. Then Luke stepped in. 'Very well done,' he said. 'Very well done indeed. How hard you've all worked.' Then during the hour that followed he stripped our performance down like a motor-bike engine and, with constant encouragement and painstaking attention to the smallest details, helped us to reassemble it.

Although Sandrine would be coming in to cook dinner in the evening, Mrs Fox was entrusted with lunch. Pâté and baguettes, quiches and salads, and – because we were after all in France – a small glass of wine for those who wanted it. After that we did the second movement of the Mozart, working on it in the same way as we'd done the first movement in the morning. And then Luke dismissed us, while he started work on the Beethoven Archduke trio with Tarquin and Lisa. Elfrieda took herself off to the other end of the house to practise. Jeremy and I, revelling in our first moment of freedom today, and our first opportunity to spend time alone together, went for a walk.

This time we turned left when we get to the road. Uphill. Mid-afternoon, with the sun-hazed air vibrant with the sound of grass-hoppers. We had no problem with that.

'Luke playing the piano in the Beethoven trio,' I said, for the sake of something to say. 'I'm a bit surprised by that.'

'Because he's really a violinist?' Jeremy said. 'Yes, he is. But he was a star at both when he studied. It was a toss-up, apparently, which way he'd branch when he grew up. He went for the violin and the rest is history. But he's no slouch at the keyboard. As you'll hear in due course.'

'He's set himself an incredibly tough target,' I said. 'Tutoring the Mozart and the Schubert. And the Beethoven, as well as playing in it. He hasn't given himself a moment off for piano practice.'

'That's why he's got you in to supervise Mrs Fox with the shopping,' Jeremy said. 'But piano practice... Well, we lesser mortals need to practise.' He shrugged. 'Lucky Luke doesn't seem to need it.'

'What does he need?' I asked.

'A woman to take care of him,' Jeremy said. Then he said, in a lower, more thoughtful voice, 'Or maybe a bloke.'

I decided not to respond to that.

At the top of the hill there was a choice of left or right. We chose left. We passed a house with a garden full of stainless steel fermentation vats the size of space rockets. At that point something lovely happened. Jeremy reached for my hand and grasped it, and we walked along the road holding hands openly in the sunshine, and holding the gaze of the drivers that passed us. None of them hooted, no-one wound down a window to give us the finger or shout French abuse. All the world loves a lover... Or so it seemed that afternoon. Even if the lovers are two boys who are in love simply with their sexual relationship.

There was a little wood to the left of the road. No more than a spinney, really. But, for two boys as thirsty for sex as we were, amidst a desert of vines, it was like an oasis.

He pulled me to the side of the road, then through the ragged hedge that fringed it. We stumbled our way across the rough ground, pulling branches of box and holly out of each other's way as we dodged through the trees and scrub. We hadn't left the road far behind when Jeremy stopped and turned. He took my head between his hands and kissed me.

We'd had sex. We hadn't kissed. Till now. His lips were soft against mine. His tongue was lovely in my mouth. He was three years younger and softer than me. For a moment I managed to forget about Chris.

I felt him fumbling with my waistband stud. By the time he'd found the top of my zip-fastener I was fumbling with his waistband stud. His underpants today were scarlet. By coincidence so were mine. We both laughed at that. But our laughs were as if in brackets: soon closed; and we were back on track with what we were really about.

Jeremy bobbed down, pulling my jeans down as he went. His lips found my very ready dick and fastened themselves on it.

The trouble was, I wanted his cock in my mouth too, or at least in my hand, but no way could I reach it without both of us off-balancing and tumbling into the mud. I had to make do with stroking the top of his head, noticing that he had a double crown nestling amongst his beautiful hair, then taking hold of both his ears and fondling them energetically instead.

'I'm going to come,' I said quietly. I didn't mean it as a cry of triumph. I just wanted to warn him what was going to happen; give him time to remove me from his mouth if he wanted to do that.

Evidently he didn't want to. He kept going and I unloaded in the warm red space between his tongue and the vaulted roof of his mouth. Looking up I saw the sky leap blue and loud between the fresh green springs of the canopied branches.

A half minute later, 'I will return the compliment,' I said. Shall was not the word that popped out, I noticed, but will. In the context it sounded ten times stronger. So

I knelt in the mud at his feet and as I took his prick in my mouth pulled his jeans down a little further, till I was staring down into them, seeing for the first time that he had tantalisingly lovely legs, which were burnished with the light fur of youth.

I didn't have time to decide whether, this first time, I wanted to swallow what Jeremy produced. He came suddenly, in a little explosion in my mouth like a sherbet burst before he had time to say anything about it. It didn't taste like a sherbet burst, though. It tasted more like something you'd scour the kitchen surfaces with. But it tasted of Jeremy, unmistakeably, and I was perfectly happy about that.

We pulled our jeans up and fastened them and then walked back to the road. Again Jeremy took my hand and we walked on together for another mile before turning back. 'With any luck they'll have finished work on the Archduke,' Jeremy said.

'Why?' I asked. 'Don't you like it?' I though the piece was rather splendid, and was looking forward to hearing it in rehearsal, hearing it take shape.

'No. I mean, yes, I like it. It's just that there's a lot of under-current between Luke and Elfrieda going on around it.'

'Oh, wow,' I said. Had I been unobservant, or was it the fact that all the others were at the same college that meant they were keenly aware of things of which I was not? Either way, I felt uncomfortable suddenly and gave Jeremy's hand, already clasping mine, a little extra squeeze for my own reassurance.

SEVEN

We took our time walking back. We dawdled and watched the birds and insects that flitted and swarmed around the vineyard expanse. There were wagtails and redstarts, and a little brown bird that went chattering up and down in the sky as if dangled on an invisible yoyo string by God.

There was a smell of supper cooking when we got back. I knew what it was. I'd done the shopping. Unpromising stewing steak with carrots. And a little red wine... But the smell of that combination maturing in the oven was better than England in those days could ever have produced.

There was also a sound. Violin and piano were being played together. Yet rehearsals of the Archduke trio were finished. Tarquin and the others were sitting out on the lawn, Tarquin chugging on a beer can. 'Who's playing?' I asked Jeremy. The music sounded vaguely familiar, though I couldn't have said what it was. 'And what's the piece?'

'Elfrieda's playing,' said Jeremy. 'With Luke at the piano. It's the Spring sonata...'

'By Beethoven,' I interrupted quickly. I didn't want Jeremy to think me a total ignoramus in the field of classical music.

I wasn't sure which movement I was listening to. It was either the first or fourth. The one that gushes like a brook after the ice melts in the spring warmth. It was full of optimism and a rush of sparkling notes. 'It's beautiful,' I said.

'I think so too,' said Jeremy. He took my hand in the empty hallway, then drew me towards him and we had a gentle kiss. Then we disengaged and walked out into the garden to join the others, trying to look nonchalant and as if butter wouldn't melt in either of our mouths.

Nobody was fooled. But nobody said anything either.

Boeuf aux carottes was, apparently, a French classic dish. A simple stew that had risen through the ranks. Beef slowly braised in stock with a little garlic, tomato paste, marjoram and a splash of wine. And carrots, of course, cut into long strips: which was something I'd never seen before. It was served with a mash of potatoes and celeriac, Celeriac was something I'd never tasted. It was just like celery but without the stringy bits.

After the stew, not alongside it, came a plain salad of herbs and lettuce. Dessert was ice cream with a hot raspberry sauce... I thought the whole meal was marvellous. I decided I would want always to eat like this.

Luke was rather holding court at that supper table. As he had every right to. He had had a very successful day. We, his students, had made good progress on the pieces we were working on. Then he had relaxed with the Spring sonata. And Elfrieda, of course. There was a light in his eyes. The special light that is born of success.

He told the table at one point, 'One of my great teachers once said that you can't really play chamber music until you've fallen in love with two violinists, a viola player and a cellist. Though I'd caution you all not to take that too literally...'

'And a pianist too, I suppose,' said Tarquin. His face was slightly flushed after the excitement of the day's playing, and after a can of beer and a glass of wine. From the little I'd seen of him I'd decided he was rather nice.

I didn't give Luke time to answer Tarquin. I came in with, 'And we mustn't forget those chamber works with things like clarinet...'

'The Trout quintet has a double bass,' Elfrieda pointed out, laughing.

'To say nothing of the Schubert octet,' added Lisa. 'Clarinet, horn, bassoon and double bass – as well as the usual suspects.'

'An out and out orgy,' Jeremy said, with a poker face.

Luke wound the discussion up like a good chairman or chat-show host. 'I did say the advice was not meant to be taken too literally,' he concluded, with a twinkle in his eye but sounding quite firm about it.

'I'm glad of that,' said Mrs Fox, and everybody laughed.

After dinner there was a general feeling – especially among the males of the group – that we owed it to ourselves to go out in search of a bar. There was a bar in Moncaret, Luke said, but it closed up at about seven o'clock. We decided to drive into Castillon instead. We had four cars between us, and we were only seven. (Sandrine had gone home as soon as dinner was served, to cook all over again for her young husband, while Mrs Fox, on being asked to join us, had wrinkled her nose and shaken her head.) There was a bit of coin tossing to decide which cars we'd take. In the end Tarquin drove his, taking Marianne and Lisa, while Luke took Elfrieda and Jeremy and me in his. Elfrieda sat in the front alongside Luke while Jeremy and I sat in the back and rubbed knees, which were out of sight of the driving mirror, while looking straight ahead of us, still trying, and still failing, to convey the impression of butter not melting in our mouths.

Rather than go down to Moncaret and join the main road, Luke wanted to show us a back way, while it was still light. It was a skein of winding lanes that eventually unravelled right in the heart of Castillon. Useful to know for the future, Luke said, especially late at night. The unspoken subtext was that we were less likely to bump into the police if we were returning home that way after a few drinks.

The route took us up the hill and past the spot where Jeremy and I had sucked each other in the copse. Our knees pressed extra firmly together as we passed the spot. Then, in the village of St-Michel-de-Montaigne we passed the handsome tower house where Montaigne had lived and written and thought. We wound through a hamlet so small that it practically didn't exist – though a road sign proudly announced it as Les Illarets – and found ourselves in the centre of Castillon about two minutes after that.

I'd never been to a pub with Luke. Why would I have? My lazy imagination had always seen a professor of music as someone of sober habits and rarefied tastes. When he'd twice given me beer at his house and we'd drunk from the can on both occasions... Well, even that had come as a bit of a shock. And now I was again surprised when he pulled up confidently in a place where he knew there would be parking space for both cars, and shepherded us to a bar he obviously knew well on the riverfront.

Luke was greeted by the *patron* of the bar and the one or two clients, and he joshed them back in French. I was wondering, and I'm sure the others were too, what we were expected to order by way of drinks. We remembered films, mostly set in World War Two, in which old codgers sat in the sun outside the bar in the town square with a glass or two of red wine on the table in front of them. 'I suppose we'd better stick to wine,' I said, when Luke asked us what we'd have.

Luke grimaced. 'It'll be awful muck,' he said. 'I know what you're thinking, but these days young people mostly have a beer if they go into a bar here. The muck is reserved for old codgers and alcoholics.'

'Then beer it is,' said Tarquin resolutely, and beer it was.

We sat out in the warm spring dusk on a pavement that was also a road – though one on which few cars passed – and did duty as a wharf. Mayflies were rising from the Dordogne, which ran, heard but unseen, just below the edge of the road or wharf. We could have seen it if we'd stood up. As it was we contented ourselves with hearing the splash and flurry of the trout as they rose to take the hatching insects before they could fly off.

The unseen but audible trout prompted the obvious question. Lisa voiced it. 'Why aren't we doing the Trout quintet?'

'Because I didn't think about it,' was Luke's nonchalant answer. 'Plus, I've never learnt the piano part. How much work do you want me to do?'

'Robbie could do the piano part,' Jeremy said. 'You've all heard him today. He's ace.'

Around me people were nodding their heads in agreement. I felt mortified by Jeremy's over-enthusiastic praise. There was no way I deserved it. I didn't even deserve those well-meant nods of heads. I was the lucky amateur who'd found myself tipped into this hotbed of young professionals. I was the cuckoo in the nest. But everyone seemed happy to have me here. I relaxed as I thought of that. And I glowed at the discovery that Jeremy wanted to give me such a public endorsement.

All the same I wanted to change the subject a bit. I had a question for Luke. 'How did you come by your wonderful house, in this beautiful place?' I realised as soon as the words were out of my mouth that I'd asked a question just as impertinent as: How did you get all that money in your bank account?

But Luke didn't seem to mind. 'I was an only child,' he said. 'There are good and bad things about that. One of the good things – I hope you don't think I'm being too cold-hearted about this – is that you end up with the whole lot of whatever there is. In my case, the house in Putney and … well, the place in Moncaret.

'Nobody of my parents' generation thought of having second homes, unless they were extremely rich. But my parents were romantics – I now realise – and they spent their retirement money on the house we're all staying at … on a whim, I'd have to say.'

'Sounds good to me,' said Tarquin.

'Just out of the blue?' asked Marianne.

'They'd read something by Cyril Connelly,' Luke said.

We all nodded. Even though I'd never heard of Cyril Connelly, and I was pretty sure the others hadn't either.

'He fell in love with this part of France before the war and in one of his books he drew a map of the region on which he drew a circle with a compass… and wrote inside it, *Quod petistis, hic est.*'

'You'll have to translate that,' said Tarquin. It crossed my mind that too many beers might make him belligerent.

'What you are seeking, it is here,' said Luke.

'And how near are we to the centre of the circle?' I heard myself ask.

Luke's face tightened for a second as he thought. Then it relaxed again. 'Never thought about exactly where he stuck his compass pin in. He was a bit of a drinker though probably not a darts champion, I think. So perhaps his circle was a bit hit and miss. But the centre of the region, for Connelly, was a few miles south east of us. We're in the north-western quadrant.'

Hearing Luke use the unexpected word quadrant actually changed my life. Difficult to explain. And I didn't know it at the time.

'Later,' Luke went on – he'd started to answer the question and seemed to have decided to make a proper job of it – 'they read another book. Three Rivers of France by Freda White. It begins with a very moving description of a day in the life of the town of Beynac, just up the river from here. Just after the war.' Luke's nostrils twitched. 'They bought the house here on the strength of that.'

'So did a few thousand others, no doubt' said Tarquin.

'Exactly,' Luke said, nodding his head. 'It's a bit ironic, really. Just along the river here...' he indicated with a westward sweep of his arm, 'is a stone slab that celebrates the end of the Hundred Years' War. The Battle of Castillon. 1453, I think. The day the English were finally driven out.'

'Hey,' said Jeremy, 'that's quite big. I mean, they taught us at school about the big English victories: Crécy, Agincourt...'

'But not much about the defeats,' Marianne said.

Elfrieda had contributed little to this conversation. Nor had Luke directed much of what he had to say in her direction. And yet somehow the situation between them was obvious to me. OK. Jeremy had tipped me off. Even so, there was nothing actually to see. They didn't even make eye contact all evening. Studiously avoided doing so, more like... It was still obvious.

Luke returned to his thread. 'Only now, all these years later, the English are coming back. Colonising the Dordogne. By peaceful means this time. Even in Moncaret there are two other English households. And there are a couple of musicians living along the lane to Vélines. He teaches composition at Bordeaux University. She teaches piano and strings to the local kids.

'Actually,' he said, turning to me suddenly and fixing me with a look, 'that brings me to another thought.'

'What?' I said. The thought clearly concerned me, and I was a bit startled by that.

'I gave us a very full timetable today. Although everybody had a bit of time on their own to practise...'

I knew what he was about to say. I said it for him. 'Except us.'

'Exactly. String players have their rooms to practise in, or anywhere in the garden or the house. But we poor pianists...'

Something in my heart swelled at hearing Luke bracket the two of us as pianists.

'Even so,' I said. 'There's only one piano...'

'Precisely,' said Luke. 'That's where my friends on the Vélines road come in. Or might do. I'll give them a ring when we get back. See if they'd let us go over there occasionally to do some practice. They've two pianos, I think. It's only two minutes in the car, or ten by bike.'

My mind jumped ahead. I could take Jeremy with me. Just the two of us. I saw us cycling side by side along country lanes, the wind in our hair... At that moment I felt Jeremy's knee rub warmly up against mine under the table, and I knew with absolute certainty that he was having the same thought.

Like Elfrieda and Luke, Jeremy and I had avoided eye contact as we sat next to each other at the table by the river. We'd been careful not to address too many remarks to each other. But I supposed the situation between us was as obvious to the others as the situation between Luke and Elfrieda was. I wondered now if Luke was thinking about taking Elfrieda with him when it was his turn to drive along the road to this suddenly thought-of bolt-hole to do his practice.

Tarquin began to fumble in the pocket of his jacket. 'Who's for another beer?' he said.

EIGHT

It wasn't terribly late when we got back, but we'd all had a pleasantly exhausting day, we'd said most of what we'd wanted to say to each other, and there was a general feeling that we would soon all be drifting off to bed.

We hadn't yet reached the front door, making our way in from the cars, when Jeremy plucked at my hand and pulled me away from the others. He said, in a voice that was little more than a whisper but very intense, 'Will you sleep with me tonight?'

I'd wanted to ask the same question but hadn't dared to. I felt my heart thump as I answered yes. Then, 'Your place or mine?' I asked him.

He seemed happy to be in charge of things – for the moment at any rate. 'You come to mine,' he said. 'As soon as it's gone quiet and we've had time to clean our teeth.' I had to smile at that last bit.

I brushed my teeth for a minute and a quarter, wondering how much time it would take Jeremy to do his. Then I had a piss in my wash-basin, rinsing it down thoroughly with water from the tap. There would no doubt be a queue for the communal bathroom by now. I surmised that Jeremy and Tarquin would have dealt with that last pre-bed ritual the same way I had.

Jeremy's room was around the corner of the corridor from mine. Tarquin's, Mrs Fox's and Lisa's bedrooms all lay in between. There were lights under all three doors still, but all was quiet. I walked quietly but not silently. If someone had popped out of a doorway I wouldn't have wanted them to have an impression of secrecy or stealth. So I didn't walk on tiptoe, or carry my shoes in my hand. I went barefoot, but was otherwise fully dressed.

I entered Jeremy's room without knocking. His reading light was on and he was lying naked on his bed, face upwards. His cock lay flaccid over his furry balls and his legs were crossed at the ankles. This was the first time I'd seen him completely naked. I thought he was a beautiful sight.

I pounced on him. We grappled and tussled together, he naked, I fully dressed. It was a wonderful feeling. New in my experience. Probably also in his. At last he said, 'Come on. Get undressed.'

'Do it for me,' I told him flirtatiously. I felt myself grinning like an idiot.

'Get up off the bed then,' he said. A moment later we were both standing on the carpet. He was undressing me in a businesslike manner while I, who had nothing else to do, was tugging gently at his cock, which was by now upright and stiff. And by the time Jeremy had tugged my trousers down my thighs he found mine in the same condition.

Once I had reached the same state of undress as Jeremy we stood and admired each other for a bit, while running thoughtful fingers over bellies, shoulders, hips and chests. 'You look nice,' I said.

'So do you,' said Jeremy. 'You feel nice too.'

'Ditto to that,' I said.

'Get into bed,' said Jeremy, and I did. We got right under the covers after a few minutes of cuddling and admiring each other while lying on the top. It wasn't that warm in the house at night.

I heard Jeremy say, quietly, close to me ear, and rather tensely, 'You know you told me about Chris. That you both fucked each other...'

'Yes,' I said.

'I've never done that. I haven't gone all the way with a girl either, actually.' By now I could feel his dick nosing its way in between my thighs – we were lying on our sides, front to front – and starting to piston back and forth. What he wanted to do wasn't that hard to guess.

'You want to try it with me?' I said, just to make sure.

'Yes.'

'Which way round? I mean, first.'

'I'm not sure I could cope with you fucking me,' he said. 'Your cock's so big. I might get hurt. Can I fuck you instead?'

'I bet you say that to all the boys,' I said, and then regretted it. It was rather an intense moment for making cheap jokes. 'Seriously,' I amended, 'yes. First time, anyway.'

'How do I…?'

I cut him off. 'I think whole books have been written on that subject, though I haven't read them yet. What Chris and I did was…'

I rolled us round so that I was on my back and Jeremy on top. Then he did exactly what Chris (and later I) had done. We went on to discover that despite his having no previous experience Jeremy was very good at it.

'I phoned my friends last night,' Luke said at breakfast. 'The musicians who live on the way to Vélines.' He looked rather beadily at Jeremy and me. 'I didn't get a chance to share this with anyone last night. Everybody seemed in a very great hurry to get to bed.'

There came the sound of someone spluttering on his coffee. Tarquin. He had the grace not to try and speak.

Luke took no notice. 'We now have a practice piano – possibly two occasionally – lined up just two miles away.' He looked at Jeremy. 'They can even lend you a cello, so if you want to cycle over you won't have to balance yours on the back.' He returned his attention to the rest of us. 'And Richard, my friend, has said he'll do his best to get us a decent audience for the concert at the end of the course. So…' He went on to outline the day's timetable. I listened with ears attentive as a dog's. I was free till lunchtime. So, I noticed, was Jeremy. There was no shopping to be done today. Mrs Fox and I had already shopped a couple of days ahead. 'So, Robbie,' Luke turned to me, 'you're free to make your way over and introduce yourself. Take my car, or one of the bikes. Do some practice.' He grinned impishly. 'If I were you, I would.' There was a general titter of laughter. It was wonderfully friendly. Collusive. My heart warmed at that. Luke continued – astonishingly, I thought – 'If anyone else is free to go and practise with, help yourself.'

'I'll take Jeremy,' I said. There was general laughter. I couldn't believe I'd just said what I had done. I was both appalled at and delighted with myself.

We were drinking black coffee from big bowls. Eating *tartines* – roundels of baguettes with butter, which we dunked in the coffee till the butter floated off – and *biscottes*, rusk-like pieces of toasted bread from a packet; we spread cherry jam on top of the biscottes. We were experimenting with being French. We were loving it. We were learning fast.

We took two bikes. There were three of them in the cellar. They had probably belonged to Luke and his parents in the distant past. We decided not to ask.

We went down the hill. It took about a minute. I forgot to look to see whether the wind was blowing Jeremy's hair about. By the time I remembered we had taken the left turn to Vélines at the bottom of the hill and it was too late. The rest of our road was entirely flat. Hills rose picturesquely to our left, but the lane itself lay on the edge of the Dordogne flood plain and we pedalled around its rose and cow-parsley corners at a sedate pace. It wasn't the same as overtaking the traffic on the descent of Fitzjohn's Avenue from Hampstead Heath with Chris. But it was just as good.

The Moulin de Jarre was not difficult to find. Its name was inscribed in a slice of log at the top of the stony track that led down to it. A big stone house with a tunnel beneath it, through which a millstream gushed. We cycled down to the door and knocked.

Knowing Luke as I did I should have already ditched my preconceptions about professors of music. This one – he introduced himself as Richard – was not much older than Luke was and his wife – she was called Odile and was French, Gary hadn't told us that – looked a bit younger than that.

We saw inside their big living-room for a moment. There was a grand piano in it. I was rather glad that we weren't offered the use of that, right in the middle of their private space. Instead, Odile took us into a separate part of the house. 'We rent it out in summer,' she said. 'Meanwhile, make yourselves at home. The piano is only an upright. But it is in tune…'

We said we were fine with that. Odile showed us another room through a doorway. 'Here is the cello I talked about to Luke. It is nothing splendid but…'

Jeremy said an appropriately big thank you and picked it up.

The piano sat in a room in which the old mill stones and workings – cogs and drive-shafts – were displayed. A lute and some other musical instrument for which I couldn't find a name hung on the walls. I couldn't help feeling that if Jeremy and I were ever going to live together in some future joint fantasy this would be the place we'd want to do it.

Odile was unlocking a glass door. 'There is a garden here at the back. Feel free to use it. Our garden is at the front. You are not overlooked.' Wow… Luke must have tipped her off last night. Why else would she have said that? Then she left us in peace and went back to her part of the big house.

The garden was beautiful. There weren't a lot of flowers in it. It was like a long, broad tunnel of grass, surrounded on all sides by wild hedgerows. There were fruit trees scattered about in it and a couple of tall poplar trees that shushed when the wind caught their tops. But the best bit was the stream that meandered through the meadow-like grass, its ripples dappling in the shimmer of the poplar leaves above. There were reeds and irises, and dragon-flies and frogs. Leaning over the water was an old plum tree in which there was a woodpeckers' nest...

'Come on,' I said to Jeremy – though very reluctantly. 'We'd better justify us being here. Go and do some work...'

Work? It didn't feel like work. Playing Mozart with the door open to the garden right beside me. With Jeremy sitting in the doorway, adding his cello's throbbing interjections to my – I mean Mozart's – piano part. We went through the whole piece once. Jeremy made a couple of suggestions concerning my playing of a few passages. I accepted them gratefully. He was the young professional after all; I was not.

Then Jeremy dived into his music case. He said, 'I brought something else. Do you think...?' He sounded diffident as he asked me if I'd like to play it with him.

It was a cello sonata by Beethoven. I looked at the piano part. 'It's difficult,' I said. 'It'd be a massacre if I tried to sight-read it.'

'Then let's just do the slow movement,' he said, full of understanding. He knew I wouldn't want to embarrass myself by ruining his piece. So we played the slow movement and it was gorgeous, and Jeremy's playing was gorgeous, and he looked gorgeous while he was playing it... And I didn't acquit myself too badly as I coped with the piano part.

Luke had been right. I heard the piece, as I now heard the Mozart, with new ears. I listened through the ears of a man who was falling in love.

After that we went into the garden and took all our clothes off. We hadn't had any sex since we'd woken earlier in each other's arms and kissed briefly before I left him – to make my prudent silent way back to my own bedroom before anyone else was about. We were more than ready for something now. I decided to take control. 'Lie down,' I said. 'I'm going to return your last night's compliment. You just need to completely relax.'

Jeremy giggled as he dropped onto the grass. 'That was a split infinitive,' he said.

'Who cares,' I said.

He did relax. Most wonderfully. I got inside him without any difficulty and barely caused him more a couple of winces as I went. 'You're more capacious than you knew,' I told him.

He smiled up at me. 'I'm just nineteen,' he said.

When we'd finished I stayed inside him, resting my chest on his chest. I'd helped him with my hand to come at about the same time as I did and the skin to skin contact was pleasantly moist. And then we heard voices close at hand. They belonged to Elfrieda and Luke. 'Oh bloody hell,' I said.

They were coming down the garden, Luke showing the place off to an admiring Elfrieda. I pulled myself out of Jeremy and we both turned over, in the position of nude sunbathers who were doing their backs. It was the best we could manage. They'd see our bottoms but at least they'd be spared the sight of our wet cocks.

'Ah,' came Luke's voice from right beside us. 'Wondered where you'd got to. Odile said she'd heard a bit of the Mozart and then some Beethoven, and that it sounded pretty good.'

I blessed him for that. He was letting us know that he knew we'd been practising. That we hadn't spent the whole time out here on the grass. I twisted round and looked up at him and a grinning Elfrieda, standing beside the poplar tree that had mercifully screened us from their view during the few seconds we'd had in which to rearrange ourselves.

'Oops,' I said. 'We weren't expecting you quite so early. If you don't mind turning your backs a moment we'll make ourselves more presentable.'

'Take your time,' said Luke and he turned and went with Elfrieda back to the house.

A few minutes later, as we walked back, fully clothed, we heard them strike up. Violin and piano. But it wasn't one of the pieces either of them was doing on the course. It was the Spring sonata. Jeremy tweaked my shoulder and grinned at me. 'Best leave them to it, I think,' he said.

I agreed. We walked around the corner of the house without going back inside. We said a quick thank you to Odile and her husband and then got back on our bikes.

We dawdled back, stopping from time to time to point out something in the landscape – a kestrel with a white feather in its tail, a ruined house – and then taking the opportunity to have what I'd learned to do with Chris: a bike-to-bike kiss, managing it without falling off.

We only just got back in time for lunch. It was a light pasta dish with olive oil and basil and tomato. Mrs Fox told us all that Luke had phoned. Elfrieda and he had been invited to stay for lunch with Odile and Richard. But he would be back in time for the next session – which would be on the Mozart – at two-thirty. We might all have exchanged knowing smirks at that moment. But none of us did. I thought that was very good of us.

NINE

Elfrieda played beautifully. I was learning to listen attentively to the way she handled the violin part in the Mozart. I wasn't falling in love with Elfrieda. But as I listened to her that early afternoon while we worked together with Jeremy, and as Luke gently took our efforts apart and rebuilt them, I realised I was hearing the voice – expressed through her violin – of a young woman in love. It was poignant, the way that violin spoke her deepest, most hidden feelings and announced them to the world. It was poignant in the way that the words uttered by a ventriloquist's dummy are sometimes poignant, when they give away something, perhaps not even felt consciously, about the innermost self of the ventriloquist.

And if I was conscious of Elfrieda's state of mind, of heart, of being, that afternoon, then how much more aware I was of what was going on in Jeremy's heart! The cello part of that Mozart trio was easy. Easy in terms of the number of notes at least. Elfrieda probably had ten times as many notes as Jeremy. I of course had about ten times as many as Elfrieda had. That's always the case with piano music. Pianists with ten fingers can, in theory at least, play ten notes together at any given time. Composers exploit that capability – they make piano players work really hard.

But if Jeremy didn't have many notes … God, what he did with them that afternoon! In the long sonorous tones that came from his instrument I thought I heard his whole soul opened up. Opened up to me. Opened up because of me. Offered to me unreservedly. Making me a present of his life. As I listened to him quite literally playing his heart out I found my eyes misting up from time to time, and it became difficult to see the score in front of me on the piano's music desk.

And what of me? What did my playing reveal of me that afternoon. I couldn't know for certain, but there were moments when Mozart had written deep silences for Jeremy's instrument, and during those moments Jeremy would turn and look at me... Am I being vain and conceited if I say there was a look of rapt wonder on his lovely face?

I couldn't get enough of Jeremy that afternoon. When the Mozart session ended I was free. I could have gone out for a walk or lain on the garden lawn and read a book. I could have gone upstairs and had a nap. But Jeremy wasn't free. He was involved, along with everybody else except me, in a coaching session of the Schubert C-major quintet. I joined that session in the capacity of audience.

Tarquin was first violin, Elfrieda second. Marianne played the viola. First cello was Jeremy – my Jeremy – and Lisa the mature student was the second cellist.

I tried to do as Luke was teaching us to. I tried to listen with equal attentiveness to each instrument's voice. And yet for me one voice stood out. The deep reverberant sighs of Jeremy's cello were the breaths that pierced my heart. Time stood still for me while angels danced whirling on a compass-point. I couldn't believe it when Luke suddenly said, rising from his chair, 'That's it for this afternoon, it's nearly seven o'clock.'

Two minutes later Jeremy and I were somehow in the kitchen and sneaking a quick kiss. He opened the fridge and handed me a can of beer while he took another one for himself. Then we walked out onto the lawn to join the others in the sunshine. I was entranced, bewitched, shell-shocked.

Dinner stole up softly, in successive wafts of aroma that drifted out into the garden through the open windows and doors. It was roast chicken with tarragon and cream. A small starter preceded that. Cucumber and mint with pepper and vinegar. Simple in the extreme, but to me it was something from another world. Why had my parents never thought of doing that? Why hadn't I? I decided that if I were ever to live with Jeremy we would have cucumber vinaigrette at least once every week. Dessert was a rhubarb jelly that glowed like the sunset. Serverd with a trickle of pouring cream. I thought we might like that every week too.

Afterwards Tarquin said, 'Anyone fancy crashing through the Pachelbel Canon? I've got all the parts.'

Everyone knew the piece, even if they'd never played it before. Everyone said yes. The invitation didn't really include me. The original scoring was for three violins, plus a bass line that could be played on a cello or double bass. Still, I joined the others in the big music room as Tarquin rummaged in his case for the music and handed round the parts. 'Want to lead?' Tarquin asked Elfrieda gallantly.

'No,' she said. 'Your idea. Your piece. You lead.' Elfrieda would do second violin.

'Luke?' Tarquin looked a little uncertainly at our teacher as he half-invited him to join in – like a child inviting a very senior adult to join in a kids' game, I thought.

'Mmm,' said Luke. 'I might sit this one out. But – tell you what – I'll lend Marianne my violin.' Marianne played the viola, of course, but like all viola players had started with the violin; she just didn't happen to have one with her. The arrangement clearly pleased her, to judge from her sudden smile.

There remained the question of the bass line. A sequence of eight notes, going down in a steady tread and then coming back up, that repeated itself tirelessly from the first bar of the piece to the last. 'Jeremy, Lisa?' Tarquin asked. 'Want to double up on that?' He was taking great pains to make sure no-one got left out if he could possibly help it. 'Pity we haven't got a double bass. We could have a bottom octave booming out as well.'

Jeremy spoke. 'We have a piano. And a pianist. Robbie? Want to give us the benefit of your bottom notes?' Everybody laughed, while I said yes. My task was considerably easier than playing chopsticks and involved the use of only one hand. The only thing that needed a moment's thought was how Lisa and Jeremy and I would sit, given that we would all have to read from the same score.

Jeremy took charge of this. He placed the score on the piano's music desk, then dragged the piano stool to the bottom end of the keyboard – I would only be using the bottom octave of the instrument after all. 'I can sit on the stool alongside Robbie,' he said. 'Lisa, bring your chair up next to me, then we can all see fine.'

It was a bit of a squash, a bit of a huddle, but we managed it. Jeremy sat facing slightly away from me, in order to be able to move his arm without shoving his elbow into me. But his buttocks were pressed firmly against my right hip while my right shoulder, which I didn't need to move, became his back-rest. Tarquin gave his leader's nod and we all began.

We played straight through to the end. It went like clockwork. A bit too much like clockwork perhaps. We all tried so hard to stay together that it sounded rather as if we were playing along with a metronome. Our audience – Luke and Mrs Fox – smiled encouragingly when the piece was ended but offered no comment, either of the positive or the negative kind.

Elfrieda said, 'Anybody want to do that again?' She paused, her eyes collecting up the nods around her, then said, 'Though maybe with just a tad more...'

'Schmaltz,' I offered, and everybody smiled.

We took it a lot more slowly. Tarquin had grown in confidence now that the first run-through of the five minute piece had gone so well; he was leading with an interpretation now, not just giving us the time. When we came to the deeply affecting passage that is at the heart of the piece he slowed right down – and so did we all. It felt quite lovely to be doing this, however 'unauthentic' our approach was. The piece was written in 1680 after all. Pachelbel had never been exposed to the romantic sounds of Tchaikovsky or Rachmaninoff. He might have been shocked by us... But Pachelbel wasn't there.

And then I thought suddenly, that Tarquin was playing his line like a boy in love – the way that Jeremy and I had been playing together all day today – the way we were playing our simple eight note sequence even now. I found myself glancing sideways at Marianne, playing Luke's violin ... but looking at Tarquin as she played.

It hit me like a gentle punch in the ribs. Why hadn't I realised this before? Perhaps because lovers are so self-absorbed that they fail to notice their own symptoms in others until they are very acute. I saw the way that Luke's eyes were focused on Elfrieda as she played...

I wasn't using my right arm. My right hand hung off the back of the piano stool doing nothing very much. I found a use for it. I put my arm around Jeremy's waist, lightly at first, then tighter and tighter, and kept it there until the end of the piece, hugging him to me as we both played.

When the piece was over Jeremy and I stayed where we were, together on the piano stool, my arm still round him, my hand tucked beneath his cello's back, discreetly resting on his hidden crotch. The others got up and moved. But we stayed put for half a minute. We had no need to discuss anything. We both wanted everyone to see what had happened to the two of us. We wanted everyone to know.

Later we all sat in the garden together, talking of other things than music and love. Talking of everyday things. It was lovely, the eight of us – Mrs Fox had consented to join us – just nattering about this and that. Jeremy and I were the first to leave the group. There were no ribald remarks or sniggers. There were just fond collusive smiles from everyone. Even from Mrs Fox, who was trying to make her face look mildly disapproving but failing to manage it.

There is something profound about the moment when two lovers confront each other in a bedroom for the second time. It's as big a moment as it was the first time round. The same in scale, but entirely different in character. Because their world has changed utterly since the first time they met and took their clothes off on this spot. And so it was for Jeremy and me that evening. We'd had sex the previous night. We'd had sex earlier today in the other garden, by the millstream. Tonight we made love.

I woke to see Jeremy's face, serene, full-lipped, eyelids closed, beside me. I didn't say the words. They just came out. 'I love you.'

Jeremy didn't stir. He didn't open his eyes. 'I love you,' I heard him whisper back.

I went shopping with Mrs Fox in the morning. We went down to the river quay at Castillon – following Sandrine's instructions. We found ourselves at the spot where, two nights before, we'd had a drink. Now in the mid-morning the quay was lined with stalls that sold river fish. There were perch and shad and zander, and great tiger-striped pike with jaws that snapped if you approached too close. But Sandrine had instructed us to buy lampreys.

Henry I of England was popularly supposed to have died from a surfeit of lampreys. At first glance they didn't look the kind of thing you'd want a surfeit of. Or even want to eat at all. They looked like eels, and writhed like eels in the baskets in which they lay piled up on the stall in front of us. But when you looked closely they were far from eel-like abut the mouth. Instead of jaws and lips each one had a sucker at the front of it. The *prey* in the word lamprey gave a clue as to their eating habits. They fastened their sucker on other fish and, vampire-like, drank their blood. They fed on nothing else.

Mrs Fox hung back while I negotiated the purchase of a kilo and a half of the things, and as we walked back to the car I was careful to keep the bag I was carrying them in – they were still squirming – on the opposite side of me from the one on which she walked. Back at the car I locked them securely in the boot. All the way back I was in dread that one or more would find its way through some minute aperture and join us in the passenger compartment and of the effect this might have on Mrs Fox. I feared such an event might precipitate a crash of some sort. Happily no such disaster occurred. We got the lampreys home safely and I put them in the fridge.

Though something did happen in the car on the way back. Mrs Fox said suddenly, 'Young love.' She breathed sternly and went on. 'Young love comes in many guises. It's a tricky thing to handle. Maybe you already know that. But if you didn't... Well, mark my words, Robbie. Mark my words.'

Very demurely I answered, 'Thank you, Mrs Fox.'

The whole morning was being given over to the Schubert quintet. That meant Jeremy wasn't free to spend his time with me and neither was anybody else. I had a bit of book-keeping to catch up on. Book-keeping was too grand a word for it, perhaps. I just had to total up the shopping bills and keep a tally of us boys' beers-from-fridge accounts. It still had to be done, though. I did it in the kitchen while half-watching Sandrine prepare food in an authentic French manner – I was learning a lot from doing this – and half-listening to the Schubert. When I'd finished my arithmetic I went into the music room and gave my entire attention to the quintet. Luke had been absolutely right. It makes a huge difference to the way you think about a piece of music when you're in love with one of the people who are playing it.

Lunch was a dish of warm sliced potatoes and onions with olive oil, herbs and smoked herring fillets. Like nothing I'd ever tasted before. I was enchanted by it, as I was by everything that Sandrine prepared for us. I enjoyed it so much I had two helpings of it. That was probably unwise. It proved quite difficult to concentrate on the Mozart, which we worked on – Robbie and I, Elfieda and Luke – immediately afterwards. At one point Luke was sufficiently disappointed in my piano playing as to turf me off the stool and play the passage we were working on himself. 'That's how it goes,' he said when he finished demonstrating it. 'You know that, because you did it beautifully yesterday. Just don't let up. Concentrate.' He smiled very warmly at me. 'I'm being demanding, urging you on, simply because I care a lot.' He paused, looked away for a half second and then looked back at me. 'And I don't just mean about the music.'

'I'm sorry,' I said. 'I think I just ate too much at lunch.' Jeremy guffawed at that, and Elfrieda snickered.

After the Mozart Luke, Tarquin and Lisa were scheduled to work on the Beethoven. Elfrieda and Marianne went to their rooms to practise. Jeremy and I went off to do our own practice – plus anything else that came into our heads – at the mill house. This time Jeremy drove me in his car. It was less fun than bicycles, but it meant he could take his own cello, which he would feel more comfortable with. The instrument simply went on the back seat.

We saw the kestrel with a white tail feather again, perched on a pole beside the road. It was like seeing an old friend, we said. I spent most of the journey with my hand resting on the inside of Jeremy's thigh, reaching across the gear lever. I had a go at undoing the zip of his jeans but didn't manage to. I'd never tried to do this from this particular angle; I'd need more practice. Also the journey, in a car, was simply too short.

TEN

We whizzed through the Mozart trio in no time. Practice might not make things perfect but it makes them easier, and swifter to accomplish. Almost without my realising it this had happened with the Mozart. Then, at Jeremy's shy request I did sight-read the whole of his favourite Beethoven cello sonata. The sunny one, in A.

The garden doors were open the whole time we played. By the time we'd finished the Beethoven... well, the sunlit vista outside, the sounds of rushing weir and rustling poplar leaves, the call of the golden oriole among the high branches were more than beckoning us, they were tugging us out into the millstream garden by the waistbands. We made no further resistance.

We lay naked in the long grass, trying to spot the well camouflaged orioles as they flitted among the golden leaves fifty feet above our heads. Their calls were liquid and fluting. Just three notes. Rising a minor third or thereabouts then down again. Sometimes one of the thrush-size yellow birds would add an extra note for the sake of variety. The sound of them among the sun-dazzle and breeze-shush of the high poplar leaves was enough to melt the heart. Well, it would melt the heart of anyone who'd just fallen in love. I decided that if there was a heaven it would have not angels but orioles in it.

We played with each other's dick in the sunshine. But there was no urgency or frenzy about this today. We'd had the luxury of going to bed in the same bed twice now, of waking up to each other's smiles. The knowledge that we had that all to look forward to again tonight. The knowledge that we had all the time in the world...

For the next nine days.

We put our clothes back on when we heard Luke's car drive up and tactically withdrew, to allow him and

Elfrieda their space and time in the enchanted spot. We drove back with both our dicks out, and fondled each other's across the gear lever just out of naughtiness. Anybody peering down from the height of a passing tractor could have seen us but no tractor came by. We were spotted only by the hawk-eyes of the kestrel, the one with the white tail-feather, as he stared down at us through the side window from his roadside post.

A rich aroma of cooking was pervading the house when we got back. Jeremy and I took a beer each out onto the lawn, joining Tarquin and Marianne there, but not sitting too close.

The *lamproies à la Bordelaise* – Bordeaux-style lampreys – were a stunning success. I knew, because I'd asked Sandrine, that they had been exsanguinated, then cooked in a mixture of their blood and claret along with baby leeks. I decided not to share this information with the others unless anybody asked me. Nobody did. If this was simple French country cooking then I couldn't get enough of it. But I remembered Henry I and his fatal surfeit – some people could have too much of a good thing evidently – and when I was offered a second helping I declined it.

'We're making much better progress with the pieces than I'd dared hope,' Luke announced between mouthfuls. 'We're not going to need all the time available for rehearsal over the next few days. You'll find you've a bit more time for exploring the area than we'd expected. But…' he paused and looked serious, 'I don't want anyone to feel short-changed. That they're not getting their money's worth in terms of coaching. So I have another suggestion to make.'

Luke's proposal was that in addition to the semi-public performance we'd be giving at the end of the course, we could prepare a few other pieces among ourselves and play them to each other at a less formal concert. Luke would give us a little coaching as we went along if we asked for it. Everyone jumped at the idea, but I had a twinge of misgiving about it. When string-players want to play their party pieces they always need a willing pianist to play the piano part. What if everyone wanted to do a sonata and would hand me their scores to learn in a week? There were two violinists, a viola player and two cellists... Love them all as I did there was no way I could manage all that. It would be a tall enough order if Jeremy wanted to do his Beethoven A-major.

The discussion about who would do what went on long after dinner, and involved a good many 'listen-to-this' moments around the piano in the music room, with everyone getting their instrument out of its case and playing a few bars of this or that. I never actually had to open my mouth and say I wasn't going to be willing or able to learn half a dozen piano accompaniments in a week. I think I must have given off vibes that indicated what I would have said if I *had* opened my mouth.

It all worked out rather wonderfully in the end. Lisa would do one of the Bach unaccompanied cello suites. (I let out a small breath of relief when she said the word *unaccompanied*.) Tarquin and Marianne decided they wanted to do the Bach double violin concerto. That meant someone would have to play the piano reduction of the orchestral score at the keyboard... I think I actually smiled when Luke said that he would do this.

Luke himself would do the Spring sonata with Elfrieda. Or vice versa, I should say. The violin is the leader in a sonata with piano. In theory at least. And then Jeremy would do his beloved Beethoven A-major, with yours truly at the piano. That was two pieces by Bach and two by Beethoven. The running order, when it came to performance, could be decided nearer the time. This gave me just the one new piece to practise. It wouldn't be easy in just over a week – parts of the cello sonata's piano part were fast and difficult – but I thought I could manage it.

It was a new experience for me to be having a sexual relationship with someone I was also making music with. Though *sexual relationship* pinpoints only one aspect of it. Jeremy and I were lovers. We loved each other, we were in love, we didn't want any of this to end. Playing with his dick at night, and fucking him and being fucked by him... well that was part of the package. Sunbathing with him in the millstream garden between rehearsal sessions and talking about life and love, about the things of earth and the things of heaven... that was another part. Yet just as significant, just as deep and just as magical, was the interplay between our musical personalities. I felt that we were becoming interlocked as securely and satisfyingly as the two halves of a zip-fastener, as Beethoven's music drew us inexorably together.

We were fine-tuning the Mozart now. It no longer took hours of every day. Although now the Beethoven did... And yet the wonderful thing about learning a piece of music is that, provided you put in enough effort to kick-start it, it goes on working away inside you, sorting itself out, becoming part of you, even when you're not concentrating on it, even when you're doing something else. So, in between shopping trips and quick updates to the accounts, and when Jeremy and I weren't rehearsing, or lying by the stream, we found time to enjoy the place we'd come to.

We drove, by a back road through tiny hamlets called Belvès and St-Genès, to the wine town of St-Emilion. It was a fairytale place, looking much as it must have done for centuries. An outcrop of picturesque stone buildings, church towers, medieval walls and ruined arches, it was set in a sea of vines that undulated in great waves as far as the horizon, and which at this moment of spring glowed with fresh emerald green. The sun shone into it and glanced back from it. We parked just under the town wall, in what had been the bed of the vanished moat, and explored on foot. The streets within the walls were no more than alleys of stone cobbles, winding and enticing. Some were so steep that they turned into flights of steps. Shops were caverns of wine, with bottle upon bottle stowed in racks that concealed behind them yet more of the same.

There were shops that specialised in selling little macaroons. The toasted almond smell of their cooking process pervaded the streets. Wisteria and rambling roses climbed the shop-front walls, while the roofed but un-walled structure in the marketplace was hung with baskets of geranium, flame-red. 'I could live here,' Jeremy said.

'Me too,' I said. I could live here with you, I thought, but didn't dare let that thought escape in words. I wondered if Jeremy thought the same, and whether he too had had to bite back the words. It was a fantasy of course. Jeremy and I had fallen in love, but that was a far cry from the matter of living together. Living together anywhere, let alone here. I didn't need to look in the windows of estate agents to know that any place to live in this beautiful, world famous, little town would cost a bomb. And what would Jeremy and I do here anyway? Make wine? Make macaroons? Set up in competition with French families who had been here for hundreds of years?

Obviously not. Yet that brought me to thinking, what would Jeremy and I do anywhere? Live together? I didn't know any gay men who lived together openly. I didn't know many gay men, full stop. The one I knew best – had briefly fallen for a few weeks back – Chris, lived with his wife. Perhaps that was the usual way of it.

I felt myself heaving a sigh. Jeremy heard it too. 'Are you all right, Robbie?' he asked.

'Yes,' I said. 'It's just that it's so beautiful here.'

'I know,' he said. His tone of voice said, *I know what you're thinking.* I knew that he was thinking the same thoughts that I was. They passed between us as unspoken things. Things we understood together; yet we understood too, with a great sudden sadness, that they were things we could never discuss.

Another day we took the car across the Dordogne at the village of Pessac, and walked the banks of the river there. I wanted to be doing this for ever, I thought. Roaming the banks of the Dordogne with Jeremy. Trying to name the trees whose overhanging branches we pushed aside as we followed the bankside. It was all magical, all heavenly, yet the balance of the fortnight had tipped. The mid-point of the fortnight was past.

I remembered how, as a small child, I had liked to walk up the sloping plank of a seesaw until it tipped forward and sent me scurrying onward at a much greater rate, downhill. It now seemed that the days were doing the same as my childish footsteps. They had finished their slow climb to the middle of the fortnight and were now running unstoppably downhill. We were looking towards the end of our time in the Dordogne. Towards the end of Jeremy and me?

I'd heard the expression holiday romance. I'd never had one. Now I was in the middle of one, and I was fast learning what the expression meant.

Jeremy and I continued to share with Luke and Elfrieda the practice venue that was offered at the Moulin de Jarre by Richard and Odile, and we continued to share their secluded garden for the pursuit of love and sex. When Luke and Elfrieda arrived, then Jeremy and I would vacate the place, exchanging a polite and anodyne sentence or two. None of us ever spoke about what we were doing there. We were two couples who each inhabited glass houses. We didn't rattle each other's windows with stones.

As Jeremy and I made our tactical withdrawal from that Garden of Eden one morning Jeremy said something I might not have remembered had things turned out differently. He said, in a throwaway fashion, 'Do you think Elfrieda's beautiful?'

I said I did. Because she was. She was petite and slim, was always prettily dressed, and had shoulder-length flaxen hair which she only put back – for obvious practical reasons – when she was playing the violin. She had a pale complexion and a pert nose. Her eyes were the misty blue of a summer morning at the seaside. 'Yes,' I repeated to Jeremy. 'I find her very attractive.' He didn't say anything in reply to that. We'd reached the car and his mind was taken up with the practical matter of stowing his cello along its back seat.

Suddenly we were there. We were within twenty-four hours of the end of the course. The final concert was tomorrow. The return to England the morning after that. It was hard to believe.

We had just finished a splendid dinner of guinea-fowl stewed with button onions, mushrooms and grapes, when someone suggested a nearly final run-through of the Schubert quintet. That would involve pretty well everyone except me. I was fine with that. I would happily have listened to Jeremy's playing in that piece every evening for the rest of my life; I was more than happy to sit on the sidelines and be the audience. But to my great surprise I heard Lisa say, 'Do you mind if I don't join you all? Poor Robbie will be all on his own this evening if we're all Schuberting. And I've hardly met him yet. Maybe I could keep him company for a bit.'

Her intentions were clearly not flirtatious. If they had been she would hardly have said what she just had in such a public way. Also, she was ten years older than me. I didn't know at that time – I was still very green around the gills – that women in their thirties could be just as interested in younger people of the opposite sex as men of the same age were.

I took what she said at face value. It was true that we had hardly spent any time together. Of all the people on the course she was the one I knew least. She wasn't in the Mozart, but was involved in everything else – which I wasn't – so she was rarely free when I was. And when we were all free at the same time, in the evenings, then I spent all my time with Jeremy these days, and everyone knew that.

Instinctively I looked at Jeremy's face for guidance. He gave me a nod. Then he said, 'Why don't you both enjoy a drink by the river at Castillon? But don't be long. I'll want to see you back here when we've finished the Schubert.' He said that in a mock-stern way. It made everyone laugh in the indulgent way that people laugh when lovers have taken advantage of an audience to say something publicly that is clearly meant to be understood in a private sense.

I borrowed Luke's car, and we took the back road through Les Illarets. I found I was asking myself whether I found Lisa attractive. By the time we reached Castillon I'd decided the answer was no. Elfrieda, OK, but Lisa... Well, she was ten years my senior, as well as being a woman. And I was coming to the conclusion, following my experiences with Chris and Jeremy, that I definitely was gay anyway. I found I liked her though.

I was old-fashioned enough to insist that I bought Lisa's drink for her despite my lack of years, and she was kind and wise enough to accept without protest. She had a peppermint cordial with iced water. I had a beer. I felt slightly miffed by Lisa's choice. Somehow I've never felt happy at parting with good money for drinks that don't contain alcohol.

We sat out by the river in the dusk, hearing the thrushes sing from the trees on the far side of the dark flowing current. 'Jeremy's an excellent cellist,' Lisa said.

'I'm glad you think that,' I said. I gave the reason there and then. 'Of course I think he's brilliant, but then I would do...'

'Of course. Because you're in love with him.'

To hear her say those words sent a thrill through my whole being. It was the first time I'd heard anyone voice the thought out loud. Until now the idea had been just a whisper, or the mere echo of a whisper, in the caverns of my heart. I had a sudden urge to prattle on endlessly about Jeremy, and about my feelings for him, to this woman I hardly knew, while the night fell across the river and the stars came out and I drank more beer than I could handle.

But Lisa didn't let me do any of that. 'Don't worry,' she said. 'He's really very good indeed. Quite objectively so. He has a great career ahead of him.' She paused for half a second. 'Or he will have if he doesn't get sidetracked.'

I felt my blood go cold. 'Sidetracked?' I said. 'What do you mean? Are you saying that I... that what's between me and Jeremy ... is sidetracking him? Preventing him from reaching his goal.'

'Oh Robbie.' I heard Lisa sigh. 'I'm saying this for your own good. For Jeremy's sake, but for yours as well. 'Jeremy's younger than you are. He still doesn't know his own mind. Doesn't know his own heart yet. You're – what? – twenty-two? Twenty-three?'

'Twenty-three,' I said in a small voice.

'You've probably got a good feel for who you are by now. You probably know to what extent you're straight, to what extent gay. But Jeremy's nineteen. I've been at college with him for nearly two years. That's a lot longer than you've known him, even though obviously I know him less intimately than you do. But from what I've seen of him... look, Robbie, what I'm trying to tell you is that I'd be very surprised if he was fundamentally gay.'

ELVEN

A matter of minutes ago I'd decided I really liked Lisa. Now a few seconds passed during which both of us were silent and I found, in a truly dreadful moment of self-discovery, that I wanted to hit her. My blood had run cold a few seconds ago. It now felt as hot as the sun.

I breathed deeply a couple of times, after which I felt I'd probably regained control of myself. 'Oh?' I said nonchalantly. 'Why do you say that?'

'Robbie... look, I don't want to upset you. I'm not going to tell you he's had strings of girlfriends at college, or anything like that. He hasn't done, as far as I know. If he's told you differently, well, that's fine. I don't presume to know him as well as you do. It's just that I've known him longer and ... oh dear, I hate to say this ... it's just that I'm older than both of you... No, OK, I don't mean older than both of you put together...'

I heard myself giggle. 'No,' I said. 'Of course I knew you didn't mean that.' Then we both started laughing rather crazily with relief and somehow we were clasping hands on the table top. I said, 'Lisa, have you ever been in love?'

She turned and looked me full in the face. Her eyes were dancing with laughter and – I saw and was deeply touched – affection for me. 'You dear sweet boy. Yes, I've been in love. Though why should you know? No young lover can look at someone older than himself and imagine for a second that they've experienced anything like what you are going through. All right. I've been married. I've been divorced. I did both those things very young. There's another man who wants me, back in London. I'm here, on this chamber music course, because I need some time away from him – a breathing space – to decide how much I want him. Does that answer your question?'

We were still holding hands. I felt her hand give mine a squeeze as she finished that.

'I'm sorry, Lisa,' I said, and felt something stab at my throat and eyes. At twenty-three it wasn't a feeling I was very familiar with. I squeezed her hand in return for the squeeze she'd given mine a second or two before. It was the only possible way I could complete my reply.

We drove back home – well, I drove – by the back lanes, the way we had come. I felt we were co-conspirators now, Lisa and I. Together avoiding the cops, the *flics* they called them here, together experienced in the ways of love and the traps love sprang beneath your feet. I'd driven the route only once – earlier this evening, in the opposite direction, in daylight. Now my heart raced at the thought that I'd miss a turning in the dark, get lost, and look an idiot in front of Lisa. It was a huge relief when Montaigne's tower house appeared in front of me. I knew we were on the right road. We were nearly home. Jeremy and I had walked almost as far as here…

'Montaigne,' I heard Lisa say. 'He had a friend, a male friend. And people asked him what the attraction was. His answer was famous. Do you know it?'

'No' I said.

To my great surprise Lisa quoted it in full. In very English-accented French. *'Si on me presse de dire pourquoi je l'aimais, je sens que cela ne se peut exprimer, qu'en répondant : "Parce que c'était lui, parce que c'était moi."'*

I said it back to her in English, to check if I'd understood it right. 'If you press me to say why I loved him I feel I can only … respond: because it was him, because it was me.'

'That's right,' Lisa said. 'You'll find that's how it always is.'

There were lights on in the garden when we drew up. We didn't go indoors when we got out of the car, but walked straight round the corner of the house to join the others in the garden. They were all sitting out there with glasses of wine. I knew where my place was. I made a beeline for Jeremy, sat down next to him on the grass, and was gratified when he reached for an empty glass from the table above his head, called to Tarquin to pass the bottle over, filled the glass from it and gave it to me. Only after that, and after he'd given my knee a tweak, did he say, 'Where've you been? We finished ages ago.'

'Doing exactly what you suggested,' I told him. 'Drove the back road to Castillon while you were doing the first movement. Finding a parking place, walking to bar and getting served would have accounted for movement two. Sitting chatting, drinking a beer without rushing it... You can hardly be surprised if you finished before we did.'

'What did you talk about?' Jeremy asked suddenly, in a tone of voice I'd never heard him use before.

'About Montaigne,' I said airily. 'And about us. And about love. Did you know Lisa had been married?' I asked.

'Of course,' said Jeremy. 'Everyone at college knows that.'

'I'm not at college,' I said. There was a bit of a silence after that. But we filled the silence with our understated caresses, leaning head against head from time to time and kissing occasionally. It was only half light out there under the garden lighting, and the others could only half see.

We went to bed after a bit and made love there with more abandon than we'd ever previously done. Whether I would need to remember Lisa's warnings at some future date I couldn't guess. I put all thoughts of them aside. Just Jeremy tonight, just us tonight, just this night … was heaven enough for me.

We rehearsed the whole official programme in the morning. I was excused the shopping. For once Sandrine accompanied Mrs Fox into town.

It was lucky that I worked in the theatre. I had learned the axiom: Bad dress rehearsal, good First Night. I shared it with the others at the end of the morning. Even Luke had to smile. We'd all suddenly given way to nerves. Elfrieda twice lost her place in the Mozart score – although she knew the thing from memory now – and we had to go back. Jeremy managed to fluff some perfectly easy phrases in the bass. As for me, in the last variation of the slow movement I played as many wrong notes as right ones. I thought Luke would make us go back and do it again but he didn't. Only much later did I realise how wise he was.

Similar mishaps befell the Schubert quintet and the Beethoven Archduke trio. Happily I was only a listener now. Anything that went wrong could not possibly be blamed on me. And plenty did go wrong. Even Luke took a wrong turning in the first movement of the Archduke, and they had to stop and sort it out.

Lunch was good, but nobody could eat much of it. Afterwards Mrs Fox and Sandrine started to bring more chairs into the music room and arrange them in readiness for the arrival of our small audience. I made a move to help them, but Luke stopped me, one hand laid on my arm. 'No, Robbie,' he said. 'You've joined the ranks of the professionals today. Even if it is just for today. No moving of furniture or anything else. Respect your hands on concert days, the way professionals do.'

I felt myself glowing as he said that. It more than outweighed what I considered the disaster of my own making in the Mozart middle movement. Luke's playing had also stumbled during the morning. It could happen to professionals at final rehearsals. I was one of them now. Just for today...

Richard and Odile arrived first, for which I was glad. The sight of familiar faces helped to steady my nerves. I think the same went for Jeremy, but I couldn't ask him. Pre-performance nerves are a very private thing. Like taking a crap – one of the few things that most lovers prefer not to share.

Other invitees included the mayor of Moncaret and his wife and a few other local music lovers. More terrifyingly, the head of piano at the Bordeaux music school, Yves Tasquin, turned up. So did his wife, Geneviève. Who was the principal.

I had hoped all along that we'd go in chronological order. Mozart first, then Beethoven, then Schubert. That way I'd get my ordeal over first and would be able to enjoy the rest of the concert in a relaxed frame of mind. But no such luck. Luke had decided to begin with the big Beethoven Archduke, and finish with the big Schubert quintet. The little Mozart trio would be the light sorbet in the middle of the feast. This meant that my piano playing would be heard after Luke's rather than before. A daunting prospect. *Follow that.* Even if the Mozart I was doing was very much less demanding than the Archduke – at least from the technical point of view.

Suddenly the concert was under way. Luke and Elfrieda and Lisa were doing the Archduke. I was among the audience. Jeremy was next to me, pressing his knee hard against mine. I pressed his back just as hard. I felt I was in a dream.

Even more dreamlike was it to find myself standing up, once the applause for the Archduke had died away, and moving to the piano stool now Luke had vacated it, then sitting down. I struck the tuning triad confidently, assertively: D, F, A. This was the easiest thing I would have to do today. Then Elfrieda nodded her head towards me and we began. Sustained Cs from Elfrieda and Jeremy, the first real phrase from me...

It went OK. I was shocked at how well it went. When the applause came at the end I was in a state of near disbelief. Nothing is ever perfect – especially when you're striving to perform Mozart – but even so, I was aware of one near-perfect thing: I hadn't played a single wrong note in any of the three movements. In my struggle with concert nerves that was no mean feat – even for a professional, such as I was this day.

The relaxed exhilaration I experienced as I listened to the Schubert! And listened to Jeremy's poignant notes in the bass. I was in love with Schubert too now. In love with the way Jeremy played Schubert. I was in love with the way Jeremy did everything.

Then it was all over. The tensions inside all of us subsided and collapsed like half a dozen houses of cards. We moved into the dining-room. The table was laid with cakes and pastries and glasses of sweet white wine from Monbazillac nearby. As the old-fashioned expression has it, we fell to.

Yves, the head of piano at the Bordeaux school asked me where I'd studied. I said I hadn't. I was amazed he'd asked me that. When he expressed surprise – I didn't think he was faking it, the look in his eyes seemed genuine enough – I was even more amazed. When I heard him saying that some of his final year students wouldn't have made such a good show of the Mozart I was ready to faint with disbelief. I took refuge in praising Luke's inspirational example and his teaching skills.

Luke was telling people, in a by-the-way sort of aside, that there was going to be a second concert, a very relaxed private one, in which we students were going to do our own pieces, just for one another, just for ourselves. And as he said this to more and more people, so, little by little the plan shifted. Most of our audience didn't want to go. They'd stay, they said – or most of them did, or all the ones that could – and hear us again, in more informal mode.

Well, fairly informal. Playing after one glass of wine is as informal as it gets for most classical musicians. More than one glass tends to shift the seesaw from informal to disastrous. Happily we'd all stopped at the one glass.

What is it that E.M. Forster says in A Room With A View? I've had to go and look it up. *The kingdom of music is not the kingdom of this world... The commonplace person begins to play, and shoots into the empyrean without effort, whilst we look up, marvelling how he has escaped us...* Or she in this case. For that is how it was with Lisa. She played us the Bach C-major cello suite, and was transformed by it. Lisa, ordinary Lisa, mature student of music, married and divorced, with a new man – maybe – in her life, in London, waiting for her... She was transformed by the Bach she gave us, just as an ordinary wineglass is transformed when it becomes a vessel charged with other-worldly wine.

Beethoven came next. (He was Forster's favourite composer, by the way.) Elfrieda and Luke gave us, unsurprisingly, the Spring sonata. It was beautiful, as it always is, and it was beautifully played. It held up a musical mirror to the spring sunshine now streaming in through the open French windows. It was played by two people who were in love. You couldn't help noticing that. Even if you'd never met Luke and Elfrieda before. One day I would learn that piano part, I decided. I'd find someone to play it with... I'd play it with Jeremy... Find a version transposed down an octave or so for cello... If there wasn't one I'd transpose it myself... Even if the process took a year.

The Bach double violin concerto. Luke played the orchestra's part rather self-effacingly on the piano. It was Tarquin's and Marianne's moment, and he let them have it. He let them soar. Again it was obvious that the two of them, Tarquin and Marianne, were in love. What must our audience of relative strangers have thought of us all? And they hadn't yet heard Jeremy and me…

Suddenly I wasn't afraid of what was coming next. That Jeremy and I would do our Beethoven sonata together as the finale to the whole event. A few days ago the idea (which hadn't yet been mooted) that we would do the sonata publicly, with an outside audience, would have had me waking in the night in a cold sweat. But now, heady with the success of the Mozart earlier, and inspired by the performances my fellow musicians had given, I was full of confidence, ablaze with the desire to play better than I'd ever played in my life. Not to show off. But to be worthy of Jeremy. To demonstrate my love for him in a very public way.

Over-confidence though, like Pride, 'goeth before a fall'. So did I take a very public and humiliating tumble during the exhilarating gallops of the A-major? Feet coming out of stirrups, losing hold of the reins? Not a bit of it. We gave a barnstorming rendition that laughed and sparkled in the fast movements, and was deeply affecting in the slow mid-section. And if anybody in the room was unaware when we sat down and began that they were watching and listening to two young men in love, they could have had no possible doubt about the matter by the time we got to the end.

Dinner that evening was a celebration. A victory for music. A victory for love. We began with cold trout fillets in a white-wine jelly with parsley. The main course was roast duck with orange – a novelty for most of us back then – and it was followed by a tart made with early wild strawberries. With cream.

We drank more than was good for us, and nobody cared. Even those of us – Luke, Tarquin, Jeremy – who had long homeward drives next day. Lisa came up to me in the course of the evening. 'I've decided,' she said.

'Decided what?' I asked.

'The chap I told you about,' she said. 'The one I wasn't sure about. Somehow now I am. Today's decided it for me. I'll throw in my lot with him if he still wants me to. I knew he loved me. I wasn't sure if I loved him. Even when you and I talked last night I wasn't sure. Now, after today, I am.'

I could see the truth of that. Her face was full of it. The new radiance I saw there owed something to Bach, of course. Also to Beethoven, Schubert and Mozart. Owed something to them. Owed much. But not everything.

In bed that night Jeremy and I burrowed deep into each other. And not just physically. But neither of us could bring ourselves to think, let alone mention, that this was the last night we would spend together, at least for now. Neither of us had any idea when the next time might be, or how it was to be arranged. Or even if it was to be.

TWELVE

It was as if I'd gone deaf. Stone deaf. That's the only thing I can liken it to. I felt the sudden awful absence of Jeremy as keenly as if one of my five senses had been ripped out of me. Returning to my room along the greenhouse tunnel of stairs I felt as a ghost must feel when it haunts in death a place in which it once lived and loved and laughed. Going back to work next day was just as bad. The theatre seemed empty of all life. My workmates mouthed words at me. I mouthed back. Nothing meant anything. As for the little piano in the foyer, I could hardly bring myself to look at it. While the thought of opening it up and sitting down and playing it sent a shudder across my heart.

I'd said goodbye to Jeremy at the tube station nearest to his parents' house. I'd driven back with him across France, taking the wheel turn and turn about with him. In the open countryside we'd got each other's cocks out and played with them, though tucking them away each time we came to a town and circumspectly zipping up. I wasn't sure where French law stood on the matter of mutual masturbation while driving a motor vehicle. I wasn't sure where English law stood on the matter, come to that.

Jeremy had arrived in France with Elfrieda and Marianne. It was no surprise that Elfrieda went back in Luke's car, with Mrs Fox, or that Tarquin took Marianne back in his. Lisa was offered a lift by everyone but turned the offers down. She knew what being a gooseberry meant, and insisted on using the return half of her train and boat ticket, consenting only to be driven as far as the main-line station at Libourne.

So Jeremy and I had arrived in London together, just the two of us. His parents lived near Tooting, and he dropped me off there. 'I'd ask you in,' he said, as we approached the place. 'Only I think we'd look a bit too obvious.'

'I see,' I said, trying to mask my astonishment. 'Well then.' I was thinking quickly. Tooting Broadway underground station was in sight. 'You must come and stay over at my place very soon,' I said. 'It's just about in walking distance from the college. Or a couple of tube stops.

'I'll see,' he said, again surprising me. 'My parents might think that odd.'

'But what if I was a girl?' I asked.

'That might be different. But they're still a bit old-fashioned in their views.'

'You wouldn't have to tell them we sleep together,' I said. 'You could just say…'

I wasn't sure what excuse I was going to put in his mouth and I didn't get time anyway. 'We'll see,' Jeremy said. He drew up alongside the kerb on a double yellow and we both hopped out to get my stuff from the boot. We managed a quick hug and a kiss on the pavement. Somebody somewhere nearby wolf-whistled us. 'We'll find a place to meet somehow,' Jeremy said, which was marginally better. But I was only half reassured.

'You've got my phone number?' I queried urgently. 'And my address? Both home and work?' He said he had. Then he gave me a final quick peck on the cheek and hopped back into the car. I'd stood on the pavement with my luggage. I'd watched him drive off. I'd watched and waved till he was out of sight.

It was at that moment that the world became a silent place.

A few days passed and then I got a phone-call from Luke at work. The fact of his calling me, as well as the sound of his voice, cheered me quite a lot.

'I've wangled a concert at the college,' he said. 'Repeating our programme of Beethoven, Mozart and Schubert. It's been agreed that you can take part – as a sort of visiting artist. I hope you'll say yes.'

'Of course I'll say yes!' I almost shouted it. My spirits leaped. 'That's wonderful. When is it?'

We talked dates and times and practicalities. I was in a state of great excitement. After I'd put the phone down I realised with a twinge of disappointment that there had been no mention of a second concert – no repeat performance of the event in which I'd got to play the Beethoven A-major cello sonata with Jeremy. I told myself it was wonderful enough that I'd be playing alongside Jeremy in the Mozart trio – at his college and in front of other students. I had much to be grateful for. I would not look this gift horse in the mouth.

Next day I brought the score of the Mozart in to work with me. During my evening break I opened up the piano in the foyer and started to re-practise my part.

I spent the next few days hoping that Jeremy would ring me to discuss this good news but he did not. I was afraid to phone him at his parents' house. If he was afraid even to ask me in for a cup of tea after a five-hundred-mile journey he wouldn't take too kindly to a phone-call either, I guessed.

'You're still practising the same piece?' Tanya queried as she came past one afternoon. 'I thought you'd have that done and dusted on your chamber-music course.'

'Yes and no,' I said. 'It went very well out there, but we're doing it again at the Kensington College of Music, where all the others study. They've invited me to take part, which is wonderful.' I paused, wondering whether to tell her the next bit, but then it just came tumbling out anyway. 'It's especially wonderful because I get to play with the cellist again. He's a lovely young chap called Jeremy. He's the new man in my life.'

'God, you're quite a goer,' Tanya said. 'That's the second new man in a month.'

'Oh come on,' I said, grinning now. 'A month and a half.'

'Well, all right then. But what happened to the last one? What was his name…? Yes, Chris.'

'He pulled up the drawbridge,' I said. 'And I found out why. I discovered he had a wife.'

'Oh cripes,' said Tanya.

'Anyway,' I went on. 'Clouds have silver linings. I've got Jeremy now.'

Tanya's face assumed a cautious expression. Had she been a railway signal she'd have gone to yellow at that point. 'Well, be careful of him,' she said. 'You don't want to lose him too.'

'Don't worry,' I said. 'I won't.' My words were brave and my tone was jaunty. But I knew I was doing little more than whistling in the dark. I'd told Tanya not to worry, but actually I was worried. I hadn't heard anything from Jeremy in over a week.

I didn't hear anything from Jeremy for the next two weeks. I thought about him all the time, of course. Especially when I masturbated in the morning before getting up. Then I got a phone call from Luke. The concert was only two days away now, so I wasn't surprised to hear from him. 'We're doing a run-through in the morning,' he told me. 'Do you think you can make that?' He was talking about the morning of the concert, two days hence.

I said, yes I could. I'd need to get away soon after one, though, as I needed to spend a couple of hours at work. My evening duties would be covered again by the woman who had stepped in while I was in France. I explained all that.

'Good,' said Luke. Then there was a silence at his end. I was on the point of asking him if he was still there when he said, in a rather serious and subdued voice, 'There's something I suppose I ought to say.' Another pause.

'Yes?' I said.

'About Jeremy. I think I have to warn you not to expect too much.'

A chill ran through me. 'Meaning what?' I said.

'I don't think there's any more I can tell you on the phone,' he said. 'Just – as I said – don't expect too much.'

'OK,' I said, in the most adult manner I could muster. Then we said goodbye and hung up.

I suppose I'd sort of expected it. That didn't stop me from feeling like a balloon with the air gone out of it.

It was a bright sunny morning on which I made my way to the college for the second time in my life. But the sunshine didn't penetrate my heart. I was dreading my re-encounter with Jeremy. I wasn't looking forward even to rehearsing the beautiful Mozart.

The rehearsal was to take place, like this evening's concert, in the main hall of the college. I went in through the front doors and up some steps. The hall was dauntingly big. I walked the length of it and walked up more steps onto the platform, where a concert-size grand piano stood, all nine feet of it, shiny and black. I'd seen a cartoon by Hoffnung in which a concert soloist, making his way to the piano in front of his expectant audience is transformed into a matador, his brooding adversary morphing into the bull he has to fight. I identified with the poor man at that moment.

I was a few minutes early. But I was expected. I was no trespasser. Swallowing my fears I walked up to the nine-foot instrument – it was a Steinway – and placed my score on the music desk. Then I sat down, played the scale of G major boldly with both hands in three octaves, and immediately afterwards launched into the first movement of the Mozart.

After a minute I saw from the corner of my eye that someone had entered the hall from the back. I had no intention of stopping. If the new arrival wanted to challenge me or ask who I was and what I was doing he would have to walk up to me and stop me himself. But then I found myself focusing a bit more on the newcomer. I saw that it was Jeremy. Then I stopped.

I stood up, walked towards Jeremy, descending the platform steps. Jeremy began to walk towards me.

There's a piano sonata by Beethoven called the Farewell. It depicts Beethoven's sad farewell to a friend, his patron the Archduke Rudolph (yes, that Archduke again) who had to go into exile for political reasons during the Napoleonic Wars. At least the first movement depicts their parting. The second, slow movement represents the sadness of absence. But the third shows the pair of friends reunited. Their rushing joyously towards each other and embracing can be heard clearly in the exuberant scurry of the notes. That is how it should have been with Jeremy and me. That is how I'd imagined it in advance. I'd even heard the exultant Beethoven finale in my head as I'd pictured the scene. But sadly my reunion with Jeremy was not like that.

We walked towards each other slowly. I tried to smile at him but couldn't. Was he trying to smile? I don't know. If he was he didn't manage it any better than I did.

I took him by the elbows. He made no attempt to embrace me. But at least he didn't try to shake me off. I kissed him on the cheek. He accepted the kiss with grace, but coolly, the way I'd always imagined Jesus receiving his betrayer's kiss in the Garden of Gethsemane.

'Good to see you,' I said.

'Good to see you too,' he said.

Jeremy looked me in the eye for a second. His eyes were so clear and blue and beautiful that my heart skipped at the sight. But only for a second. He quickly looked away again. Looked sideways. He didn't want to hold my gaze longer. Or he couldn't. That avoidance of my eyes by his eyes didn't tell me everything. But everything I really needed to know just then was written in it.

'Do you want some tea before we start?' he asked.

'Good idea,' I answered.

'We'll go to the canteen,' he said. Then he led me along twisting corridors and down some stairs, and I hoped he'd be with me on the journey back as I hadn't thought to put a ball of string in my music-case.

While we were queuing for our tea Elfrieda materialised alongside us. 'Oh hi,' Jeremy said in a rather artificially breezy voice. Elfrieda gave a nervous snicker, looked quickly, almost anxiously at Jeremy for a split second, then turned to me and gave me a kiss. I now knew everything. I also had the knowledge – hidden from me until today – of exactly what Jesus had felt at that most dreadful moment of his life.

Surprisingly the rehearsal went swimmingly. I listened to the Beethoven first. Actually I did more than listen. I made myself useful by turning the pages for Luke. Then we breezed through the Mozart. Jeremy and I needed to look at each other a few times to synchronise our entries. We didn't look at each other apart from that.

I excused myself after the Mozart was finished. I said I ought to go and do some work at the theatre. I'd be listening to Jeremy's soulful cello playing in the

Schubert this evening. I didn't think I could face hearing it twice. Tarquin caught my by the sleeve as I was leaving. 'See you later,' he said. 'Have a chinwag after the concert tonight.'

I hadn't realised how much I liked Tarquin till that moment.

Good dress rehearsal, bad First Night. That was the other half of the theatre adage. But for once it didn't work like that. The concert went as well as the run-through had done. About a hundred people showed up, and the applause at the end of each of the three pieces was warm and heartfelt. Nothing bad happened and all my notes were intact. The bad thing had happened already, and it was not in the music.

Luke took us all out for a meal afterwards. We went to a fish restaurant near South Ken underground that was called The Contented Sole. It was very good. Even so, the food wasn't a patch on what we'd got used to being served by Sandrine in France. There were no lampreys for a start.

Tarquin did seize a moment to talk to me. 'Bit of a bummer for you,' he said. 'Jeremy, I mean.'

'Win some, lose some,' I said, trying to be manly about it. Tarquin was quite a big, manly young chap.

'Well I'm sorry anyway,' he said, and gave my hand a squeeze.

'Thanks,' I said. 'Though it's a bit of a bummer for Luke too.'

'Oh, Luke will find someone else, no doubt,' Tarquin said. 'He always does.'

That took me by surprise a bit. It didn't fit at all with my idea of Luke. 'In that case,' I said, attempting a bright tone, 'No doubt I will too. As I'm lucky enough to be ten years younger than Luke.'

'Stay lucky then,' said Tarquin. 'Handsome guy like you. You'll do all right.'

Little did I guess just how prophetic that little conversation would turn out.

THIRTEEN

I felt like someone who has lived inside a box for most of his life without knowing it. Like a battery hen that had no idea there was a bigger world out there. Twice in the last two months I'd been let out of my box and had seen what lay out there, my eyes wide with wonder. Now for the second time in those two months I'd been firmly shut back inside it.

My days were dark.

I don't remember how much time passed. Was it days or was it weeks? Or even months? I thought often of Tarquin's lovely words. 'Stay lucky. Handsome guy like you. You'll do all right.' I remembered the tone of voice in which he'd uttered them. Remembered his smile. Those things, those things alone, bore me up during that dark time; they kept me afloat on that black ocean of the night.

It wasn't months. It can't even have been weeks. I was deadheading the columbines that grew like weeds outside the theatre door. They'd been in flower when I came back from France. It could only have been a week at most. Then there he was, walking up the path. I was astonished. Shot up from my crouching position in the flowerbed. Bolt upright. 'Luke!' I said.

'Oh hi,' he said, then grinned like a nervous schoolboy. 'I wondered, do you have a spare ticket for tonight?'

'I'm sure we do,' I said. 'Come in and I'll sort it out.'

We only seated a hundred and twenty-seven. When we sold out, as we often did, we bent the rules and sold sitting space on the gangway steps at a pound a pop. With Luke at my side I bent over the box-office desk. Maggie, the box office manageress was on duty. She was my favourite. She called me her toy-boy. That's why she was my favourite. I said, 'What have we got for tonight?'

'Robbie,' Maggie said, her eyes twinkling, 'You know we're sold out.'

'Just a single,' I said. 'Stairs?'

Maggie made a face. She mouthed rather than said the words, 'You know we don't do that before seven o'clock.'

I was senior to Maggie in the official hierarchy. But she'd been here eight years against my fourteen months. And while I was twenty-three she was fifty six. I took a breath. 'This is Luke,' I said. 'He's my best mate.' I felt myself go hot after I'd said that.

Maggie sighed. Then her eyes twinkled again. She turned them towards Luke. 'I'm very pleased to meet you, Luke.' She gave him her be-ringed hand to shake. He looked a bit startled for a moment but quickly regained his composure and shook her jewelled hand warmly and with a smile. I heard Maggie say to him – and I felt my toes curling with embarrassment as she said it, 'It's high time he had a best mate.' She marked the gangway area on the seating plan in front of her with a single cross.

I put my hand in my pocket and took out a pound note. 'My treat,' I said to Luke.

Luke looked at his watch. It was six o'clock. 'In which case may I treat you to a beer across the road?' He grinned and added mischievously – he'd heard me talk about theatre routines at tedious length while we were in France – 'Before the Half.'

We went across to the Swiss pub and Luke bought us a pint of Worthington 'E' each. The evening was was warm enough for us to sit out on the small triangular terrace, with the rush-hour traffic roaring past on either side. It felt like being in the prow of a tempest-tossed ship.

'Thank you for coming,' I said.

Luke shook his head from side to side. He said, 'I couldn't very well not.'

I would need some time to digest that. I said nothing. I took a very slow swallow of beer instead.

Luke said, 'I don't know if you'd be free for dinner after the show tonight…'

I'd be free for the rest of my life. I was just old enough – though only just – not to say this. I said, 'That sounds nice.'

'Good,' said Luke. 'I don't know where's good round here…'

'There's a Chinese place,' I said. 'Though I haven't tried it.' I pointed along the Finchley Road. 'Then there's the Cosmo. That's where the critics hang out on First Nights.'

'Well,' said Luke. 'If it's good enough for the critics it should be good enough for us.'

So that was where we decided to go

An interesting two hours passed between that drink at the Swiss pub and our walk to the Cosmo. When the doors to the auditorium opened each evening they were manned by two volunteer ushers – one sold programmes while the other tore the tickets in half and pointed out the seats. That was the principle at any rate. In practice, though, the volunteers would often exercise the right of volunteers everywhere to simply not turn up. Then I would tear the tickets and juggle the programmes and money bag or, if I had a friend or parent in the audience that night, dragoon him or her into helping me out. And that's how it went tonight, since neither of the volunteers arrived. I was treated to the sight of the professor of chamber music at the Kensington College of Music standing opposite me and touting programmes, fumbling for the correct change in the cloth bag he was wearing round his neck and exchanging banter with his customers. He kept laughing and grinning at me; he was clearly enjoying himself.

Then he went in and sat down on his step at the last moment. I resisted a sudden silly urge to join him. I stayed in the foyer, on the watch for latecomers, and wrote out the beer and spirits orders for the next day. At the interval I had a gin and tonic ready for Luke, and one for myself.

He talked a little about the play he was watching. Though only as a matter of form, I rather thought. It was a worthy piece about migrant workers in Germany. I didn't think it was something that would especially engage Luke's interest. I had to conclude that the main reason for Luke's visit here this evening was me. And that thought was rather nice.

I'd already explained to Luke that he'd have to hang about afterwards until the bar closed and I'd locked up. He'd realised that already, he said: he had no problem with it. In the event he was perfectly happy chatting with the cast over a drink after the show was ended, and when the place was empty he helped me take down the optics and tidy things away, close windows and lock up. It took me back to that time with Chris a couple of months back. So much had happened to me since. The whole of Jeremy had happened. His arrival in my life, his departure from it. I'd had my heart broken twice in those two months. Now here I was again, looking forward to my dinner, locking up the theatre with Luke.

'How did you come here?' I asked.

'By tube,' he answered.

'I'm on my bike,' I said. 'I'll walk it to the Cosmo with us. Don't like to leave it chained up here after the theatre's shut.' So we trundled it alongside us.

'It's on me,' Luke said when we'd sat down and menus had been given to us. 'Just in case I hadn't made it clear earlier.'

'Then you choose for me,' I said.

'I guess that won't be difficult,' Luke said. 'I have the impression you'd eat pretty much anything that was put in front of you. You certainly did in France.'

'You'd be right,' I said. 'And the same goes for drink.'

'I'd noticed that too,' Luke said. Then his mouth turned up at the corners and he gave me the warmest smile I'd yet received from him. He suddenly stopped being thirty-three or whatever and became the teenage Luke that he, obviously, once was.

We had tomato soup with basil in it. That was new to me. Then we had veal Holstein. An escalope of veal fried in egg and breadcrumbs, with a fried egg and anchovies on the top. Chips with it, and asparagus. Luke had chosen the wine too. We had a bottle of Chablis.

'People at the college said very nice things about your piano playing,' Luke said. 'And I agreed with them. You've made splendid progress. It's a pity they didn't get to hear you playing the Beethoven.' That was as close as either of us had got to mentioning Jeremy. Luke looked me carefully in the eye at that point but I didn't react so he went on. 'I must find a way to get you playing again at the college. It'd be good for you. Not quite sure how I can fix it yet but I'll think of something.'

I said, 'If my piano playing has improved it's entirely because of you.'

'No it isn't,' Luke said very sweetly. 'You always had it in you. All I've done is to help you draw it out.'

The expression *the elephant in the room* hadn't been thought of then. Or if it had, I'd never heard anyone say it. But that evening the dining area of the Cosmo was full of elephants. There was the Jeremy and me thing, the Elfrieda and Luke thing, the … I hardly dared formulate the thought … the Luke and me thing. We sat and looked into each other's eyes and talked about everything under the sun except the elephants listed above.

I turned and looked round the room at one point. 'Oh my God,' I said.

'What?' said Luke.

I jerked my eyes in the direction of another table.

'I see,' Luke said. 'It's Kenneth Williams.'

'Yes,' I said. 'I knew he lived round here...' I tailed off. The man was eating on his own. Unlike us.

Luke said, 'How fast can you play the Minute Waltz?'

'Um... I don't...'

'Maybe we could have a race,' said Luke. Then he reached with his hand across the table and touched mine. He said, 'I am joking of course.'

Something in my heart spilled out then. But it was inside myself. I didn't let it be obvious to Luke.

The pudding we had was a bit ordinary. Lemon meringue pie. My mother made that just as well at home. But I wasn't bothered. I was with Luke. And everything about this evening was turning out to be both surprising and non-surprising, moment by moment, at the same time.

Luke paid the bill. We walked out into the street. I unchained my bicycle from the lamp-post to which I'd tethered it and we walked back towards the tube station.

'Which way do you go from here?' Luke asked when we stood under the searchlight beam of the underground entrance lamps.

I jerked my head across the road. 'I bump down the steps   . Belsize Road...' I resisted the urge to recite the names of all the roads   between here and Colville Terrace. If ever Luke came back there with me – and my imagination balked at that – it would certainly not be tonight.

Luke seized me suddenly by the elbows. 'The parting of the ways,' he said. Then, 'Will I see you?'

It was an expression I'd never heard before. It sounded both very American and very grown-up.

I found I couldn't meet his eyes. I looked down at the pavement. To my surprise I found my gaze focusing very intently on some tiny weeds growing along the cracks. 'I'd like to see you,' I said.

'Me too,' said Luke. The words came wrenched out of him in a sort of animal growl. I'd never before heard him sound like that. But I was learning a lot about Luke tonight. I was learning a lot about myself.

Luke leaned in towards me and kissed me lightly on the lips. Then he turned and ran down the Underground steps.

Did I sleep that night? Actually I suppose I did. A totally sleepless night is a rare event. Yet we all have nights that fill the spaces of our minds with unmeasurable reams of thoughts. As I lay rolling and squirming on my mattress I thought about Luke. I saw him as I'd seen him this evening. Wearing jeans that were pressed and knife-edge creased. Had no-one told him that in today's world nobody wore jeans like that? Was it going to be my responsibility from now on to tell him things like that? He'd been wearing a clean white shirt with the top two buttons undone…

Yep, I had told myself by the time I finally fell into a deep sleep as it was getting light outside, I fancied Luke.

I had no reason now to go on practising the Mozart trio. Or the piano part of the Beethoven cello sonata that I'd played with Jeremy over in France. On an impulse I went to the public library (it was conveniently next-door to the theatre) and hunted down their copy of the Beethoven violin sonatas. It included the Spring sonata of course. With no very clear idea of where this might take me I started to practise the piano part.

Tanya heard me working on it in the foyer. 'A new piece,' she observed. I told her what it was. 'It's the right time of year at any rate,' she said, looking out through the glass door at the sycamore trees that shielded us from the sight of the public library – and shielded the library from the sight of us. 'Your playing sounds very dynamic these days,' she said. 'How are things with the new man? Jeremy, is that right?'

'Actually,' I said, 'that went pear-shaped. Jeremy was only nineteen. He discovered he was really more into the female sex.'

'Oh dear,' said Tanya. 'Poor Robbie. You're not having a lot of luck. And yet your piano playing...'

'I know,' I said. 'It's come on by leaps and bounds. I learnt a lot on the chamber-music course. It really stretched me. A lot of it was down to the guy who tutored us. He's a professor at the Kensington College of Music. Actually...' I hesitated, not wanting to give hostages to fortune by saying too much. But then I said it anyway. 'He came here the other night. Took me out to dinner after the show...'

'My God, Robbie,' Tanya said through a surprised laugh. 'You don't half move quickly. But a professor...'

'I know what you're thinking,' I said. 'But he's only thirty-three. He just happens to be very good at his job. Anyway,' I backtracked slightly, 'I haven't heard any more from him since.'

Tanya looked at me in a manner I can only describe as appraising. 'You will,' she said. 'Handsome boy like you. You'll hear from him soon enough.'

FOURTEEN

The show ended that Saturday night. I joined the 'strike', the taking down of the set during the night, ready for the get-in and fit-up of the new production on Monday. Working as one of the casuals, I made a bit of extra pocket-money out of these monthly forays into the world of manual labour. And the strikes and fit-ups were fun, the activity quite social. This particular Saturday night I put on a pair of winter gloves before I joined the strike. My temporary workmates ribbed me about that. 'Have you got your hands insured for millions, then?' someone asked and the others laughed.

'Not quite,' I said. 'It's just that I'm taking my piano playing a bit more seriously these days and I wouldn't like to damage them. 'Good luck then, mate,' they said.

I got back home about three o'clock to find a handwritten letter in my post. It was from Luke. I tore it open a bit anxiously, still standing under the naked light-bulb in the hall, before even padlocking my bike.

Dear Robbie, I read.

It was lovely to see you yesterday. I'm not quite sure what to write. I'm a little afraid I might end up saying too much.

The light went out. 'Fuck,' I said, quite loudly. I groped along the wall for the time-switch button, trying not to fall over my bike in the dark. I found it, pressed it and the light came back.

I want to see you again, of course. I hope you won't have changed your mind about that. I'll try and phone you over the weekend. I don't know how easy it will be to meet, with you working six evenings a week. And I can't be sure if in the cold light of day you'll still want that.

I pressed the time-switch again before the light had a chance to go out.

Right, I'll leave it at that for now. I'll phone you soon.
Affectionately,
Luke

I chained my bike to the banisters and went upstairs. I couldn't phone Luke now, at past three in the morning. I went to bed, after setting my alarm for ten o'clock.

I got up as soon as it went off. I threw my dressing-gown around me, put some coins in the pocket and went out into the hall where the pay-phone was. There was no guarantee that he'd be in of course... But he was.

'Thank you for your letter,' I said as soon as I'd identified myself. 'It was lovely.' I went straight on, so he wouldn't have to try and think of something to say in reply to that. 'I'm having lunch with my parents at one o'clock,' I said. 'I don't know if there's any chance...'

He cut in. 'You could come and have a beer with me first,' he said. Then in a more cautious tone of voice he added, 'If you like.'

'Yes I like,' I said.

'Then come over as soon as you want to. Come now if you want.'

'I will,' I said. 'I just need to put some clothes on first.'

'Why?' said Luke. 'Are you naked?'

'I'm at the pay-phone in the communal hall,' I said with a giggle. 'I'm in my dressing-gown.'

'How disappointing,' he said. It was astonishing, yet also wonderful to be spoken to like that by Luke. I had never imagined that Luke of all people would talk to me like that.

I said, 'I'll get dressed at once and head over to you,' then hung up.

I took the precaution of phoning my parents – I was fully clothed now – before I left the flat. I told them I'd be with them at one as arranged, but that I'd been invited to Luke's for a beer first. That way they wouldn't get a surprise, or get suspicious if they happened to look out of the window as I was going in to Luke's house opposite.

Luke came to the door in a sweatshirt and a pair of shorts and with bare feet. I'd never seen his legs before. For someone of over thirty they looked amazingly good. Actually, they looked amazingly good full-stop. They were lightly tanned and with just enough fair hair on them to look masculine. His muscles were better defined even than mine were. I wondered if he worked out. 'Come in,' he said.

I found myself inside his hallway more quickly than I'd ever obeyed an instruction in my life. Luke pulled the door shut behind me and then kissed me on the lips. His arms came around me and mine went round him. I didn't put them there deliberately: they did it all by themselves. In the same way my tongue decided of its own accord to make its way into Luke's mouth.

After a minute Luke disengaged himself. 'Come through,' he said. He took my hand as he led me into the living-room that was also his music room. At the sight of his piano I found myself blurting out, 'I've just started learning the piano part of the Spring sonata. Don't know why.'

Luke turned and smiled at me. 'I do,' he said. 'And I'm glad you have.' Then he wrapped me in his arms again and resumed the kiss that he'd interrupted a moment earlier. This time, as I pressed against him, I could feel his cock. It was semi-hard inside his shorts. Mine was thickening in my jeans by the second and I knew, because we were pushing so firmly against each other, that he could feel that. I wasn't sure, though, whether to try and get his out. I was uncertain of the etiquette that the situation demanded. Me with an older man. Who was actually my teacher. He hadn't poured us a beer yet. And I was on my way to my parents' house for lunch…

Luke decided for me. He gently pulled apart. 'Come on, let's get a beer inside us. We can go into the garden. We've got plenty of time for all that.'

All that, I thought. We were going to do *all that* together. Me and Luke. I felt my legs and arms tingle at the thought.

We sat on the grass together. For a town house his garden was quite big. There were trees in it and roses, which were coming early that year. There was quite a high larch-lap fence around it and had the neighbouring houses been bungalows it would not have been overlooked. Unfortunately though, the neighbours' houses were two-storeyed ones. Like my parents'. Like Luke's.

I wrote *unfortunately.* But blessings sometimes come strangely disguised. I found that having to look at Luke while not being able to touch him actually increased my lust. Looking at him in his now extremely revealing shorts as, beer cans beside us, we sat on the grass I realised just how much I fancied him. I had an idea, picked up God knew where, that at twenty-three I shouldn't be fancying men of Luke's age. But I didn't fancy men of Luke's age, I told myself. Among that age group I fancied only Luke.

'I'm working tomorrow morning,' I said.

'So am I,' said Luke.

'Shut up and let me finish,' I said, laughing. It was the first time I'd dared to speak to him like that. He was fine with it; I could tell by the twinkly smile that appeared on his face. 'I'm doing the fit-up early on. But after that I have the whole day free and the evening. There's no performance tomorrow night, just the dress rehearsal, and I'm not involved with that. I don't have to go into work again till Tuesday afternoon.'

'I see,' said Luke. 'I guess we ought to take advantage of that. I'm sure we can sort something out.'

'I'm also free this evening,' I said. 'After I've seen my parents.'

'And I'm free too,' said Luke. At that moment I saw that a small spot of wet had appeared on the front of Luke's shorts. He caught me looking. 'I guess we might have to go indoors in a minute,' he said. 'What do you think?'

Two minutes later I was in Luke's bedroom. It was a matter of seconds only before Luke had whipped off his T-shirt and shorts. It took me a few seconds longer to match his state of nakedness. I had shoes and socks and jeans on and – unlike Luke – was wearing underpants. From the window the newly naked me could see the front windows of my parents' house. Fortunately Luke had net curtains up, and as it was the middle of the day we had no need to switch on the light. Even so it was a bizarre experience.

Now Luke was already turning out to be full of surprises. (Though in falling into his lap so quickly on the rebound from Jeremy I'd more than surprised myself.) Not the least of this day's surprises was the size of Luke's cock.

Chris and Jeremy had both commented, when they first saw it, on the size of my own dick. And the very few other people I'd had sex with before them also had. But I think that because I wasn't very big in other respects my penis looked – and still looks – bigger in contrast to the rest of me than it actually was.

But there was nothing relative about the size of Luke's adornment. He was over six foot in height, against my five foot eight. I'd managed to make my dick measure seven inches on a good day sometimes, digging in the ruler tip rather aggressively below my pubic bone. But Luke's uncircumcised and very elegant truncheon looked a good inch and a half longer than that. That was only a guess of course. This wasn't the moment to go measuring it. On the other hand I couldn't fail to comment. 'You're staggeringly well equipped,' I said.

'You're not actually small yourself,' said Luke and promptly reached out and squeezed my cock. 'You're very wet,' he said. I hadn't realised that until he touched it, though then I certainly did. He smiled into my eyes. 'It's nice,' he said.

We rolled onto his bed together and then rolled around on it, mashing our cocks together by thrusting our hips. 'Do you want to come?' Luke asked suddenly. 'Or save it till later?'

I wanted to do both actually. I told him that. I added, 'Though I don't think I've got a lot of choice right now. Not wanting to come now wouldn't make a lot of difference. It's likely to happen of its own accord any minute.'

'Then let me help you out,' Luke said. He reached his hand between us and started to masturbate me. And without asking whether he wanted me to do the same to him I did it anyway. He didn't object.

I think I came within about five seconds of Luke starting on me. It went all over both our bellies in a great wash. To my surprise Luke then pulled out of my grasp and knelt over me, bent his head down and proceeded to lick up my semen like a dog. Not that any dog had done that to me. Nor had any human being before now. This was another of Luke's surprises. Another of today's firsts.

I'd learnt my lesson about going on with the other person if I happened to be the one who came first. I laid him on his back and went at his mighty instrument with my fist. From time to time I got my lips around it experimentally, but I could only get the tip of it inside my mouth. I wondered what would happen if he tried to fuck me with it. I'd cross that bridge when I came to it.

Luke's cock seemed in no particular hurry to climax. I stole a glance at the bedside clock. It said a quarter to one. I was due at my parents' in fifteen minutes. Five more minutes passed and I was on the brink of saying that I was sorry but would have to leave him when without warning he shot, very copiously, all over his chest.

I returned his compliment of a few minutes earlier. It was the least I could do, I thought, though I realised as I licked him clean that I was also licking up my own spunk mingled in with his. Ah well, I thought, this is life. I got up off the bed and started to put my clothes on. 'I'll have to go,' I said. 'I'll be back later…'

'No, don't do that,' Luke said. 'Your parents would see you arrive here, and then leave. Or maybe not leave. We can meet up in town this evening. Perhaps I could even stay the night at your place. What do you think?'

'Oh, but I've only got a grotty bed-sitter in someone's flat,' I said. 'It's…'

'Don't be silly,' Luke said. He reached towards me from the bed and ruffled my hair as I bent down to pull my jeans up. 'You ought to realise that won't matter in the least.' We arranged to meet at The Sun In Splendour at seven o'clock.

'How is Luke?' my mother asked. She was making the gravy. Very well, I told her. I couldn't really go into more detail than that. I hoped my jeans wouldn't provide the detail anyway, betraying me with tell-tale spots.

'He seems to have a girlfriend these days,' mum went on. 'Can you pass the Bisto?'

Don't get me wrong, I really do like gravy made with Bisto. I just couldn't help remembering how much more imaginatively they did things in France.

'A girlfriend?' I queried.

'Oh dear,' my mother said. 'I shouldn't have told you that. It's being a nosey neighbour and gossiping and I really hate that.'

I had no answer to that, obviously. 'What does she look like?' I asked.

'Long blond hair. Very pretty. But very young.' She paused a moment and continued to stir the Bisto. A disapproving look passed over her face. 'Young enough to be one of his students,' she said.

'Oh that's Elfrieda,' I said brightly. 'She was on the course with us.'

My mother sniffed. 'Well, I know it's none of my business, but I really don't think that's right.' I could have smoothed her feathers by telling her than the Luke-Elfrieda thing was in the past. I didn't. It suited me very well that mum should think Luke had a girlfriend. Especially if the Luke-me thing went on developing. Mum might not so quickly become suspicious of us.

Gallantly – I thought – I drew her fire towards myself. 'Elfrieda was in the Mozart trio we did.'

It worked. She turned towards me, leaving the gravy to sort itself out. 'I still haven't forgiven you for not telling us you were playing at the college that time. Fancy not giving your parents a chance to hear you – playing with young professionals in public. And we weren't even asked.'

'I'm so sorry,' I said. 'It was arranged at short notice and I just didn't think of it.' Of course I had thought of it. But I'd wanted to have time to myself with Jeremy that evening. A futile wish, as it had turned out. I'd told my parents about the concert at the college the weekend after it had taken place and all hell had broken loose. The storm had barely subsided yet. 'But,' I said with emphasis, 'Luke wants me to play there again some time with his students. I promise you I'll invite you when it happens.'

'Well, make sure you do,' said my mother. 'Now be an angel and get the plates out.' She saw me make a move to open the oven door. 'Robbie,' she protested. 'Use the oven glove!'

FIFTEEN

When I got back home I took my jeans off and also my underpants. I walked down to the Sun In Splendour wearing just a T-shirt and my old school gym shorts with nothing underneath. I had plimsolls on my feet but no socks. This was the way Luke had been dressed this morning and it had been a major turn-on for me. Now as I shot occasional sideways glances into the reflective shop windows of the Portobello Road I found I was getting quite turned on by myself. If I looked at my reflection carefully enough I could even see the helmet outline of the head of my cock in my shorts.

Luke arrived in the big bow-fronted bar about a minute after I did. Knowing that he had to go to work in the morning I'd expected he might be a bit more formally dressed than I was. But he wasn't. He was however carrying a sort of sports bag on one shoulder. His clothes for the next morning, I guessed.

He couldn't disguise his own appreciation of the way that I was dressed. Gay men didn't rush into each other's arms and kiss in the middle of London pubs in those days. Instead he took one of my hands in both of his and yanked it so hard I thought it might come off. Actually what did come off was his sports bag. It slid down to his elbow and he had to curtail his hand-shake and push it back up. 'Good to see you, little soldier,' he said, the endearment startling me a bit. 'And, hey…' he glanced down at me admiringly, 'you're looking good.'

'I do my best,' I said. 'And so are you, by the way.' I looked down at him admiringly. He was wearing the same shorts he'd had on in the morning. Still without underpants, I was pretty certain, since inside the shorts I could see the impressive dangle of his dick.

I hadn't had time to get myself a drink yet. Now I got a gin and tonic for us both. We took them outside and managed to get the last free table in the little courtyard at the back of the pub.

'What are you doing tomorrow?' I asked.

'Schedule's not too bad,' he said. 'I've two lessons to give in the morning.' He stopped and gave me a rather searching look. Then, 'One of those is with Jeremy,' he said.

'Life goes on,' I said.

Luke reached under the table and gave one of my bare knees a surreptitious tweak. 'Thank God it does,' he said. He went back to answering my question. 'There's a heads of department meeting which I can't miss, or people will be tut-tutting. But there's nothing else I can't postpone till you're back at work later in the week. I could be free in the afternoon...You say you are...' His confidence gave way for a second. 'If you'd like that.'

That momentary show of insecurity... My heart surged out to him. I felt a crazy smile take over my face. 'Of course I'd like that.' I hadn't meant to say the next bit, I hadn't even known I thought it. 'I'd like that more than anything on earth.' That just popped out, but once it had done I knew I really meant it. I wasn't just saying it.

Luke changed the subject. 'What have you eaten today?' Then quickly, 'Oh no, I shouldn't have asked. You'll probably spend ten minutes telling me, with recipes and cooking times and the lot.'

'Oh,' I said, feeling uncomfortable suddenly. 'Do I really go on about food a lot?'

Luke gave me a smile that was very affectionate. 'I'm only teasing. You're charming and entertaining when you talk about cooking. Never stop doing it.'

I promised him I would not.

We exchanged our alimentary information. I'd had a roast Sunday lunch, I told him. Luke hadn't done one of those for himself, of course. He'd had a sandwich. 'You'll need a proper meal this evening,' I told him. I gave him a mock-stern look, 'Can't have you starving to death.'

'But you won't want to eat a full meal again,' Luke said.

I said, 'Want a bet?'

We went to a little Greek place in Hillgate Street, the other side of the Gate. It was a place I sometimes took my parents to and as it happened, Luke also knew it. I won't go on and on about the dishes. I'll just say that the meal was good.

Again there was that tantalising situation in which Luke and I wanted like mad to stroke each other's bare legs, then ease each other's shorts off, but couldn't do because we were in a public place. The experience was tantalising and tickling to our sexual appetites. All we could do was look. All... Even so it was pretty good. Pleasure deferred. I was learning the taste.

'I'm wondering how to put this,' Luke suddenly said. I wondered what dreadful bit of news he was about to break over my head. I'd cleaned my teeth before coming out. Used deodorant... 'I'd like to offer you some piano lessons,' I heard him say. It hit me with a wallop of delight. 'That might be the last thing in the world you'd want...'

'I'd love it,' I interrupted. I couldn't have thought of anything more wonderful. Not then. OK. Sex perhaps, but I already had that. Love? Hmm. That would have been a different matter. It was too soon after Jeremy. I wasn't ready for that yet. Not quite...

'Are you sure?' Luke said. 'You wouldn't feel patronized? Or that the situation was a bit awkward because of...'

'Because of what's happening between us.' I finished the difficult sentence for him. 'No, I wouldn't.'

'Obviously I'm talking about giving you lessons – not selling them to you. It could be at the college or in

Putney, or a mixture of both.' He looked down at his plate and showed the charming, diffident side of himself again. 'It's the only thing I can think of to give you that would be worth something – that would be worthy of what I feel for you – and that wouldn't cost me the earth.'

Wow. That was an avowal and a half. There was something buried in the middle of that lot that I'd need to take home and think about in a private moment next time I had one. 'I think that's wonderful of you,' I said. 'I'm not sure how I'll be able to thank you...'

'You can thank me just by being yourself,' he said.

We walked together back up the Portobello Road. Sunday evening one of its rare times of tranquillity and peace. I'd done the walk a million times. Past the little terraced cottages. The first of the antique shops where a little old lady sold elaborate old tea-sets. Past a cul-de-sac called Simon Close. I'd sometimes thought about that name and that, if I ever had a boyfriend called Simon that's where I'd want him. Close. Across the intersection with Chepstow Villas and past the big antique arcades. The murky-looking Duke of Wellington pub... How utterly new and different a familiar walk is when you do it the first time with someone else. We turned right into Talbot Road, then left into Colville Terrace. 'Here it is,' I said. We walked up the stone steps and I unlocked the huge front door.

Luke was very taken with the greenhouse tunnel-bridge of steps. 'Like going down a rabbit hole in a children's book,' he said. 'Entering a different world.'

'It's a bit basic,' I found myself apologising.

'I love it,' Luke said. 'Do you know why?' He didn't wait for me to try and answer. 'Because it's part of you.'

I counted myself an observant listener. He'd used the words *I love* in the first of those three sentences. The third sentence had ended with the word *you*.

He shed his sports bag from his shoulder, took me in his arms and started kissing me. I was only too happy to respond in kind. I pushed my crotch into his and he pushed forward into mine.

In the morning we both had to get up early. We seemed to wake at exactly the same moment. I found myself looking into Luke's eyes suddenly and thinking how right this felt. We hadn't attempted to fuck each other during the night. I was still afraid of the size of Luke's erection and of getting hurt by it. And I was diffident about taking the initiative with a man ten years my senior and asking, or just trying, to fuck him instead. And Luke didn't ask me to fuck him. In fact neither of us said anything on the subject. Instead we simply masturbated each other three times under the bedclothes – those times spaced out over the whole night – each time coming abundantly over each other and into the sheets.

I worked through that morning's fit-up in a bit of a trance. I wasn't sure what was happening to me. Surely nobody could fall in love three times in the space of a couple of months? Not and it be serious each time. Perhaps I was a very shallow person, and my emotions were not the full ticket, not to be taken seriously by myself or others. Then I thought about Luke. He'd been pretty serious about Elfrieda a month back. Or so it had seemed to us all at the time. Now he was equally heavily into me. Perhaps he wasn't a serious person either. Perhaps he just played with people. Had trifled with Elfrieda's affections and was now trifling with mine before moving on to someone else. Quite apart from the added complication: that Elfrieda was a girl and I was a bloke.

But you could worry endlessly about such things, I told myself, and with no useful result to show for it.

Nobody could look at the start of a new relationship and know what lay further down the line. Nobody in the world was old enough or wise enough in the ways of the heart to know how a new thing would turn out. Young or old, experienced or completely green, you would always be in the same boat as everybody else. It was only afterwards – after you'd split up – that you knew enough to say, well *that* was doomed to fail... or – after the other party was dead – well, *that* worked out all right.

I decided I had no option but to go with the moment – like someone travelling down a river sitting on a barrel and encountering exhilarating rapids – trusting the instincts of my unschooled young heart and hoping that Luke's smile on waking this morning meant what I thought it did. It wasn't really even a question of being hopeful. It was simply about getting on with life. Trying to deal with what life bunged at you Though during the course of that morning I did hear a little optimistic voice somewhere in my head. Foolish or misguided it might have been. Or just plain wrong. But the words were positive enough. 'Third time lucky,' the voice said.

We met a little after midday in Hyde Park. Luke bought us each a sandwich and lemonade outside the Lido Café beside the Serpentine, then we set off across the lake in a rowing boat. As we rowed together across the glassy water Luke told me a story. About Edward Elgar, Yehudi Menuhin and this very lake.

Menuhin, then a boy of 16, was chosen to play Edward Elgar's violin concerto for the HMV recording of June 1932. The piece was to be conducted by the venerable Sir Edward, then in his seventies, himself. A whole day had been set aside for the recording by the studios at Abbey Road. They had played through the whole thing once, as a sort of warm-up. 'Capital,' said Elgar when the run-through was finished. He beamed at young Yehudi. 'It couldn't possibly be done better. I'm off to the races.' And with that he picked up his hat and left. The remaining sessions were cancelled and the orchestra packed up and went home. Yehudi had nothing left to do for the rest of the day, so the recording's producer, the legendary Fred Gaisberg, took the young chap rowing on the Serpentine… Just like us.

On another occasion Elgar took Menuhin to the races with him. Senior musician and rising star… I tried not to pursue the comparison. Elgar was the most famous British composer of his generation, Menuhin a prodigy who was soon to have the whole world at his feet. Luke and I were … well, we were just me and Luke.

We walked around the park. We stopped at another café for ice cream and tea. Then Luke said – his diffident side presenting itself again – 'Would you be OK with me staying a second night at your place?'

I said, 'Don't be daft, Luke. Of course I'd be OK with it. You know I would.'

We went to a film at the Odeon, Marble Arch and then had something to eat at Pizza Express. No need to explain, I guess, what the something was.

With Luke I was learning to expect the unexpected. Even so, I was slightly taken aback when he said, just after ordering a tiramisu for both of us, and topping up my wineglass, 'Did you and Jeremy use to fuck each other?'

I didn't blink or flinch or blush though. I just said, 'Yes. Why do you ask?'

He smiled very sweetly at me. 'Because I thought that you and I might like to do that. But I wasn't sure what sort of experience you'd had.'

That cut both ways. He might be ten years older than I was, but I couldn't know without him telling me what sort of homosexual experiences *he* had had. I didn't say any of that. I said, 'Yes, I would like to do that with you.

With Jeremy we did it pretty much turn and turn about…
If you see what I mean…'

'Your way of expressing it is more than clear,' said
Luke, his voice deadpan but his eyes laughing. 'If
anything, almost too graphic.'

'Sorry,' I said. 'I'm just trying to say that I'm happy to
receive as well as to give. Only…' I lowered my voice to
a whisper. *'You know what I'm going to say, Luke.
You're just so fucking big.'*

'Big but gentle,' said Luke. 'Like a good gun-dog. I'd
be very careful not to hurt you. If we decided to go that
route.' He paused and took a sip of wine. Then he
looked at me very seriously and said, 'I promise you,
Robbie, that even though I'm a bit more massive than
you are I'll never do anything to hurt you. And I'll never
try and make you do anything that you don't want to. As
long as I live.'

I've said I was an observant listener. I picked up on
that last sentence all right.

Vinum, oleum et frumentum. Wine, olive oil and
wheat. The three staples of Ancient Roman life. We
didn't bother with the wheat that night. Not after we'd
finished the pizza at any rate. But we made full use of
the other two. Back at my place Luke plied me with
wine – with my full agreement – in order to relax me.
The olive oil (from my kitchen shelf) he applied to my
other end. He got me into a sort of headstand on the bed,
naked, and poured from the Sainsbury's bottle into my
rear end as if he were filling a carafe. We'd got a towel
from the bathroom beforehand and Luke held it in
position carefully so as not to spill too much of the oil on
the sheet. Then he lowered me into a more normal
position, put the oil bottle on the bedside locker and slid
his maypole dick inside me as easily as if it had had been
the size of a wine-bottle cork.

A little later during the night I returned Luke's compliment. The olive oil was not so much of a necessity this way round. Nevertheless I used it. It was still on the bedside locker, after all, so why not?

SIXTEEN

And then that was it for a bit. We wrote each other daily letters. They grew longer – and stronger – as the days passed. We phoned when we could. It was weird, the knowledge that Luke and I worked just a few miles from each other yet because of our different work schedules couldn't easily meet up.

I saw him on Friday at last. All right, only two full days had passed since Tuesday when I'd said goodbye to him at the front door. We'd only written three letters each and phoned twice in the intervening time... It just seemed an awful lot longer than that. Fridays were the day that I did the wages at the theatre in the morning, then had the afternoon off, returning to work for the show in the evening. This Friday I used my afternoon to go down to Kensington and have my first piano lesson with Luke at the college.

I knocked at the door of his room. It seemed weird to be doing that. He welcomed me in and when he'd shut the door gave me a kiss. I immediately clutched at his cock. But he stepped back. 'We can't,' he said. 'Not here. If anybody caught us I'd get chucked out. We just both have to be patient for a bit. Sunday, come to my place. That's only a day and a half to wait.'

I had to accept that. I didn't want Luke to lose his job. And actually he was slightly less of a temptation in the twill trousers he wore for teaching – together with a shirt and tie – than he was in bare feet and shorts.

I played a movement from a Bach keyboard suite, the D-minor English suite that back then everybody seemed to like. 'He does go on a bit in this one,' Luke said, when I'd come to the end of it. 'But you play it very nicely.' He then proceeded to coach me on it. Which is another way of saying that he gently, sweetly, tore my performance of it apart. Then I asked if he had time to hear me play some of the Spring sonata's piano part.

I played through the first movement. 'It's coming on nicely,' was his comment. 'You're on the right track. Bring it again when you've got the tempo up a notch and I'll have a proper look at it. Meanwhile...' He crossed the room and took his violin out of its case then walked back with it towards me. 'I'm sorry but I can't resist. Slow movement, can we?' He gave me a comical, silly-me look, which I loved. 'Can you give me an A?'

I knew the slow movement well by now. I'd practised the piano part. Before that I'd heard Luke play it at the piano with Elfrieda doing the violin part. But there's no experience in the world like doing it for the first time ever together with someone you... With someone you like a lot. Luke positioned himself beside me, so he could read his part from my piano score over my shoulder if he didn't remember all the notes.

The slow movement is deeply moving from the outset. The piano carries the heart-melting tune over the light footsteps of the bass, while the violin does little more than give a few answering sighs to the lover's serenade. Then in bar ten the violin takes up the lover's haunting tune... I felt my chest start to shudder and my throat choke up. Thank God I didn't have to try and sing it. I looked up and sideways at Luke.

He'd suddenly shut his eyes. He didn't need to read that opening melody, he knew it soul and heart. I thought I saw a faint tremor around his closed mouth.

The door opened and someone burst in suddenly. We stopped at once and looked. Elfrieda stood in the room. Her usually serene face was red and contorted with anger. Her eyes blazed at us. 'You're playing our sonata, Luke,' she called across to him. 'How could you... How could you do that?!'

My choked emotion turned to anger in an instant. Petrol blazing when you threw a lighted match on it. 'And how could *YOU*...?' I was standing up, I discovered, as I shouted at Elfrieda. But I didn't finish my sentence. Elfrieda had turned abruptly, gone out through the door and slammed it behind her. We heard her sobs and wails receding down the corridor as she went.

I looked at Luke. 'Do we go after her?' I was new to this kind of situation. I didn't know what the standard procedure was.

'No, Robbie,' Luke said. 'Not a good idea. Who knows what might get said.' He fixed me with a look. 'By any of us.' Then he put his hand on my shoulder and lightly pushed me back onto my seat. 'But I think we'd better not go on with the Spring right now. It was a bit insensitive on my part. Save it for when we're at my place.'

I told my mother over the phone that Luke was giving me piano lessons. That I'd be going to his house at ten thirty this Sunday before coming across to them for lunch. 'Giving you lessons?' my mother said.

'Yes,' I said. 'It's his way of saying thank you for my help on the Dordogne course.'

'A pretty big thank you if you ask me,' my mother said. 'After all, you went on the course without having to pay anything.'

'I did the shopping, translated from French and kept the accounts,' I said. 'I fixed the lavatory cistern when it started overflowing and drained the washing-machine twice. I earned my keep.'

I heard my mother sniff. 'Anyway, what's happened to that girlfriend of his? Elphine. I haven't seen her for weeks.'

'Elfrieda,' I corrected. 'Oh, she's still about.'

Luke had made a tape-recording of our first lesson together. He told me about it during a phone-call. 'I hope you don't mind,' he said. 'And I couldn't tell you about it in advance. It would have made you self-conscious.'

'I'm already self-conscious when I'm playing to you...'

'Exactly,' said Luke. 'But there was method in my madness.' He explained what his plan was.

I thought it very funny and laughed down the phone. 'But you must remember to edit Elfrieda's interruption out, and my response to it.'

'Thank you, thank you, thank you,' said Luke. 'Thank God you brought that up. I hadn't thought of that.'

When I got to his house that Sunday morning we went first into the music room. Luke slipped the cassette of my previous lesson into his tape machine, turning the volume quite a good way up. Just in case my parents should be listening from across the street.

Then we went up to bed, leaving the tape to play itself. We had sex to the sound from below us of the Bach D-minor English suite.

That set the pattern for the next couple of months. There were lessons at the college. Always recorded for use on Sundays at Luke's house. Sunday nights he usually came to my place. He also took to coming over and sleeping with me one day in the middle of each week. He would arrive late, a little before midnight, coinciding with the time I got back from work. He explained his reason for these midweek visits. 'So you won't have to masturbate too much,' he said.

'So *you* won't, you mean,' I said.

Then one day he said to me, 'End of term is coming up. Long college holidays. I'm planning to spend August at Moncaret. You'll come with me, I hope?'

'I get two weeks' holiday then,' I said. 'But not a whole month.'

'What about the lady who covered for you back in the spring?' he said.

'I don't know if she'd be willing to put in another whole fortnight,' I said.

'Of course you don't,' said Luke with a shrug. It was a very French sort of shrug. I guessed he'd picked it up over there. Perhaps it came automatically with having a château in France. Then he said, without particular emphasis, 'Those who don't ask don't get.'

So I asked. I got.

'A month?' my mother said. 'A whole month? Just you and Luke?'

'I expect some of his other students will turn up as well,' I said. Though I had no evidence for that.

'If you weren't such a sensible fellow,' she said, and now her gaze into my face was as serious as I'd ever seen it, 'I might be worried about you and Luke.'

'We're just good friends,' I said. I said this in the full knowledge that she wouldn't believe me. I also knew that she couldn't for the moment query it. I'd fired my warning shot, though. She would have to think about it, and I knew she would. We'd both have to deal with the repercussions in due course.

'Will Mrs Fox be coming?' I asked Luke. I'd only seen Mrs Fox once since the first trip to France. Her position in Luke's world seemed imprecise to me, though the two of them appeared to know exactly where they both stood. I'd got it out of Luke – he hadn't divulged this very readily – that she'd been his nanny when he was a small boy. She'd been retained up to a point by his family for occasional help in the house, and Luke had kept that up after his parents' death. She occasionally cleaned for him and even more occasionally cooked him a meal...

'No,' Luke said. 'She's going to Austria with her daughter, son-in-law and grandchildren.'

'To Austria?' I don't know why but it struck me as the unlikeliest of destinations for Mrs Fox. 'Well, good,' I said. 'I'll be able to cook for us myself.'

'And wash up?' Luke asked, rubbing his hands and making a pantomime expression of hopefulness.

I said, 'Now I do draw the line at that.'

We drove to the ferry at Portsmouth and took the car ferry to St-Malo overnight. In the morning we breakfasted as the ship made its way through a scattering of little islets just off the craggy Brittany coast. The sun shone on the green grass of the islands, its rays skipped flashing among the blue waves of the sea; the mewing gulls that rode the air currents with motionless wings alongside us gleamed grey and brilliant white. If I'd been a painter I'd have tried to paint the happy vision at that moment. In an excess of romantic fervour I'd have called my painting Landfall with Hope.

The golden green of spring had darkened to olive since I'd been in the Dordogne last. Gardens were no longer filled with delicate early columbines but with rudbeckia flowers the colour of marmalade. I didn't mind. Every season has its own particular beauty. The weather was hot, the Dordogne sky was cloudless and I was with Luke.

That first night back at Moncaret he took me out to dinner at a restaurant above the Dordogne river in the upstream town of Porte-St-Foy. We had foie gras and toast with a glass of sweet golden Monbazillac, then a ballotine of rabbit, the whole animal boned out and stuffed with bacon and mushrooms, and sliced in rings onto our plates. Below us late swallows swooped among the arches of the road bridge, harvesting the river's evening crop of gnats.

Back at what I continued to think of as the château – though Luke said it was no more than a *manoir* or a *gentilhommerie,* a word I liked: it meant simply a gentleman's residence – we strolled in the garden in the near dark and listened to the country's sounds of night.

'It must bring back memories of Jeremy,' Luke said.

'It does,' I said. 'But I can cope with them. I think I'm over Jeremy.'

Luke didn't say anything. No *I'm glad of that.* Or *Good.* I appreciated that moment's silence of his. I went on, 'And I think I'm over Chris.'

'Chris?' Luke struggled for an instant. I hadn't mentioned Chris for about a month. 'Oh yes,' he said, remembering. 'The one who lives at Gospel Oak in a basement with his daughter and a wife. Has a tapering cock slightly smaller than yours is but very nice. Uncircumcised, I think.'

'Well remembered,' I said.

I hadn't set foot in Luke's bedroom back in April. Hadn't even seen through the open door of it. Now I inhabited it as my own. It's funny how things change suddenly like that. When our walk was finished we went straight up there, undressed and climbed into bed. It was luxuriously comfortable after a long day's driving, the sheets clean and smelling fresh. We both had ramrod erections when we jumped into that end-of-day haven. That was par for the course. When we got into bed together the two of us always did.

Perhaps I'd gone to bed too soon after eating. As I lay asleep, flat on my back, that bloody rabbit started to make its way back up. I woke in terror. I wanted to breathe in but couldn't. My windpipe was obstructed and all I could do was to choke and cough.

Luke was woken at once by the noises and flailing of my panic. I felt his big arm come round my back and haul my shoulders up. Then he was banging on my back with his hand and talking to me. I had no idea what words he was coming out with. I was in terror of my life. I heard only the agonised rasp of my own breathing, rasps of in-taken breath that were cruelly cut off before they'd properly started, and the choking splutters of my unproductive coughs. My chest was at the limit of its endurance. I knew then that this was what drowning would feel like. A few seconds more and I would be dead.

Luke continued to thump my shoulders. Then suddenly my throat and nose were filled with something. I found the energy to spring out of bed and rush to the window. I opened it before Luke managed to follow me there, though it was less than a second before he did. I leaned out...

A minute later I was in Luke's arms, still standing by the window naked, bawling out my fright. My tears were running everywhere. There was snot, and God knew what else...

'It's OK, my darling,' he was saying. Over and over again, 'It's OK, my darling.'

I managed to hear the words this time. I registered the D-word. He'd never called me it before. Until this moment no-one except my mother ever had. And I realised that Luke too was crying. That, like me, he'd had a terrible fright.

No more words were said by either us of till he'd taken me to the bathroom and got both our faces cleaned up. Not until we were back in bed. Then he pulled my head tight against his own and held it as if this time it was he who was drowning. 'Oh my darling,' he said in a very small and frightened voice. I felt a tremor run through him as he said it. 'I thought I was going to lose you. To lose you before... Before I had time to tell you what I felt.' He had to stop for a bit. Then he got his voice back. Just about. 'I love you, Robbie. Whatever the consequences. Whether you love me in return or whether you don't. I love you as I've never loved anybody else. I've waited too long to say it. I nearly didn't get the chance.'

I wanted to tell him I returned his love totally, unreservedly, but I couldn't. I was crying too much. My chest was hurting again now, just as much as it had done during the choking fit. He had to wait a whole minute to know whether I returned his feeling. Then I did just manage to squeeze five words out. 'I love you too, Luke.'

But that was all I could manage still. He had to wait till the morning to hear the other five. *Darling. With all my heart.*

SVENTEEN

It was as if we'd been assembling an unfamiliar piece of furniture and having difficulty with it, and then someone had come along and told us we'd got the thing the wrong way up. Now we knew we loved each other, now we'd admitted it to ourselves and each other, everything in life made sense.

The things we said to each other in the days that followed!

I want to live with you.

I want to be with you for ever.

We're never going to be apart.

Nothing and no-one can come between us.

It's the big one, isn't it.

For always...

And when raising a glass, 'To Us.'

They weren't complex sentences, any of them. Nor was the vocabulary difficult. Nor were any of them original. They'd been said in every human language and in every conceivable accent and dialect by millions upon millions down the centuries. But by God Almighty, were those words big!

And weren't the days big. I don't think a drop of rain fell throughout the entire month. We spent part of every evening with watering cans and buckets, trying to keep the flowers upright. In the mornings we made music together. We did the Spring sonata, of course. Doing this repeatedly I discovered I could play it without actually shedding tears, the way that professionals have to learn to manage it, even though the emotions that welled up every time were just as intense. Luke then made me sight-read all the Beethoven violin sonatas and all the Mozarts. The three little sonatas by Schubert. The jewel-like sonatina by Dvorak...

And Luke encouraged me to raise my game among the repertoire of solo piano works. He got me onto the Chopin études. The frighteningly difficult number four of the opus ten set, and the last one of all, opus twenty-four number twelve, which seemed all-encompassing in its intensity. It seemed to me that it towered as big as the mountainous seas of the Southern Ocean. It shone bright as the midday sun when the clouds of minor harmonies broke apart and C major appeared in majesty at its zenith. I'd always thought C major a pretty humdrum key, a take-it-or-leave-it key. Chopin showed me now how wrong I'd been. C major was the grandest key, the most magnificent, the most life-affirming, the most numinous key in the universe. I've compared it to the sun already. I've talked about seas that run higher than apartment blocks. What else can I compare it to in my inadequate words, in my puny voice? It was as big as my love for Luke.

We entertained occasionally. Richard and Odile came over. I cooked. Cooking for French people can be a bit of a nightmare if you're a Brit. I did them a classic French stew, a *navarin* of lamb. It's made from cubes of lamb shoulder and baby spring vegetables, including turnips no bigger than your average radish. The key to its success is the cooking liquor, a mixture of white wine and a brand of vegetable juice called V-8, which came from the supermarket. Odile, who was French and a good cook herself, enthused about it. She even asked for the recipe. I considered that a triumph.

I also cooked for Sandrine and her husband when they came to dinner. I did another French classic – wings of skate in black butter with capers. I served it with new potatoes cooked, in the English way, with mint. I wasn't sure how this would go down with our French guests and waited for their verdict with bated breath. To my relief their reaction was positive. Sandrine thought new potatoes with mint was, just for once, an improvement on the way the French did things. I suspected, though, that she wouldn't be trying it out on her own guests.

In the afternoons Luke and I went for walks among the vineyards, or along the river's banks. We took drives around the region, explored its quaint market towns, Le Bugue, Rocamadour, Perigueux, Sarlat... The whole region was a tapestry of beauty. As Cyril Connelly had written: *Quod petistis, hic est.* Here is what you seek.

The nights we spent together in bed. And that turned out – as it always does when you're in love – to be the best place of the lot. I'm not sure if Cyril Connelly also said that.

We began to talk about future plans. Was there a way, we asked each other, that we could live permanently together at Moncaret? We could more easily live together in Putney, we had to admit. I could give up my flat and move into Luke's nice house. But live together directly across the road from my parents? Both our minds boggled at the thought of that.

We got a phone-call from Tarquin astonishingly. He was in the area, with Marianne, touring the countryside. Could they look us up? They could. They did. In the end they stayed two nights. In the early evenings of those two days we played – sight-reading – piano trios and quartets. In the late evenings we went to the bar in Castillon, sitting out on the riverside quay and putting the world to rights as we drank. We came home both times by the winding back road through Les Illarets to avoid any possible confrontation with the *flics*. Before he and Marianne left us Tarquin took me aside for a moment inside the house. 'Told you you'd do all right for yourself, didn't I?' he said.

'You didn't,' I answered. 'You told me Luke would do all right for himself.'

'Same difference, it turned out though.' He looked at me. 'You all right with it?'

'All right with it? I'm a bloody sight more than all right. Over the moon's more like it. It's the best thing that's happened to me in my life.'

To my enormous surprise Tarquin threw his arms around me quickly and kissed me on the lips. He wiped his own lips afterwards with the back of his hand instinctively. 'Don't know where that came from,' he said. 'Never done that before in my life.'

August ended and we drove back north through France. It was a wrench to leave Moncaret. Neither of us knew when we'd be going back. At least it was a question of *when* this time. It wasn't simply *if.*

Our London routine resumed. I continued to have piano lessons from Luke at the college. Luke always taped those sessions and played them back while we made love on Sunday mornings, for the benefit of my parents who might or might not be listening from inside their house. It meant that, if I cared to listen and wasn't otherwise too distracted, I got the benefit of Luke's wise coaching twice.

I nearly got caught out once. After lunch one Sunday my mother said, 'Would you play that piece to us? It's a Chopin study, I think.'

Without thinking, I said, 'I'm not sure I could do it justice. I haven't touched it for two days.'

'But we heard you playing it this morning,' mum said with a bit of a frown.

'Yes of course,' I said, my mind now working at full-rev. 'I meant apart from that.'

'It sounded very good when we heard it earlier,' my father said.

'Well, if you say so.' I went to the upright piano in the sitting-room and sat down at it. The Chopin étude in question was the final big one, the one in which the clouds of C-minor are dispelled by the dazzling C-major sun coming out. As I played it I thought about Luke and my love for him and because of that I played it better than my small talent deserved or warranted. My parents certainly thought it went all right. My mother gave me a strange look afterwards. As if she had discerned the cause of my new mastery of my instrument.

Christmas loomed. That season of parted lovers. I was going to spend it with my parents. My sister and her husband – a soldier who was at that time posted in northern Germany – would be joining us. Luke said he had been invited to Yorkshire to stay with friends. Friends. How dared Luke have friends!

Halfway through December my mother asked me, 'What is Luke doing for Christmas?' I said, oh, he's staying with friends. 'Ah,' my mum said. 'Well, if he wasn't I'd have said he could come and spend the day with us.'

'Oh wow,' I said. 'I'll tell him you said that. I'm sure he'll be delighted that you asked.' My mind was in a whirl. Was it too late for me to backtrack? Get Luke to cancel his visit to Yorkshire? It would be wonderful to have his company on Christmas Day. But in the evening he'd have to go back to his own empty house. He could hardly take me with him and take me up to bed for Christmas night. Then he'd be on his own for Boxing Day... I wondered whether it was time to come clean with my parents and tell them everything. In my head I ran a scene in which I told my parents and my sister and her soldier husband that I was gay and in love with Luke while dad carved slices from the Christmas roast. Somehow my imagination balked at the next bit...

I talked to Luke about all this. We agreed that it would be a deeply uncomfortable experience for both of us if Luke joined my family for the festive meal. That I should come out to my parents when the time was right, or ripe; not spring it on them just because of a date on the calendar. I thought that all over the country – indeed all over the world – a million unofficial couples, of whatever sex and whatever orientation, were having the same conversation ... and many of them coming to the same conclusion as Luke and I had.

Christmas came and went. So did my sister and brother-in-law. Luke went to Yorkshire and came back.

The New Year was welcomed in. It looked as though this coming year would be a repeat of the previous one. It was hard to believe it was nearly a year since Luke had innocently asked me, out in the street where my parents lived, if I wanted to join him on a chamber music course. The seeds of our futures are small grains indeed.

Then, in the middle of January Luke phoned me at work. 'Something's come up. I need to talk to you about it. But not over the phone. Can I meet you for a drink during your five o'clock break? In the Swiss pub?'

'Yes,' I said. 'But I've got a better idea about the venue. Get the tube to Hampstead. Meet me at the Holly Bush.'

I cycled up Fitzjohn's Avenue. Actually, for most of the way I had to push my bike. I'd reap the benefit, though, on the way back. I hadn't been inside the Holly Bush since those two times with Chris. That too was almost a year ago. Being there with Luke might, I hoped, lift the curse from my memories of the place.

As it happened I didn't meet Luke inside the Holly Bush. He was coming out of the exit of the tube station as I came past. We walked together up Heath Street and then mounted the steps that led up the grass embankment to the pub. 'What is it you need to tell me?' I asked. I was anxious by now.

'Don't worry,' he said. 'It's nothing bad. But I'll wait till we're sitting down with a drink in front of us.' That would involve a wait of about a minute. I could live with that.

'I've been offered a job,' said Luke as soon as we'd sunk into two of the leather armchairs beside the gas fire.

'Doing what?' I asked. 'And where?'

'You met the head of the Bordeaux music school back in the spring. Geneviève Taskin, wife of Yves. They're setting up a branch in Libourne.' Luke stopped and took a swallow of beer.

'And?' I said.

'They want me to run it.'

'My God,' I said. What would happen to me if he accepted? I thought in panic. I saw my life collapsing like a house beset by a demolition ball.

'There'd be a job for you too,' I heard Luke say. 'We'd need somebody to deal with the admin.'

'Bloody hell,' I said. That would involve more than a bit of book-keeping, ordering bar supplies and doing the daily banking. And it would all be in French. 'What did you say to them?'

'I told them you and I would have to talk about it. Which we are doing. That I'd get back to them within a few days.'

'When would it start?' I asked.

'With the opening of the school year in September,' Luke said. 'But there'd be some setting up to do beforehand. Especially on your side of things. It might mean your going out there a couple of times for a few weeks at a stretch, It would be pretty full-time, I'd think, from about July.'

'How would I square those weeks of absence with the theatre?' I said.

'Same as you did last time,' said Luke.

'I'll need to think about it,' I said.

'That's fine,' said Luke. 'You're thinking about it now.'

'There's my parents...'

Luke gave me one of his most tender smiles. 'I know.'

We carried on talking about the practicalities of the move. Then Luke said, 'Oh, there's another thing. I almost forgot to tell you in all the excitement. There's a staff-student concert at the Kensington College in a month's time. I've booked us in to do the Spring sonata. Are you OK with that?'

'Yes,' I said. It was a much easier thing to say yes to than the offer of a job in a foreign language.

I told my parents about the concert over lunch that Sunday. I promised to invite them to it. They were both very pleased. But then my mother said, 'You and Luke again. Always you and Luke.'

I realised this was the moment. I took a deep breath. 'Yes,' I said. 'Always me and Luke. And I think it always will be now. We've been offered jobs together a few miles from his place in France. Luke wants us to accept. And he wants me to go and live with him.'

My father put down his knife and fork. He said, quite kindly, 'Are you trying to tell us something?'

'Yes,' I said. 'I'm gay. I always have been, though I didn't always know it. But I do know it now. I'm in no doubt at all about it. And Luke's my man.' I looked at my mother. 'As you said, always me and Luke.'

My mother heaved a rather noisy breath. 'Perhaps you should have told us this before. It seems it's been going on a rather long time.'

I said, 'It isn't easy to tell all of the truth at once. Especially when you're not sure at first what the whole truth is.'

'No,' said my father unexpectedly. 'It isn't easy to do that. You're absolutely right. And I'm proud of you for telling us the way you have done. Proud of you for being brave.'

I broke down in tears at that moment and had to run out of the room.

EIGHTEEN

Things got into gear pretty fast. No sooner had Luke and I formally accepted our two jobs than the Bordeaux music college asked me to fly over there to spend a few days getting to know the ropes. For the first time in my life I was on an expense-account foreign trip. They gave us a quarter bottle of champagne on the flight out. I thought that was a pretty good start.

Beginning any new job is a little bewildering, and a little frightening. They show you a few things you've never done before, you wrestle with them a bit and with any luck you conquer them; you think you've cracked it, and then they say, 'And now there's this.'

Except that in Bordeaux they didn't say, *And now there's this*. They said, '*Et maintenant, voice ce que vous avez à faire...*' Everything I did, from filling in tax returns to phoning plumbers, from querying invoices to hiring – or God forbid, firing – staff, would have to be done in French. But there it was. I had the opportunity to do what very few people newly in love get the chance to do. To work with my partner as well as live with him. It was a wonderful new start in life. I would have to overcome the difficulties and to get on with it.

The day of my arrival I spent meeting people at the Bordeaux school and familiarising myself with the place. They had found a hotel for me to stay at near the Porte d'Aquitaine. I had a free evening in front of me...

The Porte d'Aquitaine was at a five-way crossroads, with bars and restaurants on all the corners. I had a beer sitting out on the pavement. Although we were barely into February the weather was unseasonably and nicely warm and Bordeaux was, from the perspective of a Londoner, quite a long way south. I watched the people go by. Some I watched more closely than others. There was a pair of mop-haired male twins, perhaps a year younger than I was. They were as like as two peas in a pod. They were also very beautiful, and were drawing attention to the special nature of their relationship by wearing identical navy-blue blazers above blue denims and a striking pair of magenta-and-white striped shirts, which they wore with the tails un-tucked and hanging flag-like below the hems of their blazers. They seemed to be at the centre of a crowd of young people of both sexes but among whom beautiful boys were in a majority that was bigger than statistical norms would have predicted.

When I went to another place to eat, the crowd with the twins arrived there shortly afterwards and I watched them settle to their convivial meal with a little envy, given my solitary state. I cheered myself up with oysters followed by sliced rare duck breast on a bed of Puy lentils. Then I made my way back to the bar I'd started at, for a final glass of beer before bed.

The twins and their entourage arrived a few minutes later. One of the twins recognised me and gave me an almost involuntary smile and nod. A minute later I was somehow part of their group, drinking beer and Pastis. I couldn't help finding the twins gorgeous, while the flow of alcohol was doing wonders for my French.

'We're going on to the Polluxe,' one of them said lightly, a teasing smile about his lips.

'What's the Polluxe?' I asked – not all that innocently.

'It's a ... how you say? ... a gay club,' my new friend explained.

It seemed a most delightful prospect at that moment. But I had enough self-knowledge still accessible through the rising alcohol tide to know that if I joined this expedition I would almost certainly end up in bed with one of the twins or both of them and that in the unlikely chance that didn't happen, then I would definitely end up in bed with somebody else.

I just managed to say no, although very regretfully. Perhaps another night, I said. But I was starting a new job and needed to be fresh as a daisy for my next morning's work. They accepted my excuse at face value. It was my first ever experience of this situation since I'd entered the state of belonging to someone. I was a little proud of myself for making the right decision. But I'd discovered that doing the right thing didn't come easily. Much as I loved Luke I found that saying no to people could hurt. A bit thoughtfully I walked back to my hotel and had an early night and a wank.

In the morning Geneviève drove me to Libourne, a distance of some twenty miles, and we inspected the building that was going to be my new domain. It was old, stone-built and charming, situated in a quiet side-street. It hadn't been used for a few months and smelt musty when we got inside. The first thing we had to do was to open the big shutters that darkened the windows. You opened the windows inward, un-latched the wood panels that hung beyond them and heaved them open, flinging them wide and against the wall where they clanged into sprung fastenings. I felt quite proprietorial while I was doing it. People in the street looked up at me and smiled. I waved down at them. It felt good to be doing this.

Over the coming months sound-proofing was going to be added to some of the walls and windows. It would be my job to oversee this. There would be accounts to be kept, liaison with the local authorities... There were an awful lot of local authorities, in France, I discovered. Including the Police. I would also need to establish a rapport with the local press. That evening, back in Bordeaux, I bought a very up-to-date and very comprehensive English-French dictionary. It was about the size of a small suitcase and weighed half a hundredweight.

Later I spent my evening much as I'd done the previous one. Every time anyone entered the bar or restaurant I was in I looked up expectantly, wondering if it would be one of the twins or both. It never was. I spent my evening alone. Perversely I found myself saddened by the twins' not turning up.

It seemed I'd been back in London only days before I had to start re-learning the Spring sonata for the college concert. I told my parents the date and time of it, put their tickets into their hands well in advance and said, 'Perhaps I could bring Luke round here for lunch one Sunday?' I heard a hint of shyness in my voice.

'Please do,' my father took it on himself to answer. 'But would you mind asking him also to call round and see me some time very shortly? Not with you. Just himself.'

I passed this message on to Luke, who made a big-eyed face with raised eyebrows and did a pantomime gulp. But he phoned my father shortly afterwards and made an appointment for a chat.

Luke phoned me after the chat had taken place. 'Your dad was very sweet,' he told me. 'He asked me if we were sure we were serious about each other. I said I had no doubts about that. Then he made me promise that I'd look after you. I promised him I always would.' I was quite shaken to hear this promise, even this reported-speech version of the promise, coming down the phone line. Luke had promised to look after me... 'Oh, bloody hell,' Luke,' I said.

'I meant it,' I heard Luke say, in a voice of the greatest seriousness. 'And I mean it now, as I'm saying it to you.' Luke would look after me. The words echoed through my head as I put the phone down. It was very wonderful, very stirring, to have been told that.

There was a rehearsal at the college. Arriving for it I had a strong sense of history being about to repeat itself. When I entered the big hall Jeremy and Elfrieda were up on the platform running through passages from the Brahms 'Double' – the concerto for violin and cello. It is a heavenly piece. And if you can use the word heavenly about music that is being played by the man who jilted you and the woman who helped him do it ... then that is a pretty big compliment to Brahms's music.

When he saw me Jeremy had the balls, the courtesy and the loveliness to stop playing, to come down from the platform and to greet me with a handclasp. No, we didn't run into each other's arms. Nor did we hug. It was perhaps eight months since we'd spoken last. But here we were, touching hands and, although nervously, speaking to each other again at last.

'It's good to see you,' Jeremy said.

'Good to see you too.'

There was a silence then. I put my other hand over Jeremy's. He put his hand over that. No doubt if we'd been octopuses we'd have gone on doing this till we'd run out of feet.

'I'm sorry,' Jeremy said.

'You don't have to be,' I said. 'Life's like that. Last year ... I mean, us last year ... is one of the happiest memories I have about anything...'

I felt a shudder go through Jeremy's hands. 'Don't... Please don't...'

'It's just that it was good,' I insisted. 'I don't hurt. I no longer hurt.'

'I hurt,' said Jeremy, and he crumpled into my arms as he said it.

I don't know how I remembered the way down through the bowels of the college to the canteen after just one visit there many months ago. But somehow I found it and I bought coffee for Jeremy and myself. We drank the coffee. We talked. Wonderfully, neither Elfrieda nor anyone else came down to look for us. We had a chance to sort things out, up to the point we were able to, just the two of us. I found I'd lied when I'd told Jeremy I no longer hurt. Our meeting opened up the scars. We both bled. But after half an hour of talking we both felt better. Jeremy had Elfrieda now and I had Luke. We discovered we could be friends again. We rekindled between us the wonderful thing called love. But we'd lost the other thing – we had to accept reluctantly that we'd lost it – we'd lost the more difficult thing, the more dangerous thing, the more frightening thing, called Love.

That conversation between Jeremy and me, private though it was, seemed somehow to clear the air throughout the whole college, the way a lightning flash clears the air for miles around. Perhaps I'm exaggerating the importance of it, exaggerating the importance of myself. But the atmosphere that surrounded the concert that evening was joyful in the extreme. Lisa, who I hadn't seen in nearly a year, did another of the Bach solo cello suites. Her performance, which was magisterial, evoked awe and wonder as well as mere applause. She had told me during the rehearsal that she was now living with the man she'd talked to me about last year. She didn't need to tell me how deeply she now loved him. Her playing of the Bach suite told me that.

Item followed item. The Spring sonata, whose piano part I managed to play without a single wrong note or a second's self-doubt – buoyed up by the knowledge that Luke would look after me – was received with jubilant clapping. I told myself I could distinguish my parents' proud handclaps from among the rest. Marianne and

Tarquin... I'll take a break from superlatives. They played, as was fitting, like young people in love.

The evening travelled upwards after that, quick and evanescent as smoke. We descended on The Contented Sole en masse. We ate, we drank, we were merry. And Jeremy in his exuberance plucked the two gerbera flowers from the vase on the table and ate them both.

During the next few months I paid several more visits to Libourne, my new place of work. Sometimes travelling with Luke and sometimes without him. Little by little the plan for the opening of the college took shape. My huge dictionary proved its worth as one of the better investments of my life. Perhaps one incident can stand in as representative of all the rest. Walking with Luke around the building in the side street in Libourne where we were going to work I hear him say, 'Those windows could do with a clean.'

'I'll get someone onto it tomorrow' I said.

'No, don't do that,' Luke said. 'Money, money. We'll do it ourselves. Today.'

I got a bucket of soapy water. I got cloths and meths. Luke dragged a ladder up from the cellar and we set to. Most of the task was easy. The windows were large-paned with few fiddly bits. We took it in turn to climb the ladder and foot it, though for the most part the latter was just a matter of courtesy, of reassurance and friendliness.

But there was one corner of the building that had a window in an awkward place, high up. 'We could just leave that one, I suppose,' I said.

Luke looked at me with what might have been a gentle rebuke in his eyes. 'Surely we won't,' he said.

We wedged the bottom of the ladder into an awkward corner where there was a drain and rested the top of it in the angle between two walls at the top. It was quite a climb for me, trying to keep my balance with bucket in one hand and cloths in the other. As I neared the top I felt the ladder begin to twist away from its top resting point. The balance shifted and I realised – I'd been the witness to more than one theatre backstage accident – that the ladder was about to fling me off.

I felt rather than saw that Luke was running up the rungs behind me. There was an out-jut of wall, like a buttress, that had a flat top, about halfway between the ground and where I was. I felt Luke jump sideways off the ladder and onto this. I heard him say, 'It's OK, my darling, I've got you.' I felt the weight of him sprawl across the ladder, stabilise it and return it to the straight. Then I felt his hands grasp my calf muscles. So tightly he held them that I was conscious of their size. Like small – actually very small – melons in his hands.

Luke would look after me. That was the promise he had made. He was proving it now. In the most practical, physical terms, balancing precariously on a wall while he held me tight. He was the angel that had been sent to bear me up. I went on to clean those difficult-of-access top windows more thoroughly than anyone has ever cleaned a window in his life. And he went on holding my legs long after the need to do so was past.

My old job was winding down... It wasn't really; it just seemed like it. It was simply that there were other people doing it. I trained up an enthusiastic young man for whom the routines of ordering ice-cream and Coca-cola, banking the box office take and hobnobbing with the occasional theatrical celebrity were exciting enough to justify a financial reward that was meagre by most people's standards. I didn't try to disillusion him. His hopes and expectations, the stars in his young stage-struck eyes, were what mine had been two years before. I was off to work in a provincial music school in France for not much greater financial reward than my successor at the theatre could expect. I was going there because I loved Luke. And I wouldn't have let anyone dare to try and disillusion me about that.

NINETEEN

We opened in September. I don't know how. When you're flying by the seat of your pants you just do it. Then somehow it is done and you no longer know how it was you managed it. There was a bit of a launch party. Local press. First intake of students. The mayor... In France there is always the mayor. Luke and I went to bed exhausted that night. Too exhausted to have sex. But we woke up at four in the morning and made up for it. Luke wasn't yet thirty-five. I wasn't yet twenty-five. We were in love. It was par for the course.

We lived full time at the manoir at Moncaret by now. I had left my room in the Colville Terrace flat. Someone else would now be watering the plants in the glasshouse tunnel of steps. Or so I hoped. Luke's house in Putney had been rented out. Mrs Fox was keeping an eye on the place. The piano, and Luke's music, had come with us. So we now had two six-foot-nine Bechsteins in the music room of the manoir, and bookcases full of scores that ran to ceiling height. Having two pianos meant that we could play piano together if we wanted to. We sometimes did. More often though, if we wanted to unwind together with music-making, it would be Luke on the violin with me as his piano accompanist. Never the other way round. Luke did ask me once or twice if I wanted him to teach me the violin or cello. No, I told him; I drew the line at that. For a mere dabbling amateur like me, one instrument was quite enough.

I had plenty of opportunity to play the piano, though. I was constantly in demand at the college as an accompanist – at exams, rehearsals, student concerts.... I was always on site and on salary, after all, and it saved bringing in outsiders each time. It helped to balance the books.

In my spare time, what little there was of it, Sandrine taught me how to cook. That I considered myself already quite accomplished in this department cut no ice with her. She took me back to basics. Watched me fry an egg, make an omelette, grill Melba toast. She nodded and smiled approvingly, then tore my techniques to shreds and painstakingly sewed them back together again in such a way that they became recognizably French. I couldn't help remembering how Luke had demolished my early attempts to play a certain Mozart trio before building it carefully back up ... in such a way that it became recognizably Luke.

I too was being rebuilt. As someone who was recognizably Luke's.

During that first year Luke gave himself an absurdly heavy teaching load. Granted, the number of students was not yet that great. But he took on by far the greater part of the piano and violin tuition – as well as viola and cello. He coaxed and wheedled Richard and Odile into doing what time prevented him from doing in these departments, and then used local specialists for what lay outside his range of expertise: brass, woodwind, percussion and voice. Yet somehow he still made time to supervise my own progress as a pianist: he gave me the occasional lesson, and would listen attentively to my private practice, giving me encouragement and advice in turn – and sometimes even unadulterated praise.

And somehow too we found time, the two of us, to enjoy being in France, to enjoy the Dordogne. I learned to play Pétanque, the sedate – yet somehow also fierce – French version of bowls. We introduced the local 'pillars' of the bar in Moncaret to the joys of conker matches when the autumn came. The game caught on, and a match between Moncaret and a rival bar in

Castillon would become a regular annual event for the next few years.

In its second year of operation the Libourne school doubled in size. It was no longer feasible for Luke to do half the teaching himself. We took on a gifted young pianist called Jean-Claude Ivry to mop up the demand for piano courses, and two new people to teach strings. They came from England. They were the newly qualified Tarquin and his young wife Marianne. We found them a small house to rent on the outskirts of St-Emilion. It had a view down to the Dordogne river and a garden full of vines.

Luke was offered a violin recital in Bordeaux. It would be the first time he'd played a concert in a big public venue outside the UK. His piano accompanist was to be Yves Taskin, the head of piano at our Bordeaux parent-school and the husband of Geneviève, my boss and Luke's. Yves and I had first met, I didn't need to be reminded, when he'd heard me play the Mozart trio, and the Beethoven cello sonata with Jeremy, on that chamber music course more than two years ago.

Yves and Geneviève came to dinner one evening at Moncaret to sort the programme out. Yves and Luke decided to begin with the best known of the sonatas by Bach for violin and keyboard. And that the second half should consist of the kind of virtuoso things that were guaranteed to send an audience home happy. Sarasate, Paganini, Fritz Kreisler...

I listened without contributing much. Well, I didn't contribute much in terms of words. Though I had prepared the meal. A warm salad of endive and crisp bacon with vinaigrette, then trout pan-fried in a robe of vine leaves. And after the cheese course, a *mousse au chocolat* which I'd learned to prepare using a recipe from – and under the strict supervision of – Sandrine. Geneviève had just complimented me on my success with the mousse when I heard Luke say, 'I'm not sure about doing a Brahms sonata after the Bach. Couldn't we do one of the Beethovens instead?'

'Hmm,' said Yves. 'Which one do you have in mind?'

'Let's do the Spring,' Luke said, in the tone of voice that clearly expected Yves to say the French equivalent of, *Oh yes, do let's*.

But instead Yves wrinkled his brow and put his head on one side. 'It's not one of my favourites,' he said. 'A little hackneyed, wouldn't you say?'

I couldn't help it. I just jumped in. 'Hackneyed?' I said, in as injured a tone as if I'd written the thing myself. 'It's popular, certainly, but that's because it's so good. It's about happiness, pure and simple. It's a representation in music of the feeling of being in love.'

Yves turned to me. He was smiling. 'I once heard you play a Beethoven cello sonata very splendidly. You played it not only technically and musically very well, but you played it like a young man in love. And though it was none of my business I rather concluded that the object of that emotion was the young cellist you were playing it with. Now, nearly three years later, I find myself on the brink of asking an impertinent question.' He glanced across the table at Luke, on whose face a beaming smile had suddenly appeared. Encouraged, he went on. 'OK. I'll be impertinent. Would I be right in thinking that you play the Spring sonata in the same way?'

I felt myself blushing. 'I wouldn't know,' I said.

Then I heard Luke say in the most matter-of-fact way imaginable, 'I would. He does play the piece in that way. At least he does when he's playing it with me.'

Geneviève came in unexpectedly. 'Then the answer is evident. Yves, you must bow gracefully out of the second item in the concert's first half and give way for fifteen minutes to Robbie. He can be introduced as a surprise guest artist, a pupil and protégé of Luke's.'

I heard this with the same shock and awe as if I'd just heard a thunder clap while sitting under a blue sky. I didn't know who would speak next – though I knew it wouldn't be me – and I certainly didn't know what they would say.

Yves spoke first. 'I think that's a perfect idea.'

Luke's protégé. Luke's protected one. That was who I was. At all times, in every way. Geneviève had described me to a T.

A protégé is one thing: a protected person. A prodigy, the word and the idea often confused with it, is something altogether different. A prodigy is a prodigious thing, a person born with wonderful, almost supernatural gifts: a Mozart or a Menuhin. I was not a prodigy. Not in the field of music. Not in any other. If I was going to play to an audience of hundreds in the Grand Théâtre de Bordeaux, even for fifteen minutes, just this once in my lifetime, I was going to have to practise jolly hard.

I did.

The concert took place on a December evening that was bitterly cold. I held my hands together in the taxi that took us to the Grand Théâtre, thinking they'd never felt so cold in all my life. I wondered how I would ever get them warm. If they stayed as cold as this I wouldn't be able to play a note. My fifteen minutes of public exposure, my fifteen minutes of fame, would end in ignominy before they had begun. I reached across in the darkness of the taxi's back seat and gave my hands to Luke. Neither of us spoke. He just took my hands inside his own slightly bigger ones and held them, and in within a minute they were warm.

We sat in the artists' room, the three of us. Luke. Yves. Me. Perhaps it was a furnished, cosy space. But my mind has stripped it of any furnishings it may have had. The intensity of my apprehensiveness resulted in my remembering it bare.

Some musicians can have a drink before they perform. Rock musicians and folk musicians in particular. (Jazz, of course, is fuelled mainly by cigarettes.) But among classical players it is understood that only brass players benefit from a drink or two before the show. The licence extends a bit in the case of those who play in the safety of the opera, ballet or theatre pit. But classical soloists have to go dry. There was someone – a very famous pianist of the past – was it Rachmaninoff? Moiseiwitsch? Godovsky? – who allowed himself a single thimble of Benedictine before a concert, though never two. But lesser mortals such as Yves and Luke dared not risk even that. As for me, I was even less than they were. Even more mortal... At least, that was what I thought at the time.

Yves and Luke were called, with a knock on the door, five minutes before the concert started. I knew all about this from my time in the theatre. But what a different experience it was to find myself on the other end of it! They left the room, ready to play the Bach, and I was left alone with my frightened bowels.

Suddenly the door opened and, all on his own, Tarquin walked in. 'Thought this might be the right minute to give you a hug,' he said. Smiling, he hugged me tight and I hugged him back. I couldn't find any words. He didn't seem to expect any. He said, 'You'll be fine.' He disengaged and left the room, wanting to get back to his seat before the Bach started, wanting to leave me free to focus for a few minutes on what I had to do. After he had gone I kept smiling to myself. I was no longer frightened of the audience, or of Beethoven, or of what my bowels might do.

The Bach sounded wonderful, coming over the tannoy, crackling at times like bacon in the pan. Follow this, I had to think. Yet after Tarquin's affirming gesture I knew I could follow it. I had played the piece beautifully before. I could do it again. I'd played it more than once to audiences of a dozen or more. We had eleven hundred tonight, I'd been told. I could handle that.

My call came. I walked out onto the stage. Yves was coming off. He grasped my hand as he passed. Had we been in England he would have told me to break a leg. We were in France. He said it the French way. *'Merde'*.

When we had run through the programme in the afternoon the vast space of the auditorium had been a neutral thing: an empty, non-judgemental space into which my playing fell as into an echo-less well. Now it was transformed. It lived and breathed in the semi-darkness. Its brief applause on seeing me walk into the light was all-expectant. And when it rustled down to silence that silence was expectant too. It was a silence from which I too might expect things. It was a silence that would not hesitate to applaud if things went well. It was a silence that would not be afraid to chuck tomatoes and eggs, and boo, if things did not.

I took my seat at the piano stool. I was smaller than Yves. I spent a second or two winding it fractionally higher, using the little wheels on the sides. Luke smiled at me. I checked the music that lay open on the piano's desk in front of me. Made sure it was open at the right page. More embarrassing moments than can be counted have been caused by soloists striking up with one sonata while their accompanist plays the opening of another one. All was in order. Sonata V, Opus 24, *Dem Grafen Moritz von Fries gewidmet,* I read. The Spring sonata was one of the few things, it crossed my mind at that moment, that Beethoven hadn't dedicated to that

Archduke Rudolph. Lucky Count Moritz of Fries, I thought. Whoever he might have been.

I remembered Yves's words then. 'You played like a young man in love.' And Luke's: 'He does play the piece in that way. At least he does when he's playing it with me.' I gave Luke his tuning A. He gave me his nod and we began. I played like a young man in love. And so did Luke. I had no choice in the matter. And neither, it was immediately evident, did he.

TWENTY

I never played the piano in public at the Grand Theatre again of course. Nor in any other auditorium of that size. Though naturally Luke did. Nevertheless, that evening was one of the high points of my life. Luke and I finished the sonata to the sound of thunderous applause. Nobody in that audience could have had any doubt about the nature of our relationship. I listened to the second half of the concert wrapped in a cocoon of happiness. The dinner afterwards was celebratory, the wine and food were good.

In defiance of the theatre's regulations Tarquin had managed to tape-record the concert. I still have that recording, now transferred to disc. It's one of my most treasured possessions. One of the loveliest souvenirs of my time with Luke.

The years passed. Luke continued to be principal of the Libourne music school while I continued with the practical administrative tasks. The two of us still climbed ladders and washed the windows a couple of times each summer. It became a tradition, and I always looked forward to the moment when, dealing with that one awkwardly placed window high in the corner, he would stand on the wall and hold me by the legs.

Luke's concert career grew and developed. He played concertos with some of the best French and British orchestras. We travelled together to Paris, London, Manchester, Birmingham, and Glasgow. To Monpelier, Marseilles, Toulouse. Luke got a concert agent eventually, but I still looked after many of the more domestic arrangements when we were travelling together. Sorting out train and plane tickets, booking hotel rooms… I was also his rehearsal pianist. And over the years, with Sandrine's help I taught him to cook almost as well as I did myself.

Richard and Odile retired and moved into a smaller house. Tarquin and Marianne, with their growing family, moved into their mill house, the Moulin de Jarre. Tarquin and Marianne were the mainstays of the Libourne school now. In view of the time that I had to dedicate to Luke's concert career (not to mention the amount of time that he did!) we couldn't have managed without them. From time to time during those halcyon years Jeremy and Elfrieda were among the guests that holidayed at the Moulin de Jarre and whenever they came to stay we saw quite a lot of them. The pair of them were treasured friends of both of us, the pains of all those years ago assuaged by the passage of time, by the power of friendship, and by the endurance of love. Of Elfrieda's and Jeremy's love for each other. Of mine and Luke's.

It wasn't just that Luke and I still loved each other. We remained totally besotted by each other. We were still crazily in love. We remained faithful to each other. We never looked at anybody else... Well, actually, we did look. We allowed ourselves and each other to do that, and we would enjoy comparing notes...

There's a story I have to tell here.

Luke and I were holidaying on the island of Madeira once. We found it a very relaxing place. Sunshine, forested mountains, flowers everywhere, even in winter's depths. And it's the measure of how much you manage to unwind on a holiday that your ambitions from day to day diminish. At first a visit to a museum seems quite a big challenge, compared to simply walking by the sea hand-in-hand, or sitting sipping a fruit drink on the beach. Then as the days pass even the museum challenge seems too great. Buying six postcards becomes quite a big thing to do. To say nothing of the effort involved in buying stamps...

It was when we'd reached that stage of the holiday that Luke said, 'I'd like to get a letter-opener while we're here.'

'A letter-opener?' I queried.

'Yes,' he said. 'You know. A paper-knife.'

We made that our big ambition. We pottered into all the tourist knick-knack shops and out again. We found postcards, handkerchiefs, a new pair of oven-gloves for the kitchen, beach shorts, a belt... But never a paper-knife.

Sitting outside the Golden Gate one lunch-time, Luke spotted a handsome youth ambling down the street. 'He could come and open my letters for me,' Luke said.

'Mine too,' I said. And from then on the expression became our code-word for a handsome young man spotted at a bar or in the street. 'Nice little letter-opener,' we would say to each other or, if the situation or our proximity to the object of our interest made this too obvious, one of us would say simply, 'Anything in the post?'

We did eventually buy a paper-knife. It had a carved wood handle that was painted black and red, in the form of a cockerel's head – one of Madeira's national emblems. It had... It still has... For I still have it. I use it still when I have a letter to open. And I think of Luke.

It was 2004. I'm hardly likely to forget that date. We were cleaning those famous windows at the school. We'd reached the difficult bit. Luke was holding me by the legs. He slipped. We went down together, like two railway carriages coupled together and sliding off a broken bridge. We landed together in a heap, with me mostly on top.

It wasn't a massive fall. I'd been reaching up to clean a first-floor window and Luke wasn't even as high as that. All the same it was unpleasant and painful, and it gave us both a terrible fright. I picked myself up but Luke couldn't manage to do that for himself. He was in much more pain than I was, I realised. 'Where does it hurt?' I asked, suddenly seeing a void open in front of me, more frightened now than I'd been during the fall itself.

'My leg,' said Luke, touching his thigh gingerly.

My panic subsided. It wasn't his head, or an internal injury. It wasn't his violin-playing hands. Even if he'd broken a bone he wasn't going to die of it. If his leg was broken it would be a major inconvenience for both of us, but we'd manage somehow and time would take care of it over a couple of months. I had my phone in my pocket. I dialled 15 for *SAMU* and they came at once.

The efficient people who dealt with us in the Bordeaux hospital were surprised that a man who was not yet out of his fifties should have fractured his femur in a fall of only six feet. 'I did fall on top of him,' I reminded them by way of explanation. 'Hmm,' they said.

They kept him in for a few days following an operation in which they fixed the bone with a metal plate. They showed us a picture of it. It was the same technique they'd used until recently to fasten lengths of railway line. Tried and tested since about 1836.

They did some tests on Luke too. Purely routine. Took a sample of bone for analysis. X-rayed his chest. They do things very thoroughly in hospitals in France.

I got used to the daily drive to Bordeaux and back. It was a beautiful journey, up and down over rolling wave-like hills that were vineyard-clad. Entre-Deux-Mers was the name of the area whose hills I sailed across, back and forth. Familiar from many a wine-bottle label. I brought fresh clothes for Luke on the day I went to the hospital for the last time. The day I was going to collect him, to bring him back.

They talked to us as we sat together. Those tests... I took Luke's hand and we listened together. I said, 'It can't be lung cancer. He's never smoked.'

'I did when I was younger,' Luke said.

'That's neither here nor there,' I said.

They agreed with me. Whether Luke smoked or had done or never had was not an issue. He had lung cancer and it had spread to his bones and was far advanced. We needed to focus now on next steps. *Les prochaines marches.*

I took Luke home to Moncaret. That I was able to do this was something at least. But our home had changed since I'd left it a few hours earlier. Sunshine filled the house and gardens, yet it shone with a mocking spirit. A shadow filled the house. A shadow that could never lift. The place was familiar, but unrecognizable all at once. I struggled not to break down as I cooked us the duck breasts I'd bought for this home-coming treat.

For more than twenty years Luke had looked after me. It hadn't needed my father – now dead – to tell him to do that. He'd held me as I stood on ladders. He'd saved me once from choking in the night. He'd taken care of every aspect of my life. He'd made a halfway decent pianist out of me. He'd taught me most of what I knew about love. Now the time had come suddenly for me to repay my enormous debt.

It turned out we still had six precious months together. For some of that time Luke continued to run the school and teach – a little bit. He even gave one concert. It was at the Salle Pleyel in Paris. It was a recital of sonatas by Bach, Mozart and Brahms. His pianist for the occasion was a rising young star, a French lad, whose name was now on everybody's lips.

Luke knew this would be his last public concert. Watching and listening alongside Tarquin and Marianne, sitting in good seats, I knew this too, but was determined to enjoy the occasion, to experience it in a positive light. I wanted a happy memory of this event that I could cherish for the rest of my life.

During those months a lot of time was spent driving to and fro across the beautiful rolling countryside of Entre-Deux-Mers, going to the Bordeaux hospital for appointments and treatments. Luke would spend much of those journeys in silence, gazing at the landscape, feeding on its beauty hungrily as if nourishing himself in readiness for the longer journey that lay ahead of him, the one he would have to face in loneliness.

We talked, the doctors and Luke and I, about sending him to Paris, about chemo-therapy and other treatments that might be possible and appropriate. It was talk of treatment only, though: not cure. Extending life by a week or two maybe. There were no options beyond that. Eventually the only treatments would be palliative.

I looked after Luke as best I could. But he looked after me too. Even attending to my sexual needs, in the simplest way, when we were in bed, some weeks after his own sexual needs had faded and become ghosts. He still wanted holding, though. Hour by hour I could at least do that, doing my best to comfort us both.

The end came with a blessed suddenness. He hadn't been admitted to hospital as an in-patient, though it was expected that that would have to happen within a few weeks. He woke up suddenly in the night with a startled grunt and sat up. I remembered the time I'd nearly choked after eating rabbit in Porte-Ste-Foy. I sat up alongside him, frightened, and held him tight. I said, 'Are you all right?'

'I love you,' he said.

'I love you too,' I said. I know he heard me. He moved his head. Then suddenly his body went limp in my arms. He became so heavy that I couldn't take the weight and I had to drop him back on the bed.

I just lay with my arms wrapped round him. I couldn't cry. I couldn't think. I was in a state of great shock. I lay like that for an hour or more. Then I felt him cooling. I got up then and made for the telephone. The rest of my life stretched ahead of me like a dark cold tunnel. A glasshouse tunnel of steps, from which someone had now removed the living plants. There was nothing for it but to make my lonely way onward into it.

I found myself to be quite well off. I was the owner of a substantial property in the Dordogne. I was also raking in the rents from a sizeable house in Putney. And, my parents having died several years previously, I had made some money on the sale of their Putney house: it had been left jointly to my sister and me; we'd sold it and split the proceeds. Did any of this cheer me up? You bet it did not.

I still had my job at the Libourne school. But now I and the principal of the Bordeaux school – Geneviève's successor – had to find someone to do Luke's job. Tarquin and Marianne had found themselves obliged to take on more and more of Luke's responsibilities at the school during his final months. It seemed a sensible plan to make the de facto situation official. They became co-principals, and we worked together as a triumvirate.... Perhaps in these politically correct times we should have said, a tripersonate.

Thank God for Tarquin. If he was driving home from work and I was already at home alone at Moncaret he would always make the five-hundred metre detour to my house and look in on me, even if only for five minutes. It took the curse off the house's emptiness. At least once a week he and Marianne would join me for an evening meal, or else I would go to theirs. And at the end of those evenings, after I'd kissed Marianne goodnight, Tarquin would hold me tightly for a few seconds and say, as if repeating a mantra, 'You're doing OK, Robbie. You're going to be all right. You're going to be all right.'

Where would I have been without Tarquin? Without his goodnight hugs? And yet I wasn't all right. So many times I wanted to say to Tarquin, 'Can Marianne go on home without you? Will you stay with me tonight? Just one night?' Of course I never did say that. He and Marianne belonged together. But I couldn't help wishing that Tarquin, still handsome at fifty, could have been just a little bit gayer than he actually was.

And thank God for work.. It didn't ease the pain, but at least it gave me something else to think about. The school was going from strength to strength. Tarquin and Marianne began to get a bit more concert work, and they taught from time to time at Bordeaux as well as in Libourne. I never asked Tarquin to help me clean the windows in the summer. But neither did I have the heart to tackle the job myself. I got a professional team in every time. Most of them were nice little letter-openers. Though I hasten to add that they were just for looking at.

For actual sex... Well, there were places in Bordeaux I knew about. I'd rather lost the knack of going out and looking for sex. At least, I thought I had. But I discovered that it was rather like riding a bicycle. Even if you hadn't had any practice for years it soon came back.

I caught up with the twins again. The ones I'd met in Bordeaux on my first night there over twenty years ago. They no longer looked quite so much alike. They certainly didn't go round with identical shirt-tails hanging out. And I never had sex with them. On the other hand, they became quite supportive as friends during the dark years that followed the death of Luke. And in the matter of sex... At least they were able to tell me where to look.

Four years passed. We were in 2008. It seemed like the most prosperous year in the history of the planet. The world's stock markets were roaring ahead. Then came the thing the French called *le crunch*. Translation not needed, I guess. *Le crunch* was a phenomenon that occurred in what the French like to call *le monde Anglo-Saxon*. It was a crisis that engulfed the banks of this

English-speaking world, resulting from a catastrophic accumulation of bad debt. But it was only an Anglo-Saxon thing. Limited to America and the UK. The French tut-tutted and commiserated by turn. At least the contagion would never spread to France...

It was in 2009 that the Libourne school finally had to close. The Bordeaux school needed to retrench. There were jobs for Marianne and Tarquin there. It meant a daily commute that was three times as long as they were used to, and they both took a severe pay cut. They were grateful enough for that. At least they still had jobs. All over France, all over Europe, all over the world, hundreds of thousands of people, through no fault of their own, suddenly did not. Me for a start.

I was luckier than most. I owned two big houses and had money in the bank. I would weather the financial storm, with any luck. There was just the question of what I would do with the rest of my life. Was I to retire to Moncaret and write Essays, as Montaigne had done, just two miles away, four centuries before? Spend the evenings playing the piano to myself? Playing for my own amazement, as an old school-friend of mine had once joked.

One day during those first few weeks of enforced idleness I learned that my neighbour Sandrine's husband had not only lost his job but had died of a heart attack just three days afterwards. It never rains but it pours. I went to the funeral. Just as, four years before, Sandrine and her husband had attended Luke's.

I found myself in a bar in Bordeaux one April night. It was a seedy place near the station. It had the twin advantages however, of being a gay pick-up place and having a default lighting-state that verged on the pitch dark. As I walked towards the bar I saw that someone was sitting at it who looked ... how is it that we tell these things from a back view only? ... about the same age as I was. He had his feet up on the front rung of the bar stool on which he sat. I saw only the perched backs of them. His white trainers. The bottoms of his denim legs. Between jeans hem and trainers was an inch or two of elegant white ankle-flesh. Either he was wearing those sockette things inside his trainers, or was without socks. I saw the axles of his ankles. Those little ivory hubs. For some reason I found them beautiful. I hadn't come here to play with fifty-year-olds. I was more than surprised by my response to the backs of this man's feet.

The back bits of the rest of him? I couldn't see much. A blue denim jacket screened most of his jeans-clad buttocks from sight. The collar of the denim jacket was turned up. The hair above it was iron-grey and medium length. I hopped up on the bar stool that was next but one to his. I let one stool stand between us like a firebreak. I ordered myself a large Scotch single malt. Here in Bordeaux, wine capital of the Old World, Single Malt was the fashionable drink.

As I drank my lonely whisky I shot furtive sideways glances at the man on the next stool but one. I liked his profile. There is a theory that says we all know when we're being looked at – something to do with the astonishing, almost unconscious range of peripheral vision – and that's why we all turn and look back in response. It always happened when I shot a half-second's glance at a letter-opener from the inside of the car I was driving. But on the gentleman perched next to me at this bar tonight it had no discernible effect. In fairness though, he hadn't come here to pick up a fifty-year-old any more than I had.

I ordered a second whisky. A moment later he ordered another drink. He had been drinking beer. To my surprise he ordered a single malt Scotch. Same one as I'd had. His French was assured and impeccably correct.

Yet in his delivery of his order and the moment's banter that followed it I detected a faint trace – like the scent of lavender in the bedroom of a long-dead relative – of an English accent.

Again I turned sideways to look at him. This time he looked back. There was something about him... I found myself suddenly confused and puzzled. I didn't know why. My mind did a double-quick Identikit thing with his features. Did I know him from somewhere, perhaps?

By now the man was staring at me quite rudely. His eyes were an astonishing blue for someone of his age. But he had no business to be staring at me like that... Things started to come together suddenly. But before they could do so he opened his mouth. The words that came out of them could not have astonished me more. 'Cocks and kippers,' the man said.

'Oh bloody hell,' I said. It took me a second to get control of this. Then, 'You're Chris,' I said.

'You're Robbie,' he replied, deadpan. 'Though of course you already know that.'

We shouldn't have driven back to Moncaret that night. Neither of us. Not after the quantity we'd had to drink. But we both did. I led, of course. I knew the way. Over the switchback hills of the Entre-Deux-Mers we went. As I mounted the brow of each hill Chris's headlights disappeared from my mirrors and I plunged down the slope alone in the dark. Seconds later his lights flooded my rear-view and lit up my endarkened life. Up towards the crests we rode together, mile after mile. Down again into the troughs. Crossing the Dordogne by the iron-cage bridge at Branne, the spire of St-Emilion five miles away coming into view for a second as the moon sparked across a brief cloud gap. After Castillon I took the back road through Les Illarets for habit's sake. Then we drove up the track to Luke's … I mean, my … house, parked and got out.

We'd kissed in the bar in Bordeaux. We'd even gone into the toilet together and briefly reacquainted ourselves with each other's cock. But that was nothing to the way we kissed when we got inside … my … house. Oscar Wilde invented the phrase *a madness of kisses*. I can't do better than that.

'I can't believe this place,' Chris said as we explored it.

'Neither can I,' I said.

We stood in the music room / living-room. I flicked on the light and the two Bechsteins stood to attention despite the lateness of the hour. 'You have to play me something,' said Chris. His hands were on my head, around my waist, about my dick.

'I can't possibly,' I said. 'You got me far too pissed.'

'I got you pissed?!… I beg to differ. You pounced on me. You got *me* pissed. Anyway, you drove back here without mishap.'

'That was a miracle,' I said. 'That was my guardian angel, alias Luke, looking after me. It won't happen again.'

'Play me something really simple then,' Chris asked me. 'Something you can't possibly go wrong with.'

'Want a bet?' I asked. But I did find something. I reached down the score of the Bach keyboard Partitas. With one eye shut I played the Sarabande from the C-minor suite.

'Beautiful,' was Chris's one-word response when I'd finished it.

'You're beautiful,' I said.

TWENTY-TWO

We were soon in bed. Entwined together naked we couldn't help noticing we'd both thickened up a bit over the decades. Me more than Chris if I'm honest. But then I'd been as thin as a rake when we first met. Chris commented on this. 'You've filled out a bit,' he said.

'Because I enjoy cooking, I suppose,' I answered, in between mouthfuls of his shoulder, nipples and neck. 'And eating.'

'As I can vouch for.' Chris giggled as he said that.

'And I drink far too much. Especially since Luke's death.'

'Like me since the divorce.' Of course he'd told me all about that. We'd told each other all the bad stuff in the first few minutes. Then some of the good stuff...

Men's faces are the giveaway to their age. But their arms and legs and torsos change less than their faces do between youth and middle age. Wrapping myself around my new discovery of Chris's nakedness I was glad about that. Even better, it seemed that our cocks and balls had the gift of eternal youth, at least in feel and look. Perhaps because they'd been fairly wrinkly from the outset? Anyway, Chris's parts and mine were unchanged from the way they'd looked together all those years ago. And Chris's dick tasted just as it had done when, after an absence of more than twenty years, it found its way home to my mouth.

I awoke when it started to get light. Chris was still asleep. I studied the contours of his face. Lines had come to places where there'd been no lines. There was no longer a moustache. But he was still the same Chris. His sleeping head was still the one that I wanted to wake up next to, now that I no longer had Luke. At this moment I found I had only one wish. To wake up every morning and find Chris next to me for the rest of my life. But I didn't know how, or even if, we'd ever manage that.

Chris had worked in software development. (I'd often wondered what became of young theatre electricians when they grew up. Chris's career path had been typical, he said.) Then along had come 2008 and, like me, he'd lost his job. He'd been searching Europe desperately for a new one in the last few months. He'd had an interview with a high-powered company in Bordeaux yesterday. Otherwise he wouldn't have been here. Our meeting was an incredible piece of luck. Or destiny. Or chance. Or what you will. Take your pick.

He had a room in London, sharing a flat with two other divorced men in straitened circumstances. His wife had ended up with the flat in Gospel Oak. It wasn't unexpected or unreasonable. Their daughter had been only twelve when they'd split up. She'd needed a home in which to grow up. She was now nearly thirty... It was difficult for me to get my head round that. There was another interesting thing about her. It interested me at least. She played the violin, Chris had told me. He'd added, 'Like your Luke.'

If Chris got the Bordeaux job, perhaps he'd come and live with me at Moncaret. If. *If, if...* I knew that life was never as straightforward as that. Chris and I living together... It was what I wanted at this charmed moment, waking to find him asleep next to me in bed. But was it what I would want in two days' time, when he had gone back to London and distance had lent perspective to the events of the last few hours? Was it what Chris would want in two days' time? I doubted that. Was it even what he wanted now, as he slept and as his unconscious used the time to update the files in his heart and head? Was it what he would want when he awoke? I thought of Titania, waking to find herself next to an ass's head.

At that moment Chris did wake. He turned his head and looked at me. His eyes focussed. There was a nanosecond's incomprehension as he tried to sort things out. And then he smiled.

It was the smile that did it. 'I love you,' I said. I couldn't help it. The words just tumbled out. Not for the first time in my life.

Chris's smile brightened. 'I love you too, mate,' he said.

'I'm sorry the larder doesn't stretch to kippers,' I said as I rootled around the kitchen. We'd dealt with the cocks already, while still in bed.

'That's fine,' Chris said. 'Just coffee'll do fine. Maybe a bit of toast...'

'We could have breakfasted on lampreys,' I said. 'Like Henry I. But there aren't any of those either.'

'I'm glad of that,' said Chris.

I revived the remains of yesterday's baguette in the oven. We took our coffee out into the garden, and ate the baguette *tartines* with cherry jam.

For a few minutes we ate and drank in silence. Chris gazed at the garden and the view beyond it with the same rapt attention I remembered Luke giving to the landscape of the Entre-Deux-Mers as we drove through it, back and forth to the Bordeaux hospital, during his last few weeks. Then Chris spoke.

'I did something dreadful to you, Robbie,' he said. I was conscious of the struggle he had to put up in order to get the words out.

'You had to,' I said. 'You had a small child. A big responsibility. A home. A marriage. You had no choice.'

'I don't expect you to forgive me,' he said. 'I certainly will never forgive myself. I'm surprised you even spoke to me last night. In the circumstances...'

'Listen,' I said. 'The first time we tried to have sex... On Hampstead Heath... I ran away and abandoned you as soon as I'd shot my load. I haven't forgiven myself for that. But the next day you were still there for me. And we tried again. With more success...' I stopped. I hadn't thought those words out carefully. I realised how they might be interpreted. By Chris. By both of us...

Chris continued to gaze into the distance. He didn't speak. He wrapped his hand over mine and held it for what seemed ages.

I drove us to St-Emilion for lunch. We ate on the high terrace at the top of the town, overlooking the market square below. A church spire poked up improbably from the high terrace, right beside us. It belonged to the monolithic church that was hewn in the middle ages from the mass of rock below. 'It's too beautiful,' Chris said, looking out over the Roman-tiled roofs of the town to the sweep of the Dordogne valley below.

'Want to share it with me?' I asked.

He looked at me. 'On the strength of one night in bed?'

'Three,' I reminded him. 'Don't forget Colville Terrace.'

He sighed. 'I must be going mad. Because actually I would like that.'

'Don't know how, though,' I said. 'Unless you get the Bordeaux job...' He'd already told me he didn't fancy his chances. You get a feeling about interviews...

For a moment Chris chewed thoughtfully on his *bavette aux échalottes*. (It's a kind of steak, with a shallot and red vinegar sauce.) Then he said, 'Leaving me out of the equation for a moment though, and being purely practical, what are you going to do with all that big house? And with your newly jobless life?'

'I'm not desperate for money,' I said, 'but you're right. I need to have a job. Need to do something with my life. And do something with the house.'

'Same as me,' said Chris. 'Except I don't have a house.' I'd already told him I had two of them.

'Mi casa es su casa,' I said. Sometimes it's easier to say the big things in Spanish.

Chris stayed with me for three days. Then for practical reasons he had to return to London. He'd run out of clothes for a start. I thought long and hard about him after he'd gone. It was easy to fall for an old flame – or for that matter anyone you found attractive – when you'd spent a few years starved of love. But jumping into a shared life with them...? In Chris's absence I had to think very carefully about that. I had no doubt that, back in London, he was thinking the same thoughts. And after a few days of rather cautious communications between us his emails made it more than clear that he was.

I ran into Sandrine one morning in Castillon. We had a coffee together outside the bar by the riverside. On the fishermen's stalls beside us eels and lampreys writhed. I had never talked to Sandrine about serious things. We weren't close. But this morning I found myself pouring everything out. I'd just heard that Chris hadn't got the job in Bordeaux and my heart was full of a disappointment as heavy and hard as lead. Sandrine listened patiently. I realised that for more than twenty years I'd overlooked the opportunity of a real friendship with her.

And then she startled me. *'Ecoute...'* she said. Listen up. She had a business proposition for me to consider. It came out fully formed, as if she'd spent a long time with it gestating in her head.

That evening I drove over to Tarquin and Marianne's and invited myself in for a drink. We sat out in the dusk by the millstream, drinking Monbazillac, while the weir made its comforting eternal rushing noise beneath. I told them what Sandrine had suggested. They seemed impressed. They had met Chris during his three-day stay with me. Now Tarquin said, 'I think it's time you reeled him in. Get him back out here. Make a start. Do it together.' When we parted an hour of so later the goodnight hug I got from Tarquin was surprisingly … or perhaps unsurprisingly … intense. I gave him a well-earned kiss.

Chris was back in the Dordogne a week after that. He's been with me ever since.

It helped that I'd had the experience of setting up the Libourne music school all those years before. I knew what I was at. It helped even more that Chris was fiendishly clever with everything connected with computers and the web. When it came to marketing the new venture we'd have had to look a long way before finding someone as savvy and expert as Chris. But none of this would have got us very far if it hadn't been for the exceptional cooking skills of Sandrine. She was the jewel in Le Kangarou's crown. Le Kangarou French Cooking Holiday School, to give the enterprise its full name.

We've been going four years now. We don't run fifty-two weeks a year. We do twenty-four and reckon that's quite enough. Most of our client base is British. Holiday-makers and ex-pats. I do some of the teaching, though Sandrine, the star, does the advanced stuff. She talks in French always, so when she's teaching, Chris or I have to be on hand to translate. Chris is an excellent cook, though he hasn't yet had the nerve to teach and demonstrate. Not yet…

He has another string to his bow, actually. You don't need a city-centre office to work from in today's world. From our shared office at the *manoir*, a first-floor room that looks out across the Dordogne valley, Chris designs websites for other people, charging them a fair but worthwhile fee for his services. Pocket Kangaroo is the name of his company. Don't ask.

In between the holiday courses Chris and I find ourselves often playing hosts to family and friends. Jeremy and Elfrieda and their teenage kids have spent several holidays here with us. Even Mrs Fox, now in her nineties and escorted by her daughter, has been out to see us twice.

And Chris's daughter Melanie spends a lot of time with us. It's great for me to have a violinist to play with once again. She's very keen on the Beethoven sonatas in particular and over the years we've played all of them at least once. But by happy coincidence Melanie's favourite is also my favourite. Number five. Opus twenty-four. Dedicated to Count Moritz von Fries. Known to its friends as The Spring. We play it together every time she visits us. She knows – just as her father knows – how important it was to me and Luke.

But sometimes it's just Chris and me. Just the two of us. Last night we lay out on the lawn watching the annual spectacle of the summer meteor shower. We didn't need to say much. We were simply two people in total harmony with each other and at one with the cosmos. As the bright-tailed streaks appeared then disappeared in the clear luminous tent that heaven stretched over us I remembered the words I wrote before, in connection, that time, with Luke…

Nobody could look at the start of a new relationship and know what lay further down the line. Nobody in the world was old enough or wise enough in the ways of the heart to know how a new thing would turn out. Young or old, experienced or completely green, you would always be in the same boat as everybody else. It was only afterwards – after you'd split up – that you knew enough to say, well that was doomed to fail... or – after the other party was dead – well, that worked out all right.

With Luke the latter had happened. Only in retrospect did I know for certain that everything had worked out all right. With Chris, though, I was still on an adventure into uncharted territory. Even after four years together this remained the case. It always would, of course.

...I decided I had no option but to go with the moment – like someone travelling down a river sitting on a barrel and encountering exhilarating rapids – trusting the instincts of my unschooled young heart and hoping that Luke's smile on waking this morning meant what I thought it did...

My unschooled heart back then! It had been through a lot since. But it hadn't grown clever or wise. The heart doesn't do that. It lives forever in a state of hope. I hoped this night, last night, lying under the stars with the man I love and silently holding hands with him, that Chris and I could go on together for ever. We can't of course. Death will come along one day, and call on one of us. But till then... I live in hope.

THE END

****

Readers who have enjoyed the setting of this story in the valley of the Dordogne, and its hinterland of music, may also enjoy **Blue Sky Adam** by the same author.

THE PARIS NOVEL

First published (as Gay Romance in Paris) 2013

27-year-old Peter has taken himself to Paris, after splitting up with his girlfriend, to find new love - and write. The last thing he's looking for is handsome blond Fabrice, who also identifies as straight. But a love they can't at first acknowledge blooms between them. Only an enforced separation obliges them to face the truth. But where better to discover the intricacies of love and yourself than in the world's most romantic capital? The city of Paris, its inhabitants and its street life are all integral characters in this book. First published in 2013 as Gay Romance in Paris.

For Tony Linford in memoriam, and for Yves Le Juen

ONE

I opened the windows that led out onto the balcony of my hotel room. We call them French windows. The French just call them windows. *Fenêtres*.

I stepped through them and was stopped in my tracks by the view across the street. In a window directly opposite two men of about my own age – twenty-seven – stood. They were in a sitting-room or salon. The blinds and curtains were open and the lights were on. The two young men were naked. They stood facing each other. About a metre separated them. Both their penises were erect.

I wasn't gay. But I was a writer. I was researching Paris. I'd never seen a scene like this before. I stayed to watch.

The two men moved slowly towards each other. Like ballet dancers. Actually they both had beautiful physiques. Perhaps ballet dancers was what they were. They had hair the colour of dirty gold, and their skin also looked golden in the light. They were exactly the same height. Which meant that when their two extended cocks met, a little before the rest of them did, they met exactly. Tip of foreskin to tip of foreskin. Like two pairs of little lips they seemed to kiss.

Then they embraced each other tightly. I'd seen men do that before, obviously, although it wasn't something I often did myself. For some reason – and unlike most other straight men I knew – I didn't feel very comfortable with myself about it when I did.

They kissed of course. Tongues deep down each other's throat. I'd never seen men do that before, though of course I knew that some men did.

I have to say that I found them a beautiful sight. A man doesn't need to be gay to find Michelangelo's David beautiful. And because this whole book is about the difficult business of being honest with oneself, about learning to be honest, about trying to be, even if the process is a long one, I'll be honest about what happened next. I started to harden in my pants. And because it had just now got dark and there was no-one to overlook my fourth-floor hotel-room balcony I unzipped my jeans and took my cock out.

The two men repositioned themselves. One folded himself over the arm-rest of a sofa. There were two in the room. He was on the one that stood against the far wall, so he was in full-length double-curved profile from where I stood. The other came up behind him, spat on his hand and anointed his truncheon dick with it. Then, adjusting his height a little by bending his knees but still more or less standing upright, he entered his friend with a single, measured thrust.

I'd thought that these days all gay men used condoms. They didn't. I could see clearly enough to notice that. Perhaps they had both been tested, and never cheated on each other. I hoped so anyway. By now there was something I just couldn't not do. I started to masturbate.

The fellow doing the fucking started to come at the same time as I did. I shot my semen far out over the edge of the balcony, letting it fall who knew how or where or upon whom below in the street. Meanwhile the guy across the road climaxed inside his friend.

I didn't stay to see if they would follow up with a return match. Perhaps the young man who'd just been penetrated had already come on the sofa arm. I turned back into my room and shut the balcony French window behind me. I sat at the little desk the room was furnished with and began to write. Not about what I'd just witnessed. Not then. I'd come to Paris to be a serious writer, an acute observer of the social scene, not a mere voyeur. I'd come here to burn with a hard, gem-like flame, not turn into a peeping Tom.

I wrote instead about my arrival in Paris just an hour ago. About my first sight of the city since I'd last seen it ten years or so before, when I was in my mid-teens. I wrote this.

Paris. Winter. 1987.

It was the light, quite simply.

Roissy Charles de Gaulle, I discovered, was neither more nor less than a Heathrow Doppelganger or whatever the word for one was in French. Buying a coach ticket in that language (Etoile s'il vous plâit) elicited the price in English, the clerk not even looking up as he took the money, and although we set out towards the city on the right-hand side of the dual carriageway, it was raining in the desperate blackness of this February evening just as it might be, and by now almost certainly was, in England.

But the light was different.

Outside the périphérique, the ring-road that separates Paris from the rest of the world as ferociously as the vanished fortifications whose line it follows, light shone from poor bare rooms above corner bakeries now closed, from naked bulbs that dangled on suspect wires. Inside the périphérique's enchanted circle it came from warm lace-curtained windows, dripping from the thousand chandeliers that hung from sculpted ceilings in the avenue des Ternes. But whatever its source it had the same quality, this light remembered vaguely from a hundred paintings, that enticed from half open doorways, shining through the smoke of a million Gitanes, surviving its translation down the years from candle flame to gas, from gas to electricity: the yellowish, haunting, beckoning light of France.

I got off the bus at Etoile – the traffic system that circles the Arc de Triomphe. I went below ground and took a Métro train. That journey in the Métro provided one moment of shocking beauty when, in the blackness of the tunnel, the Eiffel Tower suddenly appeared at the window as if conjured. Its unmistakeable profile formed a glittering web of gold against the now diamond-studded darkness while at its feet reflections shimmered on the surface of an invisible river. It took me a few dazzled seconds to realise that my train had left its warren and was crossing the Seine high on a viaduct, its tunnel no longer a man-made one but an older one that merged with it: the night.

TWO

It was nearly seven o'clock. I would soon want something to eat. I checked myself in the bathroom mirror, and adjusted my clothing as the saying goes. I took the lift downstairs and stepped into the rue du Commerce. It was wet, cold, bleak and inhospitable. I made my way back to the Métro station at the end of the street. The line, having crossed the Seine only two stops back, had not yet returned underground but was carried aloft on an iron viaduct. The station was a greenhouse-like structure approached by a spiralling stairway. The whole effect was light and graceful: industrial architecture, and nineteenth-century at that, which had a feminine elegance unlike anything in London. I bought an orange card, passport to a month's unlimited travel in the city. I saw a beggar and gave him ten francs from out of the change. Then I climbed the stairs and caught a train.

Friends in England had told me that the best place to explore with a view to eating, drinking, night life and general Parisian atmosphere was the left-bank area around the Place Saint Michel. Others had sworn by Chinatown at the other end of the Quartier Latin. Flats were said to be cheap there still, should I feel like making it my permanent base. Yet others had recommended an early visit to the Marais, the only sizeable chunk of unreconstructed, pre-Haussman Paris still to be found on the right bank. For atmosphere, they said, there was nowhere, not even Montmartre, to touch it.

This evening I did not care where I went. I would let Paris decide for me. It was all right to let things take their course in this way from time to time, I thought, provided I kept it within bounds. Letting my shirts choose themselves as they appeared at the top of the pile in the drawer was one thing; applying the same principle to choosing a girlfriend, though, would be quite another.

Paris decided that I should get off the train, now underground again, when a station appeared whose walls were decorated with engravings of the old Hôtel de Ville, famously burnt to the ground during the 1871 Commune. I thought the pictures might be worth a look and then a comparison with the Hôtel de Ville itself, the 'new' one built a hundred years ago. With an impulsiveness that surprised me I leaped at the train doors and through them just before they snapped shut.

The sudden appearance of the Hôtel de Ville, white as an owl against the deep blue night, stopped me in mid-stride as I came up the subway steps. The whiteness, the coldness, the marble-slabbed open space around it, the floodlit formal fountains: the whole effect was like a gigantic ice sculpture so cold that it seemed to be lowering the temperature even in the surrounding streets. I fled the cold marble and the freezing fountains. I turned up a side street, turned two more corners at random. I was pleasantly lost.

I was in a narrow street of old stone houses, all different one from another, their individuality testifying to the independent spirits of their long-dead builders. Their shuttered windows were all at different heights and their crooked chimneys squirmed up from unexpected corners. Most of them had once had open arcades at street level and many now found room for a café or a grocer's, a restaurant or a tiny bar. One building in particular caught my eye, a dog's-leg twist of the road giving it the advantage of almost street-corner prominence. It rose just three storeys to its steep-pitched roof; an attractive building, but its large ground-floor windows, separated by green painted wood panels, were so filled with lace curtains and leafy plants that it was impossible to see in. A muted light shone out. Above the door a painted sign said boldly: *Bar Restaurant Le Figeac.* I pushed open the green door and went inside.

A dozen or so customers sat close together at very small tables where flickering candles wedged in old wine bottles shone through veils of cigarette smoke like harbour lights on a misty evening. An assortment of theatre posters and modern paintings hung on stone walls beneath a black-beamed ceiling. More surprisingly, there were birds. The window embrasures, each one a two-foot mortice piercing the ancient stone walls, were given over to them and, though it was night outside, they trilled and fluttered as I entered.

Just inside the door and to the left there was a small bar counter behind which an attractive young woman – petite, brunette, with a lively intelligent face – smiled a welcome. Behind her an open doorway led into the clattering kitchen.

The bar was only big enough for three people to stand at and two were already there. From the back, as I first saw them, they seemed alike: two men in heavy rook-black winter coats with hair above to match. The vermilion scarves that they both wore, brightly redolent of Moulin Rouge posters, and advertising their Parisian credentials more loudly than words, were the only concession their rear views made to colour. I came up alongside. Viewed from this new angle the two men appeared at once less crow-like and more distinct. The further one was about my age and good-looking in a rough sort of way. Streetwise, I thought. The nearer one might have been twice as old though he was only beginning to grey at the temples. His clothes had possibly been smart once, but it had been a long time ago. He wore an aggressively patterned tie whose width confessed the seventies. He had the beard, spectacles and furrowed forehead of the self-proclaimed intellectual; a copy of that day's *Libération* protruded from an outside pocket. He turned to me and, with a scowl, asked, 'Are you eating here?'

'Perhaps.' I had not yet made up his mind. I wondered whether the older man's next words would play a part in my eventual decision. Was he the proprietor, perhaps?

'Because, if you are, then beer,' (I had just ordered one), 'is no aperitif. No aperitif at all.' He glared frowningly at me and banged the flat of his hand on the counter to show his disgust. 'The hour for beer is past. Now is the time for pastis, unless you are like me whose liver can no longer support the stuff; then, *faute de mieux*, it's the time for kir.'

'Jean-Jacques...' said the young woman behind the counter, using the intonation with which a child's name is transformed into a gentle warning.

'Are you the *patron*?' I asked the bearded man. The woman and the younger man both smiled.

'No,' the man called Jean-Jacques answered, still frowning. 'Not even a shareholder.' His frown metamorphosed into a beaming smile. 'But I'm a very, very important client.' He turned his whole body towards the counter as he finished, just in case the woman should miss the point. Then he returned to me. 'Are you married?'

I said, 'No.' I had recently split up with my last girlfriend but I wasn't going to tell him that. I decided to match his forwardness with my own. 'What about you?'

Jean-Jacques peered at me. So did the younger man. 'I have a wife somewhere. Where exactly, though, I forget.'

'Take no notice of him.' The younger man leaned into the conversation, an expression of amusement beginning to animate his face. 'He talks nothing but *conneries* before nine o'clock and not much else after.' He made the sign, fist rotating on nose, for intoxication. 'You are not a tourist?'

'No.'

The young man nodded slowly, like a researcher whose most daring hypothesis has just been proved correct. 'I thought not.'

'Except tonight,' I said. 'I've just arrived in Paris to write a book but at this precise moment I don't know exactly where I am.' I was pleased with the way my French was coming back to me. I'd been considered good at it at school but it had suffered nine years of neglect since. I wondered if these two red-scarfed imbibers were typical Parisians. No doubt I would need to take a larger sample to be sure.

'You're in the Marais,' said the younger man.

'Not in the figurative sense, I hope,' said Jean-Jacques. Marais, I remembered, meant a swamp.

'But in the literal,' the younger one finished the sentence for his companion and then continued animatedly. 'You are in the exact heart of Paris. Paris has a heart, *et ben oui*. In times gone by she used to have a soul as well but now she has a liver instead.'

'Marianne,' said Jean-Jacques to the young woman behind the bar, 'Put a pastis for the Rosbif. You are a Rosbif, not a Boche? As I thought. And one for Dominique. For me another kir.'

'How do you mean, Paris has a liver?' I was working hard to keep up. I suspected I had just misheard. *Le foie* was liver, *la foi*, faith. It would be easy to make a mistake.

'The age of faith is dead or dying: the age of the liver being born.' Dominique capitalised on the potential wordplay. 'Our mortal livers exercise our anxieties as much as their eternal souls did those of our grandparents. Jean-Jacques here is a case in point. For him, kir is only venially sinful, pastis mortally so.'

'Ta gueule, Dominique,' said Jean-Jacques, who had clearly heard all this before. *'Arrête tes conneries.'*

'Thank you for the drink,' I said, and proposed their healths, privately drinking to what I thought a delightful idea: the vast, collective, metropolitan liver that was Paris.

The glasses emptied rapidly and I offered to refill them; the offer was accepted without any charade of hesitation or reluctance. 'Are you eating here, then?' I asked them. Dominique answered that he was not eating yet and Jean-Jacques's answer was delivered so firmly that it might have meant not just 'not yet' or 'not here' or 'not tonight' but that he never ate at all.

'Je mange pas,' was what he said.

The tables had been filling quickly during this time. I'd already glanced at the menu and liked what I saw. I asked Marianne if I could have a meal. 'There's only the big table left,' she said. 'Do you mind?' Why the size of the table should matter I could not imagine. Until I got there and saw that the table was a circular one, laid for six, and that five people already sat there in an animated crossfire of conversation. Too late now to withdraw, with Marianne already shoe-horning me into the narrow space, I took the sixth seat, and Marianne took my simple order.

Conversation at the table ceased abruptly. Everyone looked at me. 'I'm Peter. From England,' I said.

Seated on my left was a cheerful, uncomplicated looking woman with immaculately coiffed blonde hair and wearing a shimmering, chiffony confection of a yellow frock. She introduced herself as Françoise. It struck me that she was a little under-dressed for the end of February but this unseasonality was somehow cheering: it seemed to point towards a summer yet to come. As for other prospects, she was divorced (this came up quite early in the conversation) and I found myself taking careful sidelong looks at her when her attention was focused elsewhere. I concluded that she was attractive but a few years too old to interest me seriously.

On my right sat a younger couple, Jeannette and Denis. 'You've picked the best restaurant in the *quartier*,' Jeannette told me. 'I mean, for ambience. Not too many tourists and hardly any Parisians.'

I looked round at the busy scene. 'Then who are all these people?'

'People like us; people like you, for that matter. People who live in the *quartier*, people who work in Paris.'

'But not Parisians?' I was puzzled.

'Not real Parisians,' Jeannette explained. 'I'm from Troyes and Denis comes from Nantes. We both work in Paris. We met in this restaurant, actually. You may find it useful from that point of view yourself if you're on your own.' Denis and Jeannette had arrived in the *quartier* about six months ago, they told me. They still had about them that air of excitement and privilege that emanates from people who have just moved into a newly fashionable neighbourhood. In spite of myself I found I envied them just a little.

The other couple at the table, Régine and Fabrice, had been in the quartier for nearly two years. They weren't real Parisians either, they said. Régine came from Bordeaux and Fabrice from near Strasbourg. I put their ages at about thirty, a couple of years older than myself. They were a good looking pair. Régine was dark with large eyes, an oval face and ringleted hair: an almost nineteenth century kind of beauty. Fabrice's looks were of a more modern type. With luminous blue eyes and blond hair that was beginning to darken a little, the way honey does as it matures, he had an almost Nordic look about him. The look was enlivened by a real sparkle in the eyes and a humorous mobility about the corners of his sensitive mouth. This last feature was not at all eclipsed by a rather soft looking moustache which, like his eyebrows, was considerably darker than the hair on his head. How come we hadn't met before? Fabrice asked me. How long had I been living in the Marais?

'I don't live anywhere just yet,' I told him. I explained I was staying for my first few nights in a cheap hotel off the rue du Commerce, and that my visit to the Marais this evening was a matter of chance and impulse. 'It was the pictures of the Hôtel de Ville at the tube station,' I said. 'Does that sound silly?'

'An inspired impulse,' said Fabrice, leaning across the table towards me. 'Not silly at all.' He looked very intensely into my eyes at that moment. I wasn't sure I liked the way he did that. And yet somehow I did. Fabrice went on, 'You'll be looking for somewhere to live round here, I expect. Just the sort of place for a guy like you.'

'What do you mean, a guy like me?' I asked, a bit taken aback.

In his turn Fabrice now also seemed a little thrown. 'Oh, you know,' and his face flickered in the candle light. 'Someone on his own, new to Paris, bit of a Bohemian, that sort of thing.'

'Bohemian?' I choked slightly. 'I'm just trying to be a writer. Nothing very Bohemian about that.'

'Everything's relative,' said Régine. 'Fabrice is an investment banker.'

'And you?' I asked.

'Don't laugh. I'm in accounting. Cost control. But it is for a TV company.'

'Join the Bohemians,' I said.

'Seriously,' Fabrice came back. Again he had that oddly intense look in his blue eyes. 'If you're really looking for somewhere to live round here, I could put you in touch with someone who might be able to help. And you'd get to meet a real Parisienne into the bargain.'

207

'You mean I still haven't met one?' I turned back to Françoise. 'Surely you...'

'I was born in Paris, it's true,' she admitted, her yellow dress rustling in sympathy, 'but I'm not really one of them. My parents were from the provinces. Parisians are the end. I have a small dress shop here and I meet them all the time. If I told you how they behaved you would never believe me.'

'She's right,' said Jeannette. 'They're so rude.'

'Ils se foutent des autres,' they all agreed. The Parisians, it appeared, did not give a fuck about other people.

'Anyway,' said Fabrice, 'I'll give you an introduction to La Belle Margueritte. She's a cousin of a friend. Rumoured to be *assez riche*. She's the owner of a pretty big *immeuble* just a couple of blocks from here. She might find she had a small half-forgotten apartment going cheapish – if she decided she liked your face.' Fabrice paused and shrugged non-committally. 'And there's no reason why she shouldn't.'

'There,' said Françoise as she extracted a particularly recalcitrant snail from its shell, her voice full of triumph. 'You have a *tuyau* already.'

'A pipe?' I queried. My understanding was still anchored to the concrete meanings of the words.

'A piece of useful information,' explained Denis. 'For example, someone in the know tells you which horse to put your money on. That's a *tuyau*.'

A litre bottle of Côtes du Rhône had circulated among us and been quickly disposed of. A second had been ordered while I was still on my *saucisson* starter and my glass was being refilled as a matter of routine by the others as soon as it was empty. How the bill would be divided I could only guess.

At nine o'clock precisely a plump woman in late middle age entered the restaurant carrying a basket full

208

of fresh baguettes. 'It's Madame Touret,' Denis said, his voice hushed with respect.

I half expected the men to stand and salute. 'Who is she?' I asked.

There was no need for an answer. Madame Touret moved between the cramped tables with an agility that belied her waistline. Shaking a hand here, exchanging a word there, she circulated among the customers with the practised assurance of a royal personage. I was presented to her. She hoped my stay in Paris would be a happy one and my visits to the Figeac frequent. She passed on, a swirl of smiles, into the kitchen. Madame Touret was the owner of the restaurant.

'Her family came from the town of Figeac in the Lot,' said Régine, as if to forestall questions about Parisian origins. 'Hence the name of the restaurant. The chef, René ... have you met him yet? ... he's her son.'

Emboldened by the simultaneous arrival of my entrecôte à la Bordelaise and a third bottle of wine, I asked about the two men at the bar. For Dominique and Jean-Jacques still stood there all this time in animated discussion about something or, more probably, nothing very much.

Jeannette and Denis did not know them. The others were happy to put them in the picture. 'Dominique does a bit of everything,' Fabrice said. 'Odd jobs, selling things. Does some work as a film extra sometimes. And if I said he was a drugs dealer as well you'd get the wrong impression but – and this is another *tuyau* – if you were ever looking for an occasional supply of marijuana, he's probably where you'd start.'

I had smoked nothing so interesting since leaving university and only rarely then. I appreciated the tip less for its usefulness than for the friendliness that prompted it. I began to feel accepted in the foreign city.

'As for the other one,' Fabrice went on, 'Jean-Jacques is supposed to be a poet. I say 'supposed to be' because I've never seen any evidence for it. As far as I know his work at the bar keeps him busy most days and his muse is a liquid one.'

A hatchet-faced man at the next table turned round at that moment and tapped Fabrice on the shoulder. 'I couldn't help hearing what you said and I'm obliged to correct you. The gentleman you speak of is indeed a poet, a published one and well known in his day. And though you are certainly too young, monsieur, to remember this, he played no small role at the barricades of sixty-eight.' He returned to his own conversation. Fabrice looked suitably chastened.

'You learn something new every day,' said Françoise brightly, and poured some wine into Fabrice's glass as if in token of her support.

With the arrival of the fourth bottle I felt not just that I would like to live in the *quartier* but that I already did. During the cheese I remembered with a flash of panic that my hotel was on the other side of Paris. But over the coffee, and more especially the cognac that arrived with it, I decided that didn't matter in the least.

THREE

I wasn't the first to leave the table. Jeanette and Denis went home first, then Françoise. At that point I made a move to get up and go, but Fabrice begged me to go with him and Régine to a nearby little bar they knew. He had such a puppy-dog look on his face that I didn't have the heart to say no. The next day was Saturday anyway. There would be no work for Fabrice or Régine, and as for a writer like me ... well, I could make up my schedule as I went along.

In the end Régine didn't come with us. It was late, she said, and she'd had enough wine for today. 'But you two go and be boys together,' she said. 'Have fun.' As we left we passed the two black-coated men still standing at the bar. Jean-Jacques and the younger Dominique. We said goodnight politely but they took no notice of us.

We 'boys' both kissed Régine on the pavement outside the restaurant, then she made her way towards their apartment. It was little more than a hundred metres away.

As for the bar that Fabrice took me to, The Little Horseshoe was even nearer to the Figeac and just about in sight of it. It owed its name to the size and shape of the counter which almost filled the cramped interior. There was just room for a semi-circle of customers to stand round it and for one very small table in each of the four corners. Its appearance – well-worn woodwork, smoke-darkened ceiling and a polished brass rail around the bar – had probably not changed in the past century. It was packed solid.

Fabrice ordered us a small beer each. We clinked glasses. Because of the crush in the place, we were leaning shoulder to shoulder over the bar. 'Welcome to Paris,' Fabrice said. 'It's good to have you here.' With our faces turned towards each other we were almost close enough to kiss. Not that I had any thought of doing that, but I couldn't help remembering the two men I'd seen earlier. That wasn't something I'd forget in a hurry. I remembered they'd both had dull gold hair. Fabrice and I were, by coincidence both dark blond, though Fabrice was rather taller than average height and I was somewhat less. I was very surprised just then to feel my dick give a little twitch in my pants.

We had one beer, then Fabrice said, 'It's very crowded here. Can I take you to another place, just a short walk away, where we'll have more space and can sit and talk?'

Had Fabrice not had a girlfriend, one whom I'd met and just spent the evening with, I'd have said no to that. I'd have made the obvious deduction that here was a gay man who was trying to pick me up. But he did have a girlfriend, and so I said yes.

And so I found myself meandering up the rue Vieille du Temple with Fabrice, looking for another bar which, so he said, had the advantage of staying open all night.

At that hour the rue Vieille du Temple was a dark, forbidding place and when we turned off it into a labyrinth of alleys it seemed that the Marais had thrown off its daytime identity and reverted to an older one, medieval and sinister. As we threaded our way through the ill-lit maze I wondered how I would ever find my way home and, in a momentary reassertion of my usual disposition, cursed myself for being so easily led into an adventure such as this.

We stopped at a solitary lighted window and knocked at the door beside it. *'C'est qui?'* a voice enquired.

'Fabrice et un Rosbif.'

Bolts were withdrawn and the door opened. In contrast to the Little Horseshoe this place was large and bare. The walls were the explosive red of overripe tomatoes and the ceiling a shade of brassy, snakeish green. The lights suspended from it were shaded with the kind of tasselled fringes that seem designed to maximise the accumulation of dust and minimise the diffusion of light. A billiard table stood morosely at the far end of the room, one neglected cue lying on its green baize. The scene reminded me vaguely of a picture I'd seen somewhere, but in the state I was in by then I couldn't place it. Nearer at hand only one of the plain wood tables was occupied by customers. A group of middle-aged men sat there with glasses, a bottle and dominoes. The light gave them something of the appearance of vultures. It seemed they knew Fabrice. We joined them.

Introductions were perfunctory, names being exchanged only to be immediately forgotten, and we new arrivals were assimilated into whatever drunken game of dominoes was in progress. Someone placed a domino on its edge on the table. The next person put another one nearby, and the next two dominoes formed a bridge across the top. Turn by turn, more dominoes were added until a tower was formed. It seemed childishly simple. I wondered that there was no more to it than that. As the tower increased in height it grew more difficult to keep it stable; the upright dominoes had to be placed nearer and nearer to the centre of gravity. At last the only way upward lay in the alternating of one horizontal with one vertical domino and after two courses of this the whole edifice swayed, toppled and collapsed.

'Tournée générale,' said the man whose last domino had delivered the fatal blow, and put his purse on the table. The object of the game was revealed.

A clear colourless liquor was served. It tasted of apricots. I could only guess that it was strong. A second tower was started. This time it did not get so high and it was my ill-judged domino that sent the structure clattering to the table top where my money had then to join it. I lost count after that of the number of towers, the number of rounds of apricot liquor, noticing only that they succeeded each other more and more quickly like the passing years.

Fabrice asked our older companions if they knew Jean-Jacques. They did. Was he really a poet? he asked. A first-rate poet, they all agreed, as far as poets went. Someone said maliciously that he had sold his liver to the devil in return for good reviews for his first volume of verse. The devil was expected almost any day now to come and claim what was his own, hence the poet's recent abandonment of pastis in favour of kir. They all shook their heads. Kir was considered a sell-out.

My memory of the evening now degenerated into glimpses, as when a sea mist briefly parts to show a pale tableau of sails and sea and shore. One of the more vulturine of my companions took it upon himself to build his own domino tower. 'I shall now show you the hope of the world,' he announced when it was about seven storeys high. A joint was circulating now and the room was in soft focus. I watched, hypnotised, as the speaker withdrew two horizontal dominoes from about halfway up, like someone perversely removing tins from a supermarket stack. But the tower did not collapse. It dropped a half centimetre and swayed slightly but it stood. The builder placed the two dominoes upright on the top with a theatrical flourish. 'That is the hope of the world,' he said. 'There is no other.'

The mist came down again.

Fabrice didn't get the chance to have the quiet chat with me that he'd seemed to want. But I did occasionally think I felt his knee rub against mine beneath the table as we sat side by side. It could have been an accident though, or I might have imagined it. I think my brain had been a little over-stimulated by what I'd seen those two men doing earlier in the evening.

I began to think it was time to go, and said so. Fabrice rose to his feet. 'You're right,' he said. 'But don't try getting back to the rue du Commerce at this time of night. We've a sofa. Stay with us.'

What could I do except say yes?

Our departure was hardly noticed. Our last sight of the group was from the doorway. Two were trying to turn the dominoes into a model battleship but were unable to agree which end was the stern and which the bow. The third was fast asleep, his head on the table like the dormouse at the Mad Hatter's. Had the others later attempted to squeeze him into the empty apricot liqueur bottle I would not have been surprised.

I was surprised, though, to find that I felt good with Fabrice, lurching a bit as we retraced our steps.

'In principle I don't let. You must understand this.' Margueritte d'Alabouvettes sat in an armchair opposite me, her legs elegantly crossed. She was a still attractive woman of about fifty. Her poise, perhaps her willpower, made the studio apartment seem bigger than it was. 'But to a friend of Fabrice...' She smiled coolly. 'Do you smoke?'

'Only just occasionally, to keep a lady company,' I said.

Madame d'Alabouvettes flushed slightly. I was in two minds about my answer. Had I been gallant or merely fawning? In the end the feeling of satisfaction at finding the right words in French and managing to trot them out so quickly overcame my scruples. I allowed myself to feel pleased. Things were going well. I was still hungover from the previous night, and my sleep on Régine and Fabrice's sofa had not been the most comfortable of my life... But I felt I was making friends here, and Fabrice had been as good as his word in giving me Margueritte d'Alabouvette's phone number and address.

'Ordinarily I keep these studios for the use of my family and friends when they are visiting Paris,' she continued after we had both embarked delicately on menthol cigarettes. A lifetime of producing oboe-like vowels of the finest quality had given her the slightly protruding lip structure that is shared by people in the act of whistling and members of well-born French families. I was conscious of being in the presence, at last, of a true Parisienne.

'Most of the rest of the building is in the hands of my manager who deals with the office space lettings. I keep only two flats for my own personal use on the first floor. And there is my daughter's flat on the second floor and my second son on the fourth. My eldest in on the third and the third is in Paraguay. You see, we are a *famille nombreuse*.'

'It must be nice to have so many of your family around you,' I suggested while I tried to sort all this out.

'Around me?' She did not understand at first. Then she did. It was I who had not understood. 'Oh no,' she said, 'I don't live here. I am normally in Barcelona and for weekends, Rome. In Paris I'm only ever passing through. My husband travels so much, you see. London and Los Angeles.'

'I see,' I said, though I did not.

'I do hope you will like Paris. For me, no. I know it is full of beautiful things and places but the Parisian is someone who gets on my nerves. You know them of course. The nouveau riche women in the sixteenth who wear silk gloves to go to the supermarket. Those red berets and that forties-style make-up. So bourgeois. And they don't care, you know. *Ils se fichent des autres*.'

'You are not a Parisienne yourself?' I felt a twinge of disappointment, cheated of my promised example of the species.

She looked slightly shocked. 'I was born here, of course,' she allowed, 'but the family is from the Haute Savoie, further from Paris, you must admit, than Brussels is or London. We still have a little property there: a small manor house and a few farms. You must come and stay with us down there some time if you have a holiday.'

I began to realise that, if I had failed to bag a real Parisienne, I had at any rate encountered a specimen of an even rarer breed: the seriously rich.

'You do understand,' she continued with no change of tone, 'that you will have to pay cash.'

'Fabrice did mention that.'

'You see, I have no bank account in France to put a cheque into. There, I knew you would understand.'

A tour of the apartment was conducted swiftly. We discussed the electricity bill and the vagaries of the cooker. We smoked a second cigarette. We negotiated a price. I was nervous at doing such a thing in French but I found the cigarette seemed to help. Perhaps it was not for nothing that tycoons and movie moguls were always depicted smoking cigars.

'On no account let Monsieur Guyot know that you are paying rent. If anyone should ask, explain that you are a cousin. Perhaps, now that I think about it, it would be better if you did not put your name by the bell-push. Or if you do, write it very small. It is always easy to explain in advance to visitors that the bell is at the top on the left.'

I said yes to all of this. I did wonder who Monsieur Guyot was, and I was certain that explaining in an English accent that I was a cousin of the d'Alabouvettes would replace a small suspicion in the mind of anyone who was curious with a rather larger one. But something told me not to question. The meeting was going very well even if its momentum was generated by an engine unfamiliar to my English way of dealing.

We met the concierge at the bottom of the stairs. She was a woman not much older than I was. That surprised me; I had expected a crone. 'This is Luisa,' said Margueritte d'Alabouvettes.

It was arranged that I would move in, with the cash, this very afternoon because, although the next month did not officially begin until Tuesday, my new landlady would be flying to Los Angeles later tonight and would not be returning to Paris for a month. I had been lucky to catch her between hops. She wanted the rent in advance and could hardly keep me out of the flat once I had paid it. So my first two nights in the studio would be a kind of present. As to what Margueritte would do with the French francs in Los Angeles, I was too discreet to enquire.

Luisa showed me out into the street. She caught sight of someone across the road, a lanky young man with a mop of dark hair, and called to him. 'Joe.'

'He is an American man,' she explained to me while he crossed the road towards us. 'He lives two streets away. Perhaps, with a language in common, he will be a friend for you.'

I doubted that very much. Why do people seem to think that if two foreigners share a common language they are bound to be friends?

But I was wrong and Luisa was right. By the time the American guy had crossed the road, and we'd been introduced, and he'd shaken my hand and smiled at me, my defences had been breached. I found I couldn't not like Joe.

FOUR

'You got time to go for a coffee?' Joe said almost as soon as Luisa had retreated behind the huge varnished street door and shut it with a clang.

I said, 'Why not?' Joe led me abruptly down a side turning, in the opposite direction from the one I already knew. He seemed to pause at the door of a café. I said, 'Are we going in here?'

'No, not that one. *They* use that one. We'll go across the road.'

'I see.'

Joe took out a packet of Gitanes. 'Smoke?'

'Occasionally....'

'Mind if I...?'

'Go ahead.' I don't think he'd heard my previous answer.

'Hey, look out! We drive on the right, you know.'

'Thanks.' I'd been distracted by the Eiffel Tower, which now appeared to be striding into the street to meet us as we crossed. 'Who are *they*?'

'People we don't want to meet. Different ones different days.'

I accepted that. It made a kind of sense.

'You know what?' Joe looked at his watch. It was well after midday. 'Let's have a beer.'

We went in and stood by the zinc-topped counter. The café was not very full but an impression of frantic activity was given by the urgent sounds coming from the espresso machine and by the manic pace set themselves by the waiters. A barman approached us, shook hands with Joe, was presented to me, exchanged pleasantries and then hurried off to serve another customer who had arrived after us and was calling loudly for a pastis.

'This'll take a bit of getting used to,' I said after five minutes had passed and I'd been introduced to two more waiters without Joe managing to secure us a glass of anything.

But good things take time. *'Deux demis,'* Joe was able to command at last. 'Draught beer OK for you?' I said it was.

'So what brings you to Paris?' Joe asked. 'Cheers, by the way.'

'Cheers. British Airways brought me.' I realised at once that must have sounded rude to someone who had just bough me a drink. But I wasn't sure how much I wanted to tell this rather forward if likeable stranger. I said, 'I've come to write a book.' But that was all I was ready to give away at this stage. I threw the question back. 'What brought you here? It's a hell of a lot further across the Atlantic.'

Joe looked straight at me. 'Love,' he said. 'Love brought me here and love left me here and now my job keeps me here. *C'est comme ça.'*

'I see,' I said, unsure whether Joe was sending me up or sending himself up or just being honest and commendably brief. 'Should I congratulate or commiserate?'

'Neither. That's just the way it is. Enjoy your beer. And then enjoy Paris. Why do you think any of us are here? All of us Yanks and Limeys and Aussies and Paddies? Get to know any of the ex-pats here and you'll find the same thing: there's always a story behind their being here. More than meets the eye.'

I asked him about his job. He was a teacher of English, he said, in one of the larger business language schools. Then he looked very intensely into my eyes, the way Fabrice had done several times the night before. Was that something everyone did here? I supposed I'd get used to it.

Joe said, 'You're looking a bit rough, I have to say. Hangover perhaps?'

I burst out laughing. 'No,' I protested. I thought for a second. 'Oh all right, maybe a little bit. I overdid the French experience a bit last night. Spent the night on a sofa on the other side of the Marais and found today a little bit uphill as a consequence.' I gave him an edited account of yesterday evening.

Joe drummed his fingers of the side of his glass of beer. 'Couple of these at five o'clock's a great idea but you do have to give it a break before bedtime. Otherwise you're not going to make it through your first week. So tell me, anyway: who did you sleep with in the Marais?'

To my surprise I didn't feel offended by this but laughed before replying. 'Sorry to disappoint you but I didn't sleep with anyone. I stayed with a charming couple called Régine and Fabrice.'

'You didn't do bad for a first day. Your French must be pretty good.'

'It's not great but it seems to be improving very quickly. I noticed it got better during dinner.'

'Everyone notices that. You'll find it goes on improving for about two years. After that you won't bother any more. Eventually, if you see a verb you don't know, you presume it's something you do with ropes on a ship and you don't need to learn it. Least, that's what I found. Anyway.' He hopped onto another subject like a bird popping from twig to twig. 'It'll be nice to have you as a neighbour. And you're lucky to have got a place so fast. Sounds like you're lucky to have met this Fabrice guy. Most people arrive, look six months for a one-person studio, then the day they find it, bang (if you'll excuse the expression), they meet the partner of a lifetime and have to start over, looking for a place for two. With me it was exactly the reverse. Six months to find a love nest that was meant to be for eternity then out on a limb to look for a perch for one. *C'est comme ça.*'

'And how long have you been in Paris?' I asked him.

'A long and instructive three years. You'll come round for dinner one night. I have two plates and two forks so there wouldn't be a problem. Have you always had a beard?'

Instinctively, my hand went to it. It was a full beard, but I kept it short, almost like extra long designer stubble. It was black, like my eyebrows and lashes, and so created a striking contrast to my blond hair. I knew I looked good with it. Especially with the 'bright blue eyes' people always told me I had. I knew it worked a treat with the girls anyway. 'Always?' I said. 'Not always.' I could be as obstructive as anyone when I wanted to be.

'You knew what I meant.'

'I grew it when I was nineteen in order to look my age,' I said. 'One day I suppose I'll have to shave it off in order not to.'

'Pity. It suits you.'

A few minutes after that he looked at his watch and said it was time to be running along. He gave me his address and phone number and I gave him the ones that would be mine in a few hours. He renewed the dinner invitation for 'some time real soon' as he got up to go, then left the café, a lanky figure moving among the tables in a way that reminded me again of a bird, this time a wading bird perhaps.

A few minutes later I left the café, and took the Métro back to the rue du Commerce to pay my hotel bill and get my stuff. Before leaving my room for the last time I went out onto the balcony and peered at the window opposite. Nothing was going on there. I felt oddly cheated by that.

On my way back to the Métro I met a beggar again. Was it the same one as yesterday's? It was difficult to be sure. I gave the man five francs.

By the time I'd unpacked my stuff, or some of it, it was evening and already dark. I left the handsome building I'd just moved into and turned left towards the Figeac. After all, I would have to eat somewhere before bedtime even if I couldn't run to a meal on yesterday's scale every night. But – to be honest – I also had the only half admitted hope of running into Fabrice.

Instead, when I pushed the door open, I found the poet, Jean-Jacques, alone at the bar reading *Libération,* which he had spread right across the tiny counter. The overhead light, shining through the glass of kir that he had placed on top of the paper, cast a rosy glow over the day's news. He turned to stare at me. 'Haven't we met somewhere?' he growled.

Marianne, emerging from the kitchen, heard him. She looked at me, remembered me from the night before and smiled. 'The alcohol's ruining his memory,' she said. 'Switching off the brain cells one by one like the lights of the Tour Montparnasse when the workers go home. One day it will be all dark.' She turned to Jean-Jacques. 'Have you forgotten already? This is Peter who was here last night.'

'Very possibly,' he answered. 'What will you have, Rosbif?'

I glanced round the room instinctively, though trying not to let Jean-Jacques see me doing it. Trying not to let him see my disappointment that I had only him for company. None of my other, younger acquaintances were there. No Régine, no Fabrice. No doubt they, like me, would not normally eat out every night of the week. Suddenly transformed in my own mind into an *habitué*, I felt a quite unreasonable resentment against the strangers who peopled the restaurant tables. I returned my attention to Marianne and the poet, and told them I was shortly to become a neighbour. They made appropriate noises. Where exactly was my new flat? they wanted to know. I told them.

'A magnificent house,' said Jean-Jacques, suddenly interested. 'Did you notice the entablatures?'

Actually I had not.

'Look at them properly next time. Friezes of grapes and ravens carved in stone, Corinthian capitals under the parapet... A grand residence. Of course the interior has been spoilt beyond recovery. Offices... Offices and flats. It had a name once. It was called the Hôtel des Corbeaux, on account of the carvings. It was built, if I remember rightly, towards the end of the sixteen-sixties. An eighteenth-century philosopher whose name I can't remember used to live there at one time.'

'During the eighteenth century, I suppose,' said Marianne quietly, and moved up several notches in my estimation. I had been impressed last night by the way she did her job, remaining calm even in the face of the most obstreperous customers, fulfilling the dual role of barmaid and waitress throughout the busiest time of the evening. I'd thought her graceful and attractive. Now I decided she was fun as well. I noticed that her wedding finger was ring-less.

I asked if it was possible to have just one course, a steak for instance, and a carafe of wine. It was and so, after returning the compliment of Jean-Jacques's kir (*Je mange pas*, the poet had said again in reply to my polite mumbles about eating) I squeezed myself into a seat. Not at the big table tonight but at a very small one in a line of four, each of which was squashed so tightly up against its neighbours that only the fact that each wobbled separately indicated its independence from them. On either side of me two couples faced each other, both wrapped up in their own private conversations which were delivered at normal volume, each pair oblivious of their neighbours despite the elbow to elbow proximity. At least the seat opposite me was empty, which created a little space. Now Marianne brought my meal. But someone was making towards the empty seat. It was Dominique, red-scarfed and eager-eyed. He sat down. 'Good news,' he said, adding when I looked blankly at him, 'Your moving in.' I offered him a glass of wine from my carafe. Dominique did not say no.

'You're going to live in the Hôtel des Corbeaux.'

'News travels fast,' I said.

'Luisa told me. Your concierge. That's what concierges are for.' He leaned across towards me, conspirator fashion. 'But it's a house full of history, the Corbeaux.' Dominique seemed even more of a *corbeau* himself this evening: all beak, black plumage and sharp eyes.

'I know. Jean-Jacques told me.'

'Not his sort of history.' Dominique gave a delighted chuckle, something between a wheeze and a croak. 'I mean my sort of history. In the time of the old concierge, when a concierge was a real concierge...'

I wasn't too sure if I would like Dominique's kind of history. 'Yes,' I interrupted. 'What happened to all the old dragons?'

'They died as all dragons do. These days the job is done by Portuguese women whose husbands work in the building trade. It's very useful when it comes to getting jobs done around the house or finding an odd length of copper piping for example. And, by the way, we're not supposed to call them concierges any more; they're *gardiennes*. The money never was very good and it isn't now. Instead they've upped the title. *Comme toujours...* Now this old concierge was a bit deaf but she had a granddaughter, a real looker, who used to visit her during the holidays. That was when I was about sixteen. My God, that girl was something. Used to have a *chambre de bonne* under the roof. Top bell on the left...'

'My bell,' I blurted out, then wished I hadn't. I wasn't especially pleased by the coincidence. 'But I think I've got two *chambres de bonnes* that have been knocked through to make a studio.'

'Right,' said Dominique. 'It's been modernised since those days. And I hope for your sake they've put a new bed in.' He chuckled again, even more throatily. 'Saw some action, the old one. Thank God for electronic entry codes, the push buttons. In the old days it would have been impossible to get in. You used to have to bawl your own name if you got home after midnight to get the concierge to come and open up. Can you imagine? No chance in the old days. I mean, suppose you said you'd come to screw their granddaughter? I give you a toast to the electronic door code.' He helped himself to another glass of wine.

'Also, there was a suicide attempt there about the same time. One of Madame d'Alabouvette's daughters. Of course Margueritte herself won't tell you that. She'll say it was an accident.'

I didn't imagine that she would say anything to me on the subject at all. But I found I was enjoying Dominique's company in spite of myself. I thought my contact with him, like my contacts with Joe and with Fabrice, might help me to become more rapidly a part of the neighbourhood. So when the steak and wine were at an end and Dominique suggested a visit to the Little Horseshoe, *le Petit Fer à Cheval*, I did not protest. 'Why not?' I said. I told him I'd gone there last night with Fabrice.

I paid my bill on the way out. Marianne would accept money for the steak only. 'There won't be any charge for the wine. Dominique drank most of it.'

'I don't think restaurants do that in England,' I said.

'C'est dommage,' said Marianne. What a shame.

'You have a friendly face,' said Dominique. Such was the crush at the counter that it was only inches from my own. 'I'll give you a piece of free advice. That woman you sat next to at dinner last night, Françoise, in the yellow dress. You could have her if you wanted. Quite easily. She'll go with anyone.'

I said, 'Thank you for the compliment.'

'You know that's not what I meant. And she's not without funds either. Owns her own shop.'

'Yes,' I said. 'She told me that. But, though I'm grateful for the...' I struggled to remember the word I'd learned for a tip. 'For the *tuyau*, I don't think really that she's what I'm looking for.'

'What are you looking for exactly?' Dominique looked searchingly into my eyes as if he expected to find the answer there rather than in anything I might say.

I guessed this was a tactic that Dominique used frequently; also that, whatever anyone might divulge by way of a reply Dominique would probably promise to supply it. 'To tell the truth,' I said, 'I don't think I really know at the moment.' It seemed the safest answer.

But Dominique was well prepared for even that. 'You should decide soon, in that case,' he said. 'Life is a full bath with the plug already out when you get in it.'

FIVE

Paris. Winter. 1987.

The room was willing me to get up. Moving only my eyes, I surveyed it. I lay in a bed that would disappear, as soon as I was out of it, into a niche in a clever arrangement of cupboards and bookcases. In the middle of the floor was a coffee table. There were two easy chairs. Under the window was a good-sized desk, the morning sun now falling full upon it, which doubled as my dining table. There were two dining chairs. The outside wall sloped inwards – gently from floor to window height, more steeply above – on account of the mansard roof. Posters would be a possibility there but pictures in frames were out. The floor carpet had a jazzy pattern that wouldn't have been my choice, although I admitted that it was at least cheerful. Out of sight was a very small kitchen and next to it an even smaller bathroom. It was the kind of apartment that estate agents flatter with the word compact. I was pleased with the place. It would do.

From the skylight in my bathroom I had a view (provided I stood on the lavatory seat and held the window open to its fullest extent with an upraised arm) of the spire of Notre Dame. This morning being Sunday the bells in the west towers, which were sadly hidden by an intervening satellite dish, were in full cry, heard by the faithful and the faithless alike as they cowered in their bolt-holes or scurried on their own pursuits about the city.

I was not a religious person: an Anglican by default, I had rarely attended a church service in adult life. But I did believe – hope triumphing over experience? – in the power of human love and was attracted to the idea that there might be a more profound reality behind this love:

a reserve of solid gold that underpinned the ephemeral currency exchanged by humankind. Whatever the reason, spiritual, nostalgic or touristic, I decided this morning, listening to the bells, that I would go to Notre Dame and hear Mass.

The air was still and sharp and a mist lay lightly over the Seine, binding together the Ile de la Cité and the Ile de St Louis just above the waterline like a silken web. Before the cathedral's west front a large crowd was gathered despite the cold: tourists and worshippers whisked together in an emulsion, like oil and vinegar for vinaigrette.

The clammy shock of the darkness inside separated the emulsion out. Worshippers were passing through a narrow gate under the scrutiny of a warden who with a well chosen question barred the way of non-worshippers and the ill-dressed and cast them into the outer darkness of the side aisles: tourists in countless swarms like lost souls. These produced an unchanging, shuffling sound of unrest: the sound perhaps of wailing and teeth-gnashing heard at a great distance. I decided to try and join the worshippers in the nave and was slightly surprised to be let in unchallenged, as if winning a competition I had not entered.

Above the high altar hung a coronet of lights through which the smoke of incense billowed up at intervals and, beyond, lances of blue stained glasslight pried their way between the soaring columns of the apse. The Mass was sung in Latin, the multinational congregation of thousands joining in the chants, and when so many voices were raised in different timbres and accents to sing the Pater Noster, I, for whom the situation was without precedent in my insular experience of churchgoing, was surprised by an emotion that caught at my throat and pricked behind my eyes.

Afterwards, when I shuffled out of the gloom of incense and blue glasslight, a survival instinct that had been sharpening with every day of my new life suggested that coffee and croissants on the terraces immediately around the cathedral would cost more than my status as a resident warranted. I crossed the bridge back into the Marais and went to look for a café that was open, a search that brought me quickly to the Little Horseshoe where, despite the chill, I installed myself at one of the pavement tables that were set out in optimistic response to the morning sun.

I guessed as I waited for my croissants to appear that if I only sat there long enough the whole population of the Marais would pass before my eyes. I'd also have been prepared to bet that Dominique would be the first.

I was wrong. The first comer was Fabrice. I was surprised to see Fabrice without his girlfriend. With a gesture I invited Fabrice to join me at my table. 'I almost didn't see you,' he said. At that moment my croissants arrived.

Fabrice ordered a coffee then watched me devour the croissants with rapt attention, as if he were going to paint the scene. 'You look as if you haven't eaten for days,' he said.

'I've been to Mass,' I said.

I told the story of my meeting with Margueritte and its satisfactory outcome, making appropriate thanking noises for Fabrice's part in making it happen. I asked after Régine. With an upward flick of his eyes Fabrice told me she'd had to go to Bordeaux for the weekend: a family problem, a grandmother breaking a leg or something. Why it had to involve Régine he could not imagine but there it was. So he was alone for the weekend. With a house stocked with food. Would I like to come to his flat for lunch? The invitation had virtually made itself. I accepted.

There was something very compelling about Fabrice. He had a warmth that was highly comforting. He seemed almost without edges and I welcomed that.

For what was left of the morning we observed the life of the *quartier* as it passed before us. There was a man who wore a live white rat around his shoulder nonchalantly as if it were a scarf; a woman who carried a dog, not much larger than the rat, in her shopping bag wherever she went; she walked with an alarming limp – alarming for the dog, that was; it rose and fell through a sixty-degree arc at each lurching step, wearing the intent expression of a yachtsman negotiating a choppy sea. At one point a tiny, shrill-voiced man accosted Fabrice, railing against a neighbour of his: a monster, a devil incarnate, a Spaniard called Carlos. Later came a mild and gentle Spaniard, equally diminutive, who complained of his neighbour, a bully and a thief, a Portuguese named Nico. 'Nico was the first one,' explained Fabrice, when Carlos had gone.

'How did I guess?' I said.

'They're two of the concierges round here,' Fabrice explained. 'Rarely if ever seen together. *Les deux ouistitis* we call them, the two marmosets.'

Fabrice told me a little of the Marais's chequered history. A swampy area of slums before Henri IV built his palace there – now the place des Vosges – it had then become the most fashionable part of the city. The house I lived in dated from this time. Later the Marais had declined with the removal of the court to Versailles and then the revolution till, within recent memory, it was a slum again, quaintly awful for the tourists, grim and insanitary for its population. 'They were going to pull it down, it was all so rotten. Luckily they didn't. Look at it now. And it's one of the few bits of Paris that Baron

Haussman never got his hands on. Virtually untouched by the nineteenth century.'

We had left the café by now and were on the way to Fabrice's apartment. We stopped at a corner shop to collect baguettes and other last-minute items. I bought a suitably generous bottle of wine. The shop was run by a Moroccan woman, Fabrice said. A Madame Almuslih. Plus her two children. Between them they kept the shop stocked and selling from dawn to dusk six days a week and from dawn to lunchtime on Sundays. 'Her husband is in prison of course,' said Fabrice casually as we left the shop. 'That's why she works so hard.'

'In prison for what?' asked Peter.

'Murder, I think,' said Fabrice. 'No-one's sure exactly. One can't really ask her.'

'I suppose not.'

'The locksmith over the road is in prison too,' Fabrice went on. 'Quite funny actually. He made copies of all his clients' keys and burgled them when they were out. It wasn't till he started driving around in a Porsche that people began to get suspicious.'

Compared to mine, Fabrice's flat appeared a palace. I'd only glimpsed it briefly and drunkenly on my first visit. I had just seen the living-room spin round once before I collapsed into sleep and I hadn't stayed for breakfast the following morning. 'Don't be too impressed,' Fabrice said, though his tone was not over-modest. 'The bank pays for it all. They sent me over from Strasbourg so they pay. It's officially for one but there's room for Régine and the bank hasn't made any problems.'

The principal room –*le living*, Fabrice called it – had a fine parquet floor covered with oriental rugs while a gilt-framed mirror occupied the whole of the wall space above a carved marble fireplace. The walls themselves were panelled, painted white, and a modest chandelier twinkled benevolently beneath a moulded plaster ceiling.

'*Quand-même,*' I said. I was beginning to get the hang of that word. It meant something like *even so*. In this instance it meant that, whoever paid for the apartment, I was impressed anyway.

Fabrice poured an aperitif and suggested that we drink it in the kitchen while he prepared lunch. In any case the kitchen was the dining-room as well. We continued to talk as Fabrice cooked, over glasses of Pineau de Charentes, which Fabrice twice refilled.

'Why did you come to Paris?' Fabrice asked inevitably at one point. This looked like the beginning of the conversation Fabrice had wanted two nights ago but which we hadn't got round to.

I shrugged. 'New start, I suppose. Wanting to be a writer... I split with my girlfriend recently. Usual story. You've heard it a thousand times.'

Fabrice nodded gravely. 'Yeah. I know.' Actually he said it in French. '*Ouais, je sais.*' He was paying my own French a compliment by speaking it.

Fabrice's competence in the kitchen was of a pretty high order, I thought. Joints of rabbit appeared from somewhere, had themselves coated in Dijon mustard, were popped into an oven dish, received great bastings of cream and butter and then left to their own devices in the oven. Salads were prepared, cheeses were sniffed for something (ripeness? off-flavours?) and either chosen or rejected. Herbs were chopped, the fruit bowl's contents deftly transformed into a fruit salad with the addition of something alcoholic and aromatic from a bottle, two-tone pasta selected and put to boil... Even if Fabrice was not a three-star chef or his results in the same class as Maxim's, I knew that, had it been me unexpectedly entertaining a near stranger to Sunday lunch, it would not have been like this.

'And Régine? Does she cook too?' I asked.

'No, not really. She has a repertoire of great dishes which she does very well but she's not an everyday cook at all. I do that. On the other hand, she mixes excellent cocktails and she chooses the wine.'

'Sounds a perfect partnership.' I was glad I'd brought a good bottle to accompany the meal. Without it Fabrice's lavish hospitality might have been overwhelming.

Fabrice told me about his family home in Alsace, near the town of Saverne. He did so in a very matter-of-fact way without any trace of boastfulness or desire to impress but it was clear from his description that he had been born rather luckier than most. His father, just coming up to retirement, was in investment banking as Fabrice was himself, and he owned a fairly stately pile on the edge of one of those half-timbered, geranium-sprouting Alsace villages that make the tourists go all misty eyed. There was an estate with tenant farmers, gamekeepers and the lot. Did I shoot? I never had done, but quickly – oh how quickly – I added that this was for no other reason than lack of opportunity. An invitation seemed to be looming in the vinous lunchtime haze, and even before it was made I watched my egalitarian principles vanish into the mist along with all the ties I felt with the extremely modest edge-of-town house in Northampton where my parents still lived and where my father, stern and principled, gave up his spare time to sit on the hard benches of the council chamber as a Labour representative.

'You must come for a weekend sometime very soon – and I mean very soon, because the shooting season's almost up. Say next weekend. What about it?' The invitation had come swiftly and, just as swiftly, I said I'd love to come.

With after-lunch coffee came a large glass of Armagnac and with that, the realisation that I would have to abandon my plans for the afternoon. I'd meant to finish settling into the flat, tidy odds and ends, sort papers. That would all have to be postponed now until after a siesta. After the Armagnac it seemed that the moment had come for me to leave. I remembered the washing up and offered to do it, but Fabrice would not hear of it. He quite understood that I had things to do; moving was such a headache. He pointed out the bedroom as we passed it on the way to the door: another magnificent room complete with enormous mirror and chandelier. I said thank you for the lunch and we shook hands. 'I'm beginning to get used to shaking everybody's hand twice a day,' I said. 'It's a bit of a novelty for us English.'

'Yes,' Fabrice agreed. 'You don't enjoy physical contact the way we do.'

I laughed. 'I don't accept that. You'd change your mind if you got to know us a little better.'

'I'd like very much to do that,' said Fabrice, at the same moment turning the wish to deed with a sudden enveloping embrace whose meaning, since we were in a bedroom, was unambiguous even to someone as clueless as me. Fabrice was the bigger and easily the stronger of us and a second later I found myself struggling on my back on the rather sumptuous silk coverlet with which the double bed was draped, with Fabrice on top of me and kissing me enthusiastically while, with the one hand that was sandwiched between our two bodies, trying to undo my zip. For several seconds I struggled with arms and legs to free myself, though vocal protest was more or less impossible. Fortunately Fabrice had both the sense and the good manners to let me go as soon as he realised that no amount of persistence would kindle any kind of reciprocal lust in me. He stood up off the bed and ran a hand through his hair as if running up a flag of truce. But he didn't look in the least embarrassed or apologetic.

I bobbed up into a standing position too. For a split second I thought I was going to hit Fabrice but the feeling passed off surprisingly quickly. Bizarrely I found myself concentrating on the sensation of Fabrice's kissing me. It was the first time my own moustached upper lip had ever brushed against another one that was similarly adorned. It had felt surprisingly ... well, different. I was astonished, the next moment, to hear myself coming out with the French equivalent of 'Well, now I really must he going,' quite calmly though a little breathlessly. *'Bon, il faut qui je m'en aille. Au revoir.'*

'Au revoir,' said Fabrice. He sounded a little disappointed but not at all angry or ashamed. Then to my further surprise – though not much further surprise was now possible – he added in effortless English, 'Oh don't be so British, Peter. I can't help it. You're just so cute.' He smiled down at me from the landing as I stumbled down the stairs.

SIX

'And were you 'shocking', as my students love to say?' Joe asked. We were sitting outside the café he had taken me to two days ago. There was an amused twinkle in his eyes. 'The French believe that the English are always 'shocking' by anything overtly sexual. The preconception and the grammar mistake are ingrained together. But really, were you shocking?'

'Shocked, no. Surprised? Well, yes, I was a little. I mean it didn't seem to grow out of anything. It was a touch unexpected.'

'Do you want to rephrase the last sentence? No, but I like the sound of your Sunday. High Mass at Notre Dame in the morning and a proposition from an investment banker under the chandelier in the afternoon. You seem to live life with an inbuilt sense of style.' He broke off. 'Or do you? No, I'm quite wrong. It's rather that things happen to you with style. Are you one of those people who never seek adventure but to whom adventures simply happen? What's that other word? Befall, that's it. Befall, befell, befallen. You're a befallen man, Peter. You should be careful.'

'What do you mean?'

'I don't know,' said Joe, with a self-deprecating smile. 'How the hell should I know what I mean? Oh but yes, I do know. Some people don't create their own lives: they're always on the receiving end of them. Watch out that you don't become one of those or the whole of life will happen to you without you doing anything to it. It'll be over and there you'll be, all befallen.'

'Anyway,' I tried to reassert myself, 'the point is, what do I say to him next time we meet? I can't exactly cut him dead. We live almost next door, we use the same cafés and restaurants, know the same people... I'd actually accepted an invitation to go to Alsace with him next weekend.'

'I don't see what you're so wound up about.'

'I'm not wound up.'

'You are, or you wouldn't have mentioned it. Despite your air of apparent calm, your English phlegm, you are wound up. But I don't get why you think you need to react in some way. You don't have to do anything, or say anything, or even think about it; it's no big deal. Treat him like nothing happened. He won't refer to it or try it again. Or if he does, just tell him to go to hell if that's how you feel about it. And if you don't want to spend a weekend in the country with him just tell him something else has cropped up. Nothing could be less complicated. But for God's sake don't go round trying to avoid him. That's just inconvenient and a good way to make both of you paranoid.' He reflected a half second. 'All the same, it might be prudent not to get drunk together in his bedroom again.'

'Thanks,' I said. 'I'll try to bear the last point in mind. But seriously, what's he doing with a girlfriend if he's like that? And if he isn't, what was he doing yesterday?'

'Well, he might be bisexual. But much more likely, he's just a normal, healthy, fun-loving frog. Why do you want to know, anyway?' Joe grinned wickedly. 'Interested after all?'

'Bollocks. Or bullshit if you prefer. I just haven't had much to do with gay people. I don't know how they tick. Perhaps I've led a sheltered life.'

I was joking when I said that, but Joe didn't seem to realise that. 'Now *that's* bullshit,' he said. 'Nobody leads a sheltered life these days. It's you, trying to be conventional and seeing only what's conventional around you. Of course you have contact with gay people; that's a matter of statistics. And anyway, here you are, having a drink with me. Or hadn't you even realised that?'

'I suppose I had. Had an inkling, anyway.'

'An inkling? You know, I was going to ask you to dinner later in the week, *chez moi*. Guess that won't be so easy now. If you're going to be afraid every other male in Paris is trying to make you...'

He broke off, peered at his glass, turned it a hundred and eighty degrees and then addressed it. 'What can we poor babies do? Let a straight guy think we fancy him and he runs one point six one kilometres. Let him know we don't and he never forgives us for it.'

I said, 'I think I can understand that. O.K. I tell you what. If I promise not to think about either possibility, perhaps you could pay me the compliment of doing the same.'

'Yeah, but I couldn't, you see,' said Joe with a twist of his head. 'You may be able to ignore it but I never can. I'm built that way.'

'Then maybe you could pretend to ignore it,' I suggested. 'At least when you're with me. Would that be possible, for the sake of ... friendship?'

Joe gave his glass another half turn. 'For the sake of friendship,' he said slowly, 'I might just manage that.'

I thought of asking Joe if he wanted to eat with me at the Figeac. I wanted him to meet Fabrice. And Régine? I tried to imagine the scene but the picture would not come. Another time, perhaps. And yet...

A flick of one switch in heart or brain would bring to my lips the formula, 'What are you doing this evening?' A flick of another and my eyes would twitch towards my watch while the words came, 'It's time I was going.' The latter occurred. For what reason? A look crossing Joe's face, registered only unconsciously by me? Pressure building in my bladder that I was hardly aware of? From such trivial causes hurricanes are said to spring. But for now there was no hurricane. 'It's time I was going,' I said, and I got up. Later I went by myself to the Figeac and Joe went off on his own to get a baguette from his local boulangerie.

The house I lived in really was very beautiful, as Jean-Jacques had said. I made a point of looking at the entablatures of carved ravens and grapes when I went back there that night. Walking through the carriage doors into the central courtyard I could harmlessly pretend that it all belonged to me and that I took the back stairs in preference to the lift for the sake of the exercise. Luisa had been helpful over the last two days, despite a little language difficulty: my accent was strange to her while her French had a disconcerting tendency to wander into Portuguese and back again in the space of a few words. Still, she had always got through in the end, telling me where to shop, offering spare light-bulbs, recommending a launderette. As for the various sons and daughters of Margueritte, contact had been limited to exchanged *bonjours* in the courtyard; they recognising me by my accent, I them by their prominent, high-born lips. Of Monsieur Guyot, whoever he might be, there was no sign. Although it was late, I sat at my little table and wrote.

Paris. Winter. 1987.

The baguette worn under the arm is one of the supreme clichés of Parisian life and as such it is a badge of belonging that no self-respecting foreign resident can be without. Every street corner has its boulangerie and every Parisian too, each certain that his or her preferred bread shop is better than all the others. Madame Dumont, for example, lives at the top of the rue des Archives but swears by the baker at the bottom.

Monsieur Dupont, on the other hand, lives at the bottom but favours the bakery at the top. They pass each other in the street twice each day like two sentries on duty, and nod and say bonjour, each carrying like a rifle what they firmly hold to be the best baguette in Paris.

I unlaced a shoe. After a moment it fell of its own accord. I was unsure onto whose ceiling. Monsieur Guyot's perhaps. I'd dined relatively soberly at the Figeac with Dominique and Françoise, a little relieved that Fabrice and Régine had not been there. I felt that Sunday needed a few days to get over, especially if I decided to take Joe's advice and forget the whole episode. Perhaps Fabrice thought so too.

Françoise had been on good social form, chirruping like one of Madame Touret's canaries, a resemblance heightened by the deep orange meringue of a dress she was wearing as if in an attempt to turn early March to high summer. I guessed she used her shop as a vast personal wardrobe from which to select creations to suit her every mood or invitation. She missed the sun more with each passing winter, she told me, and, *à propos*, a man to take her to it. She looked quite directly at me while she said this. People seemed to do that a lot here. Warmer climates suited her temperament, she said. In them she blossomed. I had exchanged a glance with Dominique.

I unlaced the other shoe and let it fall to join its partner on the floor. Then I got up and loaded a tape into my cassette player.

Every traveller was in those days a desert island castaway where music was concerned because of the logistics of luggage. I had with me only a slender library of cassette tapes, a selection I'd chosen with as much rigour as any guest invited on the radio programme. Tonight I chose Beethoven, a choice that would have

241

surprised the younger me: I was a recent convert. I picked out the performance of the Waldstein piano sonata that had been recorded by Artur Schnabel in the nineteen-thirties. It was the recording against which, I'd read or someone had told me, all subsequent ones had to stand or fall.

It was a brilliant, diamantine piece, sculpted with almost Mozartean precision. Contemporary critics had described it as glacial; Wagner had even nicknamed it the Dispassionata. But with repeated listening I'd learned better. Beethoven had set springs of passion beneath the frozen surface that would explode beneath your feet and sweep you away on a cascading torrent... But only when you the listener, you the person, were ready.

After that I continued to write...

The music ended and silence and darkness filled the flat. I walked to the window and looked out. The mansards of the building opposite stood sightless but above them, on a higher level than my own, an upper attic signalled its existence by a solitary dormer that seemed to be peering skywards, casting its warm light up. It had the beckoning quality that had so struck me on my first night in the capital. So small this light was, yet so generous with its meagre resources that it seemed to want to turn night into day, so optimistically did it pour itself into the blue dark.

I looked up from my notebook and watched that lit attic window for several more minutes, uncertain of the feelings the sight evoked in me, before I pulled the shutters to and went to bed.

SEVEN

I became aware of a banging sound. It crescendoed up through my sleep, dragging me into an unwilling consciousness.

I sat up in bed and switched on the light. It revealed my Paris studio, quite unchanged since I'd gone to bed in it. I glanced at my watch, which said three o'clock, and tried to come to terms with the fact that there was someone outside the door just six feet away who very much wanted to be on the inside. Because of the entry code lock on the street door the caller had to be, in theory at least, one of my neighbours: a d'Alabouvettes or perhaps the mysterious Monsieur Guyot. But why would they disturb me at such an hour? Fire? I got up and moved towards the door, calling loudly, 'Who is it?' in English before remembering that French would be more appropriate.

The knocking ceased as soon as I spoke and a voice said, *'C'est moi: Dominique.'*

I stopped in my tracks and did not undo the door. 'What do you want?' I said.

'I want to come in,' said the voice. It sounded more than agitated but it was unmistakably Dominique's. 'I've killed my wife.'

For some reason I felt reassured by this announcement. I knew that Dominique didn't have a wife. Therefore he could not have killed her. Therefore it was safe to let him in. The possibility that I was opening the door to a lunatic at three in the morning did not present itself. It was only when Dominique stood in the room with me, fully dressed in outdoor clothes, a suddenly important two inches taller than I was that I, in bare feet and a bath robe, began to feel a bit vulnerable. 'Sit down,' I said at once in an effort to improve things by a change of eye-line. Dominique did as he was told; I stayed standing.

For someone who had not recently killed his wife Dominique managed an impressive performance as someone who had. He shook uncontrollably and his hands, which seemed to have taken on lives of their own, wandered variously over his face, his body and the armchair on which he perched rather than sat. His mouth worked as if trying sentences that would not come. My experience of real murderers was non-existent. But I did know that drunks might also behave like this.

'Tell me about it,' I said. 'How did it happen?'

'At the Figeac.' Dominique spoke quietly, haltingly. 'She refused to come home with me. I lost my rag. She dug in. I grabbed her, pulled her towards me. She began to shout. Somehow we were in the kitchen. I got hold of a knife. I didn't know what I was doing...' He burst into a fit of sobs and covered his face with his hands.

I sat down opposite him, unsure what to do or say. I pressed the tips of my fingers together like an actor playing a detective, leaned forward and said, 'She. Who do you mean by she? Who is your wife?'

'Marianne,' he said. Bloody hell, I thought.

'Are you sure she's dead?' I asked him. 'Not just hurt?'

Dominique's head jerked up and he gave me a look of pathetic intensity. 'You think perhaps she's not dead then?'

'Did you see her after you touched her?'

'No. I ran out of the kitchen. I left the restaurant. I heard her screaming but I ran.'

'When did this happen?'

'Fifteen minutes ago. I'm sure she's dead.'

'You can't be sure,' I said. I willed Marianne not to be dead. Then I said, 'Why did you come here? Why to me? You hardly know me. How did you get in?'

But even as I was speaking I remembered that, as a teenager, Dominique had had a fling with a girl who lived in this very room. He knew the door code. Ancient memories, associations of comfort and reassurance, might easily have sent him flying up here in a blind or drunken panic.

Dominique said, 'I went to Fabrice first. Looking for you both.' Looking for us both?! At Fabrice's flat? That gave me an almighty jolt. Dominique went on. 'There was no answer. I came here then.' He added, *'J'ai confiance en toi.'* I trust you.

There was silence. At last I broke it. 'What do you want me to do?'

'Don't know.'

'I think,' I said, trying to do just that, 'that we need first to discover if Marianne is really dead. If we went together to the Figeac, perhaps?'

Dominique shook his head vigorously.

'Then, if I went alone?'

This seemed to please him better. But he grabbed my arm and said, 'You won't go to the police? Promise. You mustn't. Say you haven't seen me. I'll be waiting for you here.'

I had the sinking feeling of someone who has woken up, not out of a nightmare but into one. I saw myself leaving my studio at the mercy of a maniac who might, for all I knew, be a thief into the bargain; I'd return to find my few valuables gone. Or just possibly Dominique was telling the truth; then I'd be charged with harbouring a murderer, I'd come under who knew what suspicion... and all in French. I considered telling Dominique to get out of the flat, locking the door against him, washing my hands of the whole matter. But would Dominique go quietly if I asked him to? Dominique was not a giant but I had no illusions about who would win if it came to a struggle. I was suddenly acutely conscious of my kitchen drawer, of the fact that it was nearer to me than to Dominique, and of the exact position of all the utensils in it. But some instinct told me that Dominique would in fact go quietly. There would be no ugly or dangerous scene; only Dominique would be hurt, let down, almost literally, like someone who jumps into a safety blanket only to see it withdrawn. And Dominique had said, *'J'ai confiance en toi.'*

'I promise,' I said, and heard a sigh in my voice. 'I won't say where you are if it's humanly possible not to. *J'ai confiance en toi, moi aussi.'* I made my way towards the door.

Dominique was watching me. 'You'd better put some clothes on,' he said flatly.

I let myself out into the dark street. Someone was running towards me. He passed beneath a street-lamp. It was Fabrice. I'd never been more pleased to see anyone in my life. I nearly wept with relief.

'Where is he?' Fabrice asked.

'Upstairs in my flat,' I said. Somehow I'd got hold of Fabrice's hands and was clasping them.

'Are you all right?' Fabrice asked earnestly, I felt his hands shake with his concern for me.

'Yes. Why? Is he dangerous? He says he's killed Marianne. At the Figeac.'

'Merde,' said Fabrice. 'We'd better get over there.'

'I was on my way,' I said.

As we neared the corner that would bring us in sight of the restaurant I steeled myself in readiness for the two possible scenes that would greet us: the blaze of lights and swarms of police cars that would indicate that Dominique's story was true, or the quiet, untroubled, three-in-the-morning darkness that would mean it was not. Neither possibility gave me much comfort. We rounded the corner.

The Figeac was a blaze of lights. People were clustered on the pavement round an ambulance whose doors were being shut. It drove off as we arrived. There were no police cars.

'Where's Dominique?' Madame Touret demanded almost before **we** reached the group on the pavement. Her face was set in an expression I'd not known it capable of till now, the corners of her mouth turned firmly down.

But I was not ready to abandon my promise just yet. 'Tell me what happened to Marianne,' I said. 'Is she dead? Injured? What?' The question of whether she was or was not Dominique's wife could wait.

'Is that what Dominique sent you to find out?' Madame Touret's tone was scornful. She looked from me to Fabrice then back again. She said a little more gently, 'She isn't dead. She isn't dead and she isn't in danger. You'll be able to tell Dominique that.'

We were inside the restaurant now: Fabrice and I, Madame Touret, her son and chef René, and Jean-Jacques with copy of *Libération* still in pocket though by now it was yesterday's. Presumably it would only be jettisoned in order to make way for the new one. René offered everyone a brandy. Even Jean-Jacques' liver raised no objection. The police had not been called, it was explained. Everyone had agreed that it was a purely domestic matter.

'But is she his wife?' I asked Fabrice.

'No,' he answered. 'At least, I don't think so.'

'You are correct,' Jean-Jacques told him. 'She lives with another man, quite happily as far as I know, in the *Cinquième*.'

'Dominique has a lot of imagination,' said Madame Touret. A slightly hooded look crossed her face.

'But what was tonight about?' Fabrice asked. 'That wasn't imagination. Marianne's injured.'

Madame Touret touched his forearm gently. 'Not injured badly, though she's in shock, hence the ambulance. He wouldn't really hurt someone. The knife scratched her, not much more. If he thinks he did more damage than that, then it is a *folie de grandeur.*'

'Or guilt,' suggested Jean-Jacques.

Madame Touret ignored him and continued to speak to Fabrice and me. 'Whatever impression you may have got tonight, he isn't violent. You don't have to worry about that. He has a good heart.'

'Good but crazy,' said her son the chef.

'I won't let you say that,' objected Madame. She turned back to Fabrice and me. 'He has some problems which lead him to weave fantasies about himself and about other people. I've known him since he was a child. Believe me, I understand him. A few months ago he got it into his head that Marianne was going to be his girlfriend, perhaps his wife. It was harmless at first. Just a joke. Later it became more serious. He pestered her at closing time, though he knew she lived with someone else. Tonight he became impossible. The fantasy took over. He seemed to think he was married to her already.'

'Problems?' Jean-Jacques said. 'He's a drunk, and drugged with I don't know what cocktails of *merde.* That's his problem if he has one. He needs medical help. Professional treatment. Counselling.'

'Don't talk nonsense.' Madame Touret rounded on him sharply. 'He needs a good woman to love him, that's all. Nothing more complicated than that.'

'He's hardly going the best way about finding one,' I said, and was shocked to hear myself, a newcomer and a foreigner, throwing my tuppence-worth into what was, I began to suspect, a family argument.

'I assure you,' Madame Touret told me – also a bit sharply, 'he is perfectly harmless.'

'It's good to hear that,' Fabrice said. 'You see, he's in Peter's flat right now. We're not quite sure how to deal with him.'

Madame gave us a look I shall never forget. 'Oh, don't be so wet, the pair of you. You must talk to him. Get him to go home.'

I felt a sudden urge to be supportive of Fabrice. We kept being bracketed together this evening. Well, we would stand or fall together then. 'Us?' I said. 'He's hardly our problem. And what are we supposed to say to him? One person says he needs professional help, another that he needs a woman. Then you throw him at us. I don't even know him!'

'It's not exactly we who are throwing him at you,' Jean-Jacques objected. 'He appears to have done that himself. Though why he should have chosen your place to run to rather than to anyone else's in the neighbourhood I don't know. You must have made some sort of impression.'

You obviously don't know about the old concierge's grand-daughter, I thought. I said, 'He said he trusted me.' I added, I wasn't sure why, 'He trusted us.'

'Then you must talk to him as best you can,' said Jean-Jacques calmly. 'I'm only a poet, not an oracle. But if you want one piece of advice, let it be this: it isn't the words you will use that matter – it's not what you'll say but the fact that you say it. Now *bon courage*.'

Fabrice and I had been dismissed. Together we left the restaurant.

We walked back to my place together. We didn't say much. There is something very companionable about walking side by side along a street with a friend when you have a common purpose. I'd realised that when we were walking up the rue Vieille du Temple a few nights back. The more so on the return walk, when our common concern had been to stop each other falling over.

And then there I was, showing my merchant banker friend into my small and unimpressive studio at three in the morning. Into a flat where a drunken nutter awaited us. Perhaps.

Dominique was still there. He was now sitting on my bed, elbows on knees and head in hands. We would never know whether he'd sat all the time like that, or whether he'd adopted the pose when he heard us climbing the stairs.

We hadn't planned any kind of strategy, Fabrice and I. It just happened the way it did. Fabrice went and sat on the bed on one side of Dominique and I sat down the other side of him.

'It's all OK,' I heard Fabrice say. His head was hidden from my sight by Dominique's.

'Marianne's unhurt,' I said, picking up where Fabrice had left off. 'She's in hospital but only for shock.'

'What do I do next?' Dominique asked. He seemed genuinely lost.

'A notre avis...' I heard Fabrice say. *We think...* I can't easily describe the effect that unexpected plural had on me. It filled me with complex thoughts at a moment when everything already seemed complex enough. I had to focus carefully in order to hear how Fabrice would complete the thought. I heard him say, 'We think you should go home now. In the morning early, go to the hospital and take her flowers.'

For some reason the sheer banality of what Fabrice was saying on behalf of both of us brought a lump to my throat. I heard myself say, 'He's right, Dominique. Just do that.'

And then Dominique stood up, thanked us both, and left. It was as weirdly simple as that. I felt the way you do when you try to unpick a knot or something, and think it'll never sort itself, and then suddenly it does.

And that left me and Fabrice sitting next to each other on my small bed. I remembered Joe's words: *It might be prudent not to get drunk together in his bedroom again.*

Or in mine. I stood up. 'I guess it's time we said goodnight,' I said. So then Fabrice stood up.

I walked down the stairs with him. We didn't touch. Then, as I opened the postern gate in the big courtyard door I found that we'd embraced. I held him, and he held me, for a second or two, and then he leaned in towards me, inclined his head – he was the taller one – and kissed me on the cheek.

'Oh hey,' I said, in mild protest. We unhooked ourselves and said goodnight and I shut the door after he passed through it into the street.

There was something I couldn't understand. On Sunday he'd rolled me onto his bed and smothered me with unwanted kisses. I'd been annoyed by that, though not really upset. But I hadn't felt all that much. It had just been an embarrassing mistake on his part, and perhaps I'd let myself in for it. I'd shrugged it off.

But this time I had felt something. I was a bit shaken by that fact. I didn't think I was happy with it. Even though he hadn't lathered me with kisses this time. It had just been a peck on the cheek. But I had felt something. Though I'd been taken too far out of my comfort zone to know what it was.

EIGHT

Paris. Winter. 1987

I took a walk. It was the end of the first afternoon in March but not cold. Though it was dark. Two days had passed since Fabrice had kissed me on the cheek. I hadn't wanted to see him again. I had wanted to, of course. For both those reasons I had steered clear of the Figeac. I was also steering clear of Marianne and Dominique.

My walk took me down the rue des Archives, across the rue de Rivoli, then down to the quays of the Seine, where the Ile de la Cité appeared in front of me across the water, bristling with beauty and fortresses.

I turned west along the quays. The quai Mégisserie, the quai du Louvre, the quai des Tuileries.

I suppose every gay man comes here in the end.

It seemed as though that long, long wall, the southern wall of the Tuileries gardens that flanked the river, the wall from which no turning led off, had been built for no other reason than that bare-legged, bare-arsed men might fuck each other, standing up against it. Their buttocks were round and smooth and the ambient light ricocheted back from their convex surfaces. The gentle moans that some of them made were palpable in the air. Palpable: it means I felt I could reach out and touch the soft sounds. By extension the soft buttocks, clenched bollocks and hard cocks. I did none of that. I wasn't gay, I told myself.

There was no way out of here. I could go on until I reached the Place de la Concorde after a quarter mile or so, then return by the rue de Rivoli, which ran parallel, the other side of the Tuileries gardens and the Louvre, or turn back at once, and return the way I'd come,

*reviewing the ranks of naked buttocks in reverse order
as I retraced my steps.*

*I didn't do either of those things exactly. I did walk all
the way to the Place de la Concorde, but then I retraced
my steps precisely, reviewing the whole half mile of
everything as I came back.*

'People are weird,' said Joe. 'Real weird. What about
her boyfriend? You'd think he'd be trying to kill this
Dominique character.'

Two more days had passed and this was my first
opportunity to talk to Joe. We met at a café on the place
Hotel de Ville in the early evening.

I told Joe, 'I heard they met in the hospital corridor.
Dominique really did take flowers by the way.
Apparently they nodded to each other politely and just
passed on without speaking. They won't fight each
other.'

Joe shook his head. 'Like I said, people are weird. That
includes you, Peter. In fact, especially you. I'm
astonished – even shocking – that you let the guy into
your room that night in the first place. You run a mile
when a merchant banker places his manicured hand on
your knee over the petits-fours but you open up to a
homicidal maniac at three in the morning. I fail to
discern a pattern there. Know what I mean? I'm afraid
I'd have told him to fuck off. I really would.' Joe
stopped speaking and peered at my chest as if trying to
see, in a most literal way, what was at the heart of me.

He looked up again at my face. 'You're an onion,' he
said in a conclusive tone of voice. 'Layer beneath layer
of you. The question is, though, what is the thread that
runs up the centre? The slender translucent fibre that
underlies all the layers and that you can easily dissect the
onion without finding.'

He changed the subject slightly. 'This book you're writing. Are you writing about all the people you're meeting here? The amorous banker, mad Dominique, me?'

I said, 'I didn't think I was.' There was silence for a moment. We stared out through the plate glass of the café into the square. The fountains played as coldly as ever in the centre of it and the marble gleamed no less glacially under the street lamps. The Hôtel de Ville loomed owl-white to the left of us while straight ahead, beyond the river channel the towers and pinnacles of Notre Dame spear-headed shafts of floodlight into the sky.

'I've fallen in love,' said Joe.

'Really?' I said.

'Oh yes.' Joe mimicked my English accent. 'Really, really, really. Come on. Let's go,' he said.

We paid and walked out into the cold evening air. The fountains continued to play over the white marble and the chill seemed penetrating to the marrow.

'Suddenly? Just like that?' I enquired.

'Too right.'

'I don't believe you,' I told him bluntly. 'Falling in love doesn't happen like that. Or if it does it's not falling in love; it's something else.'

Joe looked at me with mild surprise. 'Bullshit,' he said calmly. 'You're so wrong. At least you are about me. And falling is exactly the right word for it. I've never realized quite how right until now. Fall is exactly what I did. Last Monday night. Just after leaving you. Under a shower of bread and brioche cascading onto the pavement.'

'Please explain,' I said.

So Joe did. Joe had his own favourite boulangerie, just like everyone else. It was halfway between where he got the Métro at Arts et Metier when he went to work and where he lived in the rue Chapon. He'd gone there after we'd parted on Sunday evening.

The relative tranquillity of his short walk was marred by a Sunday night traffic jam and the boulevard was shoulder-high with cars aggressively demanding right of way. He told me it felt as though the traffic was fuelled not by petrol but by a distillation of pure fury under compression. Cars and buses moved in sudden leaps and little dashes, a Morse code of spasmodic progress, halted constantly with shocks to chassis and flashes – sometimes crunches too – of brake lights.

He'd threaded his way through this ill-tempered scrum, slapping hard the backs of those vehicles that showed signs of rolling back – no-one used their mirrors – to crush his legs against the car behind. He'd reached the pavement and the boulangerie. Its door had opened in his face, and out had popped a very young man with a huge openwork basket of long loaves in each hand. They'd had no time to avoid each other. Joe had collided with the boy's left shoulder and his left hand load of bread. The knock had swung the boy round to face Joe but had also made him lose his balance. He staggered, and began to fall.

Joe saw the boy was too afraid of losing the bread he was carrying to grab hold of the door or wall. He'd put out a hand to try to save him, but it had simply made things worse. He ended up shoving at the boy's chest as he fell back but, meeting no resistance, lost his own balance and fell on top of him as he landed on his back.

Falling on top of both of them came a metal trolley and a meteor shower of bread: *baguettes, bâtards, ficelles, pains longs, pains ronds, pains noirs, miches, boules*. French bread in its infinite variety fell pattering on the pavement or flew in all directions in a flurry of flour.

'Merde!' Joe had exclaimed simultaneously with another male voice. Joe found himself looking into a pair

of large hazel eyes momentarily frozen like a rabbit's caught in headlights, then suddenly illuminated by a smile. The smile had surprised itself into a laugh. Then Joe had laughed too.

People were picking them up by now, collecting scattered, flattened loaves, asking if anyone was hurt – this last a spontaneous display of public spirit rare in Paris but then, the evening ritual of the baguette was at stake. Joe had wondered if it was his imagination or if the two of them had spent just a fraction longer, a quarter-second only maybe, entangled together on the pavement than the accident strictly warranted.

'Tu n'as pas mal?' the other had said to him. Joe replied that he was not hurt at all, absurdly pleased by the *tu* that had slipped out, unguarded, in place of the more appropriate *vous*.

'You work here?' Joe had enquired.

'My first day,' the other had answered, suddenly sorrowful.

'There's nothing to worry about. *C'était un beau commencement.* My name's Joe. And yours?'

Joe had found himself looking at a young man of about twenty who faced him steadily, a frankness in his eyes that moved him unexpectedly, irrationally, almost to tears. The young man had drawn himself up as if at roll-call in the army. 'Hardrier,' he'd said, adding as if after a comma, 'Antoine.'

'So there it was,' Joe concluded. 'It was instantaneous on both sides. I can't explain how. It just was. His name's Antoine. He's a *mitron.*'

'A Mitterand?' I queried, imagining a relative of the President of the Republic.

'A *mitron*. It's an old word for a baker's boy. The mitrons are still one of the sights of Paris in the early morning, padding round the streets in shorts with their baskets of bread. It's one of the things that make going to work bearable on a winter's morning –though I appreciate that the spectacle might have less of an appeal for you. Antoine works in the boulangerie, in other words.'

For some reason I began to laugh. 'Smitten with a shop boy,' I said. 'It's too funny. I'm sorry to laugh but it is. Sometimes I think you lot are just unreal. In and out of bed one minute, in and out of love the next. Or so you'd have us believe. Why can't you face the truth? You fancy him and that's all. Don't get me wrong now. I'm not going to go all prim and proper on you. There's room in the world for a bit of honest lust. But if only you and your kind would *be* honest and see it for what it is. Don't go confusing things and calling it love.'

'Well, well.' This time Joe did sound nettled. 'Your experience with that French guy does seem to have unhinged you. For someone who knows nothing and would like to know even less about 'us lot' as you call us, you seem to have some pretty definite opinions on the subject. Two days ago you were all ignorance and bliss. You seem very good at shifting your areas of knowledge when it suits you. And, *en plus*, I've never heard you come out with such slurping generalisations on any other subject before. Where the hell's your English talent for equivocation disappeared to? It was still around last Sunday.'

Joe's answer was unsurprising and well-merited, as I realised at once. Why then my strange outburst? I didn't recognize it as coming from myself. It was an odd way for anyone to respond to a friend's announcement that he had fallen in love. 'I'm sorry, Joe,' I said after a moment's reflection.

'Are you jealous?' Joe enquired politely.

Jealous which way round? I wondered. Jealous that Joe was not in love with *me*? Perish the thought! Jealous because I might find the idea of a shop boy attractive, with or without a bread-trolley, myself? Hardly. Jealous of Joe in looks then? Not that either; I considered myself to be better favoured in that respect. What then?

'Perhaps I was a little,' I said slowly. 'I mean jealous that you've found something I have not.'

We walked together up the rue des Archives, brought closer together by the silence that followed my admission than by anything that Joe might have said for answer.

We were going to the Figeac. Joe, having heard the story of Dominique and the 'murder' coming so soon after the episode with Fabrice, had found his curiosity thoroughly aroused and wanted to meet the cast. I stopped as we turned out of the rue des Archives and came in sight of the restaurant. 'How old is he?' he asked.

'Nineteen,' Joe said.

'And you've only met the once?'

'Well no. I buy my bread from him every evening for a start. And I plucked up the courage to ask him to meet me for a *bière de mars* on Saturday. He did. He insisted it must be a bar where neither of us was known. That wasn't so easy in the *quartier* but we found one in the end. And we talked for a long time.' Joe paused. 'Just that. We talked for a long time.' There was another silence during which we got as far as the restaurant door. 'Well, all right, eventually we went back to my place and went to bed. But it isn't just a little roll in the hay, Peter,' said Joe. 'You'll see.'

We reached the door of the restaurant. I stopped Joe from going straight in. 'I'm glad you're with me,' I said. 'There was a note from Fabrice with my post this morning. Saying the weekend thing's off this time round and could we make it another time. And he said he'll be here in the restaurant this evening. So it'll be nice not to be all alone, if you see what I mean.' I hadn't told Joe anything about that late-night kiss on the cheek of course.

'I can't wait to meet him,' Joe said, with what proportion of sincerity to irony I couldn't tell. Then we pushed open the door and went in and there was everybody. It made a busy, startling contrast to the intimacy of the street.

Taking friends to a favourite restaurant is often a disappointing business. Sometimes it has changed hands the previous day, or it is the chef's night off, or the kitchen is being redecorated and everything smells of paint. I was relieved, then, to find the Figeac exactly as I'd seen it on my other visits, and peopled with more or less the same characters like a stage set. Jean-Jacques leant over the bar in his crow-black coat, nursing a kir, *Libération* spread wide on the wood topped counter. Madame Touret herself presided behind the bar, beaming a professional welcome, while Dominique hovered at a little distance, unsure whether to present himself or to wait for me to approach first. I introduced Joe.

'I'm sorry about your ship,' Dominique said.

'It wasn't really mine,' said Joe.

I explained. 'Joe isn't British, he's American. My ship, if you like, but not his.' The previous day the Herald of Free Enterprise had sunk in Zeebrugge harbour with the loss of 149 lives.

'No, you're right, Joe,' Dominique said, after a moment's thought. 'There's no such thing as a British ship or a French one, or American or Belgian. Ships are the gossamer strands that join our countries. It's a *connerie* to say anyone owns a ship. They can wear their pennants bravely at the stern – Tricolor, Union Jack or whatever – but all they can do in the end is flutter in the wind.' Dominique shrugged, and grinned apologetically, as if to indicate that there was no arguing with such an obvious fact, then drifted away to join Jean-Jacques.

Joe looked at me in puzzlement. 'What was all that meant to mean?'

'It means he's his usual self again. Come on, let's eat.'

Fabrice and Régine joined us at the table, Fabrice showing not a flicker of awkwardness. To my surprise I felt none either. The couple examined the food on my plate and on Joe's, openly and unselfconsciously asking questions about it. What kind of steak was that? How salty were the beans today? Last Thursday René had used too heavy a hand, Régine explained. Was the salad really fresh? Only then did they give their orders to Madame Touret.

'You got my note, I hope,' said Fabrice, blue eyes shining. Had he really forgotten last weekend's awkwardness and that second, gentler kiss he'd given me, or had an ingrained habit of deception turned him into a consummate actor? 'This weekend's impossible for my parents. Anyway, I was being stupid about the dates. Shooting's already at an end as far as game's concerned. But we can take pot shots at rabbits any time. So, can we make it in a week or two?' He smiled towards Joe. 'You too if you like. Fancy a bit of rabbit shooting?'

'Tell you what,' Joe answered. 'If crack-shot here' he jerked a thumb towards me 'doesn't make a total fool of himself the first time, I'll come next time round.'

'You're on,' said Fabrice.

Régine turned to me. 'Fabrice was telling me you came to lunch on Sunday,' she said. 'It's nice that he has such good friends in Paris. He gets lonely when I go away.' At this point I did find myself beginning to blush. I focused my attention firmly on my plate so no-one should see. It was a minute or two before I dared to catch Joe's eye.

Fabrice felt compelled to change the subject. 'It was terrible news about your ship,' he said.

During the meal a new face arrived at the bar counter: male, Hispanic, good-looking in a sharp-featured sort of way. 'Who is he?' asked Françoise who by now had joined us. 'Does anybody know?' No-one did, at least no-one at our table, but Dominique was talking to him so he evidently knew him or soon would do. We asked him, when the newcomer had gone.

'He's a cousin of your concierge, Peter,' Dominique explained. 'Arrived yesterday from Portugal. Did you see the gold around his neck and wrists? He says he made a lot of money selling time-shares. Well, believe that if you like. If you ask me he's looking for a job as a concierge... Sorry, we're supposed to say *gardien* now. Anyway I told him to go and talk to the two *ouistitis...* Not both at the same time of course.'

I explained about the belligerent marmosets, Carlos and Nico, on the way back to my flat. I had invited Joe up for a coffee and digestif before he headed back home.

I gave Joe a quick tour of my studio and he turned his attention to the view from the window over the neighbouring roof tops. I put on my Beethoven tape. Then, just as I had done a few nights earlier, Joe noticed the single lighted dormer window outlined against the inky sky. 'That makes a pretty picture,' he said. 'The colours, the contrast of the light and the night, could be Van Gogh.'

'Take sugar?' I asked him. He said, 'Yes please. Who lives there, do you know?'

'In the attic window? I haven't the faintest idea.'

'I just wonder,' Joe said as I poured the coffee, 'if that might not be the question that brought you here to France.'

NINE

Paris. Spring. 1987

Spring was coming and the trees that bordered the overhead Métro lines had turned a lovely translucent green overnight. That this effect of sudden spring was produced not by leaves but by catkins – as could be seen on closer inspection – did not detract from the marvel of it. On the contrary, as Joe explained to me, it exemplified a particularly Parisian trait: turning nature's little deceptions to advantage. If you could not actually have trees in full leaf at forty-nine degrees north in mid-March, you could at least cheer the heart with trees that looked it.

Forsythia followed, in sudden explosions of yellow along the boulevards, and just in the last few days the plane trees appeared to have been hung with emeralds. Day by day the sun was exploring a little further down the walls of the houses. In the clefts of streets that Haussman seemed to have cut with a cheese wire through the city, so deep and regular were they, it advanced with military precision in straight lines. Here in the Marais by contrast, where the old houses leaned backwards at different degrees from the vertical, the sun encroached in sudden spurts, building up gradually a pattern of wedges and spears of light and shade. As the sun fingered its way down in places to street level, so café tables were beginning to sprout from the pavement where it touched. The street life of the spring and summer could tentatively begin.

Joe and I were sitting outside the Little Horseshoe, waiting for Fabrice and Régine to join us for a drink before going on to eat at the Figeac. If you sat at any café table long enough Dominique would join you eventually, bringing with him a breath of something from a less predictable world and seating himself without asking in one of the chairs you were saving for Régine and Fabrice. He arrived now.

By way of conversation, and because he had just noticed one shambling up the street, Joe asked Dominique how he dealt with *clochards*. I'm afraid I had to ask what a *clochard* was.

'Not what they were,' Dominique answered. 'The *Cloche* was once an honourable vocation, the clochard a real gentleman of the road. Some were artists, some gipsies, some recluses like mobile monks. They had their codes, their signs, their rules. But in Paris now a clochard is just a beggar, wine-soaked, sleeping in a doorway.'

'I'm with you,' I said. 'There's one sleeps over a warm-air vent outside Madame Almuslih's shop.'

'That's my one,' said Dominique.

'What do you mean, your one?' Joe and I both asked.

Dominique laughed. 'This is the answer to your question, ... er ...'

'Joe,' I reminded him.

'Joe. You ought to be generous sometimes and give them what you can. That's not morality, it's common sense. French proverb: 'You never know when you're going to have need of someone smaller than yourself.' But that's where the problem starts. There are so many. What do you do? Try to give something to each one you meet? Impossible. One in every ten? Too calculating. I arrived at an answer. I chose just one. I slip him a coin or two every other day. And because I know him I have the advantage of knowing what he spends it on.'

'Which is...?' I asked.

'Bottles of La Villageoise red from Madame Almuslih's shop. The profit on the sale helps to feed her family. So everybody benefits. He's happy when he's drunk so let him stay drunk. Madame Almuslih's happy when she makes a profit so let her do that. Think of it the other way round and you'll see it would never do at all: Madame Almuslih drunk and the clochard putting money in the bank. No, no. It's better the way it is.'

Fabrice and Régine turned up just then and Dominique reached round, without standing up, for an extra chair. By the time that hands had been shaken (Fabrice's), cheeks kissed (Régine's), and everyone was settled it had dawned on me – at last – that not only was Joe a little bit interested in Fabrice, but that Fabrice returned the compliment. Perhaps it was something in the air of the Marais.

But conversation wasn't allowed to develop very far before we became aware of a scene developing at the bar behind us and we were all very soon screwed round in our seats to watch what was going on. It was the two marmosets.

Nico had been inside the Horseshoe for some time, was slightly the worse for wear, and was beginning to sing the praises of his native Portugal quite loudly to anyone who cared to listen. Had he seen that his Spanish sparring partner was at the other end of the bar he might not have started, but it was rather dark in there and he never did see very well after the seventh glass and it was too late to stop now anyway, because he had already got his captive audience. Carlos was literally captive because of the confined space; he could not discreetly leave the bar without pushing past Nico, which would have defeated the object of the manoeuvre. So he stayed where he was, chin just visible above the counter, and kept silent while the glories of Portugal were lauded together with the exploits of her famous sons. Until, that is, it came to Columbus.

'I think I should point out,' said Carlos in a voice as soft as a feather duster, 'that Christopher Columbus was Italian.'

Nico ignited. 'How typically Spanish! You claim everyone's national heroes as your own because you have none yourselves. Even General Franco was a Moroccan.'

Carlos kept his cool. 'Did I say Columbus was a Spaniard?' He appealed to the room at large. 'Did I?' It was generally agreed that he had not.

Nico could not see the difference for the moment between Italy and Spain. Carlos had contradicted him and that was enough. *'Ta gueule,'* Carlos told him but it was Carlos who in fact stayed silent while Nico continued to blaze like a small box of sparklers. Finally Carlos took two steps towards him and in a voice still feather-soft said, *'Va te faire enculer.'*

There was a moment's general silence. Then Nico said, 'Luckily for you I know your French isn't good enough for you to know what that expression means. Otherwise I'd kill you.'

But Carlos did understand what the expression meant. He proved this by explaining it in elaborate anatomical detail and reinforced it with a mime using his two hands.

Nico stepped back a pace to give himself room to aim and flung his glass and its contents at the other's chest. The glass bounced off onto the floor and shattered. Carlos took the beer itself full in the face. The bystanders were given further evidence of his command of French. A second more and the two marmosets had thrown their jackets on the floor and were squared up to each other, fists ready, dancing from foot to foot.

Then it was Dominique who stood up, in an unexpected assumption of the role of man of action, slipped between them and separated them by the length of his extended arms, one hand against each tiny chest, no higher than his own waist. Someone else grabbed Nico from behind and bundled him out of the door like a scrapping cat. 'I'm going to get a knife,' he said as he unceremoniously left.

Carlos rolled his eyes and shrugged, his hands spread wide. He waited till he had the undivided attention of all present before delivering his final word. 'It's very fortunate for all concerned,' he said, 'that Columbus wasn't Spanish.'

We moved off after that towards the Figeac, the four of us who had arranged to meet, plus Dominique, for whom plans and arrangements didn't seem to exist. As we walked, Fabrice renewed his invitation to me to spend a weekend in Alsace with him and Régine in two weeks' time. Reassured by the thought that Régine would be there, I accepted without anxiety and said I was looking forward to it.

On the thirtieth of March Margueritte d'Alabouvettes telephoned from Tokyo to say that she would be passing through Paris in two days time and if I could arrange to have the rent ready in cash she would call by for it. I was invited to an audience with her during the afternoon in one of her two first-floor flats. One of her daughters was with her. Till now we had not progressed beyond *bonjour*. *'Je vous présente ma fille,'* said Margueritte, 'Madame Guyot.'

She opened a bottle of champagne. 'To welcome you to Paris a month late,' as she put it. We sat on sofas and sipped. We smoked menthol cigarettes.

I wondered for a second if I could tell her the story of the two *ouistitis* and Christopher Columbus but quickly decided against. Nor did I mention that Margueritte's concierge, Luisa, had had her cousin staying with her now for three weeks – the cousin who claimed he made a fortune selling time-shares – and that she was at her wits' end to know how to get rid of him. 'He's no good,' she had said. 'Always in trouble with the police at home and now he has to come to France to stir things up. If only someone would take him off my hands.'

I'd later been presented with a moral dilemma when I'd walked into the Figeac to find him, the gold-braceleted Portuguese, dining à deux with Françoise, who was dressed to the teeth and still presumably dreaming of a man who would take her to the sun. Should I do Françoise a favour and tell her what Luisa said, or do Luisa a favour by letting things take their course? In the end I said nothing. If anything is more cordially loathed than an unwelcome truth it is the person who delivers it.

But such stories were not what tenants like me told *propriétaires* like Margueritte over champagne. Instead I handed over the rent money. I'd collected it that morning from the bank in crisp hundred-franc notes all fastened together with a shiny new pin like a kebab. 'You wouldn't happen to have it in notes of five hundred?' said Margueritte d'Alabouvettes.

TEN

An hour after that I was on the train to Saverne with Régine and Fabrice. I told them how my landlady had flown halfway around the world for the rent. Fabrice said that was typical. 'And who is Monsieur Guyot, in the end?' I asked. 'I've now got as far as meeting his wife.'

'His ex-wife,' Fabrice corrected. 'They're separated and she won't give him a divorce. He'd like to screw the d'Alabouvettes for every sou he can. Not that he needs it. He's a big wheel in one of the ministries... Which one is it?' he asked Régine.

'Town Planning and Housing,' she replied. 'But he's moving shortly. He's going to be some sort of functionary at the Elysée Palace, working for *Ton-ton* himself.'

'Who's Ton-ton?' I asked.

'President Mitterand,' said Fabrice. He added in English: 'It's his nick-name. Ton-ton means, like, uncle.' Then he gave me one of those brilliant smiles of his that lit up his whole face.

We were met at Saverne station by Fabrice's father, in immaculate suit and tie, at the wheel of a newish-looking Mercedes. I half expected to hear the line about having to bring the Merc because all the other cars were in use. It didn't come. Fabrice's father rose a notch in my estimation.

It took only a few minutes to reach the family home. At the edge of a village, as Fabrice had described it, it nevertheless seemed separate from the other houses, being built not in the local vernacular, half-timbered, style but was an example of restrained eighteenth-century elegance in light-coloured stone with white-painted shutters. Had it been shorn of those and transplanted across the Channel, you would have said

Georgian without a second thought. It fronted almost directly onto the road. All the land, said Fabrice – and I had to trust him on that because it was getting dark – lay at the back.

There was a homely family supper of choucroute, which I had once made the mistake of describing to a French person as a version of sauerkraute, only to be told that it was absolutely the other way round and the French did it ten times better anyway. I didn't repeat that error this evening.

What a touching honour it is to be taken to meet a new friend's family. All those intimate parts of a person's life, screened out when you meet them at work or in their own adult homes, are exposed in all their vulnerability to the outsider's potentially cold stare. I hadn't guessed that Fabrice had a little sister still in her teens whom Fabrice obviously adored. Nor that his mother, before marriage, had been a professional musician.

Still less had I imagined that after dinner and a few glasses of very fine wine, the family would sit down and make music together in nineteenth-century bourgeois tradition. That the teenage sister would play Mozart on the piano. That Régine would, after a suitable show of mock reluctance, sing a selection of numbers from Offenbach operettas in a very passable mezzo voice, accompanied by Fabrice's mother – her own mother-in-law to be? – and that after that Fabrice would be cajoled into singing something himself.

His reluctance seemed to be quite genuine. 'I really don't do this awfully well. And it's doubly unfair to make me follow Régine.' But he got out of his seat like a good lamb going to the slaughter, conferred with his mother for a moment and announced, 'Schubert. *Gute Nacht.*'

Fabrice actually did it rather nicely. He had a naturally pleasing tenor voice and a comfortable musicality even if his technique let him down occasionally on difficult corners. I'd never guessed that this was part of him. We'd never thought to discuss music in the short time we'd known each other. Fabrice sang the song in German, but I knew the story by heart anyway. 'Love loves to wander,' the words reminded more than once. 'From one love to another. God has made it so.' But when Fabrice came to the part where the lover tiptoes from his mistress's bedroom to wander the snowy landscape in search of a new life, and delivered the lines impartially around the room, I found myself hoping that the choice of song was a coincidence and that there was not a hidden message in it from Fabrice to me.

I was forced to admit, when they asked me, that I neither sang, nor played an instrument, nor painted. All I could do was write. 'But,' and perhaps it was the wine that prompted this odd announcement, 'I do have very beautiful dreams sometimes.' This went down far better than I thought it might, or deserved to, and Fabrice's mother said, 'Perhaps that's better than all the rest put together,' and smiled in a way that suggested she really meant it.

At bedtime I discovered that Fabrice and Régine went to separate rooms. The parents must know that they lived as a couple in Paris, but presumably traditional proprieties were still observed in the family home. Or maybe it was simply that Fabrice's bedroom was still the one he had had as a child, with a narrow bed in it and teddy bears and model racing cars still stuffed into odd corners of cupboards and drawers. The thought of that made me smile as I undressed for bed in the small but comfortable room they'd given me. There was no lock on the door, I noticed, and was then immediately cross with myself for thinking to look for one.

Next morning we were soon out of doors in brilliant sunshine, me learning to load a shotgun and squinting along its barrel for the first time in my life. Fabrice had lent me a pair of boots and an old Barbour jacket from England so that I looked the part perfectly. The only trouble was that everything of Fabrice's that I had about me was a fairly noticeable two sizes too large.

Rabbit shooting was not Régine's thing, so there were just Fabrice and me and, to my slight surprise, the kid sister, Stéphanie, out in the undulating meadows that lay below the forest-crested hills. Rabbits there were aplenty, though, and their numbers remained unchanged even after I fired my first two experimental shots. After that Fabrice bagged three and Stéphanie, who was considered too young to shoot, acted as a two-legged gun dog and ran and picked them up. But then I got my eye in and, no longer surprised by the kick in the chest that went with recoil, found my next shot rewarded with the sight of a pair of sprinting ears disappearing below the tops of the grass stems, then heard Fabrice's voice sing out, '*Sacré bleu, monsieur.* You've got a hare!'

I tried not to feel too pleased with myself. I suggested that the hare should stay with Fabrice's family as a thank-you present for having me for the weekend. Fabrice wouldn't hear of it. They had no end of hares and rabbits here, whereas in Paris...

'Oh sure,' I said. 'You can just see me cooking a hare for myself in Margueritte's attic, can't you, fur coat and all.' Fabrice assured me he'd take care of all that. We'd have a party for which Fabrice would do the cooking. As for the fur coat and ears, that part would all be sorted out before we even left for the capital.

There was a lunch party for a number of hunting, shooting and fishing neighbours. At which I would have expected to find myself very much out of place but for the fact of having wielded a gun and shot my own hare for the first time just an hour earlier. So I waded into the unfamiliar milieu with a bit of self-confidence and found that I enjoyed another un-suspected advantage: that of being the only person there who hadn't been wining and dining with all the others for a lifetime and listening to one another's old stories until they knew them by heart.

'We've got a mobile phone,' said one white-haired landowner lady to a little group of similar others. A mobile was still a novelty then. 'And Isolde rang the other day. You know how she talks. Well, I was in the bath. After a while the water started getting cold. I started moving to try to splash it round a bit. 'You sound as if you're in the sea,' Isolde said. 'It's not the sea,' I told her. 'I'm in the bath.' *Je vous assure*, no conversation with Isolde has ended more promptly. Try it sometime.'

There were younger people too. One couple, about Fabrice and Régine's age, who had a farm a dozen kilometres away, invited them and me to join them for an aperitif later, in the early evening. There would be a number of other people there: people Fabrice had been to school with. A day before, I'd have said this was the last thing that I and my creaky French would want to cope with during a relaxing weekend, but I was buoyed with satisfaction at the way things had gone up to now, and especially having caught my first hare, and found myself looking forward to it. Getting to know Fabrice was turning out more enjoyable than I had expected at first, and I decided that having met his family it might be interesting to talk to people from his past as well.

The afternoon was a short one. It consisted of brief but welcome siestas, everybody in their own rooms, and then a game of table football in the basement games room. Régine was particularly good at this. But then, at the last minute, when it was time to set out for the pre-prandial drinks party, she pleaded tiredness and would we boys mind dreadfully if she didn't come with us? I did mind just a little, because I had only accepted the invitation on the understanding that I would not be left alone with Fabrice for any length of time. But I couldn't find any excuse to cry off and anyway, it did seem pretty pathetic to be scared of someone who might, just might, make a pass at me. We were only going to drive a few miles together, and Fabrice was hardly going to rape me, after all.

We took the Mercedes. 'We'll go the quick way,' Fabrice said. 'It's a forest back road over the hills. Saves ten minutes over the main road along the valley.' Fabrice clearly wanted to show off his driving skill in the powerful car and, once we'd left the sedate Route Nationale behind, he whizzed us at incautious speed round the hillside-hugging bends with a great show of nonchalance. It was the sort of ride that's more fun for the driver than for any passengers. I wondered whether that was why Régine had decided not to come with us. In the middle of a particularly densely forested stretch Fabrice pointed to a pair of iron gates that interrupted a long red-brick wall. Beyond them a track-way led away through an impenetrable secrecy of conifers. 'You'll be interested to know who lives there,' Fabrice said. 'It's the cousin of Margueritte that my family knows: Pierre-Valéry d'Alabouvettes. Used to be in the government under Giscard. Of course he's retired now. We can't see the house from the road but it's one hell of a château up there in the woods.' An idea struck him. 'We could go over there tomorrow. He actually likes me quite a lot and he's very generous with the booze cabinet. I'll catch him up by phone when we get back tonight.'

'You say him,' I said. 'Does he live up here all alone?'

'He has his secretary living with him, if you understand me.'

'That seems a bit transparent,' I said, 'and yet old-fashioned at the same time. The worst of both worlds. What does she think about that?'

'It isn't a she,' said Fabrice, 'it's a he.'

Five minutes later we had come down from the hills and arrived at a farmhouse, handsome and half-timbered, that would have made a setting for a Grimms' tale. Inside was a crowd of thirty-something people, among whom the blond hair and blue eyes that drew attention to Fabrice in Paris were the rule rather than the exception, and who were circulating in a haze of cigarette smoke – for the garden weather part of the spring day was past – and an ambient scurry of dogs to trip unwary feet.

Although everyone who spoke to me addressed me in French I was aware that a lot of neighbouring conversations took place in the local dialect or *patois* as they called it. I recognized it as a form of German but was too polite to say so. We were served wine, local Sylvaner and Gewurztraminer, which Fabrice and I drank in imprudent quantities, while smoking other people's cigarettes. At least there were titbits to mop the booze up: mainly crisp hot sausages cut into bite-sized portions.

'So Fabrice has found a real Englishman in Paris,' one young woman said to me. 'That'll have pleased him. All his life he's tried to be more British than the Brits. Barbour jackets and Earl Grey tea. Of course you wouldn't have noticed.'

It was true. I hadn't. I started down another track. 'He and Régine. Are they heading for marriage, do you think? It's what, two years they've been together?' I knew I was being nosey, but I felt that my own experience of Fabrice entitled me to a certain curiosity on the subject.

'Probably yes,' said the other. She was attractive in a comfortable, round-faced way and reminded me a little of my last girlfriend but one. 'He never had girlfriends when he was younger, as far as we knew, at any rate. He was a bit of a loner. But late starters often make up for lost time quite energetically. And the two of them seem pretty serious. Where is she by the way?' I explained about her feeling too tired to come. 'The prospect of his driving, more probably,' the young woman said.

Which reminded me that Fabrice would also have to drive us back, after a hefty intake of good Alsatian wine. Well, whatever happened, I told myself, we were in it together. I looked out of the window. I couldn't believe how dark it had become. I was losing track of time. This early aperitif was turning into a full evening. I looked at my watch. No, it was not all that late: only eight o'clock. Then why was it so dark? I remembered that I was now in the eastern extremity of France where sunrise and sunset both happened that much earlier than in Paris. Perhaps that accounted for it. But Fabrice arrived and refilled my glass just then, and a bright young female student from Strasbourg came up to talk to us both and I forgot my puzzlement.

At last Fabrice noticed the time himself and suggested it was time to leave. Other people began to make a move at the same moment and, as they tumbled out of the opening front door, began to exclaim together in a murmur of *mon dieux* and oohs and aahs. A steady fall of snow was in progress and the ground and bushes were already covered in white. 'But it's April,' I said, startled, 'and this morning was so brilliant.'

'It can happen,' said Fabrice. 'High up here it can happen even in May. But it needn't worry us. We'll take the quick way, the road we came along. We'll be back before it gets to any depth.'

ELEVEN

The depth of snow in the sheltered valley from which we were setting off was very different from the depths we encountered on the high road through the forest that took us back towards Saverne. Snow lay a little more thickly on each ridge of higher ground that we crossed, and by the time we were only halfway back we were ploughing through four inches or more of nearly virgin whiteness. The view ahead was whiteness too, a tunnel of fast-flying flakes that seemed to attack the windscreen only to veer off left, right and upward at the last split second. And the wipers, on double speed, heaved protestingly at fans of settling crystals that grew heavier and more opaque with every stroke. Fabrice kept his foot down and we ploughed grimly on.

Night had really fallen and the headlights picked out just one solitary set of tyre-prints leading the way ahead of us. But even those, our only contact with other traffic on the lonely road, were growing fainter by the second. I realised for the first time that no traffic was coming the other way and I turned round in my seat to confirm my near certainty that no headlights were following us either. 'We're a bit in the middle of nowhere, aren't we?' I said, trying to make my tone conversational.

'Not really.' Fabrice was trying to do the same. 'Another few kilometres and you'll see the lights of Saverne shining up from the valley as we swing round the bends. Then it's downhill all the way home.' But downhill in these conditions seemed an even less comforting prospect than up.

A thwacking sound and the Merc shivered slightly. We'd crashed through a windswept dune of snow that had settled through a gap in the trees. Cold sparks of crystal danced in the headlights for a moment, swirling like galaxies of stars. The next drift loomed up twenty seconds later. The car porpoised through it with a thump. Then the drifts came regularly, like waves, the car transformed into a power boat, sending the semi-solid breakers up in showers of surf as it charged them one by one. 'It's like we're surfing our way home,' said Fabrice, his voice charged with an excitement that had not quite yet been crowded out by fear.

'My God. Look there!' I saw the big one first. The drift was sinuously in motion, solidifying before our eyes out of its own particular micro-blizzard. Its crest was a changing skyline that dissolved into an upward flowing fog of ice. It reared higher than the car as we approached. In a futile gesture of defiance Fabrice slammed his foot down to the floor. We struck. The Merc buffered to a stop. Wheels spun in a high-pitched whine and whir of protest. Fabrice tried reverse. Surprisingly the car inched back a metre or so. Then slewed sideways into deeper snow and stuck. He took it out of gear.

We got out of the car. The drift seemed to have stopped moving; it lay inert as if in shock from our assault on it. Rising little higher than the top of the bonnet it looked remarkably un-threatening: a different animal from the sinister rearing monster that had confronted us through the windscreen a moment ago. But it stretched a limo's length along the road in front of us. There was no shovel in the car, Fabrice confirmed. 'But you've got your mobile phone,' I said. Fabrice was about the only one of my friends who had one.

'Yes, of course,' Fabrice answered. Then, deadpan, 'I left it at my parents'.'

'Oh, right,' I said, nodding calmly, and wondering what on earth we were going to do next. Logically there were only two choices and neither appealed.

'They won't find us till the morning if we stay in the car,' Fabrice said. 'It might be buried by then.'

I stated the obvious. 'And if we keep the engine going for heat we'll die from the monoxide.'

'And if we don't we'll freeze to death.' There was a silence as we stared at each other across the bonnet of the car.

Then Fabrice said, *'T'as pas un clops?'* Got a fag?

'I don't smoke, except for other people's.' I laughed. 'Same as you.' And Fabrice laughed too.

'Look,' Fabrice said, 'we're very near the house I showed you, the château where Pierre-Valéry lives. We can make it easily on foot.'

I looked along the road ahead. But for the impenetrable blackness of trees on either side I couldn't have seen where its path lay at all. In the car's headlights the snow still fell weightily, in flakes now grown too big for dancing. Beyond the headlights' reach the dark was absolute. 'Do we have a torch?'

There was one in the car, mercifully. Only large pocket size but infinitely better than nothing. Almost better, there was a coat – though only one. Neither of us had more on than a shirt and jacket, jeans and casual shoes. Fabrice lifted the coat out of the boot. It was an ancient Afghan affair, half a generation old, with holes in it, and although it had moulted much of its own original hair this had been replaced in some measure by an encrustation of dog hairs that had accumulated over the course of a long and useful afterlife as a car blanket for family canines. Fabrice held it up apologetically. 'Best we can do, I'm afraid. We can't both fit into it though.'

'We could wear it in turns,' I said. 'Five minutes each.'

Reluctantly we switched off the car's lights and the ignition. The finality of the blackness and the silence that followed this appalled us and left us for a little while unable to move or speak. Then Fabrice threw me the coat – 'You first,' – shone the torch ahead of us, and we moved off.

Along the right-hand side of the road the drift was shallower. We waded through it up to our knees. I attempted a black joke. 'Lucky we're not in Wellingtons. Snow would have come in over the top.' Not only no boots. No pullovers, no scarves, no gloves.

The going was easier beyond the drift: the snow lay only a few inches deep. But then there came the next drift and the next. I was conscious of the presence of the car behind us, our only connection to a world beyond this white one, but silent now and dark and dead, receding into uselessness like an abandoned talisman with every step we took. I was tempted to take the torch from Fabrice and shine it behind us to see how far we'd come since leaving the Mercedes. Then I remembered Lot's wife and changed my mind.

In only a few minutes we were both shivering and wet. With a jolt I remembered the coat we were supposed to be sharing. I tore it off my back with guilty haste. 'Fabrice, take it.' If I was soaked and freezing then Fabrice must be halfway to hypothermia.

'Come on,' said Fabrice in English. 'It's my fucking fault we're here.'

'I knew there was a road along the valley too,' I said. 'I could have said, take that one.' I threw the coat round Fabrice's shoulders and started manically to stuff his arms into the sleeves as if he were an elderly invalid, until Fabrice accepted the point and finished the task for himself.

'How far did you say?' I asked. In the course of giving up the coat I had somehow acquired command of the torch and it shone still on an unchanging vista of snowdrifts framed by fir trees on either side. I knew quite well that Fabrice hadn't said how far he thought it was and that, in this whited-out forest landscape where we had come to a stop, he couldn't possibly know.

'Not far now,' was his upbeat reply.

He really is more British than the Brits, I thought. 'Perhaps we'll find a lamp post among the fir trees,' I said.

'Why a lamp post?' Fabrice was puzzled.

'It's something in an English children's book.'

'Oh, I know. We have it in French too. About a magic lion. And witches?' Perhaps it was the poignancy of the chance words, children and magic, for Fabrice suddenly reached out his hand for mine and I took it firmly, without protest. 'Conserve a little bit of heat at least, like that,' Fabrice said, and without further discussion we plodded onward hand in hand.

Fabrice didn't bother to look at his watch. He relinquished the coat when he heard my teeth chattering just below his left ear. Then, after what seemed about five more minutes, I handed it back. And so we went on.

It was Fabrice who stopped first. He was panting. 'Just need to get my breath back for a moment.'

'We can't,' I said. 'We'll freeze.'

'Well, you go on. I'll catch you up. I only need a second.'

'Don't be silly,' I said. We were still attached at the hands, and I pulled at Fabrice like a child trying to drag a parent to the sweet-counter until he started moving again.

Much later we consulted my watch by the light of the torch. We had been going for over an hour. The snow was no longer melting on the tops of our heads but clinging there, giving us a white cap each. It plastered our shoulders too and the fronts of our jackets. Only our reversed lapels had kept the worst of it from our shirts and chests. Our progress could no longer be described as walking. We were stumbling along, often using hands to crawl across the deeper drifts. It was no longer a case of holding hands but of using them constantly to pull each other up when we had fallen. We were both falling over now constantly, like farm animals about which the farmer would say the only thing to be done was put them down. Fabrice's numb fingers had let the torch go twice and we'd had to scrabble for it among the tracks our legs and bodies made, finding it thanks to the light it shed so prettily among the miniature caves and canyons we had formed.

Then suddenly I saw it. 'Look there!' The torch, which I was holding now, showed brickwork alongside the road. Brickwork with no ends in sight. 'A wall.' How long we had been following it we had no idea. I waded towards it, touched it, rested my back against it, then found myself sinking down, despite myself, dizzy with exhaustion and the cold.

I came to with Fabrice's voice a breathless shout in my ears. 'Don't do that. Don't stop. You told me that yourself a while back.' Fabrice's arms were hauling me up out of the snow, out of the sleep into which I had been falling, so nicely and so comfortably falling, like a winter dormouse, like a hedgehog, like a smallish bear. '*Viens, viens*, we're nearly there. This is the wall of the estate. Just follow it along and we'll be at the gate. We're there.' He managed something like a laugh. 'Peter, don't die on me now.'

We used the wall for support, creeping along it in snow whose shallowest deposits were now knee-deep. How big could an estate possibly be? How long its boundary wall? Nothing existed for me now except that gate and the unseen great house beyond it. Everything else fell away: weekend in Alsace, Régine, job and life in Paris, home in England and all my past. Nothing mattered any more or had meaning. Fabrice apart, the only thing that existed – I saw it clearly in my mind, though I had only glimpsed it as we rushed by unheeding during that afternoon so long ago, and not attached any importance to it – was that gate. I knew it now. As if my mind had photographed it and was just delivering the prints, I saw it before me. Brick by brick I knew its two supporting pillars and could number their stone quoins. I saw the iron-railed portals with their spikes on top. There were lamps atop the pillars...

Fabrice apart... Fabrice too I could have described in as much detail, without bothering to turn my head. Every hair of his moustache, every laughter-line on his face, every breath of his that exchanged its heat with the frozen air, all was imprinted on my consciousness and fastened there like the icicles that gripped my beard and hair.

The gate came into torch range. It came as powerfully as an apparition, like something supernatural looming through the snow. But the lamps on top of the two pillars were unlit except by the wavering beam of our torch, and the gates themselves, when we pushed at them, were locked.

'We go over the top,' said Fabrice. His voice was hoarse and breathless, thin as a thread. We didn't stop to debate this or even get our breath. We were both fired up with a terrifying sense that delay was just a stepping stone away from death. Fabrice climbed first while I shone the torch. It wouldn't have been difficult ordinarily, except for the spikes, but in his exhausted state he had to struggle to the top. He got one leg over the top of the spikes and was balancing gingerly above them prior to shifting his weight and flipping his other leg across when he let out an animal howl of pain. My blood ran cold. The spikes. I flinched and dropped the torch.

'What?' I called in panic, groping at my feet for the dropped light.

'Cramp. Got cramp.'

'Thank God for that,' I said. 'Thought you'd impaled yourself.' I rescued the torch and shone it up to where Fabrice remained, as immobile and awkward as if he really had skewered himself on the railings. 'I'm coming up.' I started to climb, with the strap of the torch between my teeth. 'Which leg?'

'Your side.'

I found Fabrice's calf and massaged it, first through his jeans and then by putting my hand up under the fabric and rubbing the muscle itself. How reassuringly solid it seemed – the cramp itself was partly responsible for this – and warm. My attentions were more comfort gesture than cure, but in comforting Fabrice I found that I was comforted myself and was startled and almost aggrieved when Fabrice said, 'Thank you, it's OK now,' and vaulted over and down the other side. A second later I had joined him.

It was difficult to guess the direction in which the driveway ran, and there was no sign of a light. 'Do they have dogs?' I asked.

'There used to be a panther.'

'You're joking,' I said, horrified. 'What, loose in the grounds?'

'It was in a cage. It's OK though. It was years ago. They sold it to a zoo.'

The snow was less deep in here. In a businesslike way we found each other's hands again and held them after a fashion as we walked, but our fingers were just hardened ridges of ice and wouldn't clasp.

'Supposing they're away?'

'Don't even think it,' said Fabrice.

And then there was a light...

It seemed almost unreal to be ringing a doorbell. To hear a crackled query from the electric box beside it. To hear Fabrice reciting his full name, hoarsely and urgently, twice. Even more unreal when the door opened and we stumbled, nearly fell, into a hallway so yellow-bright with electricity that it hurt the eyes, so warm that, like a fire, it stung the cheeks. A courteous middle-aged man had let us in. An older one with a long and claret-coloured face and an aristocratic mane of silver hair appeared in a doorway, his mouth opening with astonishment as he saw the state of the travellers who had found their way to his door. *'Mon dieu,'* he said, advancing towards Fabrice. He felt his soaking jacket shoulders and flicked snow from his head onto the floor. He turned to the other man. 'Hervé, get two dressing-gowns immediately.' Then to Fabrice and me. 'Come through at once. Get those clothes off, get by the fire, then some whisky down you. Everything else can wait. Excuse me.' He reached out a hand and flicked the snow off my head too. It joined Fabrice's contribution in a puddle on the tiles.

'I need to phone...' began Fabrice. He was swaying on his feet. I caught him.

'We'll do all that,' said the older man and guided us both through the open door to where a log fire blazed between brass-headed fire-dogs. Hervé reappeared with two towelling bathrobes and laid them side by side on the arm of a sofa. 'Get into these quickly,' he said. 'We won't watch you,' and with an air of having urgent matters to attend to elsewhere, both men left the room.

We looked at each other for a moment, almost apologetically in Fabrice's case, and then started to undress. It was not an easy process. Our clothes clung to us wetly and our fingers were so numb from the cold that when it came to undoing buttons we might as well have been using chopsticks. 'Here, let me.' Fabrice took over when it came to my cuffs and I, really to give myself something to do, returned the compliment. But I made sure to deal with my trousers myself. It was the last stage that presented the most difficulty, though. Trying to remove my socks, I discovered that I couldn't feel my feet and, simultaneously, that taking my socks off was not simply like peeling a banana: the feet themselves played an active part in the process and, unbeknown to me, had been doing so all my life. This evening though, the toes kept snagging themselves in the fabric like the fins of a fish in a landing net. Without a word Fabrice knelt to help me and in a second the process was complete.

'I think I've got frostbite,' I said.

I didn't know the word in French and Fabrice didn't know it in English but he got the general idea. He rubbed my feet gently with one of the bathrobes. 'You'll be all right,' he said. We were both suddenly conscious of being totally naked together for the first time. I couldn't help noticing that Fabrice had a nice physique but I also noticed that his reciprocal gaze was a little more interested than I would have wished. Inevitably my eyes turned to Fabrice's sex. The cold had diminished it to cherubic proportions, nearly lost in a forest of fur. Glancing down I saw that I was in a similar condition. I found myself giving a little uneasy laugh, which Fabrice immediately echoed, and we both relaxed.

'Get this on, for God's sake.' I threw one of the white bathrobes at Fabrice's head and a second later we were decently clad.

As if on cue the two older men returned, Hervé with a tray on which were a bottle of The Macallan single malt and two well filled tumblers which he pressed into our hands, actually helping to arrange our stiffened fingers into a grasp strong enough for the heavy glasses not to fall to the floor.

We fell into, rather than sat upon, one of the deep and encircling sofas, which seemed to enfold us in its silken arms. A small table at each end of it was ready to receive our whisky tumblers when those were not in the process of being raised to our lips, while in front of us the fire glowed in expansive maturity. I was so overcome with the sensation of salvage from the jaws of death that I no longer cared what might happen to me next, or for the rest of my life.

'I've phoned your father to say you're safe,' said the snowy-haired man to Fabrice. 'Then you can phone again in your own time.' He smiled. 'And talk to Régine I guess.' He turned to me. 'Now who do you need to phone?'

'Nobody,' I said 'Nobody knows I'm here.'

'What a chill those words strike in the film-goer,' he replied archly. 'But don't worry. You haven't come to Dracula's castle.'

I looked around me. It was a castle all the same.

Only then did Pierre-Valéry d'Alabouvettes introduce himself, refusing to allow me to stand up while he shook his hand. 'And please, please call me P.V. Fabrice does.'

'I think I know your cousin Margueritte,' I said. 'I'm one of her tenants at the Hôtel des Corbeaux.'

'*Chut*,' said P.V. 'Don't let's hear the word tenant. The unspeakable Charles Guyot will be jumping out of the woodwork at any second with a summons from the *percepteur des taxes*.' He introduced the younger man as, '*Hervé, mon secrétaire.*'

Side by side on the sofa, Fabrice and I could not exchange glances. Instead I felt the warmth of Fabrice's leg pressed for an instant against my own through the two layers of towelling: the leg-language equivalent of a complicit wink.

The whisky was soon gone and refills came quickly. The evening meal had clearly been eaten some time ago, but Hervé was despatched to the kitchen to find what he could in the fridge, do something with it and deliver it to us refugees.

Fabrice left the room to phone Régine and for a few minutes I found himself alone with P.V. I'd never had a private conversation with a government minister before, not even an ex-one, and wasn't quite sure what to talk about, forgetting momentarily what I already knew from my father and his colleagues on the Northampton Borough Council: namely that politicians are quite capable of setting the conversational agenda themselves.

'What an interesting character our Fabrice is,' the ex-minister began without preamble. 'So charming, so gifted and intelligent ... and so mixed up.' He smiled benignly, like someone in an eighteenth century portrait, and added, 'Don't you find?'

'What do you mean?'

P.V. looked half away from me, perhaps checking there was enough wood on the fire. 'At some point in their lives, everyone has to decide what it is they want, and who they want to be. It's not just a matter of being selfish. It's a question of making things possible for other people.' He looked back at me. 'Rather than making things gradually impossible for them. For Régine, for example. I don't think Fabrice, for all his intelligence, has got round to asking himself one or two questions. Questions that you and I, for example, probably dealt with long ago – though longer ago in my case than in yours. Maybe he finds them a bit hard to ask, or is afraid of the answers.'

I laughed faintly. P.V. continued. 'Maybe you'll turn out to be a benevolent star rising on his horizon. Perhaps you'll be the person who finally sorts him out.'

I said, 'I don't think I'm competent to sort out other people's lives. I actually came to France to sort out my own.'

P.V. smiled. 'You don't have the air of a person with a problematic life, you know. You look too … too young, too charming, too open-eyed. As you say in English, you seem *without sheeps on your shoulder.*'

'All the same,' I said 'I'm getting far more involved in other people's lives than I would really like.' The whisky must have been going to my head.

As if he had just noticed this and was responding appropriately, P.V. got up and poured me another. 'Speaking personally,' he said, 'I'd have thought that dealing with other people's uncertainties was one of the best ways to confront your own.'

Fabrice returned to the room, followed a second or two later by Hervé, who announced that he'd turned on the radiator in the *chambre des pinsons* for the visitors. Fabrice turned to me and explained that each bedroom in the house was named after a different forest bird – ours was the chaffinch room – while Hervé unloaded the tray he had been carrying. There were *omelettes aux cêpes* (tinned cêpes: he apologised) salad, and a baguette cut into chunks. And the wine – it being easier in a castle to find a good bottle than to create gourmet meals at eleven o'clock at night – was a bottle of Volnay Clos des Chênes 1979. I thought: maybe I am dead and there is a heaven after all. And when the bottle was empty, there was another one.

P.V. asked Fabrice for the registration number of his father's car, then went off to the phone to alert the *gendarmerie* to its presence on the forest road. 'Otherwise someone'll smash a snow-plough into it in the morning. That or you'll get a parking ticket.' He was only gone a moment. 'Would you believe it. They weren't the smallest bit interested. Simply said, had you secured the vehicle? As if anyone's going to pinch it, up here, in a snowdrift. In the end I gave them my name, just to make them jump.'

'And did they?' asked Hervé.

'They called me *monsieur* finally. Do you suppose that counts?'

The wine kept coming. I had no objection. I was in anybody's hands now, anyone's but my own. My body had thawed suddenly; my face burned in the fire's heat and my hands and feet had tingled themselves back to some kind of normality. The same processes must have completed themselves for Fabrice; I could feel the warmth of his body next to me, radiating through my *robe de chambre*.

'We're keeping you up,' said Fabrice eventually. 'You've been incredibly good to us.' Mumblingly I echoed his thanks. We were shown up creaking stairs to the *chambre des pinsons*. It was more like a suite than a room, comprising ante-chamber, bathroom and bedroom, all carpeted and sumptuous. Not only was it extremely warm thanks to Hervé's earlier prompt attention to the radiator control, there was also a small token log fire in the hearth, which seemed to express in its exuberant manner of burning a kind of astonishment at its own sudden kindling.

One enormous double bed occupied a large part of the principal chamber. It looked comfortable and welcoming, with a corner of the top sheet turned down. I felt it would have been ungrateful to ask for a separate bed.

'I'll leave you to it,' said Hervé, without innuendo so far as I could tell. 'No hurry in the morning. Sleep it out.'

We were alone. Standing close together, we looked at each other for a moment, but finding it uncomfortable to meet each other's gaze we both turned to look around us instead. Three of the bedroom walls were fitted with mirrors, small ones and large ones in semi-Gothic frames. They were old and not all perfectly aligned, so that as the two of us rotated slowly in opposing arcs, we found ourselves confronted by image after image of ourselves, together and separately, viewed from every conceivable angle, in every imaginable point of rotation away from and towards each other. Two young men, one somewhat bigger than the other, the smaller one bearded, the other merely moustached, both with unkempt blondish hair, both wrapped in nothing but white towelling *robes de chambre*.

The mirrors behind us finally, we faced the reality of each other once more face to face. And now we read clearer, if still cautious, signals in each other's eyes. Tentatively Fabrice put his hands on my shoulders. 'You saved my life out there,' he said. His bathrobe, no longer held together, had fallen open at the front. His cock was visible in the gap. It was thickening up.

'You saved *my* life,' I said, then stepped forward and embraced him, and was conscious of my chest encountering the warmth of Fabrice's as we began to kiss.

This isn't happening, I told myself. I thought about the naked couple I'd spied upon during my first evening in Paris. About my voyeuristic promenade along the quai des Tuileries. I told myself – this is just a one-off. Something that just occasionally happens to people once in life. Extreme circumstances. Mates who've faced ordeals together, celebrating life and solidarity and victory in the only appropriate way. It happened in the army sometimes, I knew. It would never happen again of course. Not to me. But for now, well my cock, like Fabrice's, was hard and upstanding

What would I feel about this in the morning, when Burgundy and whisky and adrenalin and everything had all worn off? I refused to contemplate that now. If this was never to happen to me again – and I was determined that it wouldn't happen again – I was going to experience it to the full now.

It was not only moustache and lips and chest and belly and fur that pressed against me. I could feel my hardness between us and Fabrice's too: together creating something double-barrelled like binoculars, like the shotgun of this morning, today, so long ago. Hard yet giving, so quite unlike the shotgun really, firmly together yet separable too.

We stood without even the pretend modesty of half-worn bathrobes. Those lay behind our heels. We looked at each other for the first time with undisguised approbation and desire. Fabrice's clothes had been a size or two bigger than mine and the same went for all those other things of his that I hadn't seen or touched before tonight: chest and biceps, thighs and cock. But I felt I had nothing myself to be ashamed of. I was as well-proportioned, on my smaller scale, as Fabrice. 'You're beautiful,' Fabrice said suddenly in English. The words gave me a frisson. I knew that he'd said it in English for a purpose. He wanted a nuance more precise than *Tu es beau*.

'Whatever you want,' he said quietly when we had rough-and-tumbled each other onto the bed, and he lay back sensually, spread-eagled and relaxed upon it as if we were about to play a board game to which I was a newcomer and therefore allowed to be the first to cast the dice.

I knew what to do. I'd seen it done. I found the anatomical novelty of the situation less problematic or off-putting than I'd imagined. I wet my cock with spittle and pushed it into the place that Fabrice was offering to me, between the cheeks of his butt. It slipped in with reassuring ease. Fabrice took responsibility for pleasuring himself, almost literally in my face. I might have expected to find that a turn-off but to my surprise it actually increased my excitement. It was more than two months since I'd had sex with anyone except myself. Perhaps because of that it was over all too soon. I came inside Fabrice as quickly as a teenager. Then Fabrice let fly his load, just beneath my face. I slumped forward and lay limp on Fabrice's wet chest. Again I said, 'You saved my life.'

'You idiot,' Fabrice said gently. 'It was me that put your life at risk. And you saved me.' I wasn't quite sure now, though I hardly cared, if we were talking about our adventure in the snow or something else. I found that I was crying. Fabrice began to stroke the back of my head, and I discovered with a finger that my own tears were not the only ones that rolled down Fabrice's cheeks.

THIRTEEN

The morning brought a cloudless blue sky and warm sunshine. It was late when we surfaced and the snow was already thawing rapidly, falling off trees and roofs in lumps as big as duvets.

I was surprised to find in myself no sign yet of the successive waves of self-hatred and guilt that I had expected would set in as soon as day dawned. There would be plenty of time for all that later, I told myself. Those feelings would no doubt steal up on me at a moment of their own choosing, like a delayed hangover – and after last night's intake I fully anticipated one of those too. But perhaps the situation I found myself in played a role in this. To wake up in a castle in Alsace on a diamantine morning of spring snow was very different from finding myself, for example, in an urban bedsit, making awkward conversation over soggy Cornflakes. And then there was the question of Fabrice. I looked at him sideways as we stood together looking out of the window, both wearing those towelling dressing-gowns again because we had nothing else.

The damage was done. I'd gone to bed with a man, had had sex with that man and enjoyed it. None of that new extension to the fabric of my life could be unpicked. But at least the man in question was a handsome, masculine one, intelligent and affectionate. I still thought so as I looked at him this morning. So it could have been worse. Just.

There was a knock at the door. It was Hervé. 'I saw you both at the window...' His face broke into an unplanned grin as soon as he was in the room with us. Perhaps the events of the night were only too legible in our faces, our body language, or even the state of the bed. But then he mastered his facial muscles and handed us the clothes that we'd been wearing when we arrived. They were now dry. There would be breakfast downstairs as soon or as late as we wanted it. Meanwhile the road beyond the gates had been ploughed and the estate manager, who had just finished clearing the driveway, was at the ready with the tractor to take us back to our abandoned car and help us get it moving once more.

As we began to dress, I ran into trouble again with my socks. The two smallest toes would keep snagging; I seemed to have no control over them at all. Fabrice saw this. 'OK, let me.' Still naked, he bent down and manipulated my socks carefully over my recalcitrant feet. That accomplished he stood up, then seized me and kissed me. I found myself submitting to this quite philosophically and even kissed him back. After all, it was absolutely certain that we would never again stand naked together like this. 'It worries me,' said Fabrice, 'how you're going to manage this sock business tomorrow morning when you have to dress yourself.' And then, partly because of the way Fabrice said that, it began to worry me too.

We rode out in borrowed coats and boots and gloves, one on each mudguard of the tractor, and holding tight to the shovel we each carried, and which our shaking progress threatened to dislodge from our grasp and grind under-wheel into the snow. The Merc, when we found it just two miles away, looked like a minor mammoth that had come to a sticky end encased in ice. The snow-plough's path had snaked around it leaving it walled up behind the embankment of cleared snow.

After an energetic fifteen minutes the car was cleared from its drift, a tow rope was attached and the tractor dragged the icebound vehicle into the ploughed middle of the road. To everyone's surprise it started up at once – Fabrice had sensibly removed a small souvenir of snowdrift from the exhaust before attempting this – and, following the tractor, Fabrice drove it and me slowly back to the castle in the woods.

Playing the chevalier to the last, Pierre-Valéry offered us an aperitif before we finally set off, but it was nearly one o'clock by now and we said a polite no and took the road again, to rejoin Fabrice's family and Régine for Sunday lunch. After that would come the train ride back to Paris.

Alone with Fabrice in the car – we'd be back at his house in ten minutes or so, barring accidents on the ice – I decided to broach the subject of our adventure together in the *chambre des pinsons*. 'Look,' I said. 'I don't want you to think that what happened last night is usual for me. I was acting a bit out of character. Perhaps you were too.' I waited for Fabrice to confirm my optimistic interpretation of the facts, but he didn't and I was forced to go on. 'I'm not bisexual – which maybe at some level you are.' This time Fabrice grunted non-committally: it might have been possible to interpret this as an assent, though perhaps not in a court of law. 'Last night was a one-off. I was in a state. We both were. It was an emotional response to an exceptional situation. We came close to dying on that road – on this road. You did save my life. You say I saved yours, well, I don't know. But it made a difference – just for last night, just that one night – to the way I felt about … well, everything.' I stopped again. Fabrice was obstinately silent, excused conversation perhaps by the concentration required to drive on the still treacherous white surface of the road among the hills. I continued. 'To be honest, I have to say it probably wouldn't have happened if you'd been anyone else. You're not only a good friend, but you have beautiful eyelashes too, if you see what I mean.' I looked sideways at Fabrice. It was no less than the truth. Still Fabrice kept his own eyes resolutely on the road. I went on. 'You'd better make the most of that compliment, though, because I'm not going to repeat it. And I'm not going to repeat the experiment with you either, in case you're wondering. Not with you or with anybody else. And, if we're going to stay friends, then I don't want to talk about what happened last night ever again, either between ourselves or with anyone else. Do you – can you – understand that?'

'You want to bury it, in other words. Entomb the whole experience in ice.' It was probably the landscape and our experience with the car that prompted Fabrice to so graphic a metaphor.

'Since you put it like that, yes I do. And so should you. If – I'm sorry to be blunt – if you value your relationship with Régine – and I mean for the long term – then you should forget it too.'

'You being the great guru on the subject of successful long-term relationships, I suppose. Sorry to be blunt.' It was the first time I'd heard Fabrice say anything even remotely critical of, or to, anybody. It stung the more for that.

We drove in silence for another minute, negotiating the looping bends that led the forest road down from its heights to rejoin the main road at the bottom, then Fabrice said, 'Your secret is safe. I won't blab about this to anyone – ever, or claim you as any sort of conquest, and, because I want to stay your friend, I'll do what you ask and never mention it again between us, unless you do first – which, by the way, is not as improbable as you may think right now. But I won't forget it, or bury it away. I'll remember it always as one of the great adventures of my life. I nearly died in the company of a beautiful, sexy young man who's more or less straight, like me, and he saved my life, and we spent the night in a castle and we made love. Nothing too complicated or alarming about that, I'd have thought. Only beautiful. And who did what to whom is just a detail. No, I'll never forget it. I'll remember it in any case tomorrow morning when I put my socks on. And I promise you, so will you.' He couldn't repress a smile at that thought. 'For me it was something beautiful. And I'll remember it even more happily because I think that, in your heart, you feel the same.'

I thought – *What?!* – but for some reason I couldn't find any coherent words with which to rebut that.

We were back a moment later. Lunch was ready, and all was bustle and kissing, and over lunch the story of the adventure got told with numerous action replays and minor disagreements about details, though of course the *chambre des pinsons* got no more than a passing mention, and the story came to an end some time before the bedroom door was finally shut for the night. After lunch, because everything was running late, it was already time to leave for the station, me carrying my overnight bag in one hand and my hare (mercifully skinned and eviscerated, and wrapped in newspaper for coolness) in the other. It was not for the first time, as I sat opposite Régine on the train, that I found difficulty in meeting her trusting brown eyes.

We said our *au revoirs* at the corner of the rue des Archives, and Fabrice took custody of the hare. He'd cook it for us and selected friends on Tuesday night, he said. I thought, how difficult it was to give yourself a break from people. You always seemed to end up inextricably entangled with them by the most trivial of connections: a bloody hare, for instance, or a pair of socks.

I dumped my bag at home and had a shower. It was my second one that day, but I took it for reasons that had nothing to do with physical cleanliness. Then I went out for a walk. I'd found the inside of my flat oppressive. But I didn't feel much better when I got outside. It was that special period of Sunday afternoon that strikes even the bravest and best-fed as cheerless: the rapture of Friday evening a distant memory, the weekend tilting inexorably towards Monday morning. I'd once thought this melancholy time a peculiarly British phenomenon but my new life abroad was teaching me that this was not so. Sunday afternoon could be as bleak in Paris as in Northampton.

The quays of the Seine were busy with well-dressed strollers examining the second-hand bookstalls. Half Paris seemed to take its Sunday constitutional here, browsing among engravings and books that nobody ever seemed to buy. They probably came to see and to be seen, though they hardly ever seemed to run into anybody they knew. I crossed the Pont Neuf. The sunshine that had blessed the morning in Alsace had not followed the train to Paris, and the Seine ran past greyly with just a few glints of quicksilver to redeem its surface from total monochrome. The plane trees were now almost fully out along its banks, though the sun was not yet strong enough to produce the dappled shade that was the speciality of the place in summer. I turned away from the bridge into the Place Dauphine and there – coming straight towards me as if to defy the rule that you never ran into anyone you knew – was Joe.

I found myself wishing Joe had given me another twenty-four hours, just this once, to compose myself and collect my thoughts after the earth-shaking events of the last twenty-four hours. Still, I managed to tune my thoughts in to another wavelength and, remembering that Joe would normally be spending his weekends with

Antoine these days, asked him what he was doing out and about on his own.

'Looking for you,' said Joe. 'I tried your bell, then the Horseshoe, then I called by the Figeac and had a coffee. You weren't there.' He paused before adding, 'But I guess you knew that. Seriously though,' he went on, 'Antoine's spending the weekend with his mother – that's why I'm on my own.'

'And the reason I wasn't in was that I've just come back from Alsace where I was spending the weekend, as you've probably forgotten.'

We began to drift along the quai des Orfèvres without thinking. Joe asked for an account of my weekend and, glad of the rehearsal opportunity that lunch with Fabrice's family had provided, I gave him the expurgated version. Nevertheless, Joe had enough prior information to add the one question that would not have occurred to anyone around the lunch table. 'God, quite an adventure. And you ending up alone with Fabrice for the night after all. Was there no...?' He let his expressive face provide the end of the question.

I didn't lie exactly. I think I set my jaw rather firmly. I said, 'Fabrice knows where I stand now,' in a rather grim tone of voice.

Joe said, rather feelingly, 'Poor Fabrice.' We continued to wander around the Ile de la Cité . Then Joe suddenly announced, 'We're thinking of getting a flat together.'

I had to think for a moment. Then I got there. 'We meaning Antoine and Joe, or we meaning Joe?'

'We, plural, but I take your point. It is me that's pushing for it. He has a few reservations.'

'I can imagine he has. He's, what, nineteen?'

Joe nodded.

'And you?'

'Twenty-six,' said Joe. 'One year younger than you.'

'How did you know that?'

'I didn't. It was an inspired guess; they're a speciality of mine. But I don't think his reservations are about me. At least, if what he says is true. He says he's concerned about the hard world outside. Parental expectations, pressures from friends, people at work. It's daunting.' Joe stopped a second, then resumed. 'I think I'm sure of him. I'm sure I'm sure. And yet, supposing he's just advancing those reasons so as not to hurt me?'

'Joe,' I said gently, 'I don't want to say anything unpopular but how can you really be sure with a boy of nineteen?'

'How is anyone sure of anything? If I tell you he loves me you have every reason to take that with a pinch of salt. It's only an inspired guess at this stage, after all. But then....'

Something rather obvious struck me. I said, 'Don't you think it's about time you introduced us? If I'd actually met him our discussion could perhaps become a little bit less abstract.'

Joe relaxed visibly. 'That's what I'd hoped you'd say. I'd been kind of putting off suggesting it myself.'

'Why on earth?'

'I'd have been hurt if you'd said you didn't want to meet him. Guess I still thought you disapproved of him in some way.'

'Just because I don't like men to make passes at me doesn't mean I disapprove of people being gay. But...'

'But what?'

'I don't want to sound stupid. But it's not being hurt by me that you need to worry about. Do you see?'

Much later that evening I sat on the end of my bed, just before I got into it, trying to make sense of the weekend's events with a little help from Beethoven. My curtains were open and I looked up suddenly when the familiar yellow light was switched on among the mansards opposite. I rubbed my still numb outer toes just as Fabrice had done that morning. I'd had some difficulty getting the socks off and wondered how I'd manage in the morning. Fabrice would not be there to help me, I thought absently. Then I realised with the sharp panic that comes with unwelcome new self-knowledge that a part of me wished he could be.

FOURTEEN

Joe had told me to come to a café called the Kabylie. It was near the place de la République. Joe and Antoine used it because no-one either of them knew frequented it. I found it eventually. There was a distinctly non-European feel to the place. The menu in the window strongly evoked North Africa and to judge by appearances – there being nothing else to go on, as Oscar Wilde said – so did the clientèle and staff. I was punctual but there was no sign of Joe or Antoine. Then a thought struck me. I looked around me. Joe had never said that Antoine was North African but he hadn't said he wasn't. A little self-consciously I leaned on the brightly polished copper counter and ordered myself a pastis. The hour for beer – as Jean-Jacques would have said – was past.

A few minutes went by and then a young European entered. He was of medium height and build, poised but unmannered in his movements and trimly dressed: his trousers were neatly pressed, his shoes polished. Straight brown hair was thick but kempt. His face tended towards the triangular but the features were perfectly proportioned. If the hazel eyes were on the large side they were at least supported by strong cheekbones and set off by lashes of a good length. The overall effect was of a normality so intense as to be striking. I wasn't sure whether the newcomer would have stood out in a crowd of his own age and race. Yet in his present setting he shone like a beacon. I had no doubt whatever that this was Antoine.

The guy caught sight of me and came up to me at once. His expression was grave; it flickered rather than smiled when he extended his hand and said – a French Stanley meeting a latter-day Livingstone – *'Peter, je suppose.'*

Ten more minutes passed and there was still no sign of Joe. 'Perhaps it's deliberate,' suggested Antoine, 'and he

wants us to get to know each other at first without him.'
We were relaxed together now and talking easily.
Antoine sipped an orange juice while I nursed my pastis;
the contrast made me feel uncomfortably old: at the
same time decadent and *démodé*.

'Do you know many of Joe's friends?' I asked Antoine.

'One or two. He doesn't have all that many. You're the
one he wanted me to meet especially. He said I'd find
you interesting.'

There was a gravity, an earnestness about Antoine that
I found inexplicably moving. He expressed himself
soberly and intelligently, choosing his words with care.
But by now I had discovered something else. Antoine
possessed a characteristic not uncommon among the
French. A face that was not given to smiling from force
of habit would suddenly open into a spontaneous smile
that dazzled with unlooked-for intensity and warmth. It
was rather like the way some sober suited moths can
spread dark wings to reveal beneath a blaze of colour
and pure light.

At this point we were joined by one of those people
encountered in bars who are called either characters or
nuisances, depending on your point of view. This one,
though dark-skinned, was not North African. That was
apparent as soon as he opened his mouth. He came from
Corsica, Antoine said.

'What's he saying?' I had to ask.

Antoine translated into a French that I could
understand. 'He says it's good to see some real French
people in here for a change. (He includes you in that.
Appearances are a strange thing, *n'est-ce pas*?) That and
Vive Monsieur Le Pen.'

'I see. Why does he use an Algerian bar, then? Do you
know him?'

'By sight only,' said Antoine. 'It's the first time he's
spoken to me.'

'Algerians?' said the other, older, man. 'Five of them set on me during the war.' He unrolled sleeves, showed scars, while Antoine relayed me the information. 'Don't talk to me about Algerians. And can I get a war pension? *Merde*.' He produced from his wallet a whole sheaf of letters in courteous bureaucratic French from various government departments, each one promising to refer his case to another one. He summoned the *patron* and ordered a pastis for himself and, refusing to take no for an answer, refills for Antoine and myself. 'Arabs,' he said, indicating the *patron*. 'All over here now. They're everywhere.'

Monsieur le Patron, who introduced himself to us two newcomers as Momo, took this in his stride and laughed. Unlike Antoine he had a smile as ready as the Cheshire Cat's and when he laughed it became positively dazzling. 'One day,' he said, 'Corsica may be independent too. Then he ...' he indicated the war veteran, 'He can be an immigrant like me.' Evidently this was as much of a ritual as the sparring of Carlos and Nico in the Horseshoe.

At that moment Joe arrived. 'What kept you?' Antoine asked innocently.

'Sorry.' Joe shrugged, then sat down. He turned to me and with an eagerness that was childlike in its lack of tact said, 'Well, you've met. What do you think of him?'

'He talks as if he'd just bought a racehorse,' objected Antoine, 'and a deaf one at that.' He turned to Joe. 'If you must discuss me behind my back, at least try not to do it in front of me.'

In *esprit* they were well-matched, I thought.

Antoine turned to me. 'I understand American but I refuse to speak it. We French have a duty to resist all attempts at cultural imperialism.'

Joe laughed. 'He's just afraid of making silly mistakes, that's all. He speaks English perfectly well.'

'That's not the point at all,' Antoine protested. 'If I give way now, where will France and the French be in forty years' time?'

'You do take a long view of things...' I began.

'For one so young,' Antoine finished the sentence for me. 'Yes. I think one should.'

'Come on,' said Joe. 'Let's go eat.'

It was only after we got to Joe's flat, when Antoine disappeared to the *toilettes* – which are always plural in French, be they never so humble – that we had a brief opportunity to talk about him, as he had instructed, behind his back. 'He's not quite what I imagined a nineteen-year-old baker's boy would be like,' I said.

'Exactly,' said Joe. 'He's not. Perhaps you can begin to see...'

'Perhaps I can.'

'It's spaghetti Bolognese by the way, because I'm the chef. At least I am tonight. Antoine's a far better cook than me and I could have asked him but tonight it didn't seem right. He likes my spaghetti anyway. Cultural imperialism with an Italian flavour doesn't seem to hurt so much. Anyway, about you for a bit,' Joe changed the subject. 'In Paris for two months and more – *en plus*, it's the spring – and there's no girl on your arm yet.'

That rather shook me. 'I suppose I haven't got round to it yet,' I said uncomfortably. 'Perhaps I'm fussy.' I wasn't happy about the change of subject. The difficulties I'd had trying to get my socks on this morning were fresh in my mind.

'But Peter, this is Paris! Just look around you. There's no possible excuse. It might be different in Timbuctoo where there's nothing but camels, but here...!' He gestured up and down the room as if to indicate that the whole delightful range of French womanhood was here on parade.

'I didn't know you were such an expert on the subject.'

'I may be gay but that doesn't make you blind, whatever they may have told you at school. What about that nice girl in the Figeac?'

Another shock. Did he mean... 'Françoise?'

'No of course not. I mean the waitress, Marianne.'

Well, it was good that he hadn't meant Françoise. But even so... 'Marianne does just happen to be attached, you know. She lives in the 5-ième with a guy you said would probably want to kill Dominique. Remember?'

'Lived with a guy. She doesn't now.'

'Come again?'

'She threw him out. She's a free woman.'

'Where the hell did you get hold of that? I didn't know anything about it.' I felt a bit put out. I thought I was the one who knew all the Figeac gossip.

Apparently not. Joe said, 'Madame Touret told me yesterday. I told you I went in for a coffee when I was looking for you. I naturally asked after Marianne – who was not on duty – and that was what Madame Touret said. But don't worry, my little concierge, you're not really behind with the news. It only happened on Saturday night.'

I said, 'Marianne's a lovely girl, I know, but to tell the honest truth I haven't taken too much interest since Becky and I split up.' I mugged a self-deprecating grimace. At least I tried to. 'I guess I'm a bit slow at getting things together again.' I was appalled at myself: appalled by the brazen lie that underpinned this rickety superstructure of half-truth.

'It isn't surprising,' said Joe, after a thoughtful pause. 'Although it is a bit different from my own experience. After Chris left me I wanted everything I saw. Fortunately I didn't always get it. Otherwise you can imagine where I'd be now. Anyway, it just goes to show how different people are.'

I was relieved that Antoine chose that moment to return to the room.

Joe's flat was just the same cramped, homely kind of space that I had, high up under the roof of a large *immeuble:* a combined office and apartment block. Unlike in mine, though, the kitchen was some way along the corridor and so I was left alone with Antoine while Joe put finishing touches to the meal. I broached the subject that had been troubling Joe. I was fairly sure that Joe wanted me to and had invited me this evening partly with this purpose in mind. I said, 'When are you two going to get a place together?'

Antoine didn't smile as he considered his reply. 'I don't know,' he said. 'I'm not even sure it'll be possible.'

'I understand,' I said. 'It is a bit soon to commit yourself to a relationship, I suppose. Nineteen is young to make a final decision about something so important. Perhaps it's a time for trying out different things, experimenting, if you like, before finally settling down. Joe's a great guy but I respect your caution. After all, you don't know who you're going to meet.'

'If you think you understand,' said Antoine rather frostily, 'you couldn't be much more wrong. My hesitation about sharing a flat with Joe has nothing to do with our relationship – about which I have no uncertainties – and everything to do with my family situation: something I don't want to bore you with the details of. Just let me say that things are not good between my mother and my father. A move like that could overturn the whole wagon of apples – is that really what you say in English? – and my mother would get hurt more than she already has been.' He went on,

'Concerning relationships in general, you may be older than me and more wise but when you talk the way you did just now I think you may be talking about your own experience, not mine. You tell me I don't know who I'm going to meet. Well, that's certainly true. But at least I do know who I have met and it's just possible that in spite of your years and experience you don't. You tell me that nineteen is an age more for experiment than for commitment and though you were too polite to remind me directly that for some young people homosexuality may be a passing phase, you hinted it all the same.'

He got up from his chair and moved to the window, looking out of it while he continued his speech. The fluency of it and the passion that clearly underlay its measured delivery were startling, especially in combination with his youthful appearance. I guessed the speech had been delivered before; either that or it was being rehearsed for a bigger occasion.

'When I think about commitment I think about some stories from the past where people who didn't share their government's or their church's views had to set sail for countries they'd hardly heard of, that scarcely existed, that they might not even reach. Perhaps only the lucky ones could get a ticket. But suppose you said to those lucky ones, 'Oh come on, think about it. You have a ticket to a place nobody's returned from, your voyage will be hell and you might in any case end up at the bottom of the sea. And if you reach your promised land it may turn out to be just a desert. Change your mind; don't go.' How do you think those people would reply? 'Like hell I'll change my mind,' they'd say. 'Like hell, because I've had the luck to get a ticket.''

He turned his back to the window and faced me. 'That is what I'm saying to you. I have my ticket: that's Joe and my love for him. I'm not going to hand that back for anything or for anyone. Do you understand?'

'Yes,' I said, 'I think perhaps I do.' I felt as though Antoine had hit me over the head with a very large heavy object. The French word for this is *matraqué*. I felt flattened.

I marshalled my thoughts. After a moment or two I realised what I had to say. I discovered, if you like, the purpose of my visit. 'If you feel that strongly, then make the move and get a flat with him. Do it soon. If you make that your aim the rest will take care of itself. For you it's the only thing to do.'

'I'll consider it carefully,' said Antoine.

After the meal Antoine got up to go. I was a bit surprised. I'd imagined I'd be the first to depart, leaving the lovers together. 'I have a very early start tomorrow,' Antoine explained. 'In any case,' he added candidly, 'you'll want to talk about me. Tomorrow I can talk to Joe about you.'

'Well?' said Joe when he had gone.

The words popped out before I'd had time to choose them. 'He's beautiful,' I said.

FIFTEEN

Joe was invited to come and share the hare dinner. Antoine was working that evening and in any case Fabrice and Régine didn't know of his existence and so didn't realise that in entertaining Joe they would be entertaining not a whole single person but one half of a couple. Joe asked me quite innocently, why not ask Marianne? I'd said it was rather short notice for her as she would have to ask for a night off. The reality was more complicated than that. I couldn't go into that with Joe, though. I didn't know what the reality was. I just knew there was this ongoing difficulty with putting on my socks without Fabrice.

But the hare would make a vast main course for just four people and so Fabrice suggested we invite Françoise. But Régine said Françoise wouldn't want to come without the dodgy Portuguese guy, and nobody wanted to invite him. In the end we decided to invite Jeannette and Denis, the other couple who had shared the big table at the Figeac on my first evening in Paris.

With everyone coming from different directions, and Joe in particular not knowing where Fabrice and Régine lived, we met to begin with at the Little Horseshoe and then walked round the block to their apartment once we had all arrived. This meant that everyone at the bar knew exactly who was dining where, and that everyone at the Figeac would also know within about ten minutes. That was the way life was lived in the Marais. I was getting used to it.

There were oysters to begin the meal. April being the last month with an R in it before September, it seemed only common sense to take advantage of them before the breeding season kicked them into touch. Denis volunteered for the martyr's role of opening them alone in the kitchen while everyone else chatted over an aperitif in *le living*, and he did this with a good deal of off-stage swearing, which helped to maintain his presence in the social gathering despite his being the other side of the open door.

I was conscious the whole time, as we sat sipping Pineau de Charentes and chatting politely about nothing very much, of my physical position in relation to Fabrice, to say nothing of the intermittent eye contact between us. Now we were sitting on opposite sofas, feet stretched out towards the middle of the room at about a hundred and fifty degrees to each other, our feet about a metre apart. Now, when Fabrice had gone to check on Denis in the kitchen and given him some moral support in the shape of a topped-up glass, and was back with a bowl of *amuse-gueules,* he stood for a moment near my shoulder. And I was astonished to find that I could smell him. Not at all in an unpleasant way. Yet under the masks of after-shave, clean clothes, deodorant and soap, there was the unmistakeable scent that was Fabrice: a scent unknown to me and undetectable a week ago but now as familiar to me as my own. And was it my imagination or could I actually feel his body heat as well?

Then Fabrice was back on his sofa. Catching my eye a moment. Settled again, legs outstretched, this time at one hundred and eighty degrees, less than a metre between our two pairs of shoes. I stole a look around the room. I hadn't memorised anyone else's position in the same way; those spatial details hadn't impinged on me at all.

At the table in the dining-room that was also the kitchen, I sat in the same seat as I'd done on my only other visit, my *à deux* Sunday lunch with Fabrice back in February. As then, Fabrice sat opposite me; meanwhile the others seemed disposed at random around the table – Régine, the lady of the house, seeming no more fixed in her orbit than Joe, Denis or Jeannette in theirs – like the positions of the planets before the invention of astronomy allotted them their spheres.

The hare had been cooking by itself in the oven, in a quantity of red wine and with shallots, juniper berries, orange peel and a bay leaf, tantalising us with its aromas, and Fabrice only had to leave the table for a few minutes after the oysters had been lip-smackingly despatched, to prepare its single, plain accompaniment: gnocchi. Even that slightly fiddly task he carried out with effortless aplomb, taking the previously shaped miniature potato dumplings from their film-wrapped inertia in the fridge and dropping them into boiling water, waiting carefully till each one floated before skimming it out with a slotted spoon.

Of course the weekend in Alsace which had produced the hare that was the focus of this gathering had to be hauled into the conversation, and its adventures rehearsed yet again in detail, for the benefit of Denis and Jeannette. Fabrice asked me, with a hint of mischief in his blue eyes, if my feet were getting their sensation back. Wanting to kick him under the table, but resisting the impulse in case Fabrice should mistake it for a gesture of affection, I said seriously that the feeling had returned to all but the tips of my two smallest toes, that they still tended to poke sideways into my socks when I was dressing myself but that, by the careful deployment of a new technique that involved both hands, I was now able to manage the daily problem quite easily. All of this was new to Joe, and he became quite curious on the subject. I was well aware that his real curiosity was as to why I'd omitted this detail, about which Fabrice clearly had intimate knowledge, from the account of the weekend that I'd given him.

In an effort to divert the company's interest away from the subject of my feet I finally said to Joe, 'What a pity Antoine couldn't make it.' And of course everyone wanted to know who Antoine was, to which Joe calmly replied, using the English words, that he was his 'Significant Lover,' which everybody understood, even if only I and Fabrice really got the joke. Joe was making a public declaration of his sexual orientation: no French female ever bore the name Antoine, but in the company then present this created no frisson or awkwardness at all. People simply asked the usual interested but not too probing dinner party questions about who and where Antoine was.

But if the heterosexual members of the gathering accepted the entrance of Antoine into the conversation as a matter of course, this was far from being the case along the axis between Fabrice and myself. I had a sudden vivid impression of this axis as something tangible connecting us, like a line of fishing nylon which, given a tweak by a third party, caused us both to twitch comically in response. Our eyes met, but that was only part of it. It seemed to me then that the things between us – what we had done together; and my rather hopeless wish that history could go into rewind and return us to the less complicated relationship of earlier times – must be visible to everyone else in the room.

Conversation had moved on. I came back to it with a start. 'For about three weeks,' Régine was saying. 'Terribly short notice. But then we're back for the summer.' Fabrice's bank, it seemed, had that day summoned him to Strasbourg for a short spell at headquarters. Régine would be going with him; she was owed some holiday. And when would they be going, I asked?

I thought, thank God for this. My feelings for Fabrice were now both complex and intense. I thought we both perhaps needed a space of time apart that would act as a fire-break between us. The day after tomorrow, Régine said. A quick drink in the Little Horseshoe tomorrow evening, because there would be packing to do, and then *au revoir* till next month.

When the party broke up finally, after quite a few bottles had crashed into the kitchen waste-bin, goodnight kisses were exchanged freely by everyone: all the men kissed each other, even Denis and Joe, who had never met before tonight. Somehow I was the last to depart from the head of the stairs; I kissed Régine, who then moved back inside the flat, and I was left with Fabrice, who had once stood on this very spot and told me not to be so British. We exchanged the polite formal kiss and then, without thinking, reinforced it with a hug, and the hug grew extended in time until it more resembled a cuddle. And though this evening we had both kept our promise not to refer ever again to our sexual adventure, I found that the memory was engraved into our embrace. I found it written there in indelible script, recorded by voices that could never be erased. And having once felt the reality of Fabrice's warm nakedness against my own bare skin, I discovered that I could feel it again now, even through our two sets of clothes, and I guessed that whenever I touched Fabrice physically in the future, were it only in a handshake, I always would do. Thank God he was going away for a few weeks.

'C'mon, Peter. You coming or what?' Joe's voice from the bottom of the stairwell recalled me to myself

SIXTEEN

Paris. April. 1987.

The night was warm. I dressed in my oldest, ripped-knee jeans and threw on my leather jacket, lined with fleece. I wore that next to my skin. Just like the jeans. No underpants. Trainers without socks. Nothing else.

I turned down the rue des Archives beneath the yellow stars of its street-lamps. Turned right along the quays. Quai de Gesvres, quai Mégisserie, quai du Louvre, quai des Tuileries... Does every bisexual man come here in the end?

Where it became dark, beneath the deep trees, there began the sounds, the rustles, the whispers, the occasional moan, of men enjoying sex. They were invisible in the darkness, their exact location betrayed occasionally by the dim red fireflies that were cigarettes.

I'd bought my own packet of Gitanes for once. I smoked one as I walked hesitatingly along. I chose a place, a dark place midway between two lamp posts, and stopped on the path where I was.

A guy came out of nowhere. He was Asian looking. About my age. About my size. His face was beautiful – like a Siamese cat's. 'T'as un clops pour moi?' he said. I let him pull one out of my packet. He put it in his mouth and lit it from the end of mine. Then with his free hand he started to fumble with the buckle of my belt.

I jerked my head towards the shadowy trees. 'Là-bas,' I said.

Now we were in shade and shadow, looking outward towards the light of the river-bank night. We dropped our half-smoked Gitanes and ground them out. I felt safe and cocooned here as we groped each other's jeans down and released each other's confined hard cocks. Standing face to face we started to wank each other. He

315

bobbed down after a moment and took my prick in his mouth. Then he bobbed back up again and gave me a grin I didn't expect. That prompted me to crouch down and return his compliment. We finished each other off by hand, standing at an angle to each other so as not to mess each other's clothes. After we'd come both come – almost simultaneously – we put a cautious arm around each other's shoulder. Then to my surprise he kissed me almost passionately for a second, before we parted, disappearing into each other's darknesses, without saying goodnight.

I hadn't said a proper au revoir to Fabrice. There had been that quick farewell drink at the Little Horseshoe the night after the dinner party with the hare. But Régine had been there, and Joe, and Françoise... We hadn't had a moment to exchange a private word – although we'd exchanged a few private if difficult-to-read looks. We'd shaken hands on the pavement. Straight men in Paris often kiss on these occasions. But that day Fabrice and I did not.

I busied myself with writing. I burnt with a hard and gem-like flame. I still went to the Figeac. I walked and talked with Joe. But somehow nothing was the same. Yet time passed quickly. It was almost a shock when the month of May arrived, with weather good enough to hint at a hot continental summer to come, and a telephone call from Margueritte – she was in Barcelona – to say she was coming to Paris to collect my rent.

I got a phone call unexpectedly from a woman friend. I'd been at university with Helen, and despite her marriage soon afterwards to a man called James we'd kept in touch ever since. She was in Paris for two days. James was at a conference; she had come along for the ride. Could we meet for dinner tonight? I said yes, of course and told them how to find the Figeac. I hadn't been there for about a week.

The Figeac appealed to Helen and her husband as I hope it would. The birds sang from the window recesses as we entered, for the evenings were light now, and Madame Touret welcomed us, more calculatingly, with an aperitif on the house. She was once more on bar duty. Marianne had gone to a new job nearer to where she lived and a suitable replacement had not been found. I guessed that Madame Touret was very particular in her requirements. Marianne was greatly missed.

Jean-Jacques volunteered a perfunctory handshake. He did not eat, he said. Then he returned to *Libération*. Dominique proved more entertaining. He arrived at the same time as our *entrecôte aux cèpes* and joined us at our table without being asked, as a child might.

'Have you heard about Françoise?' he asked me at once, with barely a nod to acknowledge the presence of the others. He did not wait for an answer either. 'The Portuguese guy has taken over her shop. Tells her how to run the business, insists on serving the customers, ordering the staff around...'

'Can't she stop him?' I asked.

'He won't take no for an answer. Difficult to forbid someone your shop when he's already in your bed. She'd have to change the locks or go to the police. She doesn't want to do that, she says. She's decided she's in love with him and that's that. She'd rather not have him as a business partner, that's all.'

'Difficult.' I wasn't sure how I could include my guests in the conversation. Or if I should.

'You know he has a prison record?' Dominique continued, still completely ignoring my friends.

'Luisa did say something of the sort, yes. Though I don't know...'

'For forging cheques,' Dominique said.

'*Mon dieu!* Does Françoise know?' I felt this keenly. I'd decided weeks ago not to tell Françoise what Luisa had said about her cousin. Maybe I'd called it wrong.

'People have tried to tell her. She doesn't listen.'

I felt slightly better. I had to introduce Dominique now if he was going to stay. Helen and James were looking bewildered. Helen had been trying gamely to follow the story, James losing the battle with the language. I attempted a brief résumé in English.

'A typical Parisian set-up?' James asked.

'They're not Parisians,' I said, as if in mitigation. 'Françoise was born here but her parents were provincials. And the Portuguese, of course, is Portuguese. To tell the truth, I haven't met a real Parisian yet. Unless Dominique...?' I turned to him. 'Where are you from originally, Dominique?'

'Look at me,' he answered. His eyes and complexion clearly said south. 'My father came from the department of the Lot. Your friends?'

'From Britain,' I said. 'Helen's a part of my past. We were at university together. James is her husband.'

'Ah, the past,' said Dominique, seizing on the word that interested him most, like a philosopher who has heard a much misunderstood concept dropped into a casual conversation. 'The past is life's capital investment. Invested well it will pay a good dividend. The dividend is your future.'

I translated.

'I see,' said James, frowning a bit. 'Er ... Should we offer him a glass of wine?'

'If you look at the bottle,' said his wife, 'you'll see from the level that your offer's been accepted in advance.' She addressed Dominique, bravely attempting French. 'What do you mean about investing the past wisely? Money can be moved from one place to another in order to ... er...'

318

'Attract a better return,' I helped out.

'But the past is immutable, surely. I don't see what you can 'do' with it.'

'I think it can be changed,' answered Dominique, 'though it's only my opinion. And you can do almost anything with it in your head.'

After a moment's thought we discovered we could all agree with the last point at least.

Helen reverted to English for her next question – which I then translated for Dominique. 'When you 'change the past' as you say you do, is it a once for all affair or something that offers multiple chances? I mean chances in careers, with relationships, chances to be happy. If this opportunity you speak of was a cherry, in other words, dangling in front of you, would you be allowed only one attempt to bite it from the stalk or could you try again?'

I put the all too graphic image into French with some apprehension. I was sure Dominique would choke on his wine.

He did not. 'It's like this,' he said. 'Imagine the sky at night. How many stars do you see? A million? A hundred million? No, an infinite number, small and large, bright and veiled, near and far. And can you have them all? Do you suppose that each single one was put there just for you? No, of course not. But suppose on the other hand that only one is there for you. Only one in all infinity. That must be nonsense too. Life couldn't be so ungenerous as to offer only one chance. That's what I think And, for me especially, I hope.'

'Why for you in particular?' Helen asked.

'I tried to kill the woman I loved,' he said simply. 'Luckily she's still alive.' He looked down as he said this and I braced myself for another emotional scene. But then Dominique's eyes lit on the wine bottle which was nearly empty, a discovery that shocked him into action: he went at once to the bar to negotiate for a replacement.

'Did he really try to kill his woman?' James asked in fascinated horror.

'Up to a point,' I said. 'Up to a point.'

Just then someone else came in and looked around a little uncertainly. With a start I found myself greeting Fabrice, who smiled when he saw me and came over. He was wearing a blue denim jacket of the same type that I was wearing this evening, or had been before I'd hooked it over the back of my restaurant chair. 'I hardly recognized you,' I said. 'This bohemian outfit.' I fingered Fabrice's jacket and gestured towards his jeans.

Fabrice looked at the table and at my guests. Might he… ?

Might he not. I introduced him, invited him to sit down, and he joined us just as Dominique, with immaculate timing, returned with a new bottle of wine. I couldn't believe Fabrice's three weeks in Strasbourg were up so soon. I'd deliberately not allowed myself to count the days. But where was Régine?

If it wasn't one thing it was another, Fabrice explained. He took his jacket off, as if in imitation of my shirt-sleeved state. No sooner had they got back, he said, than she'd been called away by her own TV company bosses. They were making a series of programmes over the border in Italy; there was some financial stuff to negotiate and she'd been needed there too. She sent her love and was sorry she hadn't had time to… I waved her apologies away. I was pleased to be able to show off the most presentable of my new friends to Helen. Better than letting her think I only socialised with the likes of Dominique. And, complications notwithstanding, it was more than just agreeable to see Fabrice again.

Soon it was late. I walked back with Helen and James to their hotel, agreed to meet Helen the following afternoon while James was at his conference, and said goodnight. Then I walked home. Buzzing the right code buttons got me through the outer doors, and the doors at the foot of my staircase were open as usual. But to get into my apartment I needed my key. I felt for it in the pocket of my jacket, which I was carrying over my shoulder. It wasn't there. I placed the jacket on the baluster head and ferreted through all the pockets. The situation quickly became clear, even before I'd confirmed it by fishing out an unfamiliar hanky and a wallet with Fabrice's name in it. Of Fabrice's keys there was no sign. I guessed he kept them in his trouser pocket or clipped to his belt, so he would have arrived home without missing them or – presumably – needing his wallet. Fabrice was all right for now, though he wouldn't be when he wanted money in the morning. I, on the other hand...

I returned to the Figeac. I got there just in time: in a few minutes the doors would be locked. René was stacking chairs on tables while the new waitress swept beneath them, and Madame Touret was busy tidying up in the kitchen. She was just calling to her son to ask if the till was done.

No, my jacket wasn't there. Did they remember if Fabrice had left wearing one? Carrying one? They couldn't swear to it, but they thought so. In any case, I'd have to go round to Fabrice's flat now to return his wallet. They wished me *bon courage*.

Unlike Dominique, I didn't carry all the door-codes of the *quartier* in my head, so I had to press Fabrice's bell and wait on the pavement for an answer. It took some time to come. For an anxious moment it went through my mind that, though Fabrice had said Régine was away, he hadn't actually said that he would be on his own. He might be ... well, I didn't want to think about that. Fabrice's private life was his own. Nothing to do with me. I was simply coming to return a jacket and, I hoped, get mine back.

Fabrice's voice came through crackle. *'C'est qui?'*

'C'est moi: Pierre.' Why I gave mys name in French I had no idea.

'Peter, you crazy boy.' Fabrice's laugh too came through the crackle. 'Come up.'

When I got to the stair-head, there was Fabrice, waiting for me, leaning over the banisters. He was wearing a towelling bathrobe. Blue. Like his eyes. Like mine.

'I think you've got my jacket,' I said as I made my way up the last flight 'This one's certainly yours.'

'You're kidding,' said Fabrice. We both walked into the apartment. Fabrice went at once to where he'd hung the garment he'd worn back from the Figeac. He looked at it briefly, dipped a hand into a pocket, said, 'Oh sorry,' as soon as his fingers encountered unfamiliar objects, and then almost handed it back to me. But he stopped in mid-movement and said, suddenly regressing, both in voice and in facial expression, to the gauche and timid teenager he might have been twelve years before, 'Would you like a night-cap?'

'Um, no, really. I only came about the jacket.' But something in my voice betrayed me. Fabrice put his jacket-encumbered arms around me, and I realised as I relaxed into that warm embrace and returned it with interest, that not only would I not be needing my door-keys tonight but that this was how I'd unconsciously been wanting this reunion evening to end for the last three weeks.

SEVENTEEN

Helen and I were on the terrace of Les Deux Magots, drinking two of the most expensive cups of coffee we'd ever tasted. In return we had the satisfaction of knowing that Sartre and his circle had passed their days in the same spot, though presumably drinking more cheaply. A notice on the wall forbade you to spin out your *consommation* for more than an hour without ordering a replacement. It would only be possible now to write post-cards here or to dash off a sonnet. To sit here and embark on any larger literary form would take the resources of a millionaire.

I stood up. 'Come on. Let's walk.' We were in the middle of a ramble round the Quartier Latin. We threaded through tiny streets little longer than their width towards the rue St. André des Arts, a huddle of old eccentric houses and deeply shaded doorways. Already, though it was only May, the street was thronged with tourists. I pointed down the rue Mazet to the place where Doctor Guillotin had honed his invention by experiments on sheep. Then we emerged onto the quai des Malaquais opposite the Louvre and, as a good guide must, I indicated the house where Voltaire had sharpened his barbed pen. Barges ploughed up and down the Seine in front of us. Across the river the Louvre's long southern wall extended in an endless repetition of identical pillars and windows. It looked like an illustration of the idea of infinity. The vista eventually lost itself in a green and white fur of trees: horse chestnuts at full candle-power in the Tuileries gardens.

Under those lovely trees, in the darkness of the night, two weeks ago, I'd sucked a stranger's cock.

'How beautiful Paris is,' said Helen.

'Yes,' I said, 'but sometimes I think it's only beautiful like dreams are beautiful.'

We turned our backs on the river and its monumental vistas and burrowed once more into the labyrinth of the Quartier Latin.

We came upon the place Furstenberg, a miniature square of brick and plane trees that opened out suddenly in our path. We sat down on a bench in its peaceful shade.

'It's good you're making friends here,' Helen said. 'I liked Dominique.' Then she shot me a very searching look. 'I especially liked Fabrice.'

I sometimes wondered if the things I didn't really know about myself were written on my forehead for everyone to read except me. I tried to shift the conversation – and my thoughts – away from Fabrice. I said, 'I have another friend I like lot. Name of Joe. American, male, sensitive, gay. He's recently got involved with a nineteen-year-old. He's decided – no, to be fair, they both have – that it's going to be the partnership of a lifetime. Of both their lifetimes.'

'Good for them,' said Helen staunchly. 'Will it work, do you think?'

I said, 'Perhaps. I've met the kid. He's good, and sensible. In fact he has a kind of precocious wisdom that's a bit unsettling when you first encounter it. In a strange way he might be able to keep Joe's feet on the ground, if anyone can. Yes, it might work out. Look there.'

I had to interrupt myself. We'd wandered up the rue Bonaparte and I pointed down a side street to a white-fronted house over whose doorway sprang a silver carved ram's head. 'That's the house where Oscar Wilde died,' I said. 'Hotel, I should say, because that's what it is and was even then. There was a problem with the bill. 'I'm dying as I've always lived,' he's supposed to have said. 'Beyond my means.' These days it's quite an expensive hotel and sought after because of the connection. The bill has been paid with interest, as it were. Funny.'

'I hope they take all the proper precautions,' Helen said.

'The hotel?'

'Your two friends. You know. Don't die of ignorance and so on.' Helen turned to look at me. I must have turned colour. I felt faint.'You OK?' she said.

I pulled myself together. 'Fine,' I said. 'Hey, look. Let's wander over to the Ile de St Louis. We can have an ice-cream at Berthillon's. Tell ourselves that summer's really here at last.'

Helen and James were going to the opera later and had invited me to go with them. I told Helen as I parted from her in their hotel doorway that I wouldn't be joining them and hoped they wouldn't mind. I'd join them for a drink before they left the following evening if that was all right.

I walked away. For a few moments I thought in desperation that I'd have to talk to Dominique. I'd say something like this. 'Look, I'm sorry to drop this on you, but you're the only person I know who ... I mean, perhaps you can advise me. A friend of mine who's bisexual is a little bit worried about, well, you know what. Because of something that happened to him recently. No, I don't know exactly what. He didn't tell me and I didn't ask. Well, I thought I could do him a favour, because, knowing you as I do, I thought you might know an address in Paris where I could ... I mean where he could... get some sort of a test, if you see what I mean...' Just running the speech in my head made me go hot and cold. Talking to Dominique was out of the question. And I certainly wasn't going to talk to Joe about this.

I made my way to the pavement outside the Little Horseshoe, ordered a beer and waited grimly for Fabrice to appear.

He did. He came sauntering down the street from the Métro in the evening sunshine and looking as if life were the most uncomplicated business imaginable. 'Hi,' he said. 'Thought I might find you here.'

I said, 'Well, I didn't. I was supposed to be going to the opera tonight, if you remember, with Helen and James.'

He ignored my chilly tone and joined me at the table. 'People do change their plans, you know.'

I said, 'Not only that. I thought it might be better – for both of us – if we didn't see quite so much of each other for a bit.'

Fabrice hauled in a breath. 'I see.'

'Only, since last night I've realised there's a question I should have asked you. Look...' I looked around us. 'Can we do this bit in English?'

'Oh all right, mister,' Fabrice obliged at once. 'It's that serious, then?'

'I need to know if you ... I mean, there's someone I know who ... no, this is stupid ... I mean, are you HIV positive? Or do you know, one way or the other?'

Fabrice smiled quickly, nervously, audibly. Then he looked serious again. 'OK. I understand. Because you found yourself last night on the ... er ... receiving end of something for the first time, you're now scared of receiving something else too. But you weren't too bothered about all that when you ... you know, in the Chaffinch Bedroom.' It seemed strange to hear Fabrice translating even the *chambre des pinsons* into English.

'Yes, but...'

'Yes, but I'm labelled bisexual in your mind, and so therefore a whore and I probably sleep with everyone I meet, whereas you're the big tough, straight guy who never...'

'Fabrice, fuck you. Just shut up and give me an answer. If I've upset you I'll apologise after.'

Our conversation was being followed with rapt, if covert, attention by everyone else on the *terrasse*, the more so for its being conducted in English at an increasingly intense pianissimo.

Fabrice consented to answer my question. 'I had a scare myself once, like you did. I went to Belleville after the agonising time lapse and had a test done. I was negative. Now you can either believe me that I'm still clear – just like I trusted you that first time – or I can give you the address and, after a suitable interval you can go along yourself.'

Was that the moment when the domino tower I'd been building all my life inside me finally collapsed? Well, no, not all of it. Not then. But a good big part of it did. I was falling, deep inside myself, into something huge and new and terrifying. I found I wanted to hug Fabrice then and shower his face with a storm of kisses, but since we were sitting on the pavement outside the Horseshoe, I just looked across the table at him with eyes that swam suddenly with tears.

'I think,' said Fabrice, still in English, but with a catch in his voice, 'that I should order us both a drink.'

I was heady with relief, stratospherically high, at what I saw as my second escape from a brush with death courtesy of Fabrice. I was high on other emotions too, but I hadn't had time to examine them yet. I accepted Fabrice's suggestion, a beer or two later, that we dine together at the Figeac and I put up no more than a token resistance at the end of the meal when Fabrice picked up the bill. After all, we both agreed, he was two years older, two inches taller, and worked for a merchant bank.

Nor did my conscience veto the way in which the evening ended.

And the way that evening ended was to serve as a model for the nights which followed.

Paris. May. 1987.

Sometimes we smoke Gitanes in bed. I never before smoked with anyone in bed. The colour of his skin is special. Somewhere between the living breathing pink of herring roe and the cool depth of honey vanilla ice-cream. His penis is the most beautiful one I've ever seen. It's an inch longer then mine is. We measured them for fun one night. It's straight, and tapers very slightly towards the tip. Like me, he's uncircumcised. Like mine, the tip of it is not so much blue as pink.

He's tall. I'm smaller. But we have other things in common. We both have a sexy gap between our top front teeth. We have blond hair and blue eyes, both of us. We both have black eyebrows, eyelashes, beards – his in the form of a moustache only – and black body hair, including pubes.

His balls are the colour of milky coffee into which strawberry juice has been stirred.

Joining him in bed at night is like climbing into a warm bath. His muscles are firm yet yielding. They yield to me, that is.

I've never felt the way I do with him in bed with anyone before. Fucking him, being fucked by him, sucking, cock-stroking... It's never been that good with anyone in my life.

To get out of bed in the morning is a real wrench. The wonderful night turns to morning surreally, with him helping to get my frost-numbed toes into my socks.

Régine would not be back until the weekend, and meanwhile I took the opportunity to spend as much time as possible with her boyfriend. We tried out restaurants where we were still strangers, because there were limits to what even our acquaintances in the Marais might be expected to turn a blind eye to, and Fabrice took me to other places I might not have found on my own.

We went to hear Olivier Messiaen playing the organ at the Gregorian Mass in La Trinité, the white church with its sugar-sifter of a belfry that stands at the end of the rue Chaussée d'Antin. The great man did not accompany the choir, a lesser mortal saw to that, but his improvisatory voluntaries punctuated the service: the organ roared and thundered like the might of God, pleaded in the voices of suppliant sinners, resolved into a final harmony of merciful reconciliation, while Messiaen, the channel down which these revelations flowed, remained unseen and anonymous in the loft at the back of the echoing church.

Fabrice introduced me to a late night music bar called the Petit Piano Zinc – *'C'est gai mais ce n'est pas le ghetto,'* Fabrice explained – where I found myself welcomed (the next words are Fabrice's, not mine) as 'a highly attractive newcomer.' And at the end of the evening, always, pleasantly just a little bit drunk, we would fall into Fabrice's – I tried not to think, Fabrice and Régine's – double bed.

I was hitting the sack, night after night, with the male partner of a woman friend who had taken me on trust as the straight guy and honest friend of my own estimation. It was impossible to make any sense of this breathtaking departure from precedent and I soon gave up trying. I dealt with the situation at a purely practical level, withdrawing strategically as the weekend approached, leaving Fabrice to deal with his own conscience vis a vis Régine. Presumably he also changed the sheets. I didn't want to know. I met Régine and Fabrice together once during that weekend, quite casually, over dinner at the big table in the Figeac and found myself behaving with exactly the same practised insouciance – that of the habitual deceiver – that Fabrice had demonstrated in similar circumstances for as long as I'd known him.

Then the weekend ended. Régine went back to work again in Italy, and I moved back in with Fabrice.

EIGHTEEN

Paris. June. 1987

The weather shifted gear from warm to hot. I bought a thermometer in Madame Almuslih's shop. She sold everything from olives to tin foil, from mouse-traps to figs. In Britain thermometers were marked in Fahrenheit as well as centigrade and I could register the centigrade figure mentally while feeling the temperature in Fahrenheit. That was something ingrained from childhood like manners and the language. (It's barely fifty, put a coat on. Or: What a scorcher, eighty-four in the shade.) In France I had to learn finally to feel in centigrade just as I had to think in French. (Trente degrés, parait-il! ... Tu rigoles. ... Faut croire!) I hung my new acquisition outside my window, an unravelled paper-clip serving as a hook to attach it to the louvred shutter, and day by day would mark the upward progress of its coloured liquid thread.

The working day finished in sunshine that still spoke of afternoon, not evening, and dusk was banished to bed-time – a time which had suddenly acquired a new intensity of meaning. Meanwhile the tentative street life of spring was giving way to the full-blooded version of summer. Doors and windows stood perpetually open while goods and salespeople seemed to cascade from the shops onto the pavement. The city was turning inside-out like a glove, its population permanently on show instead of behind shutters. Sitting outside the Horseshoe with Fabrice it was possible to wave to, even talk with,

331

Madame Touret if she happened to be taking the sun with customers outside the Figeac and, without moving, to relay news down to the café on the next corner if its importance warranted – though this responsibility more usually fell to Dominique than to me or Fabrice.

Swifts sliced the still air of the streets, manoeuvring like champion skaters, fast and black against the blue, their screams, the sound of old and ill-used brakes, making the sky shrill. Neighbours till now un-glimpsed appeared and disappeared at windows and on balconies all around like characters in an opera and, even if they did not sing, their conversations ricocheted just as energetically down the street, zigzagging from wall to wall. In more reflective moods they watered their plants – geraniums and bizzy-lizzies on every balcony in clusters of flame – and in watering them watered too the passers-by beneath, some of whom appreciated the cooling showers while some did not.

June was heralded by Margueritte d'Alabouvettes telephoning from Frankfurt. If I was short of French francs, she said, she would be equally happy with dollars or Deutschmarks. I said that francs would present no problem. My thermometer was nudging thirty-three.

That the gold-spangled cousin of my concierge Luisa was arrested and removed from the public eye came as a surprise to no-one although it made a good talking-point. Interpol had been seeking him since he had escaped from prison in Portugal while awaiting trial for armed robbery. The day after I heard about this I saw Françoise dining alone at the Figeac, dressed in sober blue. I joined her for I was alone too. It was the weekend again and Régine was back once more with Fabrice. 'I heard the news,' I said. 'I'm really very sorry.'

Françoise stared at me with wide eyes that looked accustomed to tears. 'It makes no difference to me,' she said. 'I still love him. I'll find a way to join him when I can.'

I asked boldly, 'Yes, but does he love you?'

'That,' she said with a chilling fatalism, 'has nothing to do with anything.'

I thought about this later. If that was love, and I was prepared to take Françoise's word for it since I could think of no other explanation for her behaviour, then that was not quite the same as my relationship with Fabrice. I liked Fabrice a lot, no doubt about it. He was a good friend, with nice looks and a lovely personality. I also enjoyed sex with him, very much. But I told myself that that was that.

I reminded myself that lots of men experienced a homosexual phase in their teens. I'd never gone through this stage of development. Was it unreasonable to suppose that life didn't have to happen to everybody in the same order? Surely it was conceivable that Fabrice and I were belatedly going through something quite usual: an exploration, a voyage of self-discovery that many other people undertook rather earlier in life. With any luck, I hoped., we would return to our port of embarkation, safe and sound, wiser but with no harm done to our heterosexual credentials, as soon as Régine returned from Italy in about two weeks' time.

In Madame Almuslih's shop one day Fabrice and I were surprised to find our normal greeting returned by silence from her habitually cheerful children and by a very choked *bonjour* from the lady herself. We didn't ask then and there what the problem was; we asked Madame Touret a little later.

'But hadn't you heard, Peter? She has to leave. To sell the business.'

We looked at each other. 'But why?' said Fabrice. 'It's flourishing. I know she and the kids work like dingoes for it but she must be making a small fortune.'

'She has a big bill to pay. You know, I suppose, that her husband is serving a term for homicide?'

'I knew he was in prison for something,' Fabrice said and I added carelessly, 'It seems every trader in the *quartier* is in prison for one reason or another.'

'There are exceptions,' said Madame Touret tartly, but she quickly relaxed, having the opportunity that every gossip relishes of telling an old story to people who missed it the first time round. 'Monsieur Almuslih was attacked one night by an armed man while he sat alone at the cash-desk. He used the bread-knife to defend himself and killed him stone dead. Poor man.'

It was not clear which of the two men Madame Touret sympathised with. We nodded our agreement anyway.

'As it happened, the gun was a plastic toy.'

'Perhaps Monsieur Almuslih would have got off more lightly if he had been a Monsieur Dupont,' Fabrice suggested. 'French instead of Moroccan.'

Madame Touret looked shocked. 'You are surely not suggesting that there's one law for the French and another for immigrants?'

Fabrice backed down. 'I just thought it was a possibility.'

'Anyway,' Madame Touret went on, 'Madame Almuslih is legally responsible for the court's award to the dead man's family plus the costs. Even more unfortunate is that there was an invalid son and providing for him has turned out very expensive.'

'So she has to sell up?' I said.

'That's right.'

'And instead of being able to pay her way she'll be a charge on the state?'

'*C'est ça.*'

'But it's totally crazy,' said Fabrice.

'That's the law, it appears.' Madame Touret then looked at me. 'Is it so very different in England?'

I wasn't sure but I thought probably not.

Jean-Jacques joined us. He already knew the story. 'Is there nothing we can do?' I asked him.

'What do you suggest?' said Jean-Jacques. 'Pass a hat round the restaurant for the money? I fear such sums might be beyond our modest resources. (A kir, please, *Madame ... merçi.*) And yet, and yet, maybe there is something we could try. The gnawing of a mouse may rock mountains. The voice of a child may tell the emperor that he has no clothes.' He turned to Fabrice. 'You have access to word-processing machines, I suppose? Computers? Things like that?'

Fabrice said, yes, he did.

'Good,' said Jean-Jacques. 'I can have the text ready tomorrow.'

'The text of what?' I asked. The poet took a sip from the ruby-coloured depths of his glass and explained to us what he had in mind.

We 'pillars' of the Figeac took it in turns over the next few days to sit at an outdoor table with the petition that Fabrice had had beautifully typed at work, accosting every half familiar face that passed: 'Do you shop over there? Read this. Now sign.' Everyone did.

'Go for the foreigners too, Peter,' the poet urged. 'The more international the list looks the better.' He had made me put my own name and address first. 'What's your surname? Ferguson? *Ah, bon.* Smith would have been better. Still, nobody's perfect. And something like O'Shaughnessy might have frightened them off. The bureaucrat is a shy, wild creature. He needs to be stalked with care.'

Jean-Jacques's eloquent text took the form of an open letter to the President of the Republic. In it he stressed France's traditional hospitality towards its non-native population and the practical and humane reasons that argued the tempering of the law with the spirit of clemency. Copies were sent to all government departments, to the Hôtel de Ville and, of course, to the newspapers.

'The discreet appearance of a brief list of press titles in the 'copies sent to' section does no harm in this type of letter. No harm at all. As you will see. You'll see the politicians jumping to it,' said Jean-Jacques.

I had my doubts but was ready to be impressed if the plan worked. Also, I couldn't help feeling a childish glow of pleasure at the thought of my signature arriving on the President's desk the following morning. True, it would be in the company of several hundred others, but, heading the list as it did, it would be the name of Peter Ferguson that caught the eye, even though – I realised – it would hardly be the eye of Tonton himself.

I found an answer-phone message from Joe. Antoine was in hospital. Could I meet Joe at six in the café near République, Le Kabylie, where I had first met Antoine?

'Goddam appendicitis,' said Joe when I arrived. 'It's so banal. Why couldn't he have something romantic like consumption like any halfway decent lover?'

'Or a hernia perhaps?' I said.

Joe looked at me. 'I'm not at all sure about this new tendency of yours to make jokes. I feel it could have unpredictable effects on our relationship. Anyway, appendicitis it was. We thought of food poisoning when he woke up in the middle of the night coughing up God knows what. And since we'd both eaten the same dinner –whose ingredients I no longer wish to remember – I guessed it was only a matter of time before it got me too.

But it didn't. In the end I called the *pompiers* – never call an ambulance, Peter, the fire brigade are vastly more efficient – and we were at the hospital in next to no time. Now everyone knows there's this spot you have to press to check for a burst appendix. Well, would you believe it took an hour to locate the only person on duty who could remember which spot it was? Anyway they admitted him and he was operated this morning. I stayed till he came to – that was a couple of hours ago – squeezed his hand and let him go back to sleep.'

'How was he?'

'Didn't have much of an idea what was going on. He was very concerned that his hair was uncombed. I left him my own comb on the bedside table. It'll give him something to do when he wakes in the night.'

I asked, 'How long are they keeping him in?'

'All being well, just tonight and tomorrow night. It's as straight-forward these days as pruning a rose bush. But it's when he's discharged that the problems start. I'm worried about how he'll be looked after when he first comes out.'

'Why not let him go to his parents?' I asked. 'Or to whichever one of them he gets on with.'

'His mother. That would be fine. Unfortunately his father's at home this week and he won't go there then. What a family, though. Catholic mother, Communist father, failed marriage but no divorce, no money to live separately, children taking sides et cetera, et cetera. Only good thing is, his father's a long distance truck driver and not often at home. Except this week.'

'Then maybe this is the moment for him to move in with you,' I said.

'You know,' Joe said. 'I think you may be absolutely right for once.' Then he changed the subject. 'How's the petition going? The one for whatshername – Mrs Muesli.'

'Almuslih. Too early to say. It's been sent off. Repercussions have yet to ... er ... repercuss.'

'Be careful,' Joe warned. 'Remember...'

'I know,' I said. The road to hell is paved with good Samaritans.' That was a phrase of Joe's, which he often used, and I rather liked. 'But don't worry. Nothing's going to go wrong. What could? Either it'll work – which is great – or it won't and things will stay as they were before we...'

'Started interfering?' Joe suggested.

The *patron* Momo joined us for a second. He slapped Joe on the shoulder. 'Look at him,' he said to me. 'See how happy he's become since he met his young friend. He's a new person. His eyes shine like black stars and his cheeks glow like two apples.'

'Merde,' said Joe, squirming, 'it's the sun does that, that's all.' Momo gave us a smile that could have launched a brand of toothpaste and moved off.

Looking back at me, Joe said, setting a new course without so much as a twist of his glass-stem, 'I don't see much of you these days. But your eyes are looking quite star-shiny too, if I may say so. Sure you're not having an affair of the heart yourself at long last – somewhere deep in the Marais?'

Now it was I who twisted my glass-stem, so violently that I nearly spilled the contents. 'Ha!' I said, then stopped, having no idea what I would say next. For inspiration I looked at Joe. 'Your glass is empty,' was what I came up with.

That was the beginning of a long evening with Joe. It was Friday night. Régine was back for the weekend, so I wouldn't have been spending time with Fabrice in any case. We had dinner in a restaurant Joe knew but which I didn't. We had some more drinks. We talked about pretty much everything... Except Fabrice. Then I walked home.

As I fiddled with the door-code buttons my fingers found a ragged piece of paper that had been wedged between the electric box of tricks and the wall. It had my name on it, hastily scribbled. Unfolded, it read: *Désolé que tu ne sois pas là. Il faut que nous parlions. Bisous. F.*

This was very out of character for Fabrice. Whatever he thought we needed to talk about, it was presumably something that couldn't be said over the phone or in front of Régine. Well, that last bit wasn't so very odd. Pretty well everything we said and did together these days was unfit for Régine's eyes and ears. But scrawled notes at midnight? There was nothing to do but wait, with considerable apprehension, because good news was never conveyed like this – until I had a chance to speak to Fabrice alone, which might not be till after the weekend.

NINETEEN

I went to the Figeac that Saturday evening just in case. Fabrice might well turn up, with or without Régine, and perhaps we'd be able to have the talk that Fabrice appeared to want so urgently.

Dominique was not standing at the bar of the Figeac when I arrived and neither was Fabrice or anyone else which was perhaps fortunate since – as René told me, standing in the kitchen doorway – the new waitress was late for work and his mother, who usually did not arrive till later, was not answering her phone. Not only that but some people would be arriving any minute to hang paintings in the little exhibition space downstairs. René looked to be under stress. I volunteered, for reasons that were not entirely altruistic, to serve behind the bar until the staffing situation should improve. René seemed relieved and disappeared back into the kitchen. It was then that I spotted Dominique at a table at the back of the restaurant in conclave with two other men. Clearly they wanted to be as inconspicuous as possible, since they had chosen the darkest corner of the place for their whispered conversation. On the other hand, the facts that the two strangers were dressed in full Foreign Legion uniform and that rolls of bank-notes were being furtively exchanged for small sealed packets assured them of the undivided attention of the small number of people already at the other tables. Everybody saw and everybody very deliberately didn't look. After a moment the legionnaires left and Dominique came up to the bar. If he was surprised to see me standing behind it he chose not to show it. I poured him a pastis.

A few minutes later the waitress appeared, breathless and apologetic. The traffic had been important, she said. That the English language described such traffic as heavy would have struck her as comical. Though both pleasant and attractive, the new waitress lacked those indefinable qualities that made her predecessor Marianne so special. But her arrival did at least allow me to return to the other side of the bar.

The phone rang in the kitchen. I heard René answer it. 'Oh there you are,' he said. 'Where were you an hour ago when I needed you? Clothilde has only just got here. The clients were having to serve themselves...' There then followed a remarkably long pause before he said, in a very different tone of voice, 'Yes. Yes, I'll tell him.' René appeared in the doorway. 'Dominique. Can you go to my mother's immediately? She's got someone there she wants you to meet. Apparently it's important.'

Dominique made a grimace at me and gave a resigned shrug. 'Sorry,' he said. *'A tout à l'heure.'* Then he turned and went out of the door. Not for the first time I received a strong signal that if Madame Touret said jump, you jumped.

And then Fabrice arrived – with Régine and Jeannette and Denis. They were all planning to dine and asked me to join them at the big table. It was not the moment for private chats, though Fabrice and I found ourselves exchanging what might have been meaningful glances had there been any way of communicating what the meaning was.

The main subject of discussion was the absentee from the big table that night: Françoise. She had disappeared. Her shop was shut; 'Closed until further notice' was on the door. At her apartment the concierge understood that she had gone to Portugal on holiday, had even seen her loading bags into a taxi bound for the airport. But inspection of the apartment had shown it to be almost denuded of personal effects; far more had gone than was consistent with a Mediterranean holiday. A number of possible scenarios were constructed around these bare facts over dinner and the discussion was only brought to an end by the re-entry into the Figeac's smoky atmosphere of Dominique.

But it was a new Dominique that appeared in our midst, blazing like a meteor. For an uncharitable moment I put the change down to an excess of pastis but this misapprehension was put paid to when he sat himself down in the chair from which Françoise could not have been more conspicuously absent and announced in a voice edged with hysteria, *'J'ai un boulot, un boulot, un boulot.'* Dominique had been offered a job.

Nobody had ever imagined he wanted one.

'It's with Launier, the wine-shop chain. I'm going to be the manager of one of their outlets. After a training course, that is, and a trial period.'

Blank looks of astonishment had to be hastily reworked into congratulatory smiles. But Denis blurted out the question that everyone else was thinking. 'Isn't that a bit like putting the fox in charge of the chickens?'

Dominique smiled broadly and made a lengthy pantomime out of lighting a cigarette before replying. 'I know what you mean, but you really won't have to worry. You see, I have a secret weapon. Only for the moment it's very, very secret. But in a few days' time you'll understand everything.'

'It was an old friend of Madame Touret,' Dominique continued. 'Visiting unexpectedly. He's in Human Resources at Launier. Madane Touret thought of me and so...' It all sounded too simple. I wondered if Dominique's old tendency to fantasise was getting another airing following his rapid ingestion earlier of pastis – plus who knew what besides. Dominique singled me out for his final remark on the subject. 'As we say in France, it isn't so much what you know as who you know.'

'We say something similar in Britain,' I said.

The people who were going to arrive and hang paintings had now started to do just that, and were weaving their way between tables with framed and mounted canvasses. None of these was very big, fortunately, since not only did they all have to be manoeuvred past the seated diners but carted down the small open-work spiral staircase that led to the oak-beamed basement exhibition-room and – among other facilities – the toilets. After a while I announced that I was going downstairs to have a look at the new paintings as they were hung. I didn't ask if anyone wanted to join me. If anyone did, they would.

The canvasses were certainly bright, there was no denying that. Great splodges of brilliance overlay earlier splatterings of the same in vividly contrasting tones. It was as if the bespattered ground beneath a pigeon roost had been rendered in Technicolor. But having taken on board the aggressive dynamic of the paintings, I found myself unable to come to any critical conclusion about them. Where modern art was concerned I was an ignoramus, and if I caught the eye of one or other of the people who were doing the hanging I was shamed into turning away again with a nodding pretence of sage and thoughtful appreciation. But that didn't have to last long. The pictures had nearly all been put up by the time I came downstairs and the hangers soon all departed.

Which was the cue for Fabrice, who must have carefully counted the people down the stairs and then counted them all up again, to descend the spiral stairway himself. I watched his corkscrew progress as he materialised bit by bit: familiar trainers; unmistakeable jeans-clad legs – rangy, comfortable, strong; generously cut white shirt. Then he crossed the floor to where I stood. He took both my hands in his own as soon as he reached me.

'Careful,' I whispered.

'I'm sorry,' Fabrice said, his voice also a whisper. 'I didn't get a chance to tell you before now. Italy's over. Régine's back for good.'

'It's not a huge surprise,' I said coolly. 'That was going to happen sometime soon anyway. We were hardly imagining a scenario in which she didn't.'

Fabrice let go of my hands. He looked a little hurt. 'You sound as though it doesn't bother you very much,' he said flatly.

'I don't mean that.' I grabbed his hands back and held them. 'It's just that I'm being realistic. I have been all along. It would have been stupid to pretend things were other than they were. It's been great. Special.' I looked up into Fabrice's eyes and saw this wasn't going down too well. 'Look, I'm sorry, I don't know what you want me to say. We'll still be … I mean, there may be other times…' I couldn't finish the thought, didn't want to hear myself say, '…when Régine isn't in the way.'

'Yeah, OK. But that's not all. I mean that's all I had to tell you when I called round last night. But now there's something else. The bank want me back in Strasbourg. This time for keeps.'

'I see,' I said. Then, *'Merde.'* I tried to tell myself that something simple and ordinary was coming to an end, some practical arrangement; that it was like having to part with a particularly helpful colleague at work who was going on to better things. Only it didn't feel like that at all.

'Yes,' said Fabrice. *'Merde.'*

'When… I mean, how soon?'

'Next month.'

'Then we've still got…' I didn't finish this either. We hadn't still got anything. In the silence Fabrice unhooked his hands from mine and placed their palms flat on my stomach, then, undoing the shirt buttons, ran them underneath the cloth and over my bare skin, exploring upward to my nipples, which were suddenly hard, then forced his fingers down behind my waistband into the familiar secret place inside my jeans.

'For Christ's sake,' I hissed at him. 'It's public. Someone'll come down. Régine...'

But the very public nature of this unanticipated intimacy excited me – an excitement that Fabrice's exploring fingers quickly discovered and then seized on, while I found my own fingers unable to resist fumbling at Fabrice's fly.

'I don't want...' Fabrice was whispering urgently at my ear. 'I can't bear to lose you now.'

'You can't have everything,' I said rather roughly, feeling that Fabrice was being even more selfish than I was. 'You've got a girlfriend.' I made the discovery at that moment that Fabrice had nothing under his jeans except himself, as ready for action, jumping up and wet-tongued, as a puppy invited for an outing.

'It's not the same. I sort of love Régine and we'll probably get married one day. But I don't have with her what I have with you.'

'You mean you can't make it with her?' I asked incredulously, hardly able to believe I was coming out with such prurient questions in this exposed place, where Régine's laughter and the conversation of her friends could be heard drifting down the open stairs ...while at the same time I was brazenly massaging her boyfriend's jutting cock.

'Not the mechanics: they're no problem. It's just the ... everything else.'

'Oh God, no.' Public place or no, the mechanics were working just fine right there and then for me. Perhaps it was for the best. It was after all the simplest way to bring this conversation to an end. I climaxed suddenly, hotly, causing Fabrice immediately to do the same, and then the sound of creaking boards alerted us both to someone coming down the stairs.

The feet and legs that first appeared were male, which was a bit of a mercy; they didn't belong to Régine. They belonged, it became apparent after one more heart-stopped second, to Denis. Fabrice and I were somehow zipped – *lightning closures* the French language aptly calls zip-fasteners, and thank God tonight for both our pairs of jeans being fitted with them, not buttons – but my white shirt still gaped incriminatingly.

Denis's mouth fell as wide open as my shirt and for a moment everyone stayed where they were, silent and rigid with surprise. Then Denis gave a sort of shrug, a nervous half smile and said, a little uncertainly, 'Well, we're all different, I suppose.' But it was what he said next that Fabrice and I would bless him for for the rest of our lives. 'Look, er … if you guys would like to use the wash-room first, I'll hold off out here and take a look at the paintings.'

TWENTY

Joe was initiating me into the game of Pétanque in the dust bath that served as a bowling green in front of the building that housed the national archives. I thought it was about time I did something a little more active now that, with the permanent return of Régine to Fabrice's bed, my exuberant two-month burst of sexual activity had so abruptly come to an end. Something more active, at any rate, than sitting at café tables alone and brooding over glasses of beer. I'd been a passable cricketer as a schoolboy but hadn't kept it up. I'd taken up no sport in adult life except jogging.

'The beauty of Pétanque,' explained Joe, 'is that not only is it sociable and relaxing but it's easy. *En plus*, you can be as lazy as you like and no-one shouts at you.'

'Nobody shouts at you jogging either,' I said.

'Okay, but it's pretty strenuous. Dangerous too. I heard of someone who lost an eye, jogging in the Parc Monceau.'

'Lost an eye?'

'Pigeon flew up in his face. It gets very crowded there at weekends. Neither he nor it could take evasive action and its beak...'

'All right,' I said.' You've converted me.'

'Well then. With this game a novice can play with and against the experts with no loss of enjoyment to anyone. You leave the classy shots to the old hands at first, or for ever if you want to, and go for the easy ones, like this.' He trundled a silvery ball across the uneven surface. It took a wavering path, throwing up a little cloud of white dust as it went, and finally came to rest about a foot from the *cochonnet*. Joe did not say whether its eventual position was the one he had intended for it or not. Nor did I ask. Some elderly men seated on benches in the sun nearby made non-committal grunting sounds. Now it was my throw. My ball touched the *cochonnet* with a just audible click. 'Not bad,' said Joe. 'You may go far.' His own next ball fared better than its predecessor but less well than mine. 'By the way,' he said, 'I made it up about the pigeon.'

'I'm glad,' I said.

'To go back to Launier,' said Joe, at the precise moment that I delivered my next ball, which went a metre wide, 'it's funny you should mention them.' I'd just told him the news, now three days old, of Dominique's job offer. 'Antoine and I were talking about them yesterday. We toyed with the idea of taking on one of their shop management schemes ourselves.'

That startled me a lot. 'Have you gone mad?' I said.

'No,' said Joe, taken aback. 'Why should you think that?'

'Can you see yourself, a professional man, cooped up in a tiny shop all day every day, stacking wine bottles? And not just for a month or two, for the experience – which I've done, by the way – but for a lifetime. And with Antoine. Wouldn't that spoil just everything? The banality of it. On top of each other day and night.'

'For a guy with writerly pretensions you do have a gift for disastrous metaphor. Unless it's something in your subconscious. I do know what you mean, though. Can I say, simply, that I've thought about it and I'm not worried?'

Old men on nearby benches nodded their heads in unconscious agreement. Without understanding the words they had picked up Joe's air of conviction.

'You're very sure of the strength of your relationship, aren't you?' I said.

Joe looked at me in astonishment. 'I don't get you. One week you're delighted for the pair of us. Urging Antoine to move into my flat. The next you're full of doubts about us. What's changed for you?' He looked at me narrowly. 'Something gone wrong in your own love life? The one I know nothing about?'

I couldn't say anything. I'd have cried if I'd tried to speak. I was conscious of Joe staring at me, peering deep into the emptiness of my silence. Then he said gently, 'Sorry if I've scored a bulls-eye. Didn't mean to pry.'

'I can't talk about it,' I said.

I threw my next ball idly in the air. By chance it landed, bomb-like, in the centre of the cluster of balls that vied for proximity to the *cochonnet*, scattering them in all directions. It took up its own station a snug half centimetre from the *cochonnet* itself and a metre from the nearest competition. 'Bravo!' shouted the old men. One even got to his feet and clapped.

'Je-sus!' said Joe. 'I never saw a beginner do that.'

At that moment a figure hailed us from the other side of the street. It was Antoine.

'What the hell are you doing here?' Joe asked him when he had crossed over to us, making a brave attempt to disguise the fact that he still walked with a slight limp. 'You're supposed to be still convalescing back at the apartment.'

'As it happens,' said Antoine airily, 'I've felt quite strong since lunchtime. I've spent the afternoon sun-bathing in the park.'

'Hope you didn't run into any pigeons,' I said.

I suggested that the three of us dine at the the Figeac. The others took that up. There was the removal of Antoine's stitches to be celebrated. The operation had been performed that morning.

'But be careful you don't eat too much,' Joe told him. 'You might burst.'

'*Arrête!*' protested Antoine with an involuntary shudder. 'You make my legs go all funny!'

As we arrived at the restaurant a television crew were loading their equipment into a van in the street outside.

We went in and found Jean-Jacques at the bar, improbably dressed, despite the broiling weather, in a three-piece woollen suit and a bow tie. 'What have we missed?' I asked.

'Things are beginning to happen,' said Jean-Jacques. 'Just beginning. They've filmed the shop, the interior as well as outside, and they interviewed Madame Almuslih. It went off very well. She was clear and articulate and sobbed at exactly the right moment when she spoke of her children. An actress could not have gauged it better. After that they interviewed Madame Touret and...' Modesty obliged him to hesitate.

'And you of course,' Joe put in helpfully. 'When will they show it?'

'Tomorrow at seven on the regional bulletin, just after the *météo*, all being well. If there's a riot or a plane crash they'll show it the day after.'

'Excellent,' I said.

'That's not all. *Le Monde* and *Libération* had reporters here this morning and *Le Parisien* arrived after lunch with a photographer. *Le Figaro* may come tomorrow.'

'Congratulations,' said Joe. 'You obviously knew what you were doing.'

'Would someone please explain what this is all about?' Antoine asked, not unreasonably since this was his first visit to the Figeac and he had expected a steak, not a press conference. In addition, he had been the centre of everyone's attention for the past six days and it was rather a shock to his convalescent system to be reminded that this state would not last for ever.

We put Antoine in the picture as we made our way to the big table. No-one else sat there yet. Joe asked casually, 'Your friend Fabrice likely to join us?'

Although it shouldn't have done, that gave me a jolt. I answered too quickly, without thought. 'No. Actually Régine's back now.'

Joe stared at me. I saw in his eyes a chain of connections being forged among his thoughts. He hadn't guessed about Fabrice and me before that moment. But now, I could see, he had.

Just then a most unlikely thing happened. Jean-Jacques asked if he might join us. I'm ashamed to say I felt relief at that. Joe might or might not have been tempted to pursue enquiries about Fabrice and me in front of Antoine, but he wasn't going to do so in the company of Jean-Jacques.

But also I was astonished at Jean-Jacques' request. I'd never seen so much as a crumb pass his lips before now, but as the convivial meal got under way I watched a plate of charcuterie disappear between the poet's bearded jaws, followed by a *magret de canard au poivre*, with the kind of fascination I usually reserved for watching a fire eater or sword swallower. I wondered if I'd ever feel quite the same about French poetry again.

Joe asked him casually where Dominique was.

'He'll be in later, I expect,' said Jean-Jacques, 'with Marianne.'

In the firmament of Paris's eternal feminine Marianne shone brightly where I was concerned. I missed her presence at the Figeac all the more in the aftermath of my severance from Fabrice and it had occurred to me that it would not be impossible to track her down. It was time I returned to more mainstream pursuits after my uncharacteristic – I didn't even think the word *homosexual* – dalliance with a male friend. I thought perhaps a new relationship, of whatever sort, with a woman might do my self-image some good. It might not have been appropriate to ask Dominique about Marianne but I'd thought I might try Madame Touret. I just hadn't got round to it yet.

Now it was a shock to hear she'd be arriving any minute in the company of Dominique, Only Antoine, who was sitting directly opposite me, picked up on my discomfiture. 'Who is Marianne?' he asked Jean-Jacques.

'Dominique's fiancée,' he said. 'They got engaged two days ago.' He turned to me. 'Did you not know that?'

Paris. Mid-summer. 1987

I walked down to the quai du Louvre. It was night. The lamps glittered through the trees and their gold reflections quavered in the dark water of the Seine as it rippled past. I stopped at the place I'd stopped at last time and lit a cigarette. Nobody came out from the shadows under the trees. After a while I dived deep into the shadows myself. When my eyes got used to the darkness I found I was almost on top of two men who were standing facing each other, their trousers down to their knees, each pulling on the other's jutting cock.

I started to back away, concerned for their privacy, but apparently I didn't need to do that. One of the guys turned his head towards me and with his free hand beckoned me to join them. I moved towards them, unzipping, springing my trapped hard cock, and pulling my jeans down a little way as I took the three or four steps that brought me within their arms' reach. We formed a sort of triangle with our forearms, each one of us jerking another one's cock. We carried on masturbating together, the three of us, for about a minute.

Then one of the guys gasped urgently, 'Je jouis,' and proceeded to erupt immediately, covering my hand with his hot milk. I went on tugging him until he had completely finished. He let me know when that point was reached by saying, 'OK. Ça suffit.'

The other one then said to me, 'You want to fuck?'

'Me you, or you me?' I said.

He said, 'You do me.' He reached down awkwardly into a pocket, currently at knee height. He handed me a condom. 'Put that on,' he said. I did.

He took a couple of hobbling paces away from me. Just far enough to prop himself against the nearest chestnut trunk. I hobbled after him, and so did the other guy – the one who'd just shot his bolt. He hadn't pulled his jeans back up either.

The guy who'd invited me to fuck him now had his chest against the tree-trunk. I prised apart the cheeks of his arse with my hands. Fabrice and I had never done it standing up. This guy was taller than I was. I could only get inside him with the tip of my dick. I had to ask him to bend his knees a bit. He did that, and then I got all the way inside him and started to fuck. Meanwhile the third guy got his hand between my guy and the tree trunk and went back to work on his cock.

I came after a matter of seconds. The novelty of the situation had got the better of me. I pulled out, and he, the guy I'd just been inside, twisted back around so I could see him coming when the third guy's hand brought him to his climax a few seconds after that. Then I pulled my jeans up over my still hard and condom-clad dick. The jeans would have to go in the wash.

I touched the other two lightly on the shoulders, one hand each. All three of us said a quiet, 'Bonne nuit.' Then I left them. Their trousers were still down. I had the impression they were considering another wank.

Walking along the path beside the river I found a litter bin. I got right up to it and pulled my now flaccid cock out, right over the bin. I pulled the condom off and dropped it into it.

That night the cushion of hot air that had been threatening to smother Paris for days was ripped open by shears of lightning and its substance scattered on the wind. Night had succeeded sweltering night and by now all Paris was sleeping with its windows wide open if it slept at all. It was nearly three in the morning when the wind got up that set all those windows banging, chimneys shrieking, and flower pots crashing from balconies. The opera-set sprang into life as dressing-gowned figures appeared, back-lit, all across the city, fastening shutters and reining in geraniums. Ten minutes later the sky was on fire with lightning and the air cannoning with thunder. When at last the rain fell it seemed as though an airborne ocean had been shot down over Paris. Its last remnants were still draining down when I went out in the morning. Grey clouds still blew across the drenched city like smoke over the scene of a finished battle. The Métro was out of action due to flooding and the buses were impossibly full, and le tout Paris went to work on foot.

The official celebration of Dominique's engagement to Marianne took place the following week. Dominique had invited all Paris with the exception, he said, of the Parisians. By that time the city had recovered from its soaking: water-filled awnings over shops had been emptied out by prodding with brooms, café tables had dried off in the returning sunshine and my thermometer was climbing past thirty once again in the late afternoons. Madame Almuslih's photograph had appeared in the papers and, because there had been neither riot nor plane crash, an audience of millions had witnessed her tears in between a promise of continuing fine weather and a report on the plague of aphids which were munching their way through the exotics in the gardens of Versailles.

The Figeac was transformed for the evening. Most of the chairs had been removed and stacked in the exhibition room at the foot of the spiral stairs. The tables were reincarnated, thanks to immaculate white cloths a big as sails, as a seamless buffet that lined the walls. I'd lived in France just long enough not to be surprised by the scale and variety of the refreshments but I was impressed all the same. There were salads of artichoke hearts and endive, lettuce and walnut, tomatoes and fresh basil that scented the room. In small bowls were quails' eggs to be eaten with the fingers, and sticks of carrot and celery to be dipped in garlic mayonnaise. There were cold poached salmon trout and boiled langoustines that rattled when you picked them up. For the moment that was all. Hot roasts of meat and poultry would materialise later when there was room. Room on the tables, I wondered, or room in the guests? There was champagne – rows of bottles in a trough of iced water – and crates of red wine from Cahors, courtesy of Madame Touret's family connections in the region.

'Who in the world is paying for it all?' I asked Jean-Jacques. 'Surely even the cannabis connection doesn't provide Dominique with the means for all this?'

'Madame Touret pays. At least, the business does.'

'But why? It's not as if he was family, after all.' Even as I said this I guessed that I was being stupidly naïf. I was still a foreigner and a newcomer after all. No doubt a dozen veils of nuance still came between me and any real contact with French life.

Jean-Jacques looked pained, like an adult who has to spell out for a child something that usually does not have to be mentioned. 'Strictly speaking that's true. Both Dominique's parents are dead. His surname is the same as his mother's, if you get me, but his father was Madame Touret's brother. His own widow and their children will have nothing to do with Dominique, and Madame Touret is, by default, his nearest living blood relation. Now, if I may say this to you, Peter, this is one of those things that everybody knows without having to remember all the time. Do you understand?'

'Of course. That explains...' It explained so much that I decided at once not to bore Jean-Jacques by listing it all. 'But such a lavish buffet...' I headed off hurriedly on a different tack. 'How will they cap this at the wedding?'

'That's the French way. The wedding is for Marianne's parents to lose sleep over, not for Madame Touret and certainly not for us. Madame Touret can breathe a big sigh of relief after tonight. Her opinion is that Dominique will be as safe in harness with Marianne as he could be with anyone. In other words, she's very pleased at the results of her efforts.'

This shed even more light on the power and influence of Madame Touret. She had probably even employed Marianne in the first instance with the present moment in mind. I was doubly glad I hadn't asked her for news of Marianne a week ago.

'Now, *à propos*, let me show you this.' Jean-Jacques fished a letter from his pocket. It was from the Ministry of Justice and not *à propos* at all. It concerned the Almuslihs. I read it, picking my way through the florid formulae with some difficulty, but I discerned at last a promise to re-examine the husband's dossier and to investigate all possible ways to limit the financial liability of the wife. 'So far, so good,' said Jean-Jacques. 'A little force exerted by the media can work wonders with the people who control our lives. The press is not so called for nothing. Now the room is filling up. You'd better go and get something to eat and drink before it all goes.' The name of the letter's signatory had struck me as familiar. F. Guyot. Guyot ... of course: Margueritte d'Alabouvettes' son in law, the man from the ministry.

Of the people I hadn't yet met, I was able to guess which ones were guests of Dominique's and which were Marianne's by their different dress styles: Marianne's tending to a bourgeois smartness, Dominique's displaying a more raffish brand of chic. Among those I did know, sartorial style was equally varied. Joe had come in jeans and trainers, Antoine in a suit. Fabrice and Régine seemed dressed for a society wedding while Denis and Jeannette appeared to have dressed down for the occasion on purpose. I found himself wishing for Françoise, simply to see what her dress sense would have made of the evening.

In her absence there was at least some news of her; it arrived via Jeannette. '*Grandes tractations*,' she said. 'A big carry-on. Half the stock has gone from the shop, and none of it paid for. Her suppliers are doing their pieces. So's her landlord. She was four months behind with the rent, it seems.'

'And any news from herself?' I asked.

'A postcard from Portugal. No address, of course. She says she knows she's done the right thing and intends to stay there for ever. She sounds as though she's gone crazy.'

'I see,' I said. Actually I saw a beautifully sane logic at the root of the whole thing. Françoise had wanted the sunshine first and foremost and then a man as a means to that end. She had quite deliberately pursued the wish and now she had it. The fact that the man in the case was now in prison was quite possibly not a disadvantage at all. No, I could not consider Françoise crazy.

Madame Touret asked me if I felt at home yet in the *quartier*. 'We all feel you are part of the place now,' she said, and the conventional formula touched me somehow: reassuring me after my recent discovery that I'd failed to pick up on the relationship between her and Dominique. But it was a small consolation prize for the unexpected feeling of emptiness I was experiencing following my banishment from Fabrice's bed.

'Thank you,' I said. I tried to feel positive. It was true that I'd found a social circle in which I felt comfortable. I'd made a number of friends. I'd made progress with the language to the extent that I could express everything I wanted to say clearly if not always beautifully. No-one would yet take me for a Frenchman once I opened my mouth, but then no-one ever would. I was still unsure whether the word for street-lamp was masculine or feminine but as time passed it seemed to matter less and less. I mentioned this to Madame Touret.

'Réverbère est masculin,' she said, in a tone as puzzled as if she'd been asked whether water was dry or wet.

The buffet tables were now reloaded, this time with baskets of potatoes, jacket-baked and wrapped in foil, fragrant garlic bread, leafy salads and roast joints of beef, ducks and guinea fowl. Marianne arrived with two glasses of red wine. 'Can you tell the difference?' she asked. 'One's Bergerac, the other's Cahors.'

I sniffed at both, took a sip from one, made a few faces such as I'd seen professional tasters do, and swallowed. 'Cahors,' I pronounced. 'Cahors always tastes of damsons.' I repeated the process with the second glass. 'Oh,' I said, a bit deflated. 'They both taste of damsons.'

'Cheer up,' Marianne said. 'They're both Cahors. You're the only person so far who's realised. I'm getting in practice for the training course. It starts in September. Then there's a six-month trial period in a Launier branch in boulevard Haussman. After that, well, it could be anywhere in Paris, depending on which *quartier* vacancies arise in.' She moved off to undermine the wine-tasting confidence of someone else.

Antoine appeared at my elbow. I offered him the two glasses of red wine to try. 'Which one's the Cahors?'

He gulped at both glasses of wine without ceremony and swallowed. 'They're both Cahors,' he said simply.

Joe arrived. 'There's going to be a strike tomorrow,' he said.

'Who says?' I asked.

Joe raised his eyebrows a bit camply. 'Your friend Fabrice told me. It's gonna be the Métro, the buses and the suburban trains. The whole works.'

'It's nothing to worry about,' said Antoine. 'They're always doing it. It never amounts to more than a *grève de zèle*.'

'What's that?' I asked.

Joe answered. 'A partial strike. A go slow, if you like. But Antoine's wrong. This time it looks like they're going to go the whole hog.' Now it was Antoine's turn to ask for a translation.

Jean-Jacques brushed past us. 'I'm going to look for a kir. This champagne is playing havoc with my liver,' we heard him mutter as he passed.

'Why is his liver so different from everyone else's,' Antoine wondered out loud when the poet was out of earshot, 'that a few glasses of champagne affect it but an ocean of kir does not?'

'Because,' I said, 'he sold his liver to the devil in return for his talent and now it operates differently as a result.' I was delighted at having just for once left Antoine lost for a reply.

Fabrice came up and caught me by the arm. We'd exchanged little more than a couple of sentences all evening. 'Come on,' he said. 'Let's go and see the paintings downstairs.'

'We saw them last week,' I said.

He smiled and his eyes twinkled. He said in English, 'Don't be a dick.'

We trod down the spiral stairs, Fabrice first, me following. At the bottom Fabrice turned to me and said, 'Antoine's cute.'

I said, 'You're going to have to make your mind up one of these days, you know.'

For a moment Fabrice looked older than his thirty years. He said, 'That's a luxury I just don't have. Whereas you...'

'How do you mean, *whereas me*?' I said.

'You're freer than a bird, Peter. You don't have anyone else's expectations to consider. But being gay or otherwise is not a lifestyle choice that I can make.'

I leant back against the wall, my shoulder nudging one furiously scarlet painting just a bit askew. I said, 'Look, I just don't get this. I get Joe telling me endlessly that being gay is not a lifestyle choice: you either are or aren't, or so he says. Now here you come and tell me the exact opposite. I wish you'd all make up your bloody minds.'

'It isn't a contradiction,' Fabrice said. He was struggling with his thoughts a bit. He'd had quite a lot to

360

drink. 'Joe's talking about who you are, I think, and I'm on about what you're actually allowed to do. Whatever I am – whatever that is – and I'm less sure about what that is now that I've met you than I was before (because, by the way, knowing you has made me question everything about myself, but we'll leave that for the moment) – where was I? – lifestyle, yeah. You see, I can only go one way. I come from a *bonne famille*, you see, and Régine from another. You hate all that idea, I know you do, and I do care what you think, Peter...' He reached out a hand and tentatively touched my shirt-front. 'I care more about you than I've ever had the guts to let you see.' He shrugged. 'Born with a silver spoon, if you like, so that makes me lucky. But still, that's what's expected of me in that situation: marry Régine and be a family man; carry on the line; that's how it goes.'

Fabrice looked so unhappy, almost distraught, during this speech, that I felt really sorry for him, almost experienced his pain. Yet in a way I felt gratified too. I'd clearly made a difference to Fabrice. I was partly the cause of the feelings that were tearing him apart. I might be just about to disappear into Fabrice's past, but I was evidently not going to go unremembered, without leaving a mark. Fabrice had been close to saying something just now, I realised, that would have shaken still further the foundations of both our worlds. I was glad it hadn't come to that. I didn't think I could have coped if Fabrice's ramblings had reached their probable destination of – in either French or English – *I love you.*

'Or else you have to lead a double life,' I heard myself say. I wasn't sure if I meant that Fabrice already did lead a double life, or that I was now leading a double life myself. I decided to put my uncertainty down to the fact that I too was getting slightly drunk.

'I think I mustn't do that,' I heard Fabrice say. 'I think I've got to try and give all I've got, all that I am, to Régine. To try at any rate. Hope for the best.'

This is good-bye, then, I thought; this is that moment, suddenly now. And that was the moment when the domino tower inside me – the domino tower that was me – finally collapsed. I wanted to cry. I wanted Fabrice to take me in his arms and hold me, protect me from the world and from myself, for ever.

'We move out of Paris at the end of next week,' Fabrice said flatly. 'There'll be a few drinks in here before we go.' He brushed at my close-cropped beard with the back of his fingers. I stood still for a moment and let myself be caressed, then I leaned in slowly towards Fabrice and kissed him on the lips, then, in my own time leaned back out again. That kiss marked the end of our affair.

We made an intensely silent circuit of the exhibition that was mounted on the walls around us. It occurred to me that there was a connection between the violent brightness of the canvasses that seemed so articulate of something un-guessable and hidden, and the turmoil that was going on inside the pair of us viewing them. A turmoil that could not be articulated in any other way.

The party lasted till the early hours even if the champagne did not. When the food was finished, guitars and an accordion were produced from nowhere and there was dancing, though only a little as the space was too small to take more than a couple of couples at a time. I danced once, a little unsteadily, with Madame Touret and once with Marianne and considered that I'd done my duty. At one point Joe and Antoine danced together quite unselfconsciously and without apparently shocking anyone. Fabrice made a move to invite me to follow suit with him, but I shook my head. Even though Denis had discovered our secret and Joe had deduced it I had no intention of announcing it so brazenly to Régine and everybody else. Especially as the affair was now ended.

Dominique made a speech which no-one, least of all he, would remember in the morning and then it was suddenly time to go. Numbers thinned quickly and soon I found myself, one of the last to leave, outside in the cool air of early morning.

I headed down to the river bank.

TWENTY-TWO

For the second time in ten days most of Paris had to walk to work. The first time it had been because the Métro was flooded following the storm, this second time it was the strike. I didn't have to join the marching hordes. I was a writer. My mission was, as Hemingway so memorably put it, to stay home and write.

But I wanted – needed – to be out and about. Fabrice would be gone from my life in a few more days. I was having difficulty coping with that idea. I thought it might be marginally easier to deal with it in the wide open boulevards of the city than in the confines of my small apartment.

Following the quays from the Hôtel de Ville to the Pont des Arts I crossed the river towards the elegant façade of the Institut de France. Later in the day the bridge would be hung with pictures and jammed with the people who painted, bought and sold them. But at this hour there was nothing to be seen save the original views.

To the left the Ile de la Cité lay in midstream like a giant battleship at anchor, its superstructure the brick frontages of the place Dauphine and its big guns the spires of the Conciergerie, of the Sainte Chapelle and of Notre Dame. The image was only marginally unsettled by the soft green willows that sprouted from its sharp bows. To the right the river ran past the Louvre's austere façade where pillar and window repeated like recurring decimals until halted by the elevation of the Grand Palais. Then there were the chestnut trees, a sunny froth of green along the river bank by day. In whose shadowy caverns I had casual sex with men at night.

I headed away from the river, going south. Along the straight rue de Seine and its continuation, the rue de Tournon. At last I came to the Luxembourg Garden. And in there, beneath the trees, I did what Hemingway instructed. Stayed and wrote. Trying to make the activity, the busy-ness of work, along with the summer sunshine, heal the hurt in my heart. It didn't, of course.

In the evening I walked back. I was not sorry to be stopped a little way short of my destination by an arm waving from the terrace of the Little Horseshoe. Not long ago the arm would have belonged automatically to Fabrice, but those days were past. This evening it belonged, unexpectedly, to Jean-Jacques. I'd never seen it waved before. But until the previous week I hadn't seen Jean-Jacques eat a meal or wear a suit either. Clearly his involvement with the Almuslih petition was having its effects; and when I joined the poet at his table I learnt of yet another.

He leaned across towards me. 'My old publisher was planning a reissue of some of the writings inspired by the protests of sixty-eight. It'll be the twentieth anniversary next year. He hadn't thought of me in that connection. But then he saw me on the television the other night.' Jean-Jacques paused and his face seemed almost to crack into a smile. 'This morning I had a phone-call. Have a beer.'

The streets were thick with cars making their slow way out to the périphérique and the suburbs beyond. Not everyone lived within walking distance of their work. By seven o'clock the Marais, and presumably the whole of Paris too, was gridlocked. The sounding of horns rose to a fortissimo bombardment but then died away again as one after another the drivers left their cars. All had the same idea: to telephone their wives, husbands, relatives or friends to say they would be late – and to do it now. Mobiles were still a rarity and an unrealistic queue formed in the doorway of the Horseshoe for the café's single payphone.

Jean-Jacques beckoned to the barman. 'Why don't you take drinks orders from the phone queue? You have a captive clientèle, all irritable and thirsty. There's money to be made, don't you think? I give you this suggestion for nothing.' The idea was taken up, developed, borrowed by the other cafés in the street and by seven-thirty the street was busy with pencil-thin, penguin-dressed waiters and their aproned bosses with their different figures, less pencil than brandy glass. They were zigzagging among the stationary traffic as if the cars were so many closely packed tables. Trays of glasses were balanced on their upturned palms as they uncapped bottles, took money, poured glasses of cool white wine, dispensed mint tea, shandies and mineral waters. A traffic jam was transformed into a street party.

'*C'est pas pour rien qu'on dit un bouchon,*' said Jean-Jacques. It's not called a bottle-neck for nothing.

Not until eight fifteen was the traffic on the move again. Drivers returned their empties to the cafés or at least to the nearest piece of pavement before driving away – a little regretfully, I thought. 'Not Parisians,' said Jean-Jacques. '*Banlieusards.*' The word, and especially the scornful way in which he said it made the suburbanites sound positively reptilian. 'Parisians would never return their glasses like that.'

'By the way, congratulations,' I said.

'What?'

I reminded him. 'Your poetry reissue.'

'Thank you,' he said. 'You know, I was just thinking it might be time to put together a new volume.'

'Strike while the iron's hot, you mean?'

'Such is the nature,' Jean-Jacques interrupted himself to take a small mouthful of kir, 'of what we poets call the market.'

On the news, a little later, it was announced that, the strike having been a pronounced success, no repetition was planned for the morrow.

I did see Fabrice again over the next few days. Sometimes at the Figeac. Always with Régine. We didn't have a proper chance to speak. We confined ourselves to pleasantries about the weather. Having to do that hurt. Yet had we had a chance to be alone together, what would we have said? Fabrice had already laid it out on the table for me. He had to do what his family and Régine's required of him. In a way I had to respect him for that. It was no consolation to me, though, that he looked as distressed and unhappy as I felt.

Fabrice and I had been friends who'd enjoyed a bit of a fling together. We'd had sex. That had surprised me. It still did. I still identified myself as straight. Another issue was that I hadn't thought of myself as emotionally involved with Fabrice. I'd been a bit slow on the uptake there, though. Now I was about to lose him I found to my astonishment that I was hurting more horribly than I'd ever hurt before. More painfully than I'd even guessed I could be hurt. I had trouble understanding how this had come about.

Fabrice and Régine's leaving do was a bit low-key. Well, it could hardly have competed with the engagement party of Marianne and Dominique. Those two were there of course. And Jean-Jacques. Jeannette and Denis. Joe and Antoine. Myself. There were drinks at the Little Horseshoe, followed by a steak dinner at the Figeac. At one point during the evening Joe looked at me very directly and said, 'Are you all right?' I nodded my head and said brightly that I was. Then Joe gave me that look that people give you when they know you've just lied to them but are not going to be unkind enough to call your bluff.

We parted with kisses at the end of the evening. All of us. I kissed Fabrice on both cheeks. And felt I was being Judas to myself.

I also kissed Joe and Antoine goodnight. A few minutes later that was. Outside the street door of my apartment block. It lay on their route back to theirs. 'If ever you want to talk, you know...' Joe said. 'I mean, about anything at all... Well, you know I'm here for you.'

I said, 'Thank you for that.' Then I tapped out the entry code and went inside for the night.

The yellow window opposite cast its light into the sky with its usual abandon. Whoever lived there had the casements open wide but the occupant remained invisible. Not for the first time I was tempted to call across the street to see who would actually appear but of course I did not. Shyness and a fear of being ridiculous got the better of curiosity.

But this situation quickly altered once I was asleep, when dreaming seized the reins from consciousness. For then the inhabitant of the room did appear at the window, though only in silhouette. It was impossible to scrutinise the face or even guess to which sex the head belonged. I knew only that I wished to be in that room rather than in my own, and soon I found myself climbing a broad, carpeted staircase, hauling at polished mahogany banisters, flight after flight.

The staircase narrowed, was un-carpeted and dusty; it gave way to a vertical ladder clamped to a bare brick wall. At last, though I didn't know how I got there, I stood outside the door which would lead into the lighted room. I opened the door.

But dreams notoriously fail to deliver the expected goods. The room was full of ice. Full from floor to ceiling, from door to window, from wall to wall. Of any occupant whatsoever there was no sign.

I was woken by the coldness of the tears that drained across my cheeks.

TWENTY-THREE

Paris. July. 1987.

I masturbate fiercely now that Fabrice has gone. It's as though I've regressed to being a teenager again. I'm sure it's some psychological coping mechanism that all the experts know about. But it's taken me by surprise. I do it in bed before I go to sleep at night. I do it in the morning before I get up. I do it if I wake up in the middle of the night. I do it even if I've been down earlier to the river bank.

Three weeks have passed since Fabrice went away. The pain hasn't dulled or faded in the slightest. It's like a winter split that never heals. Though it doesn't just affect a thumb or finger. My whole life has split.

As if to remind me of that, I still have difficulty getting my socks on in the morning. I manage eventually, always, but as I struggle with my numb toes I long, just as I do when masturbating, for Fabrice's tender help.

With any luck the feeling in my toes will come back eventually. Perhaps in a year, perhaps in only a few more months. And with winter splits you always have the knowledge that May will come eventually and mend your skin. But the other thing is not amenable to the healing power of time, I think. I walk around Paris in the height of summer. Bright flowers fill the parks and gardens with colour and wafts of scent. Roses, lupins, summer jasmine mingle their fragrance with the omnipresent aroma of baking baguettes.

But you know what? I have a micro-climate deep inside me and I take it with me wherever I go. To the shops. To the restaurants. To dinner at Joe and Antoine's. Perpetual winter has descended on my heart. I am the garden in the Oscar Wilde story. The story called The Selfish Giant. Summer came and went all around outside his garden, but inside his garden the winter never went. I am that garden. I am that selfish giant. With my permanently frostbitten toes.

Last night I went to the river bank again. I go there often enough now to find myself seeing – and more than merely seeing – the same people again from time to time. Last night it was the Thai fellow I'd met my first time down there. That time we'd had the pleasure of each other's cock. Last night I fucked him, standing him against the wall there with his trousers at half-mast. I was gentle with him. Although I'm not big he is the smaller of the two of us. In the end he was fine. In the end...

In the end, as I was reaching the climax, a strange thing happened. I felt that he had transformed himself somehow – or that I'd magically changed him – into the physicality of Fabrice. They are quite unalike in reality, if only in the most obvious matter of size. Fabrice is quite a big guy, and this chap is not. Yet so strong was the sensation that I found I'd whispered his name as I was coming. That made the guy snigger a moment later. He asked me, 'Who is Fabrice?'

I said, 'Sorry about that. Fabrice is someone you're unlikely ever to meet.'

A few days after I wrote that I came back from shopping to find there was a message on my answer-phone. There was also a letter on the mat. I dealt with the phone first. I didn't recognize the female voice for a second, but then she gave her name. It was Régine, She'd never phoned me before. She was saying there was news I needed to know, and suggesting I call back. My heart did something dizzy-making. I thought this could only be bad news about Fabrice. But also, this was a contact that took me close to Fabrice. Perhaps when I phoned back he would answer...

I so much wanted that.

I dialled the number. But it was Régine again who spoke.

'Fabrice has had to go away. He asked me to phone you.'

'Why? What's the matter? Is Fabrice OK?'

'He's fine. Don't worry. *Par contre* you may have a small problem. With Monsieur Guyot.'

'Who?' This was so remote from anything I might have been expecting that for a second I couldn't remember who that was.

'Monsieur Guyot. Son-in-law to la belle Margueritte. Apparently, when your petition landed on his desk he went ballistic.'

'What? My petition? I'm not with you.'

'You pay cash, don't you? To la belle Margueritte? Which makes you not strictly legal. You remember that Monsieur Guyot is looking for every opportunity to drop the d'Alabouvettes in the *merde*? Right. Do you remember too, that he worked for the ministère d'Urbanisme et de Logement?'

Light began to dawn.

'Yours was the first name – plus address, which happens to be the same as his ex-wife's – on that petition we all signed for the shop lady, Madame Al....er ...'

'Almuslih.'

'It's just really bad luck that it had to land on his desk out of all the others. But unfortunately you've handed him a pistol and the bullets to go with it.'

'What can I do?' I felt suddenly alarmed, suddenly isolated. Perhaps it was the word pistol that did it.

'Fabrice thinks you should get onto Margueritte as soon as possible. Put your heads together and you'll be able to sort something out, I know. But you must get on to it quickly, Fabrice says. She's very volatile. Faced with Monsieur Guyot she'll panic if left to her own devices and you'll be the one to lose out. If you want to talk to Fabrice he'll be back tomorrow.'

'*Merde,*' I said under my breath. But I thanked Régine for the warning, and said that I'd ring Fabrice the next day, before putting the phone down. I looked round the room. It suddenly looked less like home. I picked up the letter that was on the mat.

Its Chicago postmark would have puzzled me but for my just ended phone conversation with Régine. I tore the envelope open. In the letter, which was written by hand, Madame d'Alabouvettes informed me regretfully that her third daughter would be returning from Chile, her marriage having recently taken a nosedive – not that she put it like that – and that she would need my apartment. She would therefore be obliged to terminate my tenancy at the end of the month.

Régine's warning had come too late. No amount of negotiation would be able to dis-invent the broken marriage story. I dropped the letter into the bin and walked out of the flat.

I would have gone to talk to Joe. But he and Antoine were away. They'd gone to a wedding in Normandy. Weeks ago Joe had offered me a chance to open up to him. I'd turned the offer down. Now I wanted nothing so much as to talk to him: to say something that, whatever words I might use, would be understood by both of us to mean, *Help me*. I cursed the bride and groom whose choice of wedding date had taken my friend away to an unknown address in Normandy on this particular day.

But more than I wanted Joe, I wanted Fabrice. The image, and the sensation, came to me then of those big warm arms comfortingly around me. I longed for Fabrice. But he was out of reach, even by telephone, until tomorrow. And tomorrow never comes.

I couldn't face anyone else. Not the Kabylie café. Not the Little Horseshoe. Not the Figeac. I spent the day wandering aimlessly in the city streets.

I found myself, almost involuntarily, seeking again the mysterious bar I'd visited with Fabrice my first evening in Paris and that I hadn't rediscovered since. But it remained elusive, refusing, despite increasingly diligent searching, to show itself in the dark labyrinth of streets. I began to wonder if it had ever actually existed or if it had been simply the setting of a dream. Already the image of it was amalgamating in my mind with Van Gogh's painting of the *Café de Nuit*: the men trying to construct a battleship out of dominoes were already superimposed on the crashed-out figures slumped over Van Gogh's tables; the snake and tomato colour scheme now seemed to be common to both the insubstantial memory and the tangible painting, while the light-bulbs of the one fused with the baleful gas mantles of the other to produce a sinister hybrid light that burned into my brain. And yet it was only five months ago that the vulturine man had pulled a domino from the swaying tower and, placing it on the top, announced the hope of the world. I combed those back streets a little longer. Then I gave up my search.

The trees in the boulevards were silent so it must have been an imaginary cold wind that I felt blowing as I strove to make some sense of what I felt. I walked without thinking about a destination through streets that appeared fuller than usual of the city's dross: the *clochards*, tramps and winos who seemed to have been washed up like flotsam on prosperity's tide, stranded in doorways and on benches among a litter of broken bottles and empty hopes. From time to time as I walked, the Eiffel Tower peered at me over the shoulders of the crowding buildings, a vulgar fairground incarnation of itself, brassy and intrusive among my painful thoughts.

I didn't go to the river bank that night, though I must have walked just about everywhere else in the city. From boulevard Magenta to the place de Clichy. From the rue de Rennes to the Gare de Montparnasse. Back across the river. Tumbling exhausted into bed.

I dreamt I was having to re-take a school exam in maths.

I left it as long as possible before phoning Fabrice next day. Régine had said he would be back that day. That meant travelling back from somewhere. From where, though? I hadn't asked. But he was unlikely to have returned by crack of dawn, however short the journey. He might not be back till early evening. Or later than that...

How long is it possible to put off a phone call that you desperately want, yet don't want, to make? I lasted out till two in the afternoon. I phoned then. But nobody answered, and they didn't seem to have an answerphone. That or it was on the blink. I tried again at five, and then I tried at eight. No Régine. No Fabrice.

I phoned Joe's number. It seemed they weren't back from Normandy yet, or else had gone out. At least I managed to leave a message for Joe. I said simply that when he had a spare moment there were things I wanted to talk about. Even if I wasn't sure what those things were yet.

There was some pizza in the fridge. I heated that up and had a glass of wine with it. I was still exhausted from all my walking and thinking the day before. I went early to bed.

A hammering sound came out of the depths of my slumber like something rising to the surface of a lake. It woke me at last and I lay in bed for a second or two, trying to make sense of it.

It was my door that was being banged on. It had happened before in the middle of the night. This was Dominique again. It had to be. No-one else would do this. My heart, barely wakened, sank. Had he come to tell me a second time that he'd killed Marianne? Had he – God forbid – actually done it this time. I found myself drained of any resources that I might call upon in order to help him. No energy, no ideas, no hopes.

But I did what I had to. I got out of bed, pulled a dressing-gown over my nakedness, and moved towards the door. 'Who is it?' I asked in French.

'It's me,' came from the other side. It was Fabrice.

He took me in his arms and I took him in mine. I broke down and wept uncontrollably, drenching the shoulder of his denim jacket with my tears, waking the night-time quietness with my rending sobs.

He pawed the back of my neck and shoulders with a desperate rough urgency. His own tears came thick and fast. He kissed me, thrusting his tongue into me for a second, then he withdrew it. In English he said, 'I love you, kid.'

TWENTY-FOUR

I will never forget our love-making that night. The way he slipped my dressing-gown off me, so that I stood there with my smaller naked body pressed up against his bigger one, still fully clothed. My hard and much-used penis lay rigid against his jeans. Those didn't stay closed to me for long though: I'd soon undone the studs of his fly; released the wagging friend that lived inside.

I undressed him completely. He led me back to my small bed. He laid me on it carefully, like a little girl arranging a doll on its back... For weeks now I'd been the guy in charge of things, deciding nightly on the river bank who did what. But now Fabrice was at the helm again. In charge of what would happen this night – he was going to fuck me, that was more than obvious. But there was a bigger thing than that. Which also became blindingly, wonderfully, obvious at this moment. He was in charge of what would happen to me not only now but for the rest of my life.

'To find you, lost and crying...' he said. But his own voice choked as he said it. He was lost and crying himself.

He fucked me very gently, and coaxed me off with his hand between our chests. It was after we'd both climaxed that I heard myself say it. In a whisper. 'I love you, Fabrice.'

We'd said the big thing. We said it several times again during that night. There were other things we'd need to say in due course – the fact that he had no luggage with him was just one among many things that had aroused my curiosity – but they could wait. For tonight we just pulled the duvet up over us and slept.

And in the morning Fabrice helped me into my socks.

Later we went out for coffee and a croissant. Not to the Little Horseshoe or the Figeac, where we'd run into people we knew. People who'd want explanations about things we hadn't yet explained to each other – or to ourselves. We went instead to the Kabylie, near place de la République, where I'd been with Joe. He'd be at work now. So would Antoine. Momo greeted me cheerfully when we arrived, but then left us in peace. We sat in the July sunshine outside on the pavement and began to talk.

'I found I couldn't go on living a lie for the rest of my life,' Fabrice was the first of us to confess.

I followed suit. 'I didn't even know I was living a lie,' I said. 'How lacking in self-knowledge can you get? But then you left Paris... You left me... And I found out about myself.'

'I'm so, so sorry,' Fabrice said quietly. 'To leave you...' His voice broke.

'Nothing to be sorry about,' I said. I clasped his hand beneath the table top. 'I never staked a claim to you. You weren't to know things about me that I was denying to myself. Oh Peter, Peter, Peter,' I said, tapping myself on the chest with each repetition of my own name. 'The man who three times denied the truth. I did it a hundred times more often. Can you forgive me for that?'

'My darling,' Fabrice said in English. 'My darling.' Tears spilled suddenly among his dark lashes and ran without ceremony down his cheeks. 'Thank you for not being hard on me,' he said. Then he had to stop until he'd composed himself. He went on at last, with a bit of difficulty, 'But you mustn't be hard on yourself either. You must learn to forgive yourself.'

For both of us that last thing was harder than you might think. For some days we went about with the feeling that we'd been cruel to each other. Actually, as time passed we began to see that we'd simply done what all people who love deeply have done at some point...

Love is something that is always lived in a knife-drawer, and so it was going to be, we were discovering, with Fabrice and me. We had hurt each other very badly – but by accident.

But back to that first morning. The rest of our stories came out. Fabrice told me how he had left Régine. Learning I was about to become homeless had tipped the balance for him. He made a clean breast of it with her, he explained. He told her that he and I had been lovers. That he had been in love with me for some time, but had only just admitted it to himself. That he needed to tell her this before even checking with me to see if I felt the same. He didn't want to lie to her for even another minute. He had packed a bag and he caught the next train to Paris.

He knew he'd hurt her, and that pained him dreadfully. But in the end, he said, one had to be honest with other people, and with oneself.

When it came to hurting other people, I was luckier than he'd been. There had been no Régine in my case. I'd hurt myself and I'd hurt Fabrice, but there hadn't been anyone else within reach of my dishonesty and carelessness. Régine had said – when Fabrice announced his imminent departure – that she'd always known deep down about his gayness. She'd guessed also – hardly surprising, this – about me. I don't know if this made it better for Régine. At least it can't have made it worse.

There was another thing to deal with. Fabrice had arrived in the middle of the night without luggage, and with nowhere to stay except my small studio apartment, with its one single bed. I assumed this meant he'd lost his job or given it up. My apartment was mine only until the month's end, though. We'd both be out on our ears after that.

As for my own finances – well, you may have wondered how I was paying for my Paris lifestyle while attempting to burn with that hard gem-like flame and write. I'd been left a little money by a great aunt, actually, but it wouldn't last for ever. To tell the truth I was getting through it at a rate of knots. That first morning with Fabrice, sitting outside the Kabylie, I had to make a clean breast of that. 'But,' I told him, 'I'm OK with it if you are. I'm OK with you penniless if you're OK with me penniless.' Then I had to look down at my coffee cup, otherwise I'd have cried again. 'You're the only thing, the only person, I need or want, or have ever wanted in my entire life.' God knows how I managed to get all those words out.

'Look at me, Peter,' he said. With some difficulty I did. He took my chin in one of his hands gently, to stop me looking away again, I guess. 'That's all OK, then,' he said. 'You love me naked and without resources. I love you in the same way as that. Thank God.' Then he grinned at me. 'It's actually not quite so *dramatique*. I asked the bank if I could come back to Paris again at short notice. No, they weren't too happy about that. But they haven't fired me. They've re-posted me here in a smaller job, at a smaller salary. But it's liveable on. And the good news is they're letting me go back to the flat. We actually have somewhere to live. I dropped my baggage off there last night before I came to you. I went first to the Figeac but you weren't there. I got your door-code from Dominique.'

I took a deep breath. 'I'd still love you if you were a pauper,' I said. 'If we were both *clochards*. Share my last crust with you and all of that. And yet, if it doesn't come to that...'

He said, 'It hasn't come to that yet.' He looked up at the blue sky above us. 'We could walk in the sunshine for a bit, if you wanted to. After that, perhaps we can start moving your things into my apartment.'

In my mind's eye I saw at once those high ceilings, mirrors over the mantelpieces, friezes running around the walls... The big, big things in our lives can change so quickly sometimes. I could hardly believe any of what had happened in the last twelve hours. I was going to move into Fabrice's apartment. But that was only a little bit of it. The big thing was that I was going to share a home with Fabrice.

We were both startled at that moment to see Joe walking towards us along the street. He looked surprised to see us for a second. But then his expression changed. Reading his face as best I could, I thought I saw first wonder, then delight.

'Why aren't you at work?' I asked him when he came up.

'Just one of those days I happen to have no morning classes.' He shrugged. 'It sometimes just happens like that. On the other hand...' He looked enquiringly at me, then at Fabrice.

Fabrice didn't go into explanations. Not then, at any rate. He looked at Joe, and smiled at him, and said simply, 'I'm back for good.'

'For good?' Joe said. He grinned broadly. 'That's not good. That's not just *good*. That's the very, very best.'

It wasn't till autumn came and the evenings were getting dark that I remembered a story I'd never told Fabrice. I remembered it as we were making love one evening, naked, on the sofa, not prepared to wait (this was typical of us) until we got to bed. Carelessly we'd neglected to close the curtains or the blinds. I was on my back with Fabrice on top. Soon he would choose his moment to enter me, but we hadn't reached that point – the point after which philosophical discussion becomes impossible – quite yet. I glanced sideways towards the window. Beyond it, the yellow lights of other windows cut square holes in the blue night across the street. 'Van Gogh,' I said. 'Those windows in the dark.'

Fabrice stopped playing with my nipples for a moment. 'I see what you mean,' he said. Then he chuckled. 'Do you think anyone's out there watching us?'

I remembered suddenly my first evening in Paris. My peeping-Tom experience just hours before I met Fabrice. I told him now about that. Then I remembered the window that had so grabbed my imagination, opposite my old apartment in the rue des Archives. The question of who lived there, Joe had once suggested fancifully, was what had first brought me to France. The night Fabrice had left me, I'd had anxiety dreams about that...

I looked again at the yellow windows opposite. There was no sign of anyone. No silhouetted figures looking out. 'Do I think anyone's out there watching us?' I said. 'Can't say I'm sure, to be honest. But if they are, I'm fine with that, I think.'

Fabrice pushed his hard cock gently but firmly between my buttocks. 'I don't have any problem with that either,' he said. 'Not at the moment anyway. Tomorrow perhaps. But not tonight.'

Paris. September. 2013.

The sky is a cloudless blue. High overhead there are swallows passing over the city on their way south. I sit writing this in the gardens of the Tuileries. I am near the fountain pool by the great gates that open into the place de la Concorde. In the pool swim giant carp that seem almost as big as horses. Children who look smaller than the carp are sailing their boats across the top. Around me the flower beds are full of yellow and orange daisy-

like flowers. There are hydrangeas and geraniums still, in fiercely clashing shades of pink and red.

Beyond the wall ahead of me stand the chestnut trees of the river bank. I smile at the memory of the person I was once, the crazed caged animal I was, wandering there so hungrily at night. I've never been back there in the last twenty-five years. Never felt the need.

Beyond the gates the top of the Eiffel Tower is visible. It looks different from day to day, according to my mood. Today it has something of the look about it of a medieval knight, benevolent and smiling. Magnificent in his plumed helmet. Gracious in the victory he has won at the joust.

In a little while Fabrice will join me, making a short detour from his work in the rue de Rivoli. We shall walk home together. Past the Louvre, past the Hôtel de Ville, then through the Marais to our flat. It's the same one that Fabrice had all those years ago, when it belonged to the bank.

It was probably lucky we had that conversation on that first morning of our new life together: the conversation about loving each other even if we were paupers. Because it nearly came to that. Fabrice lost his job in the banking fiasco of 2008. For a while we thought we'd be homeless. But the bank, keen just then to dispose of some fixed assets, offered to sell the apartment to us for a knock-down price. It wasn't that cheap, even so. Fabrice's father helped him. Even my own chipped in what he could.

We lived for a time on what I was earning as a magazine editor. (I still do that.) But then Fabrice set himself up on his own as a business consultant. That business has taken off in the last three years. Now we do all right.

We still frequent the Figeac. René runs it now, since his mother retired. And although Denis and Jeannette left Paris some years ago, we still see Marianne and Dominique. Also still together are Joe and Antoine, which is nice.

Another good thing is that Régine found love not long after splitting with Fabrice. With someone whose heterosexual credentials were less shaky than Fabrice's. He, Régine's husband, is Canadian. They live happily with their teenage children (as happily as anyone can live with teenage children, that is) in Alsace.

Françoise is another matter. She flew to the sun with the braceleted Portugueses guy all those years ago and, except for the one postcard, has never been heard of since. But she set her heart on what she wanted, and that is what she got. I've never felt sorry for her. There are many mansions in the house of love.

You don't have to be trapped by your past, I've learned. Life gives you more than one star among the heavens, as Dominique said. You can remove a domino or two from the tower without the whole thing collapsing about your ears. At least, that's what I now think.

Even the effects of frostbite – that numbness of the toes – disappeared after about a year and a half, though I thought during that time that it never would. The frostbite that afflicted my heart, though, the chill of the garden of the selfish giant, was dispelled in an instant, with the arrival of Fabrice at my bedroom door that night, with his return to Paris to stake his claim to outright ownership of my heart.

I never did become much of a writer. Except for my magazine stuff. Although the book I came to Paris to try and write … well, you've just been reading it.

THE END

THE VAN GOGH WINDOW

First published (as Gay Romance: The Van Gogh Window) 2014

David, 28 and already divorced, is taken on holiday to Provence by his gay best mate. The idea is to recreate the journey Vincent Van Gogh made a century earlier, from cold dark northern Europe to the sunnier south. But in Arles, the town where Van Gogh settled, David sees a nude photo of the boy whose friendship with him brought about his divorce. Deeply buried memories surface. They force David to return to London in search of the boy in the photograph and then, like Vincent before him, to make the longer, deeper journey in search of himself. Originally published as Gay Romance: The Van Gogh Window in 2013

Dedicated to the memory of Tony Linford who, years ago, made me a present of the title 'The Van Gogh Window'. He also made me a present of his love, and of his life.

Chapter 1

It was soon after my divorce from Anne that I began to dream about Happy. And after that I started to think about him. About that year at Durham...

Anne and Happy had both come into my life at the same time. At the same moment of the same day.

I'd had a premonition beforehand. Returning to university to begin my second year, and at the very moment when the land fell away beneath the train to reveal Durham's cathedral rearing over the grovelling rooftops, I was suddenly certain that this year would be different. The certainty was so strong that I felt it physically: a tingling in the bloodstream. That year – nine years ago now – I would meet the person or people who would shape my life.

Or some of them. Or some of it.

Anne appeared in the street beneath my window the next morning. A new room, looking into the street from the second floor, and new voices down there, outside. 'Who can we call on for coffee this term? Everyone's moved.' I put my head out of the window and looked down. They were three girls and a boy, though you were supposed to think: *women* and *man*. They looked all right and I had five mugs.

'Call on me,' I said. 'I'm David.' Even in those days my occasional bursts of spontaneity tended to have far-reaching consequences.

It became a ritual. Every time they had a ten o'clock in the history lecture hall next door they would follow it with coffee in my room. Sometimes all four came, sometimes just two or three. Never only one. That was an unspoken taboo but strictly observed. Solo visits would have changed everything, giving rise to relationships where, for now, only a social situation existed.

They had names of course. There was Janie, forever knitting an endless scarf for her boyfriend, and Laura, already a comforting, aunt-like figure at nineteen. There was Anne, the pretty one, the witty one, and there was Happy.

'Why do people call him Happy?'

'A spelling mistake when he was little, apparently. His real name's Harry, short for Henry though it isn't any shorter, but the other version stuck. But you should know that. He's in your college after all. I'm surprised you haven't bumped into him before.'

'I wasn't very outgoing last year,' I said.

'Wake up, David.' It was Anne speaking. The others would not have talked to me like this – at least, not so soon. 'Or university will be over and nothing'll have happened.'

Anne had been a shrewd observer if a poor prophet. I had been virtually untouched, unaltered by my first year away from home, remaining shy, virginal, conceited. I'd looked at Anne and wondered for the first time if it would be through her that change would come.

I had to tell people about the divorce from Anne, of course. It was all done by letter in those days. (We got divorced in early '89.) I wrote to Malcolm, among other people. I'd done my teacher training with Malcolm. But he'd chucked it in a few years afterwards and moved to Paris. Malcolm was gay, I had now learnt. I don't know whether he moved to Paris because he was gay or whether he was gay because he'd moved to Paris. At any rate he now had a boyfriend there who was called Henri. Henri was nineteen. Malcolm – who, like me, was twenty-eight – taught English to French businessmen at one of the larger business schools.

Malcolm's response to my news surprised me. It was startling almost, but also heart-warming. He rang me up and asked me if I'd like to go on holiday with him. He was going to Provence in three days' time. The boyfriend, Henri, couldn't go. He, Malcolm, would like some company, and he guessed a break might do me good. I was between jobs, as they say. I was so surprised by Malcolm's offer that I said yes. I just needed to get myself to Paris the day after next, he told me. Stay the night with him and Henri, then travel onward with Malcolm from there. I phoned and booked a flight from Heathrow to Charles de Gaulle. Then I started packing. Not that I'd need many clothes. It was early July and I was heading south. I started sorting things out, tracking down my passport, things like that. And as I did all that my mind kept going back to the days when I knew Happy.

Chapter 2

Winter had come down hard that second year at Durham. All through January the green-grey ice-floes had sailed down the river, under Framwellgate Bridge, past the boathouses, round the horseshoe bend. Some had tumbled, smashing, over the weir to disappear under Crossgate and out of the city's sight while others lodged at the rim, backing up as the days passed to form a crust which froze together at the joins. This new skin the river wore was rough and lumpy as an alligator's and at night when the streets were still it could be heard squeaking under its own pressure, a sound which seemed to flitter around the valley like a summer evening's bats. 'Do you think it would be possible?' asked Happy, 'to walk across it?'

'Possible perhaps,' said Anne, putting down her coffee, 'but don't ask me to join you if you try it.'

'David will,' said Happy flatly, not even looking up.

'You should see Happy's lecture notes today,' said Laura. 'They're all seals.'

Happy's lecture notes were unlike most people's: they consisted not of written words but pictures. His surprised neighbours in the lecture room would watch designs and figures taking shape in response to a chance word in the lecture: stream of consciousness doodling, or perhaps a stream of the unconscious. I thought Happy one of the least conscious people I had met. He spoke little and seemed to wear his thick mop of hair like an insulator for the brain, protecting it from external stimulus. He was a good draughtsman though; no doubt about that.

'Show David, go on,' Laura coaxed.

Without a word Happy handed the morning's drawings over. He seemed neither reluctant nor pleased to do so; they were just there. Take them or leave them, the silence implied. That morning's lecture on the development of the royal household in medieval England had given rise to three pages of pictures of seals – of the animal rather than the Great or Privy variety. There were real seals and surreal seals, seals swimming, seals dining at restaurant tables, seals peering from the treetops, seals on the cathedral roof. Yesterday it had been grasshoppers. There was not a word of text. God help him when he came to revise, I thought. Then the possibility struck me that Happy could not actually write. In which case, how had he got to university? I'd dismissed that line of thought while Happy put the pictures away. Neither of us spoke. I'd thought the drawings brilliantly executed but pointless and their creator odd without being really interesting.

It was that day that the snow had come.

It had come hesitantly at first but with increasing firmness of purpose as the afternoon wore on. At first each flake formed an island of white on Durham's dark pavements but soon the image was reversed, as the pavement outside my window was reduced to islands of black: the footprints of the students (few other people used the street) who passed and re-passed in intermittent, alternating streams. I watched, seated at my desk. The spectacle provided as good an excuse as any to postpone the start of the essay on Shakespeare's clowns that I was due to hand in two days hence. As usual the road took longer to vanish than the pavement because of traffic but here the traffic was light and soon the time came when the double yellow lines had gone for good. I liked to see this as a watershed; the moment marked the end of the rule of law and the beginning of the snow's anarchic reign. Now you could park your car anywhere you liked, if you had a car, that was. I didn't, of course. In time, if the snow kept on long enough, the cars would be gone too and everything would be as it had been a hundred years ago. Eventually the cathedral and castle would be covered also, and I with them, in a return to a featureless, timeless age of ice. But that was going too far, even for me. I drew the curtains, as it was getting dark, and set to work on Shakespeare's clowns.

In the morning it was perfect. The snow had turned the clock back just the right amount, neither too little nor too far. The cars had gone but not the castle. I made my way across the green to college breakfast. I'd got up earlier than usual and all was dark and still, the few lines of footprints that preceded my own not devaluing too greatly the quality of the scene. With a breath-like sound a quantity of snow slid from the branch of a bush, dislodged by a bird which, breast deep, now flopped away. A few parked cars it was true, intruded like donkeys on the green but they were so comprehensively wrapped in white as not to count. The cathedral stood out against the southern sky, the castle against the northern, and as, minute by minute, the light increased it picked out every buttress, every gargoyle, every dripstone and edged them in white while hiding every dustbin, drain-cover and fire hydrant: the twentieth-century clutter swept away, the old enhanced.

The castle was the principal building of my college – my own room was in a modern annexe – and it was approached from the green through a Norman gatehouse which opened onto a central court. It would have been convenient to call this court a quad but that name was ruled out by its shape, the grass plot in its centre being round. Even the notice forbidding you to walk on it was whited out. Arguably it was without authority that day: it said Keep Off The Grass, not off the snow. Now, as I straightened after ducking through the postern gate I saw a figure standing on the forbidden whiteness. I walked nearer and saw with some surprise that it was Happy, smoking a cigarette.

'Want one?' Happy held the packet out.

'Before breakfast? Thank you, no. Couldn't you sleep?'

Happy had the reputation of a late riser. If he made it to breakfast at all he would arrive at the tail end when most other people had left.

'I just like to see it look like this,' Happy answered, 'if only for one morning of the year, before it gets spoilt.'

'I know. And look, it's starting now.' I nodded towards the postern where young people were beginning to stream in, laughing and pursued by snowballs.

'Enough,' said Happy. 'Come on. Let's go inside.' We moved off, up the steps and into the Great Hall where, because Happy habitually sat at one table under the portrait of Bishop Van Mildert, while I always sat at the one over which Bishop Tunstall hung, our paths diverged as abruptly as they had just crossed.

It was eleven o'clock in the evening and I had just put the finishing touches to Shakespeare's clowns. I was either about to take off my shoes or to clean my teeth – I had not yet decided on the order of ceremonies – when there was a knock at the door. I said, 'Come in,' without surprise. Neighbours, seeing your light on, were apt to pop in at any hour of the evening for a chat. But tonight my visitor was Happy, wearing a duffel coat, an Everton scarf and a woolly bobble-hat pulled down over his ears.

'Come for a walk,' he said.

'A what?'

'A walk,' Happy repeated matter-of-factly. 'Down by the river. It's snowed again. You'll like it.'

I was more than surprised. I thought the suggestion crazy. But I was unable quickly to find a good reason to refuse 'I'm just going to bed' might seem reasonable enough to older people but it was a lame excuse at nineteen and soon I heard my own voice saying, 'OK. If you like. Why not?'

Soon we had descended the steps that ran down between St. Chad's College and Dunelm Bridge and found ourselves at the bottom of the wooded gorge where the river ran, its presence taken on trust tonight since its sharp-edged surface was buried beneath a thick white quilt. The ice had stopped squeaking a day or two before; it was now locked tight. There was no movement to be heard or seen or felt. Without speaking we turned along the towpath towards the horseshoe bend.

Happy broke the silence when we got there. 'What do you think of it?' He seemed to be inviting my appreciation of something he had made himself: one of his pictures perhaps, or a newly decorated room.

'It suits me,' I said.

Happy seemed not to find my reply an odd one. He said, 'That's what I thought. I thought it when I saw you this morning. Before that I didn't know....' The phrase tailed away. 'Like celestial Tippex,' he said a moment or two later. Then, 'Are you in love with Anne?'

'I don't think so.' I was following easily Happy's changes of tack: so easily that it surprised me. 'Are you?'

'I don't think so either,' Happy said, 'and yet....'

That was the full extent of our discussion of the subject but it seemed somehow to have gone deeper than the many conversations on the theme of love that I and my other friends indulged in and that often lasted hours. It now occurred to me for the first time in my life that the words people said to one another might bear no more than a passing resemblance to what they were trying to communicate.

After that, conversation began to flow more easily. Ideas began to link up, sentences sometimes even to end. We talked about our childhood days, Happy's in the country, mine in the town. We were surprised to discover how much we had in common, not knowing yet that you could find as much in common as you wished with anyone you chose, provided that you wanted to. Yet somehow it seemed to matter.

We turned the horseshoe bend. Here the wooded banks rose more steeply above us, bearing up tier upon tier of trees, their scaffold of branches just visible in the dim rays of the lamps on Prebends' Bridge. The whole composition was finished with a white haze of frosted twigs, a three-dimensional latticework of infinite complexity.

'Like life, really,' said Happy, reflecting on precisely that but not bothering to check whether I understood him. 'Can you climb trees?'

'I used to. But it's a few years since...'

'Race you to the top of that sycamore.'

I would not have recognized a sycamore even in daylight and with its leaves on but Happy was blithely shinning up a nearby trunk and for a second time that evening I could find no good reason not to follow. To my surprise it was quite easy, like the dangerous feats performed in dreams, and soon we had both climbed as high as we could without breaking the slender branches we stood on. The tree was already waving about alarmingly in response to the smallest movement either of us made. 'I wonder how that couple managed to do it in a pear tree,' Happy said.

'Which couple?'

'You know. The couple in Chaucer. In the Miller's Tale.'

'Oh, right,' I said. 'I've wondered that myself. I never knew historians could read, though.' I raised my eyebrows in mock surprise. 'Read literature, I mean.'

'Supercilious bastard,' said Happy and shook the tree. 'I did English for A-level as it happens. Economics too, if you're interested.'

'German and French,' I countered and then, with no qualifications left to hurl, we each tried to shake the other from his perch. Half a minute later we were on the ground again having neither exactly fallen nor scrambled down but something in between.

We lit cigarettes in a futile attempt to warm hands that were now stinging with cold and walked on. The weir was eerily silent except at the narrow fish passes where a little water spilled down from beneath the icy cap as if to remind us that it could not be stilled completely or for ever. Here we struck matches and flicked them out across the river's flat expanse. They blazed a second like shooting stars, lighting up the snow as they arc-ed towards it, then the white swallowed them and turned to blackness. At last the matchbox, as well as Happy's cigarette packet, was empty. Without anything having to be said we knew the walk was over. We climbed the path beneath the cathedral's massive silhouette and parted on the green, Happy to his turret somewhere in the castle, I to my more conventional, modern room. It seemed to me at that moment, nine years ago, that all thought and all feeling had been banished from my mind except a sense of peace; that the internal as well as the external landscape had been whited out by Happy's celestial Tippex.

Chapter 3

There was a flight you could take from London to Paris that was operated by Air India. A Boeing 1747 used to fly into Heathrow from Bombay, then a few hours later the same plane flew out from Charles de Gaulle to Delhi. In between, cheap tickets were offered to anyone who wanted to make the short hop between the European capitals.

I thought it would be fun. With any luck they'd serve a decent curry on board...

They did no such thing. This was low cost flying before low cost flying had been invented, and the London Paris leg coincided with the cabin crew's rest break. They lay prostrate with exhaustion across rows of empty seats while the Boeing lumbered slowly into the air and bumped its way along the cloud corridor. The journey was so short and the old Boeing's rate of climb so gentle that I realised we wouldn't even climb to cruising height before it was time to descend into Paris. My mind went back to that snowy winter nine years before...

There were seven degrees of acquaintanceship at university, each one signalled by its own social convention. There were the people you nodded to in the street, the people you said hallo to and those you would cross the street to speak to. Then – number four – came the people whose rooms you might visit casually but only in the company of someone else (your girlfriend's best friend and your best friend's girlfriend were in this category) and there were those whom you would call on at any time, alone or not, for any good reason such as to discuss an essay topic or to borrow milk. This group, embracing most of your neighbours and a sizeable chunk of your department as well, was a rather large one. The sixth degree consisted of those on whose doors you would knock for no reason whatever and who in their turn would not expect your visit to have anything so prosaic as a purpose. A small group this. Finally, number seven, a plane of relationship not restricted to university but to which neither I nor Happy had yet attained, was the one which usually has room besides yourself for one person only.

Happy's late evening visit and the snowy ramble that followed it had abruptly shifted our relationship from group four to group six, missing out the large fifth group in between. My room was easily accessible, lying on the main axes between the university library, the castle, the cathedral and the shops. Happy's, by contrast, was approached by a flight of ninety steps and lay in the innermost recesses of the castle on the way to nowhere else. The room was an unusual shape: bottle-shaped, Happy called it – you entered along the neck.

In good weather the view from the window was superb. Today it was just a blur of white, its only prominent feature a building from the previous century – a period Happy called the Age of Endarkenment – a hundred of whose windows peered up at Happy's. You never saw a light turned off to indicate the migration of occupants from one room to another and when the city suffered a power cut that windowed wall became a beacon in the blackness. It was the county gaol. It was Happy's grim joke to peer from his window in the evening, indicate the lights to whoever his visitor might be and, with a sardonic smile, exclaim, 'Oh look. The prisoners are in.'

The walls of Happy's room were mainly covered with reproductions of famous paintings but right above his bed two texts in his own handwriting were blue-tacked. One was a quotation from Machiavelli which read: 'The Prince should read History'. Reading history was what

Happy was here for and he did it with about as much enthusiasm as he might have picked oakum. He had selected the text for his own encouragement. The other one was more cryptic; it read: 'This is not Dungeness'. I asked him to explain it. He said that Dungeness was a windswept shingle beach in Kent: something I already knew. Pressed further, he explained that the phrase was a quote from a dream he had once had – an idea that intrigued me. My own dreams, though occasionally memorable, were never sources of quotation.

'I've never been there,' Happy said, 'though I dream of the place often. I can't think why. It's a dismal spot by all accounts. And by the way, there's nothing wrong with quoting your dreams, or even your waking thoughts. I recommend it to you. If ever I write a sentence in an essay that seems more apt or prettier than usual I stick inverted commas at either end. Somehow it seems to commend itself more to the tutors that way. They never ask where a quotation comes from. They want you to think they know the source of all quotations. History is bluff.'

'University is bluff,' I'd said.

'And life itself.'

'Life yes. Art no.'

Our conversations usually came round to art in the end, often specifically to painting, a subject that stirred Happy to a rare degree of enthusiasm. 'I once thought I had the makings of a good painter,' he explained. 'Only the ambition went away and the talent was probably never there in the first place. Now all I have left are opinions.' Which were sometimes curious.

'Look at the *Marriage of Arnolfini* next time you're in the National,' he said. 'In the background is a mirror on the wall. People say the reflection in it is the artist's. It isn't though; it's yours. Try it and see.'

Months later I'd gone to look. The minute reflection had not been wearing my clothes that day but the face, a single brush-blob, might have been my own. It was a nice idea. Not far from Arnolfini, though, I'd come upon Botticelli's *Portrait of a Young Man* and discovered with a shock that it resembled Happy. Had he been there, I now thought, Happy might have countered that the picture looked like every man of nineteen and that that was its genius. But Happy had not been there and the resemblance had hurt.

It was in the realm of music though, that I'd held views of my own. In Happy's room we listened to Beethoven, in mine to Schubert – in addition to the pop music of the day which was the same everywhere. But it was over Beethoven that we disagreed. When Happy wanted to provoke me he would put the finale of the Ninth Symphony on the turntable and turn the volume up.

'It's rubbish,' I would say. 'Self-conscious, overblown, bombastic...'

'Any more adjectives?' Happy would enquire placidly.

'Triumphalist...'

Happy would silence me with a well-aimed pillow.

'One day,' Happy said simply, 'you will change your mind. Everyone comes to love Beethoven in the end.'

'Bollocks,' I said.

'But how?' Happy went on, ignoring me, almost to himself. 'That is the question. How will you get there and with who?'

'With whom,' I corrected.

These conversations would fizzle out under pressure from the music. In any case it wasn't considered cool to remain articulate for too long at a stretch.

Once, but only once, we talked about our dreams. At that time I was fascinated by dreams, especially my own. I recounted a recent and particularly pleasant one to

Happy. I had been walking in sunshine in a village ringed with trees where birds sang and children played. The dream had lasted a considerable time, or seemed to. The details had been fine and compelling. I finished describing it, then asked, 'And what did you dream last night? Dungeness again, or don't you remember?'

'Oh I remember all right,' said Happy.

'Tell me then.'

'You don't want to hear it.'

'Of course I do,' I said.

'Well then. I'm afraid it was shorter and more brutal than yours, though. I dreamed you shot me through the head.'

I was brought back to myself by the voice of a stewardess telling me that we were landing, and would I please do my seat belt up.

Chapter 4

Malcolm had told me to take the RER underground service as far as the Gare du Nord, and then change onto the older, slower Métro. I would get off at Place Blanche, by the Moulin Rouge. I was looking forward to seeing Paris again. I hadn't been there since I was a teenager. But even now I had to wait, as I ploughed through the city's chalky subsoil, looking blankly at the black reflections in the window of my underground train. With nothing more real to distract me, my thoughts went back to Durham again.

The snow was going. The real world was returning to the city streets. It was the world, as Happy put it, '...of yellow lines and parking fines and meter maids all in a row.' The quotes are his. We were all having eleven o'clock coffee in my room.

'Anyone fancy some theatre this afternoon?' Anne asked.

'The Assembly Rooms, do you mean?' Happy asked, puzzled. 'I didn't think there was anything on this week. Or do you mean in Newcastle?'

'Neither,' said Anne. 'I mean the Court House. The Bloody Assizes. Not that they call them assizes any more. But we ought to go and have a look anyway. Part of our education.'

Happy said that he would not go, Laura that she would. Janie, still knitting her incessant scarf, said that she would go: it was sure to be fascinating. I said that I too would join the party but on condition that Janie did not take the scarf. I drew the line, I remember saying, at sitting next to a *tricoteuse*.

The court room was not unlike the Assembly Rooms, which were the principal venue for student drama, in that both were decked out with impressive quantities of brass rail and red plush. But the court was intimate in the extreme, far smaller than I'd expected. Reaching down from the public gallery I could almost have removed the barristers' wigs had I been tempted to. I was not. But the shortage of space did not prevent the onstage action achieving an intensity rarely found at the Assembly Rooms. Here, the author of the entertainment was life itself; life the subject matter too, along with death.

When we arrived the judge was summing up a case that had been carried over from the previous day. An elderly man was in the dock, listening alertly, sometimes nodding in agreement. One bandaged wrist, prominently displayed on the dock rail testified to a half-hearted suicide attempt the night before. It appeared that he had formed the habit of firing a shotgun at his neighbours, later at the postman, and finally at the policeman who was sent round to have a word. He was on trial for attempted murder. The judge suggested that the jury consider the prisoner's mental state, then sent them out to find a verdict.

'Exciting, don't you think?' said Janie. I murmured a reluctant agreement, wondering whether excitement was really what you ought to feel, this being real life after all. Then my attention was taken up by the entrance of a second jury, new white-wigged counsels for defence and prosecution, a new prisoner in the dock. Surveying the new cast my eye fell suddenly on Happy, seated a few places away. I was doubly surprised because I hadn't heard anyone enter the public gallery and because Happy had said that he wouldn't come. He was looking away when I spotted him so no glance of greeting was exchanged. And I was too awed by my surroundings to call out.

The new case concerned a closing-time brawl. A skinhead had been kicked to death. Another one, in a suit, stood in the dock charged with his murder. More skinheads in suits testified in his defence. A few ritual thrusts and parries were exchanged by the barristers and occasionally the judge made a little joke when he judged the tension in need of easing. Soon he was summing up. I was amazed at the speed of the proceedings.

The second jury left, the first returned. Not guilty, was their verdict on the old man. A wave of good feeling swept the court room, a taut balloon of tension punctured. Indefinite detention in a psychiatric institution, said the judge. Nobody seemed to hear.

Like weathermen on a barometer, or like a Greek chorus working shifts, that jury left only to be replaced by the second. Their discussion of the skinhead had been brief. Manslaughter, yes, they said but murder, no. There were audible sounds of relief. I found that my own relief was slightly tinged with disappointment. I'd been cheated of my first sighting of a murderer in the flesh. The judge prescribed a prison term with the easy nonchalance of a doctor ordering a rest-cure. 'There's too much of this putting the boot in, as it's called, about,' he said. That night another of Happy's prisoners would be in.

The scenery was set for a third case. Now it was another impeccably dressed but even younger man who occupied the dock. His age was given as nineteen. He was a bank clerk who had been supplementing his income by offering his body for rent. But the renting process had gone horribly wrong, one of his clients demanding money from him in return for certain photographs not finding their way to his parents or to the bank where he worked. The blackmailer had grown greedy and raised the price. The boy, grown desperate, had strangled him with a silk scarf.

'You have heard the charge against you,' said the judge. 'How do you plead?'

The boy replied so softly that heads craned forward to hear him. 'Guilty, my lord,' he breathed, and in those words that so faintly broke the silence the fall of a sparrow could be heard by straining ears.

'You have pleaded guilty to the crime of murder,' said the judge in a voice now grave and sad. 'There is only one sentence that the law allows: that you be imprisoned for life.' The prisoner, who had appeared among them for no more than two minutes, the sparrow in the feasting hall, was led down steps behind the dock, down steps where the imagination could not follow, and out of sight.

I was aghast. I'd been rewarded for my patience with this glimpse of a murderer and it had not been at all what I'd expected. I looked towards where Happy sat but his seat was empty. A door on the far side of the gallery was just closing.

But now we were gliding to a stop at Place Blanche Métro station. I got up and unhooked the silver catch that allowed the door to open. It whooshed and clunked as it did so, and I got out.

Chapter 5

I made my way up the rue Lepic. Malcolm had told me that it was shaped like a sickle, though a left-handed one. The short straight handle bit climbed past the stage door of the Moulin Rouge and a line of wonderful foodie shops opposite. Malcolm's flat was halfway around the curving 'blade' of the street, higher up. The tip of the rue Lepic poked its way into the picturesque quarter of Montmartre at the top.

It was quite a climb, and though it was early evening by now the sun was still hot, but the street was so attractive that I didn't mind that. I pressed the buzzer and a few seconds later I heard Malcolm's welcoming voice and the buzz and click as he opened the postern gate. The postern gate. That took me back...

Malcolm met me at the top of his flight of stairs. We went into his big salon and I was immediately gobsmacked. It was like walking into an explosion of colour and light. First was the view out of the big window. The sun was pouring into it from the south-west, and I found myself looking out across the roofs of the city towards the Eiffel Tower, which reared up in the distance. But inside the room the sun lit brilliant pictures everywhere I looked. I knew the pictures well. It was as if someone had taken an expensive book of Van Gogh reproductions, dismembered it and plastered the pages all over the walls. When I asked him, Malcolm confirmed that this was actually the case. There were sunflowers here, sunsets there, fields of ripening wheat, the orange roofs of Auvers, the blazing blues of canal and sky at Arles. In Malcolm's flat, especially with the evening sun streaming into it, the effect was overwhelming: a battering of the senses. But what struck me more than that was a memory that came back. I suddenly remembered that Happy's room at university had been similarly decorated, his endarkened castle quarters enlightened by an, admittedly more modest, set of Van Gogh prints. How could I have forgotten that?

'I found it like this when I got back from work this evening,' Malcolm explained. 'It's Henri's doing.' Shyly he added, 'It's my birthday. Today I'm as old as you are, David. Twenty-eight'

'Why the hell didn't you say...?' I made standard apologetic noises about cards and presents. I was glad I'd bought a bottle of wine from the Nicolas shop at the bottom of the street, at least.

'Never mind all that. Look, we've got to call by the café to borrow some more cutlery. There's two other people coming as well and I don't have enough knives and forks.'

'Oh,' I said, 'that'll be nice.' I meant the other guests.

'Well,' Malcolm explained. 'Henri got a bit carried away in the market this morning. He bought a whole pike. It's one helluva big pike. *Le brochet au beurre blanc de la Loire*. Henri's in charge of the preparations, thank God. Where is he?' He looked away towards an unseen kitchen. *'Henri, viens! Laisse ton sacré poisson!'* Come here. Leave your bloody fish.

Henri emerged from the kitchen along the corridor. *'Voilà,'* he said, *'ça y est. Bonjour, David.'* And he sniffed at his fingers before giving me his hand to shake.

It was a convivial evening. The other guests were a gay couple, one English, one French, called Peter and Fabrice. We talked a mixture of the two languages. We talked about Van Gogh. With that lot plastered over the walls we could hardly not have done. I said that the view from the window here reminded me of a painting by Van Gogh: the one in which the Eiffel Tower appears half built.

'It should do,' Malcolm said. 'It was painted from the house next door, which was where he lived with his brother Theo when he first came to Paris.'

Peter said that when *he*'d first arrived in Paris two years before there had been an attic window visible from his flat that shed a yellow light at night. Against the blue dark it had reminded him of windows in paintings by Van Gogh.

'I hope you like Van Gogh,' Malcolm said to me. 'Because this holiday we're going on is partly to follow his footsteps to Provence.'

'I'm up for that,' I said. 'I've always been a fan of Vincent's. I had a friend at university whose walls were plastered with Van Gogh prints. I'd forgotten that till I saw yours when I arrived here. My friend's name was Happy,' I said. For some reason I found it was imperative just then to get that out, to speak his name.

'Intriguing name,' said Malcolm. 'Was he? Happy by nature as well as name, I mean.'

'Not at the end,' I said. 'Tell you sometime.' We had a fortnight.

Henri was a charming boy. He was very ... I suppose I'd have to say pretty. Perhaps that was fair enough. He was gay after all, and only just nineteen. Big almond-shaped brown eyes, and full lips. He wouldn't be joining his partner and me on this Provence jaunt, he explained, because his mother liked him to spend a week with her every summer in the spa town of Vichy. It was a bit dull, he said, but he loved his mother and still did this every year. He was an only child and his father was dead.

'He's very good to her,' Malcolm explained. 'Sees her every weekend and cooks her lunch.'

I was enjoying the pike with white butter sauce enormously. I thought Henri's mother was lucky to have a son who could cook like that.

After the guests had gone and the washing-up had been incarcerated in the dishwasher, Henri took himself off to bed.

Malcolm poured himself and me a final cognac. 'Holiday begins tonight,' he said. We sat beneath the Van Gogh paintings and talked.

'I want to hear about your friend Happy,' Malcolm said. That surprised me a bit. I'd only mentioned his name once.

I told him the whole story, up to the point where we were in the court room and Happy left. I sighed involuntarily. 'And I'm afraid I only saw him one more time after that. I don't feel very good about it.'

'Tell me,' said Malcolm, in the gentle voice that people use when coaxing forth reminiscences over the third cognac.

'It was later that same evening,' I said. 'I was well behind with my weekly essay and I was having trouble concentrating. That wasn't surprising. The events of the court room, the sentencing to life imprisonment of someone my own age, someone who had stood literally within touching distance but was now a murderer – all this had taken my imagination over and rather monopolised it. Even at dinner I'd found it hard to eat. I'd been impressed by the professionalism of the judge. (He lodged in the castle's state rooms while the court was sitting, and dined at high table with the dons.) There he was, cheerfully tucking into pheasant pie, the business of the day firmly behind him after six o'clock. And I wasn't surprised, finally, when Happy knocked at my door around eleven o'clock. 'Can we talk?' he asked me. 'About this afternoon?'

'Yes,' I said. 'I want to very much. But not just now. Tomorrow. Tomorrow all day if you like. But...' I pointed to my unfinished essay. 'Deadline nine a.m.'

'I understand,' Happy said. He left and softly closed the door behind him.

'I made some coffee, trying to rebuild my concentration. I put a record on the turntable. I even remember what it was. One of my all-time favourites: Schubert's *Winterreisse*. I played the whole of it – all three sides – by which time the essay was as finished as it would ever be. It was nearly two o'clock. I went to bed.' I stopped for a second. 'I remember it in so much detail,' I said, wondering at myself a bit.

'It was obviously important,' Malcolm said. 'The *Winterreisse* is the one where the lovelorn boy drowns himself in the millstream, isn't it?'

'Oh my God,' I said. 'You know that!'

'Anyway, what happened?' Malcolm asked. 'Though I think I can guess. After you told Happy to get lost he did just that?'

'In a manner of speaking, yes,' I answered slowly. 'The morning came as it always does. The history group didn't have a ten o'clock so I didn't expect to see Happy early on. I had lectures myself till twelve in the English department on the other side of town. I walked back the long way round – along the river bank. It wasn't quite spring yet, but birds were making a racket and there was a feeling that things were about to happen. I saw two policemen talking together in the trees on the other side of the river but I didn't think anything of it. I was feeling really great for some reason. You know, one of those days you get when you feel about a hundred and ten per cent. I walked up to the castle and went in to lunch. Do you remember that college lunch feeling? You went in and, in a way that almost knocked the breath out of you, There Was Everybody.'

Malcolm nodded his head.

'That day it was more than that. As I walked in I had the sensation that in that roar, the sound of four hundred people all talking at once, there was only one topic of conversation. Not only was everybody talking but they were all saying the same thing. By the time I got to my usual place I think I knew that one of us – I mean someone from the university – had been fished out of the river. Dead. By the time I sat down I knew it was someone from our own college. I asked who. As if I needed telling. 'Paddy Laughton,' someone said. 'Chap who used to run everywhere, you never saw him walking. Reads history…' And I remember the bloke trying to correct the tense.

'Not Paddy,' I said. 'His name was….' only, his name being the one it was, I couldn't manage to say it and had to leave the room. The soup was just arriving. It was mushroom.'

Very gently, Malcolm reached across and touched me on the shoulder. 'And what happened then?'

I said, and it sounded silly as I heard my words come out. 'I married Anne.'

'Incredible!' said Malcolm. 'Just like that? Before the soup?' As well he might.

Chapter 6

Anne had been so practical that first day, so sensible, so right. She was very upset herself by the news of Happy's death but she sensed somehow that my distress was of a different order to her own. Rather than discuss, painfully and uselessly, events and feelings for which neither of us had words, she asked me to embark with her on a very overdue spring cleaning of the flat she shared. It was probably lucky that there was so much to do. The carpets hadn't been taken out and beaten in the memory of the present occupants; there were chests and cupboards which had not been moved or swept behind for years. We actually found some dirty plates at the back of the cooker that Anne had never seen before. They were so encrusted with ancient grime that we threw them in the dustbin.

Happy had left no note, no explanation. The coroner recorded a verdict of accidental death. There was no evidence that it was anything else. That he had been upset the last time I'd seen him? What good could it do anyone to bring that up? That he had dreamed I shot him? I'd watched as a trunk containing Happy's things was loaded onto a lorry in the Castle Court. What would his parents do with the contents? I'd wondered. And who were they? Another month or two and I might have met them. Now I never would. Where did they live, anyway? Colchester, was it? Chelmsford? Ipswich? Somewhere down there. I only knew for certain that it was not Dungeness. Nothing but nothing of Happy remained to me. Addresses were normally only exchanged at the ends of terms, holiday post-cards only after that. It was as if in his own death Happy had cut something away from me and caused me to die a little as well. This was not Dungeness. That negative was all I knew...

I gave Malcolm a slightly edited account of that. He got up and poured us one more cognac. I didn't tell him the next bit...

A terrible depression had seized me as the spring advanced. Brighter the weather might grow day by day but blacker and deeper the hole I seemed to be falling down. The doctor prescribed some pills. They made me feel even more disconnected. Anne came to see me but seemed to sit outside. It was the same with all of them: with my college friends, with Laura and Janie. Even when Anne sat on the bed beside me, an arm around my shoulder, she seemed to be outside.

One day she lost patience with me, told me my depression had become self-indulgent, that it served no useful purpose; I had to put the past behind me and get on with life. I became angry with her, told her she didn't understand. A shouting match began and then, suddenly, a frenzy took hold of me; it was something I'd never experienced before. I found myself yelling, swearing, throwing things at Anne. She fled screaming from the room. I saw her from the window, a small figure in the street below. There was something I had to tell her, but what was it? I'm sorry? No. I love you? Something to do with Happy? Or, I hate? My fists were clenched now. They went through the plate-glass as if through butter, and the glass slid down the air like the floe ice down the weir, all shining shards that tinkled softly as they landed. Anne's figure ran from sight, blood ran from my hands, other knuckles hammered at my door.

It was probably the long wait in casualty, with roughly bandaged wrists, that had brought me back to my senses.

Months passed before I made contact again with Anne. It came about through Laura. 'What are you going to do about Anne?' she said one day while Janie's needles clicked away in the corner of the room.

'Do?' I asked.

'Yes, do! Or have you been expecting her to reappear with flowers and apologies?'

'Of course not,' I said. 'I just don't expect she'll want to be reminded of my existence, that's all.'

'The difference between not wanting to see someone again and knowing that it's not your move is enormous. Did you know that? What about writing, at least?'

I'd looked sharply at Laura. Nearby, Janie's knitting needles clicked on impassively, not missing a beat. 'Are you here as Anne's messenger?' I'd asked.

'No,' said Laura. 'I'm here as yours.'

In the end I called at Anne's flat and, without preamble or flowers, boldly proposed taking a long walk together the next Saturday. Rather to my surprise she, equally bold, accepted at once.

The day was beautiful. It was June. Larks sang overhead as we left the city behind and headed out across an open rolling landscape. We saw hares, alert on distant knolls, that in turn followed our progress with tele-photo vision. We walked into an old mining village, a slimmed-down version of its former self, where the remaining cottages overlooked a wide sun trap of a green. Here one building only stood, the village pub, and there we sat outside, eating sandwiches and drinking beer, at rustic tables made from old ale casks.

Later we lay together at the edge of a field and, under a cloudless sky, partly undressed and made love for the first time. A rite of passage, this, that I'd long tried to imagine, script, cast and direct but the reality was better, easier and more natural than anything I could have wished. It happened as smoothly as I'd slipped my hand through the plate-glass window. And I realised that it was then this rite of passage had occurred – not now but at the moment when my fist broke through the pane. What happened now, so easy, so beautiful, so right, was simply that the rest of me had followed suit...

413

I could see Malcolm looking at me oddly. I must have been silent for a while. I think he could see that I'd skipped a bit. I resumed.

'I moved out of college in my third year and into Anne's flat. It surprised none of our friends. Once it was an accomplished fact it seemed as inevitable as the completion of Janie's endless scarf. She did eventually finish it; it was seven metres long and was worn round the neck of a man she had met when the scarf was only inches long. She married him when it reached eleven feet.

'We got married the next summer. Honeymoon in Italy, return to Durham in the autumn. I began my post-graduate teaching course... And the rest you know, of course.' It was on that teaching course that Malcolm and I had met.

'And Anne got a research assistant's post in the university museum,' Malcolm said. 'Have I remembered right?'

'Yes,' I said.

'You know,' said Malcolm. 'Hearing you tell that story about Happy... I'd say, if I didn't know you better, married man and all, that you and Happy were a little bit in love. In fact, now I think about it, I wonder if Happy wasn't perhaps very much in love with you. You didn't seem to be responding... And that's what his problem was.'

'Oh shit,' I said. 'Now that's given me something to feel bad about.' I was making out that that idea had never crossed my mind. But I was being disingenuous. The idea that Happy had been in love with me had crossed my mind from time to time. At bad moments. In the dark spaces of bad nights.

I heard Malcolm say, 'None of us are responsible for the actions of others. If other people fall for us, that's their problem, not ours.'

I was grateful for that. I remembered a line of – I think – John Donne's. *That I love thee is no concern of thine.* Malcolm had just, very kindly, put that the other way round.

I looked at my watch. 'Oh my God,' I said. 'It's one o'clock. I've been rambling and keeping you up.'

'Don't worry about it,' Malcolm said. 'It's been an interesting evening. We can always sleep on the train tomorrow.'

Meanwhile we now got ready to go to bed.

I dreamt of Happy. But this time it was different. My imagination had made a leap. Perhaps because I'd been talking about him, perhaps because Malcolm had said something neither I nor anyone else had, and that I'd never confronted. Those words of Malcolm – *you and Happy were a little bit in love* – must have bitten deep.

In my dream Happy and I were sharing an armchair, seated side by side. It was a tight squeeze. I was conscious of the side of him, shoulder, arm and hip, pressed hard against me. My leg was squashed up against his. I felt the warmth of him for the first time ever. In life we'd scarcely ever touched. A handshake, perhaps, or a mock punch, would have been the most.

Did he then touch my head? Rumple my hair, perhaps? I'm not sure, because I awoke at that point. Awoke in confusion and embarrassment because I found I was coming, and it was too late to do anything to stop it, coming all over my host's sheets. I found myself using my hand to help the last of my semen out.

I was not only wet, but mortified. Why had this had to happen on my first night in Malcolm's spare bed? I should have worn pyjamas, I thought ruefully, or gone to bed in underpants. But that wasn't the worst of it. I'd never dreamt in that way about a man or boy before. Now I'd just made myself wet while dreaming of a male friend who was dead. It was a deep and unpleasant shock.

It was only five o'clock. I went back to sleep and dozed a bit, then, when I heard the others stirring, I got up.

I had to come clean about it, make a joke of it, at breakfast. 'I'm awfully sorry, Malcolm,' I said, assuming a sheepish grinning look. 'But I've had a wet dream in your sheets.'

Malcolm laughed, and so did Henri. *'Tu as fait la carte de France, comme on dit,'* he said: *You've made the map of France, as they say.* While Malcolm said, 'Don't worry about it. That's what sheets are for. Dreaming about Happy, no doubt.'

'Good God!' I said. 'Why on earth do you say that?' But then a dreadful thing happened. I began to blush deeply, and I saw Malcolm clock it. I saw him realise that, even if quite by accident, he had hit the nail on the head. He was kind enough not to say any more on the subject. He said something about the coffee we were drinking instead.

Chapter 7

The *Train de Grande Vitesse* was still a novelty. The showpiece of French engineering, it had been introduced just a few years previously and, running on a brand new track from the suburbs of Paris to those of Lyon, had brought the two cities to within two hours of each other. Like a thread yanked tight in the hem of a garment it had, at one stroke, changed for ever the shape and scale of France. Sold to the regions as the key to their own futures, the TGV was meant to break the centralising grip of Paris on the economic life of the country. In reality the opposite was happening. True, some centres of industry and population were shifting along its golden plateway but always in the direction of the capital, not away from it.

But none of this was in my thoughts as Malcolm and I boarded the flame-coloured train at the Gare de Lyon that brilliant morning in July. Few of the passengers were dressed for business; most wore the expression, half anxious, half excited, of people bent on escape. Escape from work, escape from the city, escape too, this particular morning – though the patriotic among them would never had admitted it publicly – from something else. For today was no ordinary July Tuesday. It was the Fourteenth. Malcolm (a foreigner and therefore exempt from patriotic qualms) was able to voice their unspoken guilty thoughts.

'I've been through three *Quatorzes* and, frankly, I've had them up to here. *Ras – le – bol!* It's always the same. The same tanks, the same fly past. The parade, the salute and the cavalry falling off their horses like clockwork on the same tight turn. The streets are impassable and the shops shut. You see it better on the television.

'Even the fireworks – they're spectacular, I must admit – can only be seen properly if you've got a friend with a well-sited balcony. Then to finish with there's the Firemen's Balls to tide you over painlessly from the *Quatorze* to the morning after. They can be fun, I grant you.' He paused to signal the inevitable tag. 'That is, if firemen's balls are really what you're into.'

For all the generosity of Malcolm's invitation I'd inevitably had some reservations about going to Provence with him. Holidays were notorious slayers of friendships. And I had feared that twelve days in the company of such a flamboyantly homosexual personality might prove rather wearing.

A few passengers were still arguing over the numbers of their seats and invoking the phlegmatic ticket controllers as referees when the double-length train slipped from its berth as imperceptibly as any cruise liner. It glided past the end of the platform, out from the shade of the station's arching canopy and into the embracing sunshine: a slender orange compass needle seeking South.

The south. That was the attraction, of course. It was the idea of the south that now awoke in me the eager excitement with which children begin their holidays. I determined to cast from my mind any reservations or anxieties about spending twelve days in close proximity to a gay man. It crossed my mind for a moment that perhaps those anxieties had added an extra piquancy to the venture. I told myself they had not.

Purposefully, with no sense of hurry, the train threaded its way through leafy outskirts, following at first the windings of the Seine until, without signalling the fact by so much as a click, the new track branched away from the old. Three, two, one, announced trackside panels silently to the driver and anyone who happened to be looking out of the window; then the train, already fast by any ordinary standard, effortlessly doubled its speed: a cantering horse changing up to full gallop. There was no sensation of the urgency of a plane on its take-off run or the breathless haste of a car on a race track. Rather it was as if the landscape had changed its focus; the senses that experienced it and plotted its reality in relation to time had selected a different magnification. And so the rolling pastures of northern Burgundy were conjured up from the normally endless-seeming plains of the Ile de France in a mere ten minutes. Another thirty minutes and Burgundy itself was left far behind in the slipstream of the train, now in free fall down the face of France.

Van Gogh had made the same journey, of course, as Malcolm now reminded me, although at a less exhilarating speed.

I told him Happy had once said that van Gogh's whole life had been a journey from darkness to light, from the cold north to the warm south, from the clouds to the sun.

I remembered Happy showing me the picture of the Potato Eaters. It wasn't one of the bright Van Gogh prints that had 'dis-endarkened' his bedroom walls; Happy had had to delve into a book to show me a photo of it, all black, brown and sepia. 'Then came Paris,' Happy had said. 'Two years there. And finally, off to the south where...' He'd tailed off and allowed the pictures in his book to articulate the rest of it. Van Gogh's two years in Provence had crowned his career with their celebration on canvas of his discovery of the light.

Now I remembered something else. Happy had added, 'Not everyone who begins that journey gets there at all.' Perhaps it was the unbearable poignancy of that remark that had caused me to blank the memory of the paintings on Happy's walls until it was woken by the sight of Malcolm's picture-hung apartment.

Time-charmed castles came and went among the changing perspectives of the hills while the Beaujolais mountains bided their time in the hazy distance. At last, decelerating smoothly, the train emerged from the uplands and, on a track as steep and winding as a staircase, descended to where the town of Lyon lay draped over the surrounding hills like a vast and richly patterned carpet.

'Impressive, isn't it?' said Malcolm. It was his first experience of the TGV too.

'Too right,' I said.

A few minutes later – 'Sunflowers!' said Malcolm suddenly.

We had left behind the enormous spread of Lyon and were following the Rhone on its tortuous course down the valley that had linked the south of Europe with the north since prehistoric times. On the right now ran the broad river and on the left a field of yellow faces stared at the sun. Sunflowers.

'How much did that sunflower painting fetch, back in the spring?' Malcolm asked. 'The one they sold to a Japanese guy in London?'

'A lot,' I said. 'I don't remember how much.'

'Permit me to interrupt,' said a neighbour in heavily accented English. He was one of the few occupants of the carriage to wear a business suit. He was middle-aged, with shiny slicked-back hair and unusually lustrous dark eyes. He leaned forward to address us. 'I could not stop myself hearing. If it interests you it was twenty-two and a half million pounds sterling. A world record. Compare that, if you want, with the artist's poverty. Compare it even with mine.' He chuckled and gave us a business card that identified him as a fine art dealer from Arles. 'Pass and see me if you are in the town,' he said.

'Thank you,' we said.

Now town succeeded town, each vying for the brightest orange tiles, most luminous apricot walls and most brilliant blue sky. There was not a cloud to be seen by the time the profile of Mont Ventoux filled the eastern horizon and the train was coiling slowly round the ancient walls of Avignon, where the pennants atop the Palace of the Popes hung limply in the breathless afternoon. The air-conditioned train stopped and the door opened like an oven's. Our art dealing acquaintance gave us a discreet wave as we left the train while a tide of baking desert heat engulfed us when we stepped onto the platform.

Malcolm said, 'Which one of us do you reckon that guy fancied? The art dealer.'

It hadn't crossed my mind that he might have fancied either of us.

Despite the bustle of the season, we managed to find a hotel that suited our modest budgets and that first night it was so warm that we slept with all windows open and the shutters folded back. This suited me well since it helped to dispel the vague claustrophobia I'd imagined into existence at the prospect of sharing a room with Malcolm. In the event the experience was perfectly unthreatening – we undressed demurely with our backs to each other the way straight men do, and we then each donned a pair of pyjamas that (certainly my case, so quite probably also in Malcolm's) had not seen service in years, but had been hauled out of retirement precisely for the present unusual circumstances.

It was the first time I'd knowingly shared a bedroom with a gay man. Perhaps it was because of this that I had another wet dream in the middle of the night. This time I didn't know, when I awoke to find my hand a-flutter on my pulsing, spurting cock, what or who I had been dreaming about. That was just as well, I thought.

At least I didn't have to confess to Malcolm this time round. The sheets were not his but those of the Hotel Bristol. They were used to this, presumably, and semen stains – unless DNA testing is applied – are pretty anonymous.

But disaster had struck overnight, although in a very minor way. It came from a totally unexpected source: Malcolm and I both woke up studded with the largest and most painful mosquito bites we had ever experienced. We were sheepishly aware that we had been stupid not to foresee this. Three of the largest culprits could be clearly seen parked at dispersal stations around the walls; they were summarily squashed. Later we discovered the mosquito screens for the windows in the wardrobe.

'It's not as if they just itched,' Malcolm complained, applying a preparation we got from the pharmacy – at some expense. 'They remind you of their existence every few minutes with a little stab of pain. It's worse than wasps' stings.' We had agreed in advance that we'd come to relax, do some sightseeing, drive round the region following the Van Gogh trail, and eat drink and sleep a little more than usual. 'No sport,' Malcolm had insisted. 'At least, not for me. If you want to go out jogging on your own, that's just fine, and I'll hole up in some suitable bar while you do it – unless it's at sparrows' fart in which case I'll simply stay in bed. And if you want to play a game of cricket and can find another twenty-one people with the same inclination, then that's fine by me too. Only don't ask me to be the referee or whatever it is you call it. For snooker, though, or pétanque – well, I'm up for those if you find you get a craving.' Holidaying with friends was all about compromises. I thought I could live with this one.

Chapter 8

We spent our first day wandering in the ancient squares and alleys of Avignon and in the evening we dined in the coolest spot in town: an old lane with a stream flowing beside it. It boasted a small restaurant housed in what appeared to be an antique shop. There was only one dish on the menu, a *daube* of wild boar, and only one wine, a local red, served in engraved goblets. We ate with just six other diners, all at the same table, surrounded by leather-bound books and gilt-framed mirrors that reflected the candle-light, and surveyed by a statue of Saint Lucy, who carried her own eyes before her on a dish like two poached eggs. The proprietors – he the waiter, she the cook – kept watch on us customers from across the street, sitting in the cool on the low wall that divided river from road. The bill when it came was modest in relation to the quality of the experience.

Someone had told us of a garage in Avignon that rented out cars at a third of the normal price, and the nest day we sought it out. It had been decided that Malcolm, veteran of French roads, would do most of the driving and I could make my debut, if I wanted to, in some anonymous rural spot. But this plan had to be drastically rethought when Malcolm discovered that his driving licence remained in Paris. So I received my initiation into the ways of most of the motoring world among the morning traffic on the six lanes of the Avignon ring road. The car was neither new nor pretty – not that those things bothered us. More disturbing was the rear-view mirror's habit of sliding down the windscreen like a snail in fast motion.

Never mind. The sun was hot and we were high on the effects of our surroundings: colour, scent and countryside; escape from Paris, in Malcolm's case and, in mine, escape from just about everything else.

The road took us that morning to the hilltop village of Gordes where we could afford nothing except the view, and then to the shaded valley of Sénanques where a timeless Cistercian abbey rode like a ship at anchor on a bee-buzzing lavender sea. Then the mid-day sun swept into the valley like a blow-torch. 'Want to visit somewhere cooler?' Malcolm asked.

We found the canyon of Fontaine de Vaucluse. At the narrow head of the valley green waters welled from a cave so deep that not even Cousteau had got to the bottom of it and here, centuries before, Petrarch had settled reclusively to contemplate the beauties of nature and his absent Laura. The sky at this point was reduced to a narrow blue ribbon across which kites sailed from time to time, going from one horizon to the other in half a dozen seconds. A little lower down the gorge the sky broadened out with the river. Here white-bibbed dippers plunged and darted in the icy waters that, unable to agree upon their own level, argued noisily among the rocks.

Malcolm found a smooth slab of rock that seemed to have been placed deliberately in midstream for the convenience of sunbathers and, hopping across to it, installed himself there. He was not born to be a sunbather as I could see from his reddening knees and nose but, in adopting the attitude of one, he looked as comfortable and relaxed as I, now perched on a boulder nearby, could remember seeing him. His face had lost its habitual tension and his eyes, which I had always thought of as black, now seemed no darker than hazel as they caught the reflection of the brightness above.

'What do you want to be when you grow up?' Malcolm called across to me. It was an unexpected question.

'Be?' I asked. 'Or do?' I felt happier, lighter, than I'd done for weeks. Was it Malcolm's company that had done that?

'Either. Both,' Malcolm said laughingly. 'Doesn't matter – though I appreciate the distinction.'

'I actually thought I was grown-up already. Don't you think that at twenty-eight – and you ought to be an authority now that you're twenty-eight as well – I should be?'

'Should be, perhaps. Yes, at twenty-eight you should be.' There was an unspoken reservation in Malcolm's answer. I let it go without challenging. Between my boulder and Malcolm's rock slab gushed a torrent of water a metre wide, though the noise and urgency of its progress made it seem broader than that.

'I once thought I'd grown up,' Malcolm continued, as much to himself as to me. 'Then I found I hadn't. And now...' The phrase tailed off in the splashing of the water. He turned towards me. 'How would you like to live here?'

'What? Like Petrarch? A solitary hermit in a hut? 'The world forgetting, by the world forgot.' I'm not sure I would. It is a bit extreme down here in this chasm. Winter evenings might get a bit depressing, I imagine.'

'Well all right, not precisely here maybe. But in Provence. Or anywhere in *la France Profonde*.'

'What?'

Malcolm was speaking quietly and the rushing water was very loud.

'*La France Profonde*. Deepest France. I would.'

'Would what?'

'Like to live here.'

This surprised me. 'I always thought you were a town mouse.'

'Appearances are defective, as someone probably said already or ought to have done. I was born in the wilds of Cornwall. I must have told you that. The wilds of Provence would be quite like home – if a bit warmer.

But then I'm at home everywhere. And nowhere too, of course. And you?'

'And me what?' I wasn't sure if I'd caught all the words. It would be easier without the rapids between us.

'Would you like to live in Provence?' Malcolm articulated the question and at the same moment I rose from my rocky perch and leaped across the stream. I landed neatly astride Malcolm's waist but then nearly toppled backwards into the current. To steady myself I dropped to a crouching position and accidentally found myself kneeling astride him and grasping his shoulders.

Malcolm gave me a smile of surprise. At that precise moment I found it appealing and boyish.

'That's better,' I said. 'Now I can hear you properly.' I laughed; I wasn't quite sure why. Perhaps it was the unexpected novelty of my position, almost sitting on top of Malcolm and peering into his face. The novelty of seeing Malcolm smiling up at me like that, his smile almost turning to a laugh. I said, 'Yes, perhaps I wouldn't mind living in Provence, though I'd want to see a bit more of it first. And it would depend who with, of course. What were you trying to say about being at home everywhere?'

'And nowhere,' Malcolm answered seamlessly. 'And by the same token. Like the wandering Jew, as Verlaine said in a poem called *Walcourt* – which you should read if you haven't already. Only Verlaine wasn't Jewish. I mean, not literally.' He looked straight up into my eyes. 'And neither are we.'

And then for some reason which I'm still not able to explain properly, I leaned down and kissed Malcolm on the lips. It was an equal surprise for both of us.

A second later I detached himself from Malcolm and rolled a short distance across the rock slab. I felt confused and awkward, though nothing worse than that. 'Have you got a cigarette?' I asked.

Chapter 9

There were no wet dreams that night. Not for me at any rate. As for Malcolm, well, I didn't ask. There are some things you don't.

Another of those things you don't ask friends, but wait till they volunteer the information, is the question, *Why did you get divorced?* Another, *Whose fault was it?* Malcolm hadn't asked me anything about my divorce, and I'd volunteered very little to date. To my surprise I found myself wanting to answer those unasked questions of his when I awoke the next morning, even though I knew I'd find the subject difficult. I wondered if this had something to do with the extraordinary fact that I'd given him a kiss.

The heat was quite something. We decided to move to L'Isle sur la Sorgue, a small and slumberous town whose name's every syllable suggested the plash of water wheels and encircling streams. It was about an hour's drive from Avignon, and when we arrived we found it looking every bit as lovely as the sound of its name. There were the water wheels, there were the streams. As we whiled away the end of the afternoon on one of its old plane-shaded terraces, dragonflies skimmed up and down the watercourse beside us, their reds, greens and blues providing a changing pattern of jewels against the backcloth of the jade-green crowfoot whose tresses seemed almost to fill the fast-flowing river. One dragonfly landed on Malcolm's wristwatch and stared with its shiny Martian face uncomprehendingly at the passing time.

'Only the big ones are really dragonflies,' I said. 'The little ones are damsel-flies.'

'Call them what you like, they're both beautiful,' Malcolm said.

A battered Renault Four pulled up alongside us. It was white, with a rainbow transfer applied along the side. It also had more than the usual number of dents and craters. It had been rammed from the rear, attacked frontally and subjected to the odd broadside as well. 'I bet that comes from Paris,' Malcolm said.

Out of the Renault stepped a young woman, blonde, slender, who turned her face away from us just at the moment when I realised that it was beautiful. Moving with the grace of a dancer, transforming her simple dress by the way she wore it, she crossed the road and disappeared into a shop.

'Now that,' I said, 'is the eternal feminine of France.' I realised I was rather waving my heterosexual credentials in Malcolm's face. Perhaps I needed to do that though, after yesterday's kiss.

'Her background?' Malcolm asked. This was a game we'd used to play when we were together learning to teach, though we hadn't done since.

'Ballet teacher,' I suggested. 'Or masseuse.'

'Nothing so physical,' Malcolm said. 'She does wonderful things for the poor in the third world. She's a plain-clothes nun.'

When she came out of the shop she was encumbered with an enormous though not heavy-looking parcel ('knitted blankets for Bangladesh,' said Malcolm) that got in her way when she came to unlock her car. I was sitting only inches away. I sprang up and took the parcel from her while she dealt with the door. I was rewarded with a bright though brief smile and a *merci beaucoup*. Then she drove away.

'Thus,' said Malcolm, 'does the beautiful dragonfly emerge from its chrysalis, even as from a beat-up Renault, and disappear for ever into the wide blue.'

'The damsel-fly as well,' I said. 'And which was she, do you suppose?'

'A damsel or a dragon?' Malcolm queried. 'Let's say a damsel, shall we? Be nice and give her the benefit of the doubt?'

We were returning later that evening from a substantial restaurant meal when Malcolm came to a halt in the middle of a small square and exclaimed: 'Good God! Look at that.'

'At what?' I said

'That café. The Café de France. It's a dead-ringer for the *Terrasse du Café le Soir*. Look. The light spilling out on the pavement, the round tables, the awning – even the dark street beyond with its lighted windows, even the stars above.'

'Was this the very place, perhaps?' I asked.

'No,' said Malcolm authoritatively. 'Vincent painted a café in Arles. But he got the actual idea for the picture from a description in Guy de Maupassant.'

'Of the same café?'

'No such luck. De Maupassant was describing a boulevard café in Paris. Which just goes to show how we go round in circles. Nothing is what it seems or where you expect to find it. And when you begin a journey the destination is never the one you thought you were setting out for.' Malcolm paused for a second. 'Look, we're in a direct line for home now. Reckon to call in for a route-map on the way?' A route-map was a new coinage of Malcolm's own: an alloy of night-cap and one for the road. I found I was up for that.

And so we walked up from the square onto the lighted café terrace. It was as if we were actually walking into Vincent's bright canvas. I felt a frisson among the hairs at the back of my neck.

'Hey!' Malcolm said when we were installed at one of the terrace tables among the beau monde of L'Isle sur la Sorgue. 'It's the dragonfly.'

'Damsel-fly, didn't we agree?' I prompted.

'As you want.'

The damsel, or dragon, was sitting at the next table with two other young people, one of each sex, who were clearly a couple. After a moment she nodded across in recognition and after a few more seconds Malcolm asked her if he and I could join their table, something which I, had I been alone, would not have thought of doing. Well, I might have thought of it. But only thought.

As Malcolm had said, appearances were defective. The damsel was a journalist who worked for the *Dépêche du Midi* and her friends were, respectively, a nuclear physicist and an infant school teacher. The man taught in infant school, his girlfriend wore the white coat.

The first route-map begged a second and once the internationality as well as the francophone credentials of the gathering had been established, conversation developed on a number of subjects which the world was at that time waiting to have put right.

The waiter arrived to chat and to elicit a further order. Malcolm took advantage of the ensuing buzz to say to me in English, 'You could make that woman tonight if you wanted.'

For some reason I found myself appalled by his suggestion. 'Are you joking?' I hissed.

'Only partly,' Malcolm said. 'I know you won't, of course. But if you wanted to. The couple will go in a few minutes, I can sense it. She'll stay to see what will happen. Two minutes later I plead a headache and retire. The rest is up to you. I'll keep the room warm till you get back. If you do get back before breakfast time, throw stones at the window.'

I was even more appalled at hearing this eminently practical scenario spelled out so simply, so clinically. 'Get away,' I whispered.

Another route-map was agreed and ordered. One or two more conversational hares were started only to be lost sight of in the shimmer of the summer night. The glasses empty, the three French people took their leave together.

'Guess your vibes weren't all that positive,' concluded Malcolm.

I felt an explanation was necessary. 'It's just that casual sex doesn't hold a great deal of attraction for me at the moment. Perhaps it never has done. I can't explain. Perhaps...'

The waiter arrived to offer us a drink on behalf of the *patron* – a traditional form of long-service medal. After that it seemed necessary for some reason to buy one back for the patron and another for the waiter. As Malcolm had said, we were on a straight line for home.

Malcolm leaned across the table towards me. 'We still have time to talk, don't we?' he said smoothly. That is, if you have anything you specially want to talk about.'

Was the guy a mind-reader? 'Yes,' I said. 'Funny you should say that. There is.'

'Thought there might be,' Malcolm said.

Chapter 10

Here we were, on the terrace of a café that looked uncannily like the one that Van Gogh had made world famous, and Malcolm had invited me to talk. It was the moment I'd been waiting for all that day – perhaps for longer. It was a moment, under the fading evening sky, with a friend, over a drink, that was made for opening up. 'I told you I didn't like Beethoven,' I heard myself suddenly, erratically, begin. 'And that Happy told me I'd one day come to change my mind. Well, I did change my mind a few years later. I'd like to tell you about the person who carried out the conversion. I was a Schubert freak at that time. You may remember that.' Malcolm nodded. 'Happy used to quote a famous musician who said, 'Schubert is a forest in sunshine and shadow; Beethoven a mountain range.''

'Uh-huh,' said Malcolm, making an effort to follow this. 'So who showed you the mountains?'

'I'm going to tell you,' I said. 'I didn't exactly choose to become a school teacher,' I continued. 'But what else did you do with an English degree? I was just about to get married. People started to talk about security and so on and before long, so did I. The training course beckoned. It pointed towards a life of school, of marriage and family, with long summer holidays on the plus side and late nights marking essays on the minus.'

'It was the same for me,' Malcolm reminded me. 'The same for all of us.'

'Sorry,' I said. 'You went through the training course with me. I haven't forgotten that. It's just that we haven't seen much of each other since, and I've never really told you what happened after that.' Malcolm nodded. I pressed on. 'My first year as a teacher went really well. I'd got a job just outside Durham which was lucky. You did know that, of course. Anne was still there doing research and we'd managed to rent a house really cheaply on the edge of town. The headmaster thought I was doing a good job as beginners go, that I was energetic – for that read young and naïf – and I managed all right with discipline. Don't ask me how. Most of the kids even seemed to like me.'

'Why do you sound so surprised?' asked Malcolm.

I ignored that. Now I'd started, there seemed an awful lot I wanted to get out. 'After a year or so I started to panic. About work I mean. About the results of it all.'

'I don't get you. Exam results?'

'No, of course not. I mean the real results. The results of my teaching those kids the language of Shakespeare, Wilde, Lawrence...'

'And what was the result?'

'Nearly non-existent. Or so it seemed to me for the best part of two years. Naturally I talked to my colleagues about it and they did their best to be positive. They suggested for instance that just by keeping them busy in the classroom, Shakespeare and I were stopping the kids from vandalising phone boxes and stealing motor bikes. I didn't think a great deal of that argument. It didn't make me feel any better for one thing and it didn't reflect too well on poor old Shakespeare either.'

'Oh, I don't know. Anyone from the seventeenth century who can save modern phone boxes from vandals can't be all bad. Don't forget, I've been a school teacher myself.'

'Of course,' I said I was talking as if I hadn't remembered that. It was the drink, of course. 'Sorry.' But I went on anyway.

'I was saying I didn't have any discipline problems. Well, that was almost entirely true. There was one kid though, just one in all the classes I taught, who was a perfect pest. He was fourteen when I arrived at the school, very bright but younger than the rest of his class and a late physical developer into the bargain. He made up for this by being an attention-seeker, irritatingly trying to be witty in class. His classmates found him witty, of course, his teachers just irritating. Me included. If there was a double entendre to be dredged up out of a text he was always the one to find it and then question me about it with an insolently straight face. Then he'd dream up the kind of classroom pranks the others had grown out of years before – you know, alarm clocks going off in locked cupboards, gerbils in the waste-paper basket, that sort of thing...' Malcolm nodded. He knew only too well, of course.

'Well, you get the picture. This kid was called Ian Lewis. There's an Ian in every school; you also know that. They're nice as anything outside the classroom. They just go mental inside it. And they're quite impervious to punishment. Ian was once actually thrown out of a detention class for being disruptive.'

'I'm beginning to like this kid,' said Malcolm. 'Go on.'

'For some reason I found it doubly infuriating because he was good at English and also he read better than the others – at least he could once he forgot about sending the text sky high. One day – by now he was about sixteen and had already been a pain in the arse for two years – we were doing King Lear and I'd asked him to read the part of the King. He came to the line, 'And my poor fool is hanged', where he suddenly stopped and couldn't go on. I looked at him a bit apprehensively, wondering what we were in for, expecting some kind of joke I suppose. But what I saw surprised me much more: his face was running with tears. Why that particular line had moved him I don't know. There are others more obviously pathetic. Maybe, simply, the whole tragedy had come home to him all at once in that single moment. Now it went through my head that I had the perfect opportunity to humiliate him in front of his classmates and put an end to his two years of attempted sabotage in a split second. Some teachers would have done.'

Malcolm said grimly, 'I've known a few who did.'

I said, 'The fact I even thought about it just shows how much he'd tried everyone. But I didn't make a conscious decision. I simply finished the line myself and read the part of the king till the end of the scene. A few of the kids looked at me, surprised, but nobody looked at him and he was able to recover himself without losing face. Men still weren't allowed to cry in the north-east of England and certainly not when only sixteen.

'Neither of us referred to the incident at the time by even so much as a smile but the change in his behaviour could hardly have been more remarkable – at least in my classes. I say that because I gathered from other teachers that with them he went on pretty much as before, but I never had any trouble from him again. He still liked to lark about, but the destructive thing seemed to have evaporated.'

I took a slurp of wine. 'From that day on I started to enjoy teaching once again. Quite suddenly, quite immediately. And though this was less immediate, the kid began to talk to me outside the classroom, just in the ordinary way. It was something the others all did as a matter of course but, before then, he didn't. He took to button-holing me after lessons with questions about literature, then later with chit-chat about life in general. I began to lend him books I thought would interest him. Then he found his way to our house. Of course he met Anne. Time passed and we all became – well, friends, I suppose. Though with me there was always that space, that fire-break that has to exist between a teacher and a … a non-adult pupil. I got invited to his house. I met his parents and his sister. Becoming a sort of confidant, if you like, I got treated to his views on everything from euthanasia to socialism.'

'And were they earth-shaking?'

'No.' I laughed at the memory. 'But his musical tastes... Well, I mentioned Beethoven. I once said flippantly to Ian that Schubert was worth ten Beethovens. That was a hornets' nest all right. The boy had just had a road to Damascus experience on hearing a disc of some of the piano sonatas played by Artur Schnabel.'

'Who?'

'First person to record all Beethoven's piano music, back in the thirties. Ian had been collecting all the discs one by one. So I was subjected to them, listening grudgingly. But little by little I was converted in my turn. Not just to Schnabel but to Beethoven too – as Happy predicted.'

'After music, the theatre. Anne and I began taking Ian with us to plays in Newcastle occasionally, and sometimes to the cinema. He moved very easily between his own family and us. When the summer came we'd go walking, sometimes the three of us, sometimes Ian and me, sometimes Ian and Anne. It was a beautiful summer, just before Ian began his last year at school, and perhaps the beauty of it blinded me to other things that should have been obvious.'

Malcolm said, incredulously, 'You're not going to tell me he seduced your wife?'

'No, nothing like that. Well, not really. In the autumn he was going to do the Oxbridge entrance exams. He had to have special classes in English, obviously. That meant me. Sometimes at the school, sometimes at his parents' home, or at ours. A bit irregular, I suppose, but we were all family and friends by now.

'One Saturday morning in November when Anne had gone to visit her parents for the weekend I got a phone-call, quite late, from Ian. He was on his own, he said, and was feeling nervous about his Oxford interview. Would I be able to come over for a chat? I said that I could. By that stage the request seemed quite natural and if I sensed something strangely agitated in his voice I'd have put it down to his exam nerves.

'When I got there he was more than nervous. Not exactly drunk, though he'd obviously been to the pub earlier. And I did think it odd when he announced that he'd been left alone in the house for the entire weekend. He explained that his parents thought his sister was at home and his sister thought his parents were. OK, he was seventeen by now and well able to take care of himself but his parents were the careful sort, over-protective if anything, and the last people to leave a teenager alone for the weekend by mistake. I asked him how it had come about. He just grinned and said, "I fixed it." Then he offered me a glass of his father's malt whisky.'

'Which you refused like a good boy?'

'At first, yes. But Ian launched into a crazy spiel about me and him which I couldn't – or just didn't want to – understand. It wasn't till he threw himself into his father's armchair and said in so many words that it was time he told me he loved me that it really sank in. At first I just gaped at him. He repeated what he'd said. 'It's time I told you I love you.' Then I found I wanted that drink. As I poured it I saw – like drowning people who see their lives pass before them – images whose significance seemed to have been hidden from me till then. I can't explain how. I saw Ian smiling at me from his classroom desk, not just once but on dozens of occasions over the years. Smiles which had meant nothing at the time but which now seemed to engage like gears to drive a whole engine of realisation. Now I saw him, only three months earlier, on one of our walks, slipping out of his clothes and plunging into the River Wear; only now did I see how deliberately he had done it, how he had made sure I was looking. There were other occasions... I was seeing in one moment what I'd failed to see in four years.'

A bat fluttered low over our heads under the awning before swooping up under the street-lamp in pursuit of some invisible insect. 'Go on,' said Malcolm.

'Hindsight is wonderful. It tells me now, as it no doubt tells you, that for my own safety I should have left the house there and then. I can see you're thinking that not many people would believe the story I've just told you. Well you're right. Not many people did. I'll come to that. But at the time I didn't sense any danger. Stupidly I imagined that because I didn't reciprocate his feelings I wasn't compromised by staying where I was. Huh! I used to think queer schoolmasters who got into that kind of situation had only themselves to blame when their careers collapsed in scandal and acrimony. Well, I was right of course, but not necessarily for the reason I used to imagine. OK, I stayed, and I'm to blame for that. I tried at first to persuade him he was mistaken. I suggested he had drunk too much, that he was nervous, excited, going through an adolescent phase... Anything. I thought I was being helpful. I soon realised. My words only enraged him. He searched around for the worst insult he could throw at me. "Typical fucking grown-up" was what he came up with. Before long we were shouting at each other all over the house. I'd stopped trying to be reasonable. I was furious with him for putting me in a position that was getting more desperate by the minute. The discussion was now way out of my control; I didn't know how or when it would end.

'Finally he collapsed in tears, howling, on his bed. That was another cue for my exit and this time I decided to take it. I touched him gently on the shoulder, meaning simply, "Goodnight and no hard feelings." He turned, grabbed me, caught me off balance and quickly pulled me down on top of him. He made a move, as I thought, to kiss me. Only he didn't. He sank his teeth into my neck. I yelled as much with surprise as pain – and in that moment the door opened and his parents walked in. Their plans had changed for some reason. You won't be surprised to know that I no longer remember what the reason was.' I stopped speaking and looked up. Malcolm's face was expressionless. I couldn't guess what he was thinking. I resumed,

'I'll skip the next few minutes if you don't mind. It makes me wince even now, though the days and weeks that followed were nearly as bad. Before eight o'clock the next morning – Sunday, remember – I'd had a phone-call from the headmaster. He suggested I might like to take the following week as a paid holiday and call on him for a drink on the Monday. When I did call, he was surprisingly sympathetic. He gave me a cheque for the next term's salary in lieu of notice and explained that this was necessary since Ian's parents were considering taking proceedings against both myself and the school. He reassured me that it was all talk and nothing would come of it but said it would help everyone concerned if I promised never to contact Ian again. He even had a typed document for me to sign, making the undertaking concrete. He also told me that it would be unwise of me to apply for a school-teaching post again. News travelled fast, he said, and the kindest reference he could give me would never be kind enough. He said he'd further my search for any other kind of employment in any way he could. He couldn't speak too highly of my gifts or of my services to the school. He regretted losing me deeply. It was all one of those dreadful things that happen in life. The awful thing was that he meant every word. He was quite unprepared to discuss what had happened and silenced me with his hand when I tried to speak. It appeared that my own guilt or innocence was a total irrelevance. He gave me three large gins during all this. God, I needed them. I was growing up quickly that week.'

'But you signed that paper without a fight?' Malcolm said in a tone of near disbelief. 'You didn't have to do that. If you were as guiltless as you say – and I don't have to tell you that I believe that – you could have proved it, with testimony from Ian, in a court. Innocent until proven guilty. Or did the boy put the boot in?'

'No he didn't. Anne did.'

'Oh bloody hell. How come? And why?'

'That was the worst thing. I phoned her, naturally, as soon as I got home, panicking, that Saturday night. But something in her tone made me uneasy and when she arrived the next day it became more and more apparent that she – of all people – didn't believe my version of events. It was incredible. I was lost. Not only did she disbelieve me, she minded desperately. She persuaded herself somehow that she had always had misgivings about my relationship with Ian, that she had always thought – 'subconsciously' was the word she used – that I might be homosexual and had stifled the thought for years. Can you imagine? Your own wife tells you something like that! You know it to be untrue but...' I looked at Malcolm, challenging him to disagree with this, but he said nothing. I relaxed slightly and went on. 'Well, without Anne's backing I felt unable to defend myself somehow; it was as if the foundations had shifted, and I just collapsed. I signed the bloody paper and was deprived at a stroke of my job, Ian's company, and, eventually, Anne's too.'

'She divorced you.'

'As soon as she could. Since she felt so strongly I suppose she had to. But why feel so strongly about something so mistaken, so untrue? That's what I still can't get over, still find hard to take.'

Malcolm nodded slowly, sympathetically. 'It still hurts, of course. I understand that. What happened to Ian?'

'He was very shaken up for a bit. Was even ill for a time. Messed up his Oxbridge exam. Still, he got over it soon enough as youngsters do. Did all right when it came to A-levels and got a university place at London.'

'So you've seen him since?'

'No, certainly not. I heard that by chance from one of his ex-classmates I bumped into. And that's all I heard.'

'Gosh,' said Malcolm soberly, although sober was a long way from describing his state.

'I've probably told you too much,' I said, suddenly conscious of how much I'd said.

'Actually,' Malcolm said, 'you probably haven't told me enough. Though probably just about enough for tonight. It'll take me a while to get my head round that. Perhaps it's time we headed back.'

With a bit of difficulty we got to our feet, thanked the waiter, who was putting the chairs on the tables – on every table except ours, that is – and said *Bonne nuit.*

Chapter 11

The hotel had provided us with a key to the street door in the event of a late return. That was fortunate. It was nearly two o'clock. But we couldn't make the key fit the only lock. I tried, then Malcolm tried, then we both tried, struggling as much against each other as with the key. But it was not a question eventually of the key's needing a knack to turn it. The key was simply too big to enter the slot at all. We knocked. Loudly and often. No answer came. 'There must be another door,' said Malcolm. There was. We found it with some effort about three yards from the first. This one was a hundred or more years older, a confection of gnarled oak boards and iron studs. Its key-hole was of Jack and the Beanstalk proportions. Our little modern key could poke about in it for ever and not touch the sides.

A black shadow now in an even blacker street, the hotel became a medieval fortress and we were without the means to capture it by night. The town was silent now except for the steady spurt of water through old mill paddles. Drunkenly we cursed our luck, the hotel, the town and everyone in it. Then I noticed a crack of light at the join of a pair of shutters on the top floor. I shouted up to it – something I wouldn't have done at such an hour when sober; perhaps the climate had something to do with it – *'Holà, holà,'* though that was the wrong language, and was agreeably amazed when, after a few repetitions, the shutters were flung open. Yellow light spilled out, bright and warm against the cobalt night. A silhouette was framed in the opening.

'Qu'est-ce qu'il y a?' called an Italian-accented male voice.

'Can you let us in?'

'Didn't they give you a key?'

'It's the wrong one. It doesn't work,' said Malcolm.

'Are you drunk?'

'Not specially,' said Malcolm, his injured tone indicating, why do you ask?

'Wait. I'm coming down.' The window emptied.

The door was opened easily from the inside and a smiling, suntanned young man stood before us. The suntan was more remarkable than the smile because it stretched from head to toe without the interruption of the smallest stitch of clothing. He chuckled and, forming his hand into a fist, applied it to his nose with a rotating gesture, as if attaching a false one. 'Drunk?' he repeated the question. 'Upstairs we're all drunk.' He shrugged. I hadn't realised before that a shrug involved all the muscles from the thighs up. The discovery fascinated me. 'And now you too? That's as it should be,' said the Italian, at that moment showing the first signs of an erection.

Malcolm seemed to have lost the power of speech. It was left to me to murmur, *'Merci,'* and to the Italian to point out the small keyhole we had overlooked among the crevices of the oaken door while we were focused, each of us with one eye shut, on trying to make our key fit the larger one.

'Sleep well,' said the Italian and then paused, perhaps to choose the goodnight gesture that most fitted the situation. In the end he rumpled the hair on top of both our heads – one hand each – and pattered quickly upstairs. By the time we had recovered our wits he was out of sight

Malcolm's friend Peter had talked of having a Van Gogh window opposite his flat in Paris. It shouldn't have been surprising to find another one turning up here on what was pretty much Vincent's home patch. It was more surprising to find this one harbouring neither damsel nor dragon but a flesh and blood, naked, Italian male with the body of a Renaissance athlete and not a fig leaf in sight. But, drunk as I was, I was hardly surprised by what happened next.

Malcolm was all over me before we had even got up the stairs, and my brief kiss of yesterday afternoon was being returned with a quite phenomenal accumulation of interest. And I, drunk as I was, found myself returning Malcolm's kisses quite fulsomely, despite the faint promptings of my more sober self that I didn't really want this, it was sure to lead to complications, and I'd be sorry in the morning. Once inside our room though, we were both out of our clothes in no time, fully aroused and rolling in each other's arms, on one of the beds – it had not yet been decided which was whose, and right now the question would hardly have had meaning. But then, just as Malcolm's hand began to get to grips with my dick and mine drunkenly with his, something happened. It was as if a switch had been thrown somewhere among the circuits of my dulled consciousness, and I heard myself say, 'Sorry, Malcolm. This isn't for us.' With a bit of an effort I extricated himself from Malcolm's embracing arms and legs – the effort being necessary not because Malcolm put up that much of a struggle, but because I was having difficulty co-ordinating my own movements. Then I stumbled off to the bathroom, finding that I quite genuinely needed to pee. When I returned, Malcolm was conclusively tucked up in one of the beds and not looking at me, though he did say, quite civilly, 'I guess that wasn't too good an idea after all.'

'OK,' I said. 'Let's forget it, shall we? Go to sleep now?'

We did. We slept like rocks and woke up with very bad headaches. We were too late for breakfast at the hotel and had to scour the town for coffee and croissants in the middle of the morning. We were not surprised to find the Italian, now fully clothed and with a group of friends, doing the same thing. We greeted each other with warm smiles of recognition, shaking hands among the café tables and exchanging a few hackneyed words about hangovers. We all said *tu* to one another as though the singularity of the previous night's encounter automatically licensed this familiarity. But, breakfast over, we never saw the Italian again.

We didn't discuss the embarrassing bedtime episode. We became talkative and bright after breakfast – an astute witness might have said too bright. It seemed we had both decided to declare the incident null and void.

Malcolm suggested St-Rémy as our next destination, I said: 'Why not?' I'd never heard of the place and would have said the same to San Sebastian or St Moritz. Despite my swimming head, this was the day I found the car becoming less of a problem. For the first time I began to feel it quite natural that oncoming traffic should hurl itself towards me on my left instead of approaching politely from the right as it did in England. It no longer startled me that the gear-lever should leave its knob in my hand whenever I needed to change down particularly suddenly. Even the fact that the car tended to weave from side to side at speeds of over a hundred kilometres per hour no longer bothered me; no more did the violent vibration that started up simultaneously in the steering column.

By the time we arrived in St-Rémy I had learned, thanks to Malcolm, that this was the place where Van Gogh had spent the second of his two Provence years. But I suspected that the town was important to Malcolm for some reason more personal than this.

A circlet of miniature boulevards lined with plane trees protected the tiny town centre like a charm. Once on the inside there was little place for traffic or its emissions, and no room for troubled thoughts; those things were left behind like wild dogs outside the stockade of plane trees.

Van Gogh was in evidence everywhere. The sites he had chosen to paint were drawn to the attention of visitors by discreetly placed reproductions. He had not actually lived in the charmed town centre but a little way outside it – in the insane asylum, to be brutally precise. That might have been expected to put a damper on his appreciation of the place. But the pictures that I saw all around me seemed blessedly infected with the sunny, extrovert charms of the town. Charms that had begun to work on me as soon as I arrived, dispelling troubling thoughts.

Not only Van Gogh but also Nostradamus had lived in this place. Nostradamus who had dared to reveal a fearsome future to a God-fearing past. I said, 'It's hard to imagine anyone having such terrifying visions in so placid a spot.'

Malcolm answered by showing me a Van Gogh picture. It only took a minute to find a copy of it on a postcard outside a shop. In it the painter had depicted St-Rémy as if snugly tucked up for the night, in bed among the soft enfolding hills. A few lights glowed complacently from the cheerful houses that nestled around the church spire in the centre. But the sleepy town was blissfully unaware of the celestial high-jinks in progress above. A vast crescent moon seemed to be trying to touch its toes in a radiant furnace of energy while stars and constellations exploded in Catherine wheels of sparks. The Milky Way itself rolled like phosphorescent ocean waves and broke in glittering showers on distant hills.

'The heavens at play while mankind sleeps?' Malcolm hazarded. 'There's Nostradamus in context for you, if you want. Does it help you to make sense of things, do you think?'

I chose not to ask him what things he thought I was trying to make sense of. I'd realised that I knew that picture very well. It had had pride of place on Happy's wall all those years ago. Was that the terrifying night sky he had gone out to look for on his lonely winter walks? Was it the one he had finally found on the last one?

Malcolm must have noticed my moment of silent thoughtfulness. He said, 'Ghosts of yours in the picture?' But I didn't answer, and he didn't press me. Not then.

Chapter 12

We drove out of the town past the asylum and up into the Alpilles, the cockscomb of mini-mountains between St-Rémy and the sea. From here we could see the whole Rhone delta, from Montpelier to Marseille, the distant sweep of the Mediterranean shimmering beyond its inlets and lagoons. Inland lay Avignon, asleep like a tawny beast in its loop of the Rhone, while over to the east the wispy outlines of Alpine peaks emerged and vanished by turn like summer clouds amidst the haze.

The heat was intense, energy-sapping; all life was invested in the light, the colour and the scents around. Winding down from the hills on our return to St-Rémy, we passed the ruins of a Roman town not long since resurrected from encroaching olive groves. Here we sat out the hottest part of the day in the shade of a dark green cypress tree. Actually we didn't sit. We lay on our backs on the grass. In order to stay in the shade we had to move round it in circular fashion as time went on, like the two hands of a clock. Redstarts and wheatears flitted among the ancient stones, feeding in the forum, nesting in the recesses of the baths, unaffected by the heat. The air was vibrant with the rattle of cicadas and – when anything moved to disturb them – it shimmered with their wings. A few yards away a praying mantis crouched at its devotions while a procession of ants made their penitential way across the hot stones, engaged in some alternative ritual of their own. Beyond the excavations stretched cornfields too bright for comfort, their blazing yellow not relieved but only intensified by the red of their scatter of poppies. At their edge the rooftops of the asylum rose from the valley and beyond them the needle-sharp spire of St-Rémy itself. On the other side the saw-toothed outline of the Alpilles was shaded in with blue and mauve. It all looked oddly familiar.

A thought slowly took shape in my mind. Eventually I said: 'It isn't the first time you've sat under this tree, is it?' Where the thought had come from I never knew.

Malcolm smiled. 'No. I came here with a previous boyfriend.'

'Called?' I asked.

'Aidan.'

'I don't remember...'

'I might not have told you. It was during the years when we weren't in contact very much. I thought it was going to last for ever with Aidan. We came to France together, wandering Jews. By the time we found this spot – we're where Vincent painted Les Blés Jaunes, you may have realised – we'd been lovers for two years.'

I said, 'Not bad for a gay relationship.' At once I saw what an insensitive thing I'd said. Malcolm was kind enough to take no notice. He went on.

'Aidan was the Van Gogh freak at that time, not me. I guess I caught it from him – like you got Beethoven off Ian Lewis. So here we came. It was the last really happy time we had together. But something wonderful happened to Aidan after that. Wonderful for him, not for me. He grew up at last in his own way. He met a woman and fell in love with her. Went through hell trying not to hurt me. But that was impossible. I had to be hurt. He had to live, to grow up in his way.'

'I'm sorry,' I said, thinking how strange were some of the things you found yourself saying sorry about. 'It happens, though. Not everybody knows themselves at... Well, whatever age he was.'

'I was twenty five,' Malcolm said. 'But Aidan was twenty-eight.' He gave me an odd look. The look may have been odd, but I understood its significance. 'I knew myself – from that point of view at least – when I was seven, despite a few untypical experiments in early adolescence. Stupidly I'd imagined that he knew himself equally well. But...' Malcolm gave one of the Gallic shrugs that he had had three years to practise.

I asked, 'And is he happy now? Do you know?'

'Most certainly he is. We exchange news at Christmas. It's all most civilised. He married the girl. She was – is – French. They live in Lyon and are halfway towards their two point four children or whatever the recommended ration is.'

'And you?'

'Like you, I discovered the flip side of love. You know, at least I suppose you do, that when two people fall in love they each plant a knife in the heart of the other. But it's only when the knife is wrenched out that the blood flows.'

There was silence for a moment. Then he said very gently, 'Tell me about Anne. I mean, if you want to.'

'I'm not sure if I know how to. I really don't know what was going on in her mind. You've talked about love. Well, for five years I believed Anne and I loved each other. I knew we did. But now I don't know. How could I lose a certainty like that: something so basic? I mentioned a girl called Janie, forever knitting a scarf. She got married not long before we did and we used to keep in touch. Anne and I used to laugh about Janie and her husband just a little. They seemed so contented, their marriage had an almost banal quality. We imagined they missed out on the highs and lows of love and life and the more their contentment deepened the more we – as I see it now – looked down on the quality of their relationship. It was as if their good fortune was something contemptible, something of which only idiots were worthy. Our own was always tinged with a degree of cynicism that seemed the healthy result of our being sophisticated, intelligent people. It never occurred to us to be jealous of them. Nor did we consider the possibility – which I have only just begun to think about in the last few weeks – that they were truly in love and we were not.'

'Where is Anne now?' Malcolm asked quietly.

'She has a good job in the museum in Norwich. And I've heard she's got a new man. I suppose I'm pleased for her.'

'She's getting over it like a youngster, perhaps,' Malcolm said. He smiled and shook his head. 'That's what you said last night. Don't know if you remember that. That Ian Lewis had 'got over it as youngsters do'. I nearly took you up on it but didn't. How does anyone know who gets over what? And what about your friend Happy: wasn't he a youngster? I'll put it down to a slip of the tongue, or the carelessness of cognac.' He paused a second, then said, 'You too should try being a youngster one day.'

I didn't say anything to that. Malcolm plucked a couple of stalks of grass. Then he said, 'How do you feel about the boy now?'

That startled me a bit. 'Ian? I don't feel anything about him *now*, if you understand me, because I don't know what he's like now. But about him *then*, my feelings have gone through a few changes. At first I felt sorry for him, then, with all the bitterness of the divorce, I began to hate him. Later I managed to shut him out of my mind. I could even listen to Beethoven without him coming into my thoughts. The file was closed.'

'You've told me he had feelings for you,' Malcolm said. 'Are you quite sure, in your heart of hearts, that you had nothing of the same feeling for him?'

'It takes two to tango,' I said, 'and in that particular case only one of us wanted to. Still, the hard feelings have gone. I wish him well, wherever he is.'

Then another thought struck me. I hesitated before asking this, but then I did ask. 'You say Aidan found his heterosexual side as he grew older. How can you be sure that the same thing won't happen with Henri?'

'Because of Henri himself. I know you've hardly met him, but does he strike you as someone who'll change with the wind or the seasons?'

'I have to say, on a first impression, no, he doesn't. All the same...'

'Aidan never gave the same first impression, if that's what you're wondering. He was like mercury, if you want. Henri's like gold.'

'That's very pretty.'

'It's very true.'

I said, 'Then why the hell...?' It was impossible now, after the turn the conversation had taken, not to bring this up. 'What the fuck were we playing at last night – not just you, me as well?'

Malcolm was silent a moment and looked down. He plucked at another plant stem. At once the scent of lemon thyme filled the air. 'Last night was a mistake.' he said. 'And if you want me to say sorry, then sorry. Now I've said it. But I don't really mean it was a mistake as you would understand a mistake. With your conventional rules and two point four children and divorce until death.' He spoke bitterly all of a sudden.

I found myself speaking bitterly too. 'You talk of my conventionality as if conventionality was something criminal. You may despise it and laugh at it if you want to but you can never say that it's wrong.'

'No,' said Malcolm, 'I can't. Unless, unless, just possibly it's the wrong convention. The wrong convention for you.' His tone softened. 'No, David, I'm sorry. There's nothing criminal, as you put it, about your particular conventionality. The only person it can hurt from now on is you.'

My hackles rose. 'What the hell's that supposed to mean? That I've hurt people in the past? By responding to them differently from the way you would have? That's monstrously arrogant. That I've upset you by not wanting to sleep with you? That I'm missing out on something if I don't? Christ Almighty!'

'No, I don't mean that,' Malcolm said. 'It's just that you seem trapped by this idea that everybody has to be treated, or to behave, the same.'

'You think I do?'

'And how! You think I was out of order last night because I have a relationship with someone else and that means no sleeping around elsewhere. Wrong. That's what I meant when I said I hadn't made a mistake as you would understand it. In my book I made a mistake last night because I have a relationship *with Henri* and *that particular relationship* means no sleeping with other people. Even (don't hit me) with a friend as delightful as you.'

I said more quietly, 'I admit that I behaved stupidly myself. It wasn't just you that was out of order. I was drunk and crazy and...' I stopped and stared down at the grass for a moment, as if I'd seen an abyss being opened up by my own words. Then, with a struggle, I pulled my thoughts together. 'I also admit it was stupid of me to give you a kiss, even in fun, two days ago. It was just high spirits, but it gave you the wrong message, and I apologise for that. But...' I groped desperately for something that would make sense. 'I got out of your bed principally for the one reason that you've dismissed as unworthy of your notice. And it's not particular to us. Where I'm concerned it's general. I do not sleep with men. Ever. I don't wish to and I'm not going to. Full stop.' But even as I heard myself say it I found myself wondering if I was really telling the truth.

Malcolm decided to change the subject. 'Sometimes,' he began slowly, 'it seems as if life, or God, or fate or whatever you like to call it, knocks down the building you've been trying to make of your life and gives you the chance to begin it again. When Aidan left me it was as if the linchpin had been pulled out of the structure I'd fondly called my life and that all I had left were the building blocks However bad things get, however broken, you never lose those building blocks. Your past goes to build your future; none of it is wasted. I'm only beginning to understand that now.' He got up and retreated to the other side of the cypress tree from where I presently heard the sound of him pissing. It was as sure an indication as any that the discussion was closed.

Chapter 13

Things could easily have gone downhill from then on: our conversation reduced to scratchy bickering, our companionship turned to mutual irritation, that holiday intimacy that Malcolm likened one day to a brightly coloured bubble hardened to an amber prison. Somehow none of this took place. Perhaps the climate was to thank, our northern souls finding it impossible to remain quarrelsome for long under this brief interrogation by the southern sun. In fact the heat lessened somewhat over the next few days though the weather did not break – for us tourists the only improvement to be wished. Travelling became supportable once more, while the dazzling envelope of colour and light in which we moved didn't fade at all. On the contrary the colour seemed to etch itself more and more deeply into the slate of my mind.

We explored the flatlands of the Camargue, circumnambulated the walled town of Aigues Mortes and drove eventually into Arles. Here were fewer tangible links with Van Gogh than at St-Rémy – two world wars had seen to that – but the unresolved tensions of primary colour that inspired his canvasses were everywhere still: green oleanders, yellow stucco and orange brick; blue and violet sky. Swept up one picturesque narrow street on a flood tide of clicking cameras, we were relieved at one point to be washed up in a shop doorway, but momentarily puzzled to see someone beckoning to us from the relative darkness of the shop's interior. It only took me a second, though, to remember the fine art dealer who had given us his card on the TGV.

Despite the crowds in the street his gallery was not busy. Day-trippers did not spend a lot on fine art, he told us. Perhaps time was hanging heavily on his hands: his pleasure at seeing us seemed disproportionate to our brief acquaintance. At any rate he was more than happy to show us the paintings on his walls, while a curly-headed blond youth did discreet sentry duty behind the fine mahogany table that it would have been *lèse-majesté* to describe as either a counter or a cash desk. Most of the canvasses depicted the flat, wind-ruffled landscapes of the Camargue, though here and there were street scenes recognizable as being Avignon, Aix and other towns we had passed through. Malcolm suddenly pointed to a painting of the Café de Paris, the 'route-map' bar, in L'Isle sur la Sorgue. Clearly someone else had remarked on its resemblance to Van Gogh's *Terrasse du Café le Soir* and had highlighted the resemblance by painting it from the same angle and at the same time of evening. Familiar yellow lights gleamed out of neighbouring dormers. 'We were there a few nights ago,' Malcolm explained to the gallery owner.

'C'est romantique, n'est-ce pas?' he replied. Then, after a pause while he gave us as thorough an appraisal with his dark and expert eyes as if he were judging the merits of a double portrait, he asked us if we would like to see the other part of his collection downstairs. The young man at the table looked up when he heard this invitation made, but then returned to his previous occupation of observing through the window the passers-by in the sunny street outside.

Downstairs, in an even darker exhibition room we found ourselves in the centre of a collection of photographs whose subject matter – it did not come as a surprise to me now – was the male nude. The style owed a lot to Robert Maplethorpe. Malcolm was clearly delighted, while I found myself trying not to think too hard about my own reaction. Until I was pulled up short by one particular picture. It was simple in the extreme. A blond-haired youth stood in a patchwork of sunshine and shadow, his back against the stone wall of what might have been a barn, his cock lolling, half-fat, against one downy thigh. Surely, surely, wasn't that familiar-looking form and face that of Ian Lewis?

'Who took that photo?' I asked hoarsely, too surprised to mask my desperate need to know. Malcolm peered over my shoulder at the photo, curious as to what had precipitated my reaction.

'Jean-Charles did. The young man you saw upstairs. He has a talent, has he not?'

I said, 'Do you know, I mean, would he remember who...? No, sorry, it doesn't matter. Just something that came into my head. Forget it. It doesn't matter.'

But the gallery owner, pleased with himself for picking up on the first of my signals, failed to register the second. 'Jean-Charles,' he called upstairs. 'Here a minute. Answer a question.' And the young man came pattering down the stairs.

'What was the name of this one?' asked the gallery owner.

'Oh...' The young man tapped his head. 'Oh gosh. It was, let me think ... er ... An English guy. Ian.'

'Ian?' queried Malcolm, who, after a few seconds of puzzled peering had just got to where I had arrived at once; he had been at a disadvantage when it came to recognizing the figure and face.

'Look, this really doesn't matter,' I said.

'I'm sure it was Ian,' said the young man. 'In fact I think it may be written on the back.' With a certain amount of fuss he de-mounted the photograph from the wall and there, sure enough, was written on the back a date, a location and a name. The name was Ian. But the surname wasn't Lewis. The young man depicted was apparently called Ian Smart. 'There you are,' he said proudly. 'I thought I'd remembered right.'

There was a longish silence. Then the gallery owner broke it unexpectedly by saying, 'Look, why don't we all have lunch together?' And so we did. My pleasure in the expensive restaurant meal that followed was tempered by the knowledge that Jean-Charles and the gallery owner (whose name was on his visiting card inside my wallet, but there was no way I could take it out to remind myself what it was) both took me and Malcolm to be a couple. Still, it was always agreeable to be treated to a meal by someone whose wallet was fatter than your own. We had rose-tinted trout with almonds, a *vin gris* (also pink) from the nearby hills, and a *coulis* of summer berries, and when we parted company afterwards it was in a friendly spirit.

That evening we returned to St-Rémy where we watched late-hunting swifts swirling like bats among the blossoming stars and, from the safety of a seat among the plane trees we tried, by screwing our eyes half shut, to cause the celestial bodies that watched over the town to dance as the artist had seen them do.

We knew we were going to have to talk about what had happened at the art dealer's shop at some point. In the end it was I who brought it up.

'You said, after we'd met him on the train, that that art dealer obviously fancied one of us. Well, I thought you were being a bit fanciful, if you like. Until he invited us downstairs, of course, and then it became pretty clear.'

'How clear?' asked Malcolm.

'Well that he obviously did fancy one of us. Though it wasn't clear to me which one.'

Malcolm said, 'Now I think about it, I'm not sure it was quite like that. It may have just been the idea of the two of us together that he found attractive. Nothing more alarming than that.'

'I see,' I said. I actually found it more alarming to hear Malcolm so breezily accept what I had reluctantly realised that lunchtime: that other people might take the two of us for a gay couple.

'But what surprised me,' Malcolm changed the subject, 'was what on earth made you think you were looking at a picture of Ian Lewis this morning. I mean, I know you'd seen him swimming once in the nude, but...'

'It doesn't matter,' I said. 'Just a mistake.'

We resumed our travels. We explored Aix and Carpentras and the slopes of Mont Ventoux. The private bubble in which we journeyed and lived remained unpunctured by any further adventures that might have troubled my comfortable view of my sexual orientation. Bedtimes returned once more to being – if not sober, then at least chaste. Then, on the last night of our tour, when we'd returned the car to its ring-road garage and were back at the Hotel Bristol, I woke during the night to find Malcolm's silhouette at one of the windows, leaning half out and smoking a cigarette. His naked form was all in shadow except for where the street-lighting picked out the line of his shoulders and forearm in pale ivory – a far cry from the bricky hue that the sun now painted him by day.

'Anything wrong, Malcolm? Can't you sleep?' I said.

'Uh-huh.'

'Why not?'

The silhouette turned to face me. 'Thinking about you, actually.'

'I see,' I said.

The silhouette took a pull on its cigarette. A pinprick of red light intensified in the dark. 'You're gay, David. A poof. A fairy. A faggot. Queer. Call it what the hell you like; it makes no difference. That is you. I know that and so, now, do you.'

'What?!' I thought Malcolm had gone mad. I sat bolt upright.

'I thought the other day that I would never dare to tell you so straight out. I thought the risk to our friendship would outweigh any possible gain to you. Just now I changed my mind. So I've told you what I'm thinking.'

'Malcolm, that's some accusation!'

'Not an accusation. An observation. A diagnosis, if you like. Even if incorrect it wouldn't become an accusation. It's not something bad to be. And don't act shocked; I'm hardly the first person to tell you. Even your wife...'

'Not something bad to be? For you, no, because that's the way you're made. But it would be for me; I'm not like you, don't you see? It's you now who tries to generalise all the time, not me. And don't go quoting my wife to me. My real friends have always believed me rather than her. I thought that you...'

'Come on, come on. That's baby-talk. It's crap.'

'Malcolm, what is this?'

'Have a cigarette. Catch.' Malcolm threw me one. 'And you'd better light it yourself in the circumstances.' He took a fresh one himself. 'OK. Let's get one thing out of the way first. I've always liked the way you look, the way you talk, the way you are. Fancied you, in brief. But, except for that bit of stupidity on my part the other night, that's water under the bridge and we can leave it out of the argument.

'But since then I've been doing some thinking about those two ghosts in your life that you can't shake off. Two men. Happy, who killed himself after seeing a blackmailed homosexual put in prison just a couple of weeks after falling in love with you...'

'That's a wild guess, Malcolm. Pure imagination, conjecture.'

'And there's Ian, the kid with teeth. You think you're really screwed up by Anne and the divorce. Bullshit. Divorce takes a lot longer to happen than a love bite yet you told me about your divorce in two sentences and took ten minutes over that little episode with that kid. And remember I've only heard the case for the defence. David, it's Ian and Happy that you're screwed up about. Not Anne but those two. Those two and yourself.'

'Go to bed,' I said. 'I'm not listening. Go to sleep.'

Malcolm did not obey. He left the window and crossed to his bed, then sat down on the far end of it.

'It was lovely that you agreed to come to Provence with me, to share a bedroom with a gay bloke. I've loved watching you fall in love with the colour and the light. I loved it that you jumped across the stream at L'Isle sur la Sorgue and gave me a kiss. I know that you felt the electric charge as keenly as I did when that Italian came down all naked from that Van Gogh window. So keenly that just for a few minutes you were almost as ready to have sex with me as I was with you...'

I tried to bluster my way out. I said, 'Your imagination beats a spotty adolescent's. Talk about wishful thinking! And your memory's about as objective as ... as...'

'David, David,' Malcolm said quietly, 'just be yourself at last, that's all. Now I'm sorry. You may possibly never forgive me for saying all that. You may never understand why I did. Look, I need some air. I'm going out for a walk.' He began to dress himself.

I was lost for words. My cigarette finished, I lay flat once more, pulling the sheets around me like a child, though the night was still hot. I found my tongue again just as Malcolm reached the door. 'Don't try to change people,' I said. 'To warp them into your own image. That is wrong. Very.'

Malcolm stopped, his hand already on the handle. 'It is wrong,' he said with great feeling. 'My God, it is. I couldn't agree more. But I've said nothing to try to change you; I've only tried to point to who you are. And if by any chance the cap doesn't fit, well, you won't be wearing it anyway. It was only an inspired guess. If there's anything that needs changing it's way out of my reach; I couldn't do anything there even if I wanted to. I leave that to you. To you and your ghosts. Now I'm going out. I've got the key and I won't be long.' He paused for a second. Then he said, 'The real David, I begin to think, is even now not really angry or surprised by what I've said.' Then he opened the door and went out. I didn't hear him return.

In the morning we realised that we'd forgotten to set the mosquito-screens at the windows. We took the souvenirs of this oversight back with us to Paris.

Chapter 14

Kilometre by kilometre the progress of twelve days ago was reversed. From south to north, from a great light to a lesser, from mountain horizons to the plain.

After our exchange of words the previous night the atmosphere between us might have been frosty. It wasn't. It was quite sober: that's to be expected on the return from a holiday, especially when you're returning to the northern, from the southern part of France. But there was no animosity between us. We had had to agree to differ. Malcolm mistakenly believed that I was gay – a closet case or worse. I knew, of course, that I was not.

We returned to Malcolm's wonderful flat, next door to where Vincent had lived with his brother, in the rue Lepic. Henri had returned from Vichy a couple of hours earlier. I was touched by the rapture with which Malcolm and Henri greeted each other. And I wasn't surprised when they excused themselves for a private half-hour in their bedroom. They seemed almost to be asking my permission to do this, Malcolm asking diffidently, 'Would you mind very much if...?'

Laughingly I told him not to worry. I said I would take myself out for a walk. They gave me a key to let myself in with when I came back.

I took myself up the steep rue Lepic, to where it entered the heart of Montmartre at the Place du Tertre. Painters sat at easels, capturing on canvas the famous and picturesque buildings around them that had been made famous by generations of painters before them, going all the way back to the Impressionists. I sat and had an espresso at a pavement table, watching scissor artists cutting out profiles of tourists from black paper at lightning speed. It seemed a long way from Van Gogh.

Around another corner I found myself on the tourist-filled terrace in front of the white-domed Basilica of

Sacré Coeur, standing at the rails and overlooking the whole of central Paris. There were the towers and arrow-spire of Notre Dame, the golden dome of the Invalides, the Pantheon, the Opera... and those wonderful double-sloped grey rooftops and their dozens of chimney-pots. I thought of that lovely film, The Red Balloon, and how it ended with the little boy flying, lifted by hundreds of balloons across the rooftops of Paris... Across the very vista I was looking at. I looked at my watch. I'd been out for forty-five minutes. By the time I got back Malcolm and Henri would have had time to make love at least twice. I turned away from the view and made my way back down the hill in the slanting evening sun.

Later we went out for a meal at a favourite restaurant of theirs in the rue de Clignancourt. 'I've looked at those Van Gogh reproductions on your walls again,' I said. (I'd had a few spare minutes by myself in the salon after I came back from my walk.) 'I see them with new eyes, with new feelings almost, now I've been to Provence. Actually walked through the streets he painted. Seen inside the asylum at St-Rémy. Looked at the stars through the cypress trees at night...'

Nineteen-year-old Henri said unexpectedly, 'Maybe it won't just be Van Gogh you'll look at with new eyes now you've been down there.' He didn't elaborate and I didn't ask him to. I knew exactly what he meant. Inevitably Malcolm had talked to him about me while I'd been out, walking up to Montmartre and back. They wouldn't have only been having sex.

'Maybe,' I said.

I had one more day to spend in Paris before returning to England. Malcolm had some teaching to do, and Henri would be back behind his computer screen in the travel agent's where he worked. Over breakfast they both made suggestions about parts of the city I might like to visit. I said vaguely that I might wander around by the Seine. The Ile de la Cité, the Louvre, the Place de la Concorde, perhaps... Henri told me, with a straight face, that I ought to include a stroll along the riverbank quai des Tuileries.

I took the bus that dived down a picturesque route past unexpectedly quaint churches and houses hundreds of years old and then, after a walk in which I got pleasantly lost a few times, I found myself at the river. Everywhere the views were like paintings into which you could simply walk. It's difficult to explain, but there is something particularly magical about the heart of Paris.

I walked around the Ile de la Cité, enjoying its changing perspectives; the spires of the Conciegerie, Notre Dame and the Sainte Chapelle appearing to do a stately dance around the sky together as I moved from place to place; the river appearing in teasing glimpses between green willow trees; the quays beyond... I remembered Henri's recommendation of the quai des Tuileries. I took a quick look at the map Malcolm had lent me and made my way there through the late July heat.

The quai des Tulieries turned out to be a lengthy pathway along the river, beneath the wall of the Tuileries gardens. It also turned out to be – Henri had deliberately not told me this, evidently – a major gay cruising ground.

Had I wanted to charge people for telling them the time I could have filled my pockets with francs. I could also have given away the contents of several packets of cigarettes... Men were everywhere, dressed in swimming-trunks of the scantiest proportions, the remainder of their clothes presumably stuffed into the backpacks they all either carried, if they were walking about, or used as pillows or back-rests if they were lying down taking the sun.

Some had formed themselves into pairs and were standing half-hidden among the trees, embracing, their tongues down each other's throats, their hands down inside each other's swimming-trunks. Other pairs were lying on top of each other on the ground, trunks pulled down a little way, bottoms exposed to the sun... I found myself reacting quite strongly to this scene, to this new canvas I'd unexpectedly walked into: this new window I found myself walking through. I felt queasy. I didn't like it. And yet I did. I was guiltily excited by what was going on around me. I felt my penis thicken in my pants. I found myself wondering what the place would be like at night...

Had Malcolm ever walked down here at night? I wondered. Between his break-up with Aidan and meeting Henri? And what of Henri himself? Henri who was only nineteen... Having posed the questions I discovered that I didn't want to know the answers. Yet other questions crowded in. Was this the place Happy's nocturnal rambles would have brought him to, given life and time? Aged nineteen, wandering Durham's riverbanks at night, had he, unsuspected by innocent me, actually already been doing this? A few days ago, I would have said no, of course not. But now, after everything that had happened in Provence, the whole of the past seemed up for renegotiation. It rose up before me and bristled like a porcupine, every quill a question. What if? With a mixture of relief and a curious disappointment I reached the steps that led up to the bridge

I went on mulling this over as I walked northwards through the heterosexual streets. Supposing all of that was true about Happy, including what Malcolm had said nearly two weeks ago about his having been in love with me. What did that say about me? Had I been in love with Happy too? Malcolm had also suggested that. How could I, aged twenty-eight, have had no inkling of that before coming to France?

Malcolm had suggested I was gay. Gay without knowing it! Impossible, surely. And yet Malcolm's Aidan hadn't known about *his* own disposition till he was twenty-eight. Still, there was an enormous difference between our cases. Aidan's discovery had not occurred in a vacuum, there had been nothing abstract or intellectual about it. He had met someone, a woman, another human being, who had been... Been what? A mirror in which he had seen himself for the first time without distortion perhaps; a window through which his future had come into focus for the first time; a sudden glimpse of the sun without dark glasses? But a human being, a person. That above all.

Then I found myself thinking about Ian. Had he grown up gay in the end? What was his life like now? Did he spend his spare time doing what I'd so recently witnessed in the sunshine under the walls of the gardens of the Tuileries? It was yet another disturbing line of thought.

Two nights ago I had defended myself easily against Malcolm's over-the-top harangue, if not in words at least in my own mind. My fortress walls had stood. Malcolm physically present, a naked friend with a sun-peeled nose being histrionic in a hotel room, had left me relatively unruffled. But Malcolm's words seemed more powerful now, now that I'd walked the quai des Tuileries, and had got an erection as I'd walked and looked.

The French are quite something when it comes to food. At the end of his day's work Henri came home and prepared a meal for the three of us. He did eggs in aspic jelly for a starter. They came from a shop, admittedly, but he still had to wrap a warm cloth around their little moulds and get his timing right so as to get them out in one piece each. Within the jelly a slice of ham was wrapped around a soft-boiled egg, which spilt its gold contents prettily, like a liquid jewel, when you cut into it. Then pork tenderloin, *filet mignon* as he called it, served on a bed of tomatoes and courgettes. A selection of cheeses, then soft fruit with ice cream. I'd have taken my hat off, had I been wearing one.

'I did explore the quai des Tuileries,' I said as we were tucking into the first course.

'What did you think of it?' Henri asked with a bit of a twinkle in his eye.

'An eye-opener, to be honest,' I said. 'But interesting.' Then I added, because I knew that Malcolm would have told Henri some of this, 'Malcolm is determined to make a gay man out of me. I'm not sure he's going to meet with much success. I think it's the effect that Provence has on him. All that sun and light. Another twenty-four hours and he'd probably have been saying that even Van Gogh was gay!'

'Who knows?' said Henri, with a wicked half smile. 'And who knows what will be the effect on you of all that sun and light?'

Then he stretched his hand across the table towards my bare forearm, stopping his fingers a millimetre short of my skin but then running them up to my elbow through the hairs, rubbing those up the wrong way and triggering a miniature storm of static. The effect was electric, literally so, and magical. It stirred something among my deepest feelings: something I hadn't known about. And despite the presence of Malcolm at the table with us it was a wonderfully intimate contact. It prevented me from saying anything further on the subject we'd been talking about. And I had to admit, it felt very, very nice.

When I went to bed that night, a little fuzzy with wine and cognac, and closed my eyes, my mind was filled with a kaleidoscope of images. Most were of the nearly naked male bodies I'd seen enjoying themselves and each other in the sunshine on the quai des Tuileries. But among them came repeatedly the memory, very vividly, of the naked photo of the boy called Ian Smart, who looked like Ian Lewis: the photo that we'd seen in Arles, in the art dealer's shop.

I couldn't believe how brightly those pictures all filled my imagination then. There was so much colour, so much light. My sheets were the same ones I'd had when I spent my first night here a fortnight ago. They were still emblazoned with my map of France. Nobody would notice if I overlaid that with another one. With those pictures still filling my mind's eye powerfully I reached for my erect cock and started to masturbate.

Chapter 15

Malcolm did manage to persuade me of one thing, at least. That I should do a training course in teaching English as a foreign language, just as he had done when he dropped out of school teaching a few years earlier. Then I could work anywhere in the world I wanted. I might not become rich but... He promised me that if I wanted him to he would introduce me to the powers that be at the business school where he taught in Paris.

I made enquiries once I was back in England and a few days later, after an interview at a centre in London, I was enrolled on a short course. That didn't begin for another month. We were now in August. That August in England was good, weather-wise, and I would have been quite happy whiling the spare month away in my home country, seeing friends and doing not very much. But I'd been spoiled by Van Gogh's land of light and colour. I hankered after Provence. After a few days I went back.

I went the slow way this time, as, having recently returned from a two-week holiday with hotels to pay for, I was counting my pennies. I went by train as far as Dover, then crossed to Calais by hovercraft. From there I travelled by long-distance coach. One took me into central Paris, another took me out the other side and – in the course of a long and not very comfortable night – all the way to Arles.

Why Arles rather than Avignon or Aix, or St Rémy come to that? The answer was something I was reluctant to admit to myself. I wanted to see Jean-Charles, the young assistant in the art dealer's shop, and get to the bottom of the mystery that was Ian Smart – or maybe Ian Lewis. I didn't tell Malcolm I was returning to France. And I certainly wasn't going tell him about that.

I awoke in my bouncing coach seat that next morning to see that we were sailing across a sea of sunflowers that were looking towards the dawn. Happy had talked of celestial Tippex when describing the effects of snow. I don't know. Does Tippex also come in gold?

The coach drew into the bus station at Arles. I blundered off it and went in search of coffee and croissants. The morning was cold, although it was August. A chill wind was blowing in off the Camargue. It was still only seven o'clock. I spun my coffee and croissants out as long as I could. Then I walked around the town. What time did art galleries open? I wondered. I guessed, not till ten o'clock.

Little by little the wind dropped, and then reversed itself. The scent of thyme and lavender blew into the town's streets from the blue hills inland, and the day warmed up. I dropped in at a couple more cafés while I loitered. I felt I was getting to know the town a bit. Had I been a painter I could have painted it.

I found the street where the art gallery was. I braced myself and opened the door. There sat curly blond Jean-Charles at his sentry-box desk. Although we'd had lunch together a mere two weeks ago I didn't presume on his remembering me without Malcolm, out of context. *'Bonjour, Jean-Charles,'* I said.

'Bonjour,' he said, and hesitated no more than a second before smiling, and adding, 'David.' It was a good start.

'How are you?' I asked him in French.

'I am good,' he said in English. 'You went back to England, did you not?'

'Yes,' I said. 'But now I have come back to France.'

'That is very soon,' he said. 'But we are honoured by that.'

'I came back,' I said, 'and please don't misunderstand me, but I came back especially to see you. There is some information I want from you. I need to pick your brains.'

Jean-Charles's rather beautiful young face puckered into a frown. 'Pick my brains? What is that?'

'Sorry,' I said. 'It's an expression. It just means there are some questions I want to ask you, and I need your advice.'

He nodded his understanding and his frown was replaced by a new smile as quickly as if I'd flicked a switch.

'Tirez, monsieur.' Fire away, he said. 'Although I think I can imagine. It's about that photograph.'

'Précisément,' I said.

'I remember the moment very clearly,' Jean-Charles said. 'I had the impression you thought you knew the guy. When I told you his first name you were – how to say? – bouleversé, but in a good way. But when I told you the second name you were deceived, *n'est-ce pas?'*

'Yes,' I said. Disappointed was what he'd meant.

'After that day we met,' Jean-Charles said, 'I thought about the thing a lot. I went back in my mind to remember how I met the guy and how it happened that I took the photograph. Would you like me to tell you what I remember?'

'Yes please,' I said.

'It was last summer,' he began. 'I was walking along the river out in the country near here, with my camera, taking photos of the nature. I saw three young guys, maybe nineteen years, who had taken off their clothes and were playing by the edge of the water and in the water, running in and out and laughing. They saw me. I was wearing … well, just shorts and boots and my camera round my shoulder…'

I found I could imagine the scene only too easily. Jean-Charles would have been halfway between their age and mine, I thought. He was probably about twenty-four...

'They asked me in English if I would like to take a photo of them. I thought they were serious and I started to ask them to move into a group. But then they changed their *avis*, and said, no, please do not.

'But one of them – he was actually the handsomest – came up to me and said I could take his photo naked, if I wanted, and if I would give him two hundred francs. I said that was a lot of money, and I offered him one hundred. He accepted that and I took the photo you saw. Of him with the tree behind him. I would have liked to take him to a studio and make many more pictures of him. Of him and his ... his *bite*, how do you say?'

'His cock,' I said. 'Or his dick, if you like.'

Jean-Charles smiled. 'His cock or his dick if I like. I will remember that. OK. After that we talked a little. He told me his name was Ian Smart – though I remember he hesitated before saying 'Smart'. It was like he invented that very quick. He told me they were three friends who studied at university in London and were here on holiday. I asked Ian if he wanted a copy of the photo. He thought for a little bit, then he said yes, and he gave me his address. It was not easy to find a pen and some paper, with nobody very well dressed, but one boy found those things in his backpack. Then we parted. I never saw them again.'

'And did you send him a copy of the photo?' I asked.

'Yes,' said Jean-Charles. 'He never wrote to say thank you, so I do not know if he received it.'

'And did you ... have you still got... his address?'

Jean-Charles made a little grimace. 'I had the fear you would ask me that question,' he said. 'And that you would not like my answer. No. I am very sorry. I do not have his address now.'

We both realised that my research had hit the buffers. There was nowhere else to go with this. There was a silence between us. I realised at that moment that Jean-Charles had been talking to me in the way he would talk to another gay man. He had made the assumption that I was gay, and treated me accordingly. He continued to do so now.

'Tonight we have a *vernissage*,' he said. 'Would you like to come to it?'

'What is a *vernissage*?' I asked.

'It is when we open a new exhibition and we invite people, the people who buy art from us, also their friends, and especially people who are a bit rich, and there is wine and canapés...'

'I understand,' I said. 'It's called a private view in English.'

'You can come if you would like,' he said again. 'You do not have to buy a picture. And there will be good wine. Your friend ... Malcolm, is it? ... can come too. He is here with you in Arles?'

Sometimes it was nice to be mistaken for a gay man. 'He isn't here,' I said. 'He is in Paris with his French boyfriend, Henri. Malcolm was never my boyfriend. We are just old friends who studied together. I'm here on my own this time. So, thank you for the invitation. I'll certainly come. I'd really like that.' I was really touched. 'I need to find somewhere to stay in the town, though.'

Jean-Charles gave me an appraising look. 'How long will you stay in Arles?'

'I think just one night. Maybe two.' I smiled. 'I have to go home after that. I can't spend another week in hotels, after my last visit. I'm not even a little bit rich.'

'There is a sofa at my place,' he said, a bit diffidently. 'You could sleep on that for a few nights, if you wanted. It's my parents' house actually, but they are away. At least it would be free.'

'It's a very kind offer,' I said. 'May I accept?'

I spent most of that day with Jean-Charles and with his boss, whose name – I had to ask Jean-Charles to remind me of this – was Marc. They showed me the Place du Forum, in which the café that Van Gogh had made famous still stood. Even so, it looked less like his golden picture of it than the Café de France in L'Isle-sur-la-Sorgue, where Malcolm and I had got so drunk a few weeks back. Perhaps that was a question of the time of day, the state of the light ... or how much we'd had to drink.

They showed me the rebuilt Yellow House, where Vincent had lived. Where he'd covered the walls with his sunflower paintings in readiness for Gaugin's visit. Marc bought lunch for Jean-Charles and me. In the afternoon I repaid their hospitality, present, future and past, by helping to hang the pictures for the exhibition that would open that evening.

Most of the paintings I was hanging depicted summer landscapes of Provence and the Loire: landscapes that were bright with lads and lasses, and golden with ripening corn. It was a very life-affirming collection, I thought. The pictures did my heart good. And hanging them did my muscles good.

A young man passed the open doorway at one moment. He stopped and looked in. He was wearing ancient orange bell-bottoms and a football shirt and he carried his possessions in a small plastic sack. He looked no more than twenty and his face had a composure and a serenity that reminded me, when I caught sight of it, of a picture I had seen in a book about the Louvre: Watteau's 'Gilles', the portrait of a simple clown. Jean-Charles saw me looking at the young man, who moved off down the street at that moment. 'He's a homeless guy,' Jean-Charles explained. 'He sleeps in doorways around here.

He appeared just a few weeks ago. We've tried to speak to him, but he's mute and deaf. The other thing about him is, he's interested in art. He looks always through the windows here. And he can draw and paint a bit. Sometimes he sells a sketch to tourists in the Place de la République.'

'He sounds interesting,' I said.

I met a lot of interesting people at the *vernissage*. The evening pushed my French to its absolute limit, but that also did me good. Among the people I got talking to was … Mark's wife.

You don't expect gay men to have wives, yet Marc, who I had no doubt was a gay man, did have a wife. Her name was Brigitte. There was no end, I thought, to the complexity of sexuality and life. Malcolm had been right about some things, I now realised, and I'd been wrong about them. I would see him soon, I hoped, and humbly tell him that. Now Marc's wife and I were talking about Paris…

She broke off suddenly from a story she was telling me about a recent visit to the Opera there, her attention distracted by a figure in the doorway. 'I wonder who is that?' she asked.

I looked. 'It's a young deaf mute,' I said, 'and he's interested in art.' I felt absurdly pleased with myself for being able to tell her something about someone in her town that I knew but she did not. I went on and told her everything Jean-Charles had told me about him.

Brigitte nodded approvingly. 'Perhaps he'd like a glass of champagne,' she said, surprising me a bit. 'I'll ask him in anyway.' She went out to do just that and immediately, as if filling a vacuum, a young friend of Jean-Charles whom I'd been introduced to earlier appeared at my other elbow and topped up my glass.

Brigitte returned a moment later with the young man in orange bell-bottoms following obediently like a dog. 'He doesn't speak,' she said. 'But he understands. He isn't deaf. His name's Raoul.'

'How do you know that if he doesn't speak?' asked Jean-Charles's friend.

'It's engraved on a chain round his neck,' said Brigitte.

'Is the address there too?' the friend asked. 'We could send him home by post.'

'Don't be naughty,' said Brigitte. 'Find him a chair and I'll look for a glass for him.'

A few moments later the young man was equipped with a chair, a glass of champagne and a plate of canapés, and being fussed over by all the arty well-dressed guests.

'Just look at that tableau,' said Marc, joining me. He gestured to where Raoul sat, expressionless and looking more than ever like Watteau's painting. On his left Brigitte was talking to him painstakingly, framing questions so that they could be answered with either a nod or a shake of the head. On his right crouched Jean-Charles's friend, looking up at him intently like a disciple at the feet of a guru or else a painter sizing up the face as a possible model for some religious subject. 'I suppose the symbolism doesn't need pointing out,' Marc said.

I thought about this. 'Perhaps it does, for me,' I said.

'Oh, I don't know,' said Marc. 'Blessed are the poor, perhaps, or blessed are the meek. Blessed are those who hunger and thirst – and blessed are the pure in heart. Theirs is the Kingdom anyway. We don't need to be very religious to realise that.'

Later in the evening Jean-Charles came up, with Raoul in tow, and caught me by the arm. 'Come with me,' he said. 'We're going to show this *mec* the photos downstairs.'

I said, 'Are you quite sure they'll be up his street? His cup of tea?'

Jean-Charles nodded gravely. 'I think so. Sometimes you just get a feeling about things. You know?'

The three of us walked down the stairs together. Jean-Charles had been right. The photos were very much up Raoul's street. I saw him smile for the first time as he looked in turn at each of us, pointing out interesting things in each of the photographs. Sometimes it was an interesting bit of background that caught his eye, or else he approved of the overall composition: the unity of the piece. But as often as not the thing that grabbed his attention in each photograph, and that he would point to, grinning cheekily at both of us, was the size or elegance of some young man's naked cock. Or *bite* as Jean-Charles had taught me to say in French.

We came to the picture of Ian Smart, or Ian Lewis, and he pointed approvingly at that particular young man's cock. I spoke then. I couldn't help myself. 'I think I knew that young man. He was a friend of mine once. And yes, he has a beautiful *bite*.'

Chapter 16

It was late when we finished clearing up, and Jean-Charles and I walked back to his parents' house.

I had made an assumption, I discovered, without realising it. I'd assumed that because Jean-Charles had a friend whom I'd met and talked to, that friend must be not only gay but also Jean-Charles's boyfriend, his *copain*. I assumed that the three of us would go back to the parents' house, where I'd be given the sofa to sleep on as I'd been promised, while the other two, taking advantage of the parents' absence, would head off to Jean-Charles's room together, discreetly shutting the door behind them as they went.

I was wrong about some of that. Jean-Charles's friend was met by his girlfriend, his *copine*, who arrived at the door just as the party was breaking up. They drove off together in a Citroen Deux Chevaux. Raoul had taken his leave some time before that. On returning from the delights of the basement gallery he had reverted to being his previous quiet self, his face serene and unsmiling once again, though beautiful still, I had to admit. He had bowed slightly, in an almost Japanese kind of way, to both Jean-Charles and me as he turned for the door and made his way out into the dark. An hour or more passed after that before Jean-Charles and I left.

The walk was not a long one, Jean-Charles assured me. In the course of it we were brought up short. We spotted what looked like a bundle of clothes on the pavement. It was the bright orangeness of some of them that caused us to take a closer look. We were not looking at a bundle of clothes, we discovered, but at the silent, serious young man who wore the name Raoul on a chain round his neck. His shoes, together with his plastic bag of possessions, were stowed under the back of his head, where they formed an approximately theft-proof pillow.

Jean-Charles felt in his pocket and found two ten-franc coins. Very gently he placed the money in one of Raoul's shoes, making every effort not to wake the sleeper and taking care that they were hidden from passing eyes by Raoul's thick hair. I felt myself shamed into doing the same thing. I knelt down too, and parted with twenty francs of my own. The price of three small beers or two sandwiches. We stood up and continued our walk.

A little later Jean-Charles said to me, 'Sorry, but I need urgently to piss.'

I said, 'You go ahead.'

He turned into the angle of a wall and got out his cock, which he made no attempt to hide from me. If anything the opposite was the case. But, just in case he was embarrassed about this, I followed his example, turning towards the bit of wall next to him, and unzipped my own jeans. Then for a minute we urinated side by side in a companionable silence that was broken only by the surprisingly loud sizzling of our two streams as they hit the wall and pavement.

We finished and zipped back up.

'We are nearly there,' said Jean-Charles as we resumed our walk. 'It was just that I could not wait.'

'Moi non plus,' me neither, I said. That wasn't true on my part: I could have waited easily. I wondered whether it was true on his.

A second later he put his arm lightly around my shoulder and I put mine around his.

I'd just seen this young man's dick. He'd as good as shown it off. I had to admit I was excited by the sight. It looked very nice.

I'd been excited by a lot of things this evening, though. The conviviality of the atmosphere. The champagne. The reaction of Raoul – which I hadn't expected – to the photos of young nude men in the basement. His reaction

to the naked body of Ian Lewis ... if it was Ian Lewis...
My own reaction to it.

We arrived at the door of a substantial nineteenth century house and unhooked our arms from each other as Jean-Charles got his key out. Inside, the house was large and grandly furnished. Jean-Charles took me on a very quick tour of it. He was obviously proud to be showing it off. He showed me the inside of his bedroom. I noticed that he gave me time to clock the fact that he had a double bed.

'Une pour la route?' he asked me. Did I want a small night-cap? 'I had better not open champagne,' he said, sounding apologetic. 'My parents...'

I said I'd accept whatever was going, and he poured us a small glass each of red wine from a bottle that had been opened the previous night.

We sat in the salon to drink it. Beneath a moulded ceiling and a dripping chandelier. Amidst a certain amount of gilt and plush. We sat next to each other on the sofa. We raised and clinked our glasses and said *Santé.* 'You are very kind, Jean-Charles,' I said.

He said, 'And you, David, are very nice.'

He reached forward a little and placed the palm of his hand on my thigh, at the same time looking very firmly into my eyes to see if I was OK with that.

It turned out that I was. I wouldn't have expected to be, but I was OK with that. I'd guessed that Jean-Charles was a few years younger than me. Whatever your sexuality, it's always flattering when a younger person behaves like that. 'How old are you?' I asked him.

'Twenty-four,' he said. 'And you?'

I said, 'I'm twenty-eight.'

Jean-Charles had given me about half a minute to remove my thigh from under his hand politely if I wanted to. He'd had time to conclude that I didn't want to do that. He started to stroke my thigh back and forth. I wriggled a few inches closer to him on the sofa and placed my own hand on his thigh, quite near the crotch.

His body stiffened for a second and he looked at me, trying to read my thoughts from my face. Then he relaxed and ran his hand across to where my cock and balls were. He felt them carefully through the denim, working out with his fingers exactly where everything was. He said, 'You have a very nice … cock.'

I said, 'It was small when you saw it out in the street.'

He said, 'It was still very nice.'

I recognised a cue when I heard one. I said, 'Yours was small too, but I still thought it was nice.' We leaned in towards each other and began to kiss.

There is something very special about that glass of wine that you know will be the last one you drink before you start doing something else. We didn't want to rush things – and yet we did. We compromised. Standing, we took each other's clothes off with one hand apiece, clutching our glasses of wine in the other hand and occasionally drinking from them as we progressed. Occasionally we had to cheat, and put the glasses down while we attended to some detail of clothing that was not amenable to being unfastened by a single hand. Belt-buckle. Shoe-laces. Then we finished the last drops of our wine and went naked up the stairs to bed with wagging dicks.

We got into bed and began to play with each other. We touched heads and necks, and backs and arms and thighs and buttocks. We reached down to feel each other's tough taut calves. For a second at a time we stroked each other's cock.

This was as far as I'd gone with Malcolm that drunken night. I wasn't drunk tonight, though I was relaxed and cheered by drink. I wondered what would happen next. What would we negotiate? I was the older one. Was it up to me to decide, despite my lack of experience of sex with other guys, exactly what we did? I decided to come clean. I said, *'Pour moi, c'est la premiere fois.'* Told him it was my first time with another man, and let him make what he would of that.

'But Ian...?' he said. 'Did you not...?'

'No,' I said. 'That's a long story. I'll tell you in the morning. Not tonight.'

He saw the sense of that. He said, 'We don't have to ... as you say ... fuck. We can just... You know.'

'Yes, I do know,' I said. 'For a first time I'll be happy with that.' And *that* was what we did.

It was lovely, I have to admit. In a way there was nothing new about it. It was more or less the same as I did with myself. People were beginning to use the word synergy about that time as a buzzword in business. Synergy meant two plus two made five, the definition went. Well, Jean-Charles and I experienced a kind of synergy that night. In our case it felt like one plus one made about six.

We came over each other's tummies, then held each other wetly for a minute before Jean-Charles got out of bed and fetched a towel so that we could mop up. Then we held each other, asking no questions of ourselves or of each other, leaving the morning and its thorny thickets of doubts and problems to wait for us. In each other's arms we went to sleep.

'How long can you stay with me?' Jean-Charles asked me as we got dressed.

'I don't know,' I said. The question of expensive nights in hotels had been thrown out of the equation, but other things were left. 'When are your parents coming back?'

'Sunday night,' he said. 'They're in Italy right now. A sort of business plus holiday trip.'

Today was Wednesday. I weighed a few things up. 'I could stay till Sunday,' I said. 'I mean, if you wanted me to.' I smiled at him cautiously. 'And if we still like each other by Sunday.'

'I think we will,' he said.

Oh dear, I thought. And then we'll have a painful parting. He's young. He may not know that yet. I said, as gently as I could, 'I also hope we'll still like each other on Sunday. But we mustn't get too attached.'

'You are very cold, you English,' Jean-Charles said, though he said it with a friendly laugh. 'Very un-romantic.'

'I'm just trying to be realistic,' I said. 'I'm older than you are. I know how easy it is to get hurt.'

'I understand,' he said. 'I know you want for the best.'

I walked round the corner of the bed to where he was standing half-dressed on his side of it. I gave him a little kiss and his still unclad cock a little tweak. 'What do you have for breakfast?' I asked.

I spent much of the day with Jean-Charles. In between walks around town on my own I stayed with him at the shop. A lot of his job was simply watching discreetly: checking that people didn't remove pictures from the walls, or leave smeary thumbprints on glass.

We talked a lot. I told him the whole story of Ian Lewis and me. That included the story of my marriage and divorce. He told me he'd had a boyfriend who he'd lived with. They'd split up and he'd gone back to his parents. 'Do your parents know you were in a gay relationship?' I asked him.

He looked a bit awkward. 'I don't think so,' he said. 'I think they just thought we shared a flat.'

'I see,' I said. 'That might be a bit difficult when you get another boyfriend and move out again,' I found myself thinking how difficult it must be for gay men who don't move away from their parental home towns. Realising at that moment that that was why so many of them did.

'When I get another boyfriend...' he said. 'Or if...'

I was relieved he hadn't said that he'd now acquired one and that I was it. I said, 'You'll find someone very soon. I'm sure of it.'

It felt extraordinary to be talking like this. Talking about boyfriends to a man I'd slept with. A man I'd slept with. The weirdness, the improbability as I'd always thought, of that. And yet it had been nice. There was no doubt about that. I'd arranged quite calmly to sleep with him for the next four nights also. I thought again about gay men and their parents. At least I wouldn't have to confront mine with the information that I'd had a week-long fling with a gay young man. They lived six hundred miles away from Arles and even when I was in England we didn't see each other all that often. They'd certainly never need to know about this.

And when it came to flings with young men, well, anyway, I wouldn't be making a habit of it.

We lunched together, and in the evening we cooked together at his parents' house. It was funny observing Jean-Charles observing me in the kitchen. For the first time in his life, probably, he was watching an Englishman cook. He watched with a certain amount of disbelief as I filled a pan with water, put it on to boil, added salt, and weighed out pasta to cook in it. It was as though he hadn't previously imagined any English or other British person could do this without ruining the eventual dish. My *spaghetti al limone* was a revelation to him. The pasta was simply tossed in a mixture of lemon juice, virgin olive oil and lemon zest, with Parmesan grated on top. Jean-Charles was astonished when I actually pulled it off. 'It is impossible,' he said. 'I really am enjoying this.'

He was responsible for the next course. It was a veal cutlet with a green salad. I told him it was the sort of thing I cooked myself, but I don't think he was ready to believe that. Neither of us cooked the cheese that followed, obviously, though Jean-Charles had chosen the baguette that accompanied it himself with great care, making sure he got the one he considered the best specimen in the baker's shop. Fresh peaches completed the meal, and then we went out for a brief walk around the evening streets and a beer before bed.

Before bed... Bed with a bloke. I was still having trouble getting my head round this. A one-off could happen to anyone, I supposed, but here I was now, calmly preparing for a repeat performance this second night. Not just calmly preparing. Wondering at myself, I found I was actually looking forward to it...

Chapter 17

There was a little rain that night. It gave the morning a diamond-sharp quality. In early August, in the south, the effect was uplifting and refreshing. I had enjoyed my second night in bed with a man. Jean-Charles was quite slight in build, and so was I. I thought we were a good physical match. He'd sucked my cock in bed that night, and I'd sucked his. I'd liked that a lot. Oh dear, I thought at breakfast. I'm getting to like this a bit too much. And, oh dear, I thought again, I'm getting to like Jean-Charles too much.

I was rather afraid also that he was getting too fond of me.

'You can go back to bed if you want,' he said to me over breakfast as we finished our *biscottes* and cherry jam. 'It's only me that has to be at work at ten o'clock.'

'Well, I might stay and lounge about the house for a bit,' I said. 'I don't think I'll go back to bed, though. I'd only end up thinking about you and having a wank.'

I'd taught him that word – among a number of others. He'd taught me their equivalents in French. You never knew when they'd come in handy. The verb to wank translated into French as *branler*. Though there were several variations on that.

'Come and join me at coffee time, then,' he said. When we parted at the front door a little later he gave me a kiss. Again, oh dear, I thought.

Setting off in the newly freshened air a couple of hours later I spotted a familiar figure crossing the street. A young man wearing a football shirt and orange bell-bottoms. It was Raoul, of course. For the last twenty-four hours or more I hadn't given him a second's thought. He didn't see me, he was looking the other way. I could have called out to him, he was close enough. I as almost about to call his name, but something I suddenly noticed prevented me. I was horrified and ashamed. I realised that, from the top of his thick mane of hair, down through the striped football jersey to the bottom of his prehistoric orange flares, Raoul was soaking wet.

I told Jean-Charles about this, when I met him at the gallery a little later. 'We gave him a few francs the other night,' I said. 'And Brigitte gave him canapés and champagne. It does no real good, a little gift like that now and then.'

Jean-Charles agreed. 'It only give the giver a chance to imagine himself a better person.' A truly generous person, he went on, would have reckoned his parents' house big enough to shelter Raoul for a week or two, or would at least have made the offer. It would have cost nothing.

'That's true,' I said, 'But think of the practicalities. What would happen when your parents come back on Sunday. Even I have to go back to England then. Can you imagine your parents' reaction to finding a homeless guy had moved in?'

'You're right,' Jean-Charles said with a shake of his curls. 'It's like feeding the birds in the winter. What happens when you go away?' Then he said something I thought beautiful, though, because true, also sad. 'Few people have hearts to match the size of their apartments.'

That night while we held each other tight in bed after coming together, a storm broke. Lightning flashed as brightly into the bedroom as if the heavy curtains hadn't been there, and the thunder crashed around the sky as loudly as if the distant hills were falling down. Then came the rain, bringing down in its cacophony the whole immensity of the sky.

'Oh my God!' Jean-Charles said. 'What about poor Raoul? What's going to happen to him?' His voice trembled on the brink of tears.

'I don't know,' I said. I felt Jean-Charles's sudden emotion catch me too, and catch me out. 'We can't go out and look for him. Not in this. Not in the middle of the night. He must have experienced a storm before. He won't die.' I gave Jean-Charles a squeeze to comfort him. 'He'll be OK. And in the morning, when you go to work, I'll go and look for him. We'll take it from there. OK?'

I felt Jean-Charles's nod of reluctant acceptance as a tickle, in the darkness, of unseen blond curls. Then the lightning blazed again, the thunder split the heavens, and the big house quaked.

I spent most of the next day looking for Raoul in the streets of Arles. Shy though I was of accosting strangers in my faltering French I found myself doing just that, button-holing everyone I met who didn't look like a tourist. I walked into shops and cafés. I asked everywhere. Quite a number of people knew who I was talking about. The orange flares were a pretty distinctive identity badge, after all. I got the impression he was a popular figure in the town. Someone who did no harm, someone who wouldn't hurt a fly. Someone had seen him painting by the river once at night, with candles planted around him on the ground to light his work as he sat cross-legged on the ground, sketch-pad on knees. But no-one had seen him since the previous day.

I returned to the gallery from time to time throughout the day, reporting each time the ongoing failure of my search to Jean-Charles. At the end of the day we had dinner in a café together. Though we were more than happy in each other's company, the disappearance of Raoul had cast something over our cheerfulness. It was as if someone had thrown a towel over a bedside lampshade, or a high thin cloud were veiling the sun.

We stayed out late, though, drinking Pastis – as Van Gogh would have quaffed Absinthe, though perhaps in more moderate amounts – at the Café du Forum Then we wandered back to Jean-Charles's parents' house.

As we arrived at the front door and as Jean-Charles fumbled in his pocket for the key. We practically tripped over a familiar assortment of clothes lying in a heap on the doorstep.

Jean-Charles leaned down and tried to wake Raoul with a hand on the shoulder. But he was fast asleep and unwilling to be roused. I tried another approach. I rubbed the lobe of one of his ears very gently between finger and thumb, a method I had heard of for waking people without frightening them or making them cry out – not that Raoul would have done that. It worked at once, Raoul turning a pair of calm, trusting eyes on me, and then on Jean-Charles that seemed to say, OK, now what? So Jean-Charles told him.

'You're not sleeping there tonight. This is where I live. Just come upstairs; you can sleep on my sofa. No strings. Have a shower if you want.'

Without much of a change of expression Raoul got to his feet and followed Jean-Charles through the door, while I brought up the rear. We went into the salon. 'Are you hungry?' Jean-Charles asked him. 'Do you want to eat something?'

Raoul said no with a polite smile and a wave of his fingers. It was very late after all. But the offer of a shower went down better and, once he'd been shown where it was, Raoul startled us by quite unselfconsciously taking all his clothes off in front of us, out on the landing. I might have looked away and pretended not to be interested, but I found I couldn't.

There was only so much lying to myself that I could do in one lifetime, I realised finally then, and I had done it all already. Raoul actually had a very beautiful body. It was about the same size as Jean-Charles's and my own, but softer, less wiry, and with a glowing, golden complexion that made me think bizarrely of butterscotch. He had very little hair about him: just the bare minimum that was necessary to prove that he was actually grown-up.

Once he was naked he turned towards us and smiled broadly at our state of awed suspended animation. We were awed, I think, because Raoul was sporting a full and sturdy little erection that pressed itself flat up against his belly like a teenager's and seemed to be trying to climb towards his navel in the manner of a determined but still cuddly little animal. Raoul looked around the landing quickly, then walked over to the telephone table that was there, seized a pencil and wrote something with it on the message pad. Jean-Charles and I exchanged a look of astonishment and walked over to see what Raoul had written. It was just the two words, *vous aussi*, you too, and even they were made redundant a moment later when Raoul began to undo the few buttons of our two shirts that, that hot day, had been done up in the first place.

So the three of us took our shower together, and towelled each other dry, and, all thoughts of the sofa forgotten, crept together, the three of us, into Jean-Charles's double bed and pleasured one another, not especially athletically but tenderly, comfortingly, until, arms thrown lightly across one another, we all slept.

When I awoke in the early light I didn't need to reach out a hand to know that Raoul wasn't there. I was alone with Jean-Charles in the bed. Together we got up and checked the house. The door was fastened but Raoul and all his clothes had gone. We might have thought we had jointly hallucinated the incident but for the wet bath towels and the state of the bathroom floor, and then, when we got back into bed I found I could smell the washed and youthful scent of the young man whose body had shone gold like butterscotch.

I fell into a light sleep and dreamed, for the first time in weeks, of Happy. He stood inside a lighted window that was high above me, and signalled to me to approach. I moved closer. Happy gestured to the window-pane between us. 'Break the glass,' he said.

I thought about this when I awoke again. There didn't seem much glass left to break. I'd broken the taboo I'd always carried around me about sleeping with, and having sex with, men. Last night I'd even jumped up and down on the splintered shards, it seemed to me, by sleeping with two of them at once. Where do I go from here? I had to ask myself.

I got out of bed, hearing Jean-Charles do the same on his side of the bed, and we started to dress. We were still a bit too gob-smacked by what had happened between Raoul and us to find very much to say. Then I was distracted by the sight of something shining in one of my shoes as I lifted it to put it on. The something was two ten-franc coins. I had left twenty francs in Raoul's shoes a few days ago, while he slept, and now it seemed that Raoul had done the same for me – the same two coins maybe. It was like a tip in a hotel bedroom, or a thank you for something more important than a mere night's sleep. Or – my imagination crept sideways up on this one – payment, of a sort, for sex. I smiled, and then sat down upon the bed and laughed. I'd remembered that Jean-Charles had left the same amount of money for Raoul too. He hadn't put his shoes on yet. 'What's funny?' He asked.

'Look inside your shoes,' I told him.

He looked there. *'Ah, mon dieu!'* he said.

This new day passed like the previous one. The difference was that we were both much happier.

Yesterday we'd felt we'd lost Raoul somehow. Today we had the feeling that he was very much found. The long-term consequences of that might be problematic, but then the long-term consequences of anything and everything can be problematic. There was still the imminent parting of Jean-Charles and me to deal with in little more than twenty-four hours' time.

It was Saturday. I couldn't believe how quickly this week had flown. I went again to the gallery at morning coffee time. I had a request to make of Jean-Charles. 'Can I go downstairs again?' I asked him. 'I'd like to take one more look at that photo of Ian before I have to go.'

'I knew you would,' said Jean-Charles with a smile. 'Ian Smart or Ian Lewis. He's the boy you knew. I can see from your face that you've no doubt about that now.'

'I guess you're right,' I said, though I'd tried not to let myself be too certain of it up to now.

Jean-Charles asked his boss Marc to keep an eye on the door for a minute of two, and together we went down the stairs. Together we gazed at the naked youth in the dimly lit room. 'He was very beautiful,' Jean-Charles said. 'I mean, he was when I met him. He still is in the picture. No doubt he still is in real life too. As you will see when you find him again.'

'When I find him again?' I queried, startled. 'What makes you think I'm going to find him again?'

'Because you're going to look for him.' Jean-Charles looked me steadily in the eye. 'When you are back in England that is exactly what you are going to do.'

'Oh, I don't know,' I said. 'Everybody always says it's a bad idea to go looking for your past.'

'It depends what the past was, surely,' Jean-Charles said. 'If it was a good thing…'

'It wasn't a good thing,' I tried to say.

'That's what you thought at the time,' he argued. 'You were trying to save your marriage, and some ideas you had about yourself... Well, now they are all burned up behind you. That's the bad past that has gone. You should look for Ian and find happiness with him.'

Because of his French accent he made *find happiness* sound like *find a penis*. I had to smile.

I changed the subject very slightly. 'And what will become of you after I've gone? What are you going to do?'

'Oh, I don't know,' he said. 'Perhaps I will look for Raoul.'

'Come here,' I said. 'Give me a kiss.' We stood embracing in the half-dark of the basement gallery for a long, long time.

Chapter 18

Jean-Charles didn't have to look for Raoul that day at any rate. In the middle of that hot afternoon Raoul came to the gallery looking for... For Jean-Charles? For me? For us? Whatever the case, there he was. Jean-Charles asked him if he would have dinner with us that evening. He made it clear that Raoul would eat as his, Jean-Charles's, guest. We both watched Raoul's beautiful, impassive face as he thought about the invitation and its possible implications. This took several seconds. I felt my emotions stirred as I saw Raoul's face break into a smile, and then watched him nod his yes.

The next thing that happened was that Raoul indicated with a gesture of hand and head that he wanted to see the photos in the basement again. I was acutely conscious that it was I who would be departing from both their lives tomorrow. I wanted to be gracious in my manner of leaving the two of them. I said, 'You take him down there,' to Jean-Charles. 'I'll man the desk.'

They returned, beaming, about ten minutes later. I was more than happy to see the smiles on both their faces.

We went to the Café du Forum. The café Vincent painted in the evening, with the light spilling out from under its awning onto the terrace and the tables. When we arrived it was still daylight, and the café hadn't yet adopted its evening look. But little by little as we sat on that well-known terrace the light changed. It became the light of Van Gogh. The buildings opposite darkened as the dusk thickened, and the lights under our yellow awning came on. Lights began to glimmer at the open-shuttered windows across the street. As we drank our *soupe de pistou* and ate our duck with olives it felt as though we were inhabiting the actual canvas of Van Gogh.

I let Jean-Charles talk most. He let Raoul know that I was returning to England the next day for good. Also that his parents were returning to their house tomorrow night. He told him that he'd be a welcome guest again at home with us tonight. That he didn't need to get up and leave at the crack of dawn. His parents wouldn't be back till the evening, he repeated. After that... Well... All three of us exchanged a very expressive smile and Gallic shrugs.

I left the table at one point. I'd spotted a pay-phone on a back wall. I was pretty sure it wouldn't have been installed yet in Vincent's day. Never mind: it was today that I wanted it.

I dialled Malcolm's number in Paris. I listened to it ringing out. Saturday night, I thought glumly. Everyone goes out. I'd have to leave a message... Ring back...

But Malcolm's voice spoke. *'Allo?'*

I said simply, 'It's David. I'm passing through Paris tomorrow. Can I stay with you tomorrow night?'

'Of course you can,' Malcolm said. 'Where are you speaking from?'

'I'm in Arles,' I said.

'Good God,' he said.

'It's a long story,' I said. 'I won't try and do it on the phone, but a hell of a lot's happened since we last spoke.' We arranged a time for me to turn up at his apartment.

I returned to the table, to find a second bottle of wine standing on top of it. 'I'm staying at Malcolm's place tomorrow night,' I said.

'That's good,' said Jean-Charles. 'Meanwhile, are you happy if Raoul sleeps again with us tonight?'

'Very happy indeed,' I said.

I fucked Raoul that night. On top of the bed. Raoul lay back and spread himself, open and inviting. Jean-Charles lent me a condom. Well, not lent me a condom. Nobody wants to be given it back afterwards. It was a free gift. I'd thought that men might be difficult to enter. But I guessed there were differences between them, as there are between everyone and everything else. Raoul was delightfully straightforward in this respect. Jean-Charles knelt on the bed, naked and erect beside us, massaging both his own and Raoul's cock.

I came all too quickly. I wasn't surprised by that. A little later, as I lay back and rested, Raoul eased his own sheathed small cock into Jean-Charles and pistonned him elegantly while I watched. I'd never have imagined previously that I'd get pleasure from watching such a scene, but I did.

And after that... Well, I couldn't be left out. Everything else had happened to me by now, or pretty much everything. This might as well be the night I lost my anal virginity. And who could I have wished to have as my deflowerer in preference to Jean-Charles? Jean-Charles with his petite and slender, unthreatening, foreskin-hooded, *bite*.

I loved every minute, and every inch, of it.

At last, after a very long time of shared sensual pleasure, we pulled the duvet up over us and, still fondling one another till the last, drifted into sleep.

We got up late, the three of us, and breakfasted together on the croissants that – fetched piping hot from the bakery by a designated family member while at home the coffee brews – form most French family's Sunday morning treat. The designated family member that day was me. There was no question, this morning, of Raoul's leaving either of us a tip.

I left in the middle of the morning, heading for the station, walking past Van Gogh's Yellow House. 'Are you sure you will be all right?' Jean-Charles asked me before I went. 'You told me it would be hard to part. As the older one of us, you knew that. And you were right, *bien sur*. Already it hurts.' It hurt for me too, of course, but I didn't tell him that. He went on, so sweetly that it made the hurt even more painful, 'I am the lucky one. I have ended up with Raoul. You are journeying on your own for a bit.'

'Even with Raoul,' I said, 'it won't be plain sailing for you. Your parents are coming back tonight...'

'That's later,' he said. 'We've got a few hours for think about that.'

'I wish you all the luck in the world,' I said.

'And you too,' he said. 'I will worry a lot.'

'No need,' I said. 'I'm a big strong boy. And we'll always keep in touch.' We held each other then, tightly, like parting lovers. *Like* parting lovers? We actually *were* parting lovers. It just happened that we'd been lovers – it had been understood between us at the outset – on a leasehold rather than a freehold basis.

Raoul joined in our au revoir embrace. On the doorstep. In full view of the street. He didn't have a stitch of clothing on him. None of us minded that.

I wasn't a big strong boy really, I discovered. On the train I cried my heart out, and not always silently, all the way to Paris.

'I lied to you,' I said. 'Lied to myself too, which is probably worse. But in the end I had to stop doing that.'

'Don't be hard on yourself,' Malcolm said. We'd gone out to a bar – one of the few that opened on Sunday evenings – opposite the stage door of the Moulin Rouge near the bottom of the rue Lepic. Henri, realising that I needed a little time alone with Malcolm, had stayed back at the apartment, preparing a supper of langoustines with garlic mayonnaise and salad, and a gateau of omelettes.

It crossed my mind that if ever I was lucky enough to have a boyfriend I'd want him to be French.

I told Malcolm everything that had happened. How I'd wanted simply to question Jean-Charles about the model in the photograph but had ended up in bed and having sex with him. How I'd then gone on to sleeping with two men together on the same night. How that had cumulated with all three of us fucking one another and getting fucked by one another ... I looked at my watch ... within the last eighteen hours.

'Christ almighty, David,' said Malcolm. 'You don't believe in doing things by halves...'

We walked together back up the steep curved incline of the rue Lepic. I had the sensation that I was returning home to a very familiar place. And I knew that supper would be good...

The dream of Happy in the window returned again that night. 'Break the glass,' he said again. And this time my dream-self did. Just as in real life years ago, my fist sent shards and splinters flying. But unlike in real life I now stood side by side with Happy. We walked together on a pebble beach. I had no doubt now where I was. This was Dungeness, a wild expanse of shingle, pounded by waves and blasted by wind, remote from human life, remote from everywhere. I began to wake. Urgently, because I feared to let him go a second time, I seized Happy's wrists and said, 'Where? Tell me where...'

But Happy's answer cut my question off unformed. 'Look in your address book.' The shocking incongruity of the answer woke me with all the finesse of an alarm clock in a cake tin.

'And did you look in your address book?' asked Malcolm. 'Well, did you?' We were sitting in the café near the Institute where Malcolm worked. I'd put off my return to England for a day or two. I needed Malcolm to talk things through with. I needed to sort myself out. The day's work was over for Malcolm and there was a small beer in front of both of us.

'Did I look in my address book? No, of course not!' The question made me laugh. 'I wouldn't expect the promptings of the unconscious to be so crudely literal,' I said.

'Maybe that was your problem all along,' said Malcolm.

I gave him a look. 'I do not believe, and never have, that dreams have any prophetic or guiding power.'

Malcolm slowly turned the stem of his beer glass. 'But they do come from the subconscious, you'd agree with that. And that in that case they might do a useful job, just occasionally, in reminding us of things that are important but which our conscious memories have forgotten. Either by accident or...' He hesitated, but then finished the thought anyway. '...Or deliberately buried.'

I knew full well that Happy's address had never found its way between the pages of my address book but nevertheless, since I'd brought the thing to France with me, in one of the side pockets of my backpack, that night I looked.

Malcolm, at breakfast, was exasperated. 'Well, do it now! Ring the bloody number. Use the phone here. We won't listen in.'

'It's just a coincidence, that's all,' I said. 'Both surnames beginning with L. I'd never thought about it before. I always knew Ian's parents' number was on that page; it's no big deal.'

'Yes, but not that London number pencilled in. Where did that come from?'

'From that ex-classmate of his I met a year ago, I guess. I really don't remember.'

'Erased from the mind but not from your phone book. What an awesome thing the pencil is.' And Malcolm bullied me until I phoned.

I returned to the breakfast table. 'Moved last Christmas,' I said. 'So that's that.'

'You are incredible, David. Don't tell me they didn't give you a new number for him.'

'Well, they did actually, but...'

'Then go ring it!'

'Maybe when I'm back in England tomorrow,' I said. I wasn't returning across the Channel today. Malcolm had arranged for me to have an interview with his boss at the Institute. 'But hell,' I said, 'I don't know why I'd want to do that. It'd only be to say hello.'

'Ring it.'

I did. Ian had moved again, a pleasant voice informed me. Someone in the flat who was out at present would have the number. Could he ring back? He rang back. It was all more complicated than that, a new voice told him. Ian had moved again. I was given the number of someone who might possibly know where.

As the task grew more frustrating so, paradoxically, I began to warm to it and Malcolm's urging was reduced to a mere background hum. The pursuit for its own sake was becoming more interesting than its object which was, after all, only to say hello.

It took two days. On each of those days I had an interview with someone at Malcolm's place of work. It seemed as though, provided I qualified on the course I was planning to do in London, and got my certificate, I could expect to come here and get a teaching job. But apart from going to those interviews I had little to do. I might as well spend my time making useless phone-calls, I thought. And so I did. But then at last the telephone gave me a voice there was no mistaking. It was my own physical reaction to it that surprised me.

Afraid of what my voice might do, I hesitated before saying, 'It's David here. I rang to say hello.'

The silence from the other end seemed as if it would last for ever. Anxiously, all too anxiously, I broke it myself, my voice finally betraying me. 'Ian, are you still there?'

'Yes,' came back firmly from the other end. Then more softly, 'I always was.'

Chapter 19

We arranged to meet at the Sun in Splendour, at the bottom end of the Portobello Road. I had been away from London for little more than a week. But the shock of that return! It wasn't that London had changed a lot in the intervening days. All the change was in me.

Ian had only to walk for twenty minutes to get to the Sun in Splendour. He lived in a shared flat near Powis Square. I made the pilgrimage by tube. I was staying with a group of friends of mine, singles of both sexes, who also shared a flat, but in Stockwell, south of the Thames. They had sheltered me, in between my travels, quite a lot during the past year.

And so I found myself walking up the steps, and then the road, from Notting Hill Gate tube station to the corner where the pub stood, its unique bowed frontage following the curve of the pavement between Pembroke Road and the Portobello. I took a nervous breath and opened the door.

I'd known the Sun in Splendour well in earlier days. I hadn't set foot inside it for years, but I still knew its layout well enough to know that what I could see was what there was. And what there wasn't... Ian wasn't there.

At least he wasn't there yet. The rules of chivalry dictate that when a guy arranges to meet a lone woman in a pub he shall arrive early, so as not to expose a lady to the awkwardness of waiting among strangers on her own. I wondered now how this played out among gay men. Was the senior one supposed to arrive first? If so, it seemed I'd obeyed the rule.

Now what would I have to drink? What would Ian drink these days? I had no idea. It was nearly two years since we'd seen each other. Then he'd been a boy of seventeen. Now he would be nineteen, and a man. A world-full of life and experience, of change and adventure had been his in the meantime. I had no idea who or what I had arranged to meet this early evening. Though neither, of course, had he...

The door opened and in he came.

He'd grown.

When we'd last we met he'd been about the same height as I was. Now he was about two inches taller. He was better muscled than me, now, though only just. He was beautiful. The photograph I'd seen of him in Arles, taken a year ago, was beautiful. I had no doubt at all now that he was the boy in the picture. But the way he looked this evening was something else. I found I wanted to say everything all at once. I didn't. I said, 'Ian, it's good to see you.' I held out my hand and we shook.

'Good to see you too,' Ian said, very adult, very cool.

We couldn't go on like this. I said, 'Ian, is it OK if I give you a hug?'

A hug is a very revealing thing. It's like a thermometer. Tells you what you need to know in the space of a minute. Or less. Ian's hug told me that he was OK about hugging me, but only just. My hug told him – told both of us – that suddenly, unexpectedly, I'd realised I wanted him very much. There was a degree of mismatch between where we were each at.

'I don't know what you drink these days,' I heard myself saying. 'Tell me what you'd like.' He chose a pint of Stella and I ordered the same thing for myself. We looked around for a vacant table. There wasn't one, but a second later a couple got up and left one and, as if executing a joint Rugby tackle, we dived for it and grabbed it round the legs before anyone else could.

'Why did you get in touch?' Ian asked me as soon as we'd said Cheers.

I said, 'Because I wanted to. Because I like you. There's a long story behind that, but it'll keep. Are you OK with that to be going on with?'

He nodded. 'How is Anne?' he asked. He was a smart kid.

'I think she's fine,' I said. 'There's a new man in her life. We got divorced. Did you know that?'

He winced slightly. 'I'm not sure if I knew it or if I sort of guessed.' Oh, he knew all right.

There was a hiatus during which we found it difficult to look at each other. I glimpsed his blue eyes through his long dark lashes. I saw them remembering his hurt. He spoke. 'We fucked each other up.' A sentence that tore into me like a knife.

I was the older one by nine years. It was for me to deal with this. 'For any hurt I've done you ... I'm deeply sorry. It's a hopeless word, an inadequate word, but it's the only one there is. Any hurt I've suffered – if I have – I've inflicted on myself. There's nothing in anything that happened that was your fault.'

'I'm sorry anyway,' he said.

'I love you, Ian,' I almost said. And then I was horrified at myself.

I found myself smiling at him. 'Would you agree with me that we don't need to discuss that right this minute? That we might want to meet again another time? And that for the moment we could just enjoy each other's company for an hour and chill out?'

He rewarded me with a flash of eyes and a smile that became a laugh. In that moment he became again the teenager I'd known for years, the boy I'd watched grow up. Just for a second it was as though nothing had happened in between those days and now; it was as though we'd never been apart. I said, 'Tell me what you've been doing with yourself this week?'

We talked for an hour. We talked about small things, not big ones. Perhaps that was wise of us. At one point I asked him, because I genuinely couldn't remember, if he was a fan of Van Gogh. 'A bit of one, perhaps,' he said. Then he astonished me. He said, 'I know that Happy was.'

'You knew that?' I didn't know he'd even heard of Happy, let alone that he knew that about him. 'Did I tell you about Happy? I don't remember doing that.'

'You didn't,' Ian said. 'Anne did.'

'Oh,' I said. We eyeballed each other across the table for a moment. Oh dear. How lovely he looked.

'She told me how upset you'd been about his death. I think she thought that you...' He shook his head with a jolt, as if his train of thought had hit a rough patch of track. 'No, forget that.' He started to talk about something else.

I hadn't known how or when our meeting would wind up. I'd left that to him deliberately. I wanted him to handle it his way, and so he did. He looked at his watch. 'I'd better go,' he said. 'We're eating in tonight and it's sort of my turn to cook.'

I took this on the chin, or at least pretended I did. 'Fair enough,' I said. 'It's been lovely seeing you.'

'It was good to see you too,' he said, and his eyes dropped, so that I got a view simply of his long lashes.

I was very calm as I said, feeling my way with this, like an angler reeling in a fish that he has only very lightly hooked, 'I wonder if I might buy you dinner one night next week. Would you be OK with that?'

He didn't meet my gaze. Not yet. I had the feeling he was speaking from behind the shelter of his eyelashes as he said quietly, 'Yes, I'd like that.'

I was tempted to try and nail an evening there and then. Something told me not to do that. I took a bigger risk. For much higher stakes. 'Can I phone you in a day or two?' I asked. 'Then we can fix a day.' I just managed not to say date. 'Is that all right?' He said it was.

We stood up then and walked out into the street. His way lay leftward, mine to the right. We embraced momentarily on the pavement. It's funny how you always know whether there is or isn't going to be a kiss. We knew there wasn't going to be. Not tonight.

As I walked away, resisting the almost overpowering urge to turn round and look back, I thought at once of all the big questions we hadn't asked. Neither of us had said, are you in a relationship? Neither of us had volunteered the answer to that. He hadn't asked me if I was gay. Though I wouldn't have expected him to. I was nine years older than him and had been a married man when we'd last met. He on the other hand had declared his love for me drunkenly when he was seventeen. He might well have spent the intervening years feeling painfully foolish about that. It was good of him to agree to meet me, in the circumstances.

And yet… That first exchange of words of ours on the telephone a fortnight back was etched on my memory. I even remembered exactly his tone of voice. Are you still there? I'd asked him. Yes, he'd said. *I always was.*

I hadn't asked him if he was gay either. Not yet. Give him space, I thought. Give him time and space. I heard my breath come out as a large loud sigh as I reached the top of the steps at Notting Hill Gate. So great a sigh, so painful a heave. It was nearly a sob.

I tried a T-shirt on and turned in front of the mirror, this way and that. It looked too obvious that I was trying to age down, to take away those nine years that lay between us, that always had done, that always would. I replaced it with various open-necked shirts, one after another, then took them off. I spent over half an hour in front of the mirror that evening. It was the kind of thing

Anne used to do – and she wasn't alone among womankind in that. I used to tease her about it, as most husbands do. But as for me, I had never done such a thing before in my life.

In the end I chose a plain white collarless linen shirt. Then I agonised over how many buttons I should leave undone. Just two? Or three? Or - *four?* Bloody hell, mate, I told myself... I knew that my chest looked good however much or little of it I might expose. But that was not the point... I settled for three in the end. It was a hot night. I didn't bother with a jacket. I just jammed everything into my jeans pockets and went out.

We met in the Sun in Splendour as before. I was happy to see Ian looking much more relaxed tonight. That made me relax too, and I saw Ian clock that. I also saw that he'd taken some trouble, just as I had, to look his best. I found myself surprisingly, and deeply, moved by that.

At my suggestion we had a gin and tonic this time. A large one. I was paying, after all. I'd had my experiences of going to restaurants after several pints of beer and then having to keep leaving the table during dinner to let the water out. I didn't want either of us to have to deal with that particular embarrassment tonight. If we ever got to know each other better, then maybe that would be all right. We weren't at that stage yet...

We walked together across Notting Hill Gate and into Hillgate Street, where there was a small Italian restaurant I'd known for years. It was home territory, and I felt safe.

When we were seated I returned to the subject of Van Gogh. I'd now had plenty of time to rehearse this scene: I wanted to try and get it right. I told him how a friend had invited me to go to Provence with him, with a view to helping me get over the trauma of my divorce. How he'd been a Van Gogh freak, just as Happy had, and had taken me on his track. I saw his ears prick slightly at the mention of Provence. I now said, 'We went to Arles…'

He almost gave a start. I pressed on. 'I saw something very beautiful there in an art gallery.'

'Oh,' he said. 'What was that?'

'I just wondered,' I said, 'if you might guess.'

He looked cross for a second. 'Don't tease me,' he said.

'I won't,' I said. 'But if I get this wrong I'm going to be hideously embarrassed. OK, I'll tread carefully. I saw a photo of a young man on a river bank.'

This time he really did start; he couldn't disguise it. I smiled, trying to relax him, wanting to show him I was OK about it. 'A very nice looking young man, naked. I might be wrong, and if I am, that's the embarrassing bit…'

He didn't let me go on struggling. Bless his lovely heart. 'You were right. It was me,' he said.

'I'm very glad of that,' I said, and we both laughed. With a sound like breaking ice, or breaking glass.

I had to tell him, because he was curious, about how I'd met Jean-Charles and his boss. I didn't tell him I'd had sex with him – let alone had a threesome with him and Raoul. There might one day be a time and place for telling everything, but this was certainly not it.

I changed the subject. I told Ian I was going to do a short course in teaching English as a foreign language. 'My friend Malcolm introduced me to the bosses of the business school he works at in Paris,' I said. I adopted an expression, or tried to, that would convey the idea of *Qué será, será*. 'See what happens,' I said. 'It's one option. I haven't decided yet.'

Ian wasn't going to go down on his knees and beg me not to go to Paris but to stay with him in London. He wasn't going to tell me he'd rather I got a job washing dishes in this very Italian restaurant than move three hundred miles away across the sea. And of course he didn't.

It wasn't until that very moment, though, that I discovered I wished he would.

A young Italian was playing a guitar in one corner of the small space. As we came towards the end of our meal two young couples at a nearby table got up and started to dance. It was brave of them: the space was extremely cramped. After two dances they called it a day, vanquished by that constraint. They began to sit down again, and the two girls actually did. But the boys did not. Halfway to sitting down they seemed to change their minds – jointly. They both got up again.

They were back on the dance floor together. On was Italian, the other English, I guessed. They held each other, their cheeks so close they could have leaned in easily for a kiss. But then the Italian one turned aside to speak to the guitarist. 'Play 'Feelings',' he said. And the guitarist did.

To say the two boys danced together would be overstating it. Their feet didn't leave the floor. But they held each other, swaying with the music, with the unmistakeable intimacy of two people who – even if they don't actually love each other - are deeply attracted and closely attached. They were two people who – even if they didn't know this consciously – would at some level have liked to have sex.

The dance didn't last more than a few seconds. The boys broke apart, their faces expressing both disappointment and awkwardness. Frustration too perhaps. The guitarist's accompaniment petered out. The men joined their girlfriends - or wives - back at the table. Ian and I looked at each other. To say the looks we exchanged at that moment were heavily freighted would have been a major understatement.

One of us had to speak. I found it was me. 'When I was in Provence,' I said, 'I made more than just one discovery. Among other things I discovered was the fact that I'm gay.' I adapted Ian's own phrase. 'I probably always was.'

In a very small and diffident voice, almost a whisper, Ian said, 'I'm gay too. I probably always was.'

Chapter 20

At one time I thought that being gay – if you were – was about the biggest thing you could find you had in common with a fellow human being. That it was the biggest bond you could have. I was wrong. It isn't. It's quite a small thing actually. Think of it the other way round. Two guys are heterosexual... Automatic bond between them? I think not.

So we didn't rush into each other's arms across the restaurant table. We didn't go to bed together that night. But we parted friends. Rather good friends. There was a bond of understanding between us. There was affection. And we'd told each other we were gay. All right, it wasn't a big thing. But it wasn't nothing.

A week after that I became enormously busy. My training course began. I thought it would be easy. I'd been teaching English for years, after all. But it was far from that. Our trainers made a point of smashing to pieces all the assumptions I had about teaching. I saw what they were about. They needed to rebuild me, as a teacher, from scratch. It was a very different kind of teaching I was about to do. Instead of English school-kids with whom I shared a language, a culture and a load of assumptions and other baggage, I would be working with adults with whom I shared none of the above. It was pointed out to me, as one example, that while the word dog evokes up a warm cuddly feeling in British people, for people in many countries it conjures up primeval fears, of the jungle, of the lawless, rabid, scavenged back streets. I could make no assumptions about even the things I thought of as basic.

I had a lot to learn. They made me learn it. Because I'd been a teacher – I was the only specimen in my group of fifteen – they often picked on me in front of the whole class, to make an example. To rub home the fact that what we were learning to do was nothing like we'd experienced at school. I didn't like it. I bore it. I didn't let it get me down, although it might easily have done had there been no-one in my life. What buoyed me up was … Ian.

At the end of the day I would phone him up and we'd have a chat. He'd tell me his daily woes. About his English degree course at UCL. I'd tell him my about my tribulations too. Once a week we'd meet for a drink or dinner. Once I went to his flat. Once he came to mine. We enjoyed each other's company. That was as far as it went.

'Are you still planning to go to Paris?' he asked me more than once.

Please ask me not to go, a voice inside me begged. *Tell me you need me. Ask me to stay and I'll do that. I'll get a job here in London washing dishes. Just say one word.* The outward me said, 'Probably. I'm still not sure, though. Do you have a better idea?' He did not. *Just say the word.* But he did not.

If I was going to work in Paris I would need somewhere to live. I couldn't stay in Malcolm and Henri's small spare room for ever. Through a friend they found me what they called a *chambre de bonne*. It meant a maid's room, an attic bedroom in effect. The mansard roofs of the Paris skyline were crammed with these. The maids had long gone, and their empty nest-holes had been for the most part converted into small studio flats, inhabited by students and the likes of me – single young workers who were not yet rich.

My four-week intensive (extremely intensive!) course finished. A week later I got my results. I got a grudging pass. But a pass is still a pass, as time goes by, and the grudge fades into meaninglessness.

Still, I would have cancelled everything, and risked the wrath of Malcolm's employers had Ian said or done anything to stop me at the last moment. But still he didn't. We had a farewell dinner together. I said, 'You promise you'll come and spend a weekend with me in Paris as soon as I'm settled?'

He said, 'I will.' Then he smiled beautifully at me across the table. It was far from being a marriage vow but it was the best I was going to get.

I didn't ask him to come with me to the airport. That would have been too cruel to both of us. Instead I went on my own. Van Gogh had left London, all alone, for Paris in March 1896 – I was following him in September 1989. The parallel was not exact. A neat centenary would have been pleasing, but never mind.

Van Gogh had travelled by ship. There was no other way, back then. Unlike Vincent I had a choice. I went with Air France, taking off from Heathrow just before four o'clock. I wondered what, if any, refreshments would be provided by the French flag-carrier during the forty-minute hop. It turned out to be a quarter-bottle of Moët et Chandon, red-sealed and gold-foil-wrapped, placed without fuss on every seat-back table as we crossed the French coast overhead the docks of Dieppe. I had to hand it to them. Nobody has style like the French.

Things don't always go like clockwork, though. The Institute wanted me to start on a Monday, naturally, while my studio wouldn't be ready until two days after that. Nor was Malcolm able to put me up. He was away with Henri for those few days, and Malcolm's brother and his sister-in-law were staying in the flat in rue Lepic. I checked into a cheap hotel at La Motte-Piquet.

And then I began my new life.

I had ordered breakfast for seven-thirty. It was served to me and to half a dozen twitching travelling salesmen by a pale Pole who doubled as a night porter as he passed bleary nights studying economics text-books in French. There was coffee in bowls, and baguettes cut in chunks to dunk in it. There were no croissants at seven-thirty on a Monday.

It took me exactly twelve minutes to walk to the Institute. The wind took my old Durham Castle scarf and wrapped it twice around my throat as if it meant to strangle me with my own umbilicus before I could snatch even my first breath of this new life. Then, as I crossed the threshold of my new place of work it occurred to me that existing in a new language was going to involve a marathon repetition of firsts. That first day at school – an event as impossible to repeat, I'd thought, as the death of a hero – now had to be undergone again, this time in French. So it would be with the first visit to the doctor, to the hairdresser; with the first altercation, with the hesitations of the first new intimacy, the sorrow of the first parting. Only in English were these rites of passage behind me and unrepeatable. I realised now that my relative unfamiliarity with the language would leave me as fragile and unprotected an arrival in this francophone world as a newborn child. The door shut behind me and I began once again my first day at school.

There had been two first times in my case, of course. On the first occasion I was five. My mother had towed me by the arm down the slope to the entrance, uncoupled with difficulty my tightening fingers from her own and hooked them into another hand which belonged, I soon discovered, not to a woman or man but to a new thing called a teacher. It was not a happy morning and everyone had cried, including me. The second time I hadn't cried, though I'd felt just the same, but that time I'd been twenty-two and myself a new thing called a teacher.

'*Monsieur Walton?*' said the receptionist, pricking up her ears as I announced my name. '*Vous avez un groupe à neuf heures.*' I had a group at nine o'clock, apparently. It was now eight fifty.

'*Ce n'est pas possible,*' I said, trying not to let my panic be heard in my voice. I had nothing prepared. Really, this third round in the David versus School contest was going to be as bad as the others. 'Madame Suger told me that my first class would be a one-to-one this afternoon. I came in early just to see where things are and to prepare for later on.' This speech sounded less impressive in my halting French.

The director of studies, sailing into the reception area just then, came to my rescue, or so I thought. She was a tall, elegant Englishwoman who had been trying out Parisian chic for twenty years and had very nearly got the hang of it. 'You're David, aren't you?' she said, smiling. 'I'm Rebecca.' She offered varnished nails. I tweaked them nervously. 'Madame Suger told me about you. Now this class at nine o'clock. We can't possibly expect you to do it, of course.' Her smile widened reassuringly. 'Not at zero notice. It isn't on your programme and you've only just arrived.' I nodded with gratitude and relief. 'On the other hand...' The smile vanished and she gave me a penetrating look through fashionable spectacles. 'We've got two teachers sick this morning and we'd be ever so grateful if you could ... at least, just till eleven o'clock. By then I'll have found someone else to hang in till lunchtime. You'd still have time to prepare for the afternoon.'

'But...'

'They've got books.' Rebecca had played this scene before. 'At least I think they have. It's *Salle Numéro Sept.*'

Faced with the choice between accepting and refusing additional work on your first morning, what did you do?

I'd found himself rapidly and expertly manoeuvred beyond choice or decision. Within five minutes I was in *Classroom Number Seven*, teaching English to a computer programmer, an air hostess, a journalist, an accountant and two secretaries and trying, as Rebecca had advised, to *make it relevant*.

'How much are they paying you?'

'Pardon?'

'How much are they paying you?' The question came from under thatched eaves of hair, well coiffed but designed to leave the face beneath a shadowy, enigmatic affair. The voice and hairstyle belonged to a small, mouse-like woman who was seated at the staffroom table. Other people, preparing lessons as I was, had left me temporarily *à deux* with this stranger who had not responded when I'd introduced myself to the room in general. 'Well, how much?'

'The normal rate, I suppose,' I said. 'Like everyone else.'

'Don't you believe it,' said the voice under the thatch. 'There isn't a normal rate. We're all paid differently. You wouldn't credit it, would you? But it's true.' The woman's face now seemed to be peering out of a burrow, nose a-twitch and small eyes darting. 'They do it so that none of us can trust one another. It stops us from getting together to improve things.'

'I suppose it would do,' I said blandly.

'It's disgraceful,' the other went on. 'Do you know, we're not allowed to join a *syndicat*?'

'What's a *syndicat*?' I asked, though I could guess.

'A trade union,' the woman said. 'I don't know why we put up with it. You ought to do something, you know.'

'Me?'

'Strike while the iron's hot,' said the woman in an impassioned squeak. 'You had to do an extra class this morning without notice. You shouldn't let them get away with that. They'll be walking over you in no time.'

'It's still only my first day.' I wasn't sure whether to be alarmed or amused. 'It might be just a bit soon to proclaim the revolution. I mean, coming from me. How long have you been here?'

'Twelve years. I don't know why. They don't thank you. They don't appreciate loyalty.' She lowered her voice to a rustle. 'This hell hole, it's run by a coven of witches. Did you know that?'

To my relief two other people came in, talking together, and my own conversation ended. I buried my head unnecessarily deeply in a text-book until it was time for lunch.

The afternoon's one-to-one lesson presented me with a large, jowly man who faced me across a table and informed me, 'I don't want grammar or exercises; I want to talk.'

I closed the text-book. 'OK. We'll talk.' And my student turned out to be as taciturn an individual as I'd ever passed an afternoon with, while my watch crept towards five o'clock like a train passing a succession of signals set at amber.

It was a delicious novelty to finish a day's work and to be at the same time in a foreign country. Today, for the first time in my life, I found that I could step abroad and into all its associations just by stopping my class on time and walking out into the street.

Near at hand a bright shop window displayed charcuterie, champagne and those jewel-like hors d'oeuvres of eggs and seafood set in aspic. All up the street other lighted windows gave promise of the same and more. At the end of the vista one giant leg of the

Eiffel Tower appeared, framed by the surrounding buildings. It seemed to be stepping on stage teasingly, like a showgirl: this glimpse of leg a coquettish preliminary to the grand entrance the Tower would make if I would only cross the road and move towards it. I did cross the road. I'd seen a phone-box. I went into it and phoned Ian. We talked for ages, and when I put the phone down I felt that all was well again with the world.

Chapter 21

Two days later I moved into my bright-windowed apartment under the zinc roof of an *immeuble* just off the Place Blanche. The little square lay at the bottom of the rue Lepic, and was just five minutes' walk from Malcolm's flat. Even better, by now Malcolm was back.

We met for the first time at the end of the day's work. There was so much I wanted to tell him. He forestalled me. 'Let's go for a beer,' he said. 'There's a café round the corner the others don't use. Then we can talk.'

And talk I did. I told him all about Ian. About where we'd got to. About where we had not. 'The trouble is, I've rather fallen for him,' I ended up.

Malcolm said, with a little laugh, 'Oh, I knew you'd do that.' Then, 'When are you seeing him next?'

'I've asked him to come to Paris once I've settled,'

'Ah,' he said, nodding wisely. 'I wouldn't leave it as long as that.'

'I'll bear that advice in mind,' I said. 'I phone him every evening anyway. I'll be phoning him later tonight.'

'Good,' Malcolm said. 'I'm glad to hear that.' Then he changed the subject, and we began to talk about the place, a mere two hundred metres away, where we worked. 'What did you have today?' he asked.

'A four-hour intensive group in the morning and a one-to-one in the afternoon,' I told him. 'And you?' I asked.

'About the same,' Malcolm said. 'Except my morning was 'in-company'. That's quite good. It means you spend some of your time riding around Paris on buses and trains and things. When you're new it helps you get to know the city and when you're not it serves to remind you that it's all still out there – Paris I mean – looking beautiful. When you work in a place like this for a while it's dead easy to forget that. And you can do your lesson prep on the bus as well if you get tired of sightseeing. Mind you, they won't let you loose on the company classes for a month or two. You'll have to stay here under Madame Suger's petticoats a while yet. Till they feel sure they can trust you. Have you had any problems with Sarah today?'

'Who's Sarah?' I asked. Then I guessed. 'Is she the woman who looks like a mouse peering out of a thatched roof?'

'Got her in one,' Malcolm said.

I had indeed had a run-in with the thatched woman earlier that day. There had been an electric heater in my classroom which I'd switched on a while before my morning lesson. Returning to the room a few minutes later with a book I'd forgotten, I'd caught Sarah in the act of removing my heater in order to install it in her own room next door. I had already noticed that her room had its own heater. 'I feel the cold more than other people,' she'd claimed when I protested. An unseemly argument had ensued in front of the students, taboo among teachers everywhere, which had only ended when I physically wrested the heater from Sarah's grasp, winning not through any persuasive power but mere male might. I still felt rather bad about this.

'She's a witch,' Malcolm said matter-of-factly when I'd finished the tale. 'I guessed you might have trouble with her. That's why I asked. Who else have you met?'

I'd met two American guys who were very different from each other. 'I've met George,' I said. 'And I've met Huck.'

'Ah,' said Malcolm. 'George first. Well, he crossed the Atlantic to forget his divorced wife and her kids. Now do you know Katie?'

'Haven't met her yet. But don't tell me. She came here to forget her husband. Right?'

'That's not the half of it. George was the husband she came to forget. And here he was in Paris, working at the same school. God, I'd like to have been a fly on the wall when they first met up in the *salle des profs*. It's a small world, I know, but George and Katie couldn't have guessed it was quite that small. Now Huck. He came all the way from New York to forget he was positive.'

'Positive?'

'HIV. He seems to think that now he's in Paris it'll sort of go away. Dear, lovely Huck\. I mean I know Paris has its magic but there are limits...'

Later I phoned Ian and we chatted. Our chats got a little longer each night, I was noticing. I liked that. I just hoped he didn't feel the opposite. I jumped in now with both feet. 'Can you come to Paris this weekend?' I invited. 'I'd pay your fare, of course. I'd really like that.' I heard my voice falter as I added, 'If you would...'

There was a moment's silence. It was long enough to give my heart time to sink. Then I heard Ian say, 'I can't do this weekend. It's too short notice. I've got coursework. Or the next one. But I could do the one after that. Would that be all right?'

My heart leapt and sang and capered. 'It would be wonderful,' I said. I couldn't say less than that.

And then I caught up with Malcolm again, and had supper with him and Henri in their apartment in the rue Lepic. We sat in the salon, surrounded by Vincent's golden fields of wheat and sunflowers. I told them the news about Ian's forthcoming visit, and they said well done, and drank my health.

I walked back to the Place Blanche with my heart full of light.

The phone rang just after eight. It was Rebecca, the director of studies. I could feel the clutch of her varnished nails through the bedclothes. 'I know you're not due to teach before two o'clock,' Rebecca said, 'but could you, exceptionally, cover a class from nine-thirty till twelve-thirty? I've got someone to hold it for the first hour.'

'I'm in bed,' I protested.

'Would you be able to make it for nine-thirty?' Rebecca said.

I felt the nails digging in. After a tiny pause, the voice on the phone – now modulated into a more sombre key – added, 'You know we'll always try to accommodate teachers when they have their own timetable problems. These things have to work two ways, I feel, or not at all.'

I had felt the nails meet, somewhere just below my diaphragm. 'All right,' I said. The class I found myself teaching, a rushed hour later, was in a bad humour, its equilibrium upset by the non-appearance of its usual teacher. I struggled to kindle in the group some enthusiasm for gerunds and infinitives, but finished the lesson wishing – at one with the students for the first time that morning – that I hadn't bothered. The afternoon passed only marginally more happily and it came as a great relief at five o'clock to step out into the street and watch the Eiffel Tower do likewise as I crossed the road towards the café. I'd arranged to meet Malcolm there in fifteen minutes.

We'd met at lunchtime already, though. He had asked me, out of the blue, 'How are you getting on with *la Sorcière*?'

'With what?'

'Sarah. Have you thrown any more heaters at each other?'

'Heaters, no,' I said. 'We had a set-to over the photocopier, though. She decided she had the right to jump the queue because she only had four copies to make and had arrived late for her class into the bargain.'

'Trying it on. Did you let her?'

I laughed. 'Hell I did. I took the opportunity to do some of my copying for tomorrow as well while I was in front of her. She was pretty livid but there wasn't much she could do. On the other hand she had the gall to ask me for five francs during the coffee break, saying she had no change for the coffee machine – which only requires two francs anyway.'

Malcolm chuckled. 'That's our Sarah.' We'd gone on to talk of other things.

I reached the café now and went inside. I ordered myself a *panaché*, a shandy, and at the same moment, to my great surprise, Sarah entered. *La Sorcière*. She was wearing dark glasses, which gave her the conspicuous appearance of someone who did not want to be recognized – and made her all the more conspicuous since we were indoors and the café was not particularly brightly lit. The effect in combination with her thatch-like coiffure was striking. But if the dark glasses, like the hair, made it impossible for outsiders to peer in, they apparently didn't diminish her own ability to see out. She made straight for me and said, 'There you are. I thought I'd find you here.'

I didn't feel under any obligation to be courteous. 'I was hoping to see Malcolm,' I said. 'And now you're looking for me. Must be my lucky day.'

For answer Sarah opened her purse, took out a five-franc coin and rapped it smartly on the counter like a small hammer. 'I owe you that,' she said. 'From this morning.'

I said, 'You haven't come here specially to give me five francs.'

She turned black lenses on me. She might have been looking searchingly into my eyes. On the other hand her own might have been shut. 'No,' she said. 'I'd like you to order me a Côtes du Rhône.'

I laughed. Finally, when people were so preposterous, that was all there was to do. When I ordered the drink it arrived at once. In France that was one of the additional benefits to be derived from female company – even, it now appeared, from Sarah's.

'There's going to be a *Comité d'Entreprise*,' she announced after a small sip of wine. She had said neither cheers nor thank you.

'A what?'

'I'll explain. Every company over a certain size has one. Ours has just reached that size. Due, in actual fact, to your recent arrival. You appear to have hit the jackpot. That or been the last straw.'

'You don't make yourself clear at all,' I said. 'What is this committee?'

'The *Comité d'Entreprise* is a social committee that'll organise things like cheap theatre tickets, painting classes, staff outings...'

'Ouch,' I said.

'Staff outings not your *tasse de thé*? No, I was fairly sure they wouldn't be. But that's actually not what I came to talk about.'

'So...?'

'Along with the *comité* they want two *délégués du personnel* and if your French isn't up to understanding what that means I'll spell it out. A *délégué du personnel* represents the staff to the management – in the case of a dispute about pay, for example; conditions of employment, contracts and so on.' She switched her attention away from me, rapped another coin on the counter and called for change for some purpose which I couldn't catch, so rapid was her French.

'In other words they want two poor sods to stick their necks out,' I summed up. 'Who's standing?'

'No-one so far. The list of names for the *Comité d'Entreprise* is full, but the other one next to it is conspicuously empty. – *Ah, merçi.*' Her change had arrived.

'I can't say I'm surprised,' I said. 'Madame Suger and Rebecca together would make a formidable pair of opponents at the negotiating table, I imagine. At the table and beyond.'

'Exactly. For that reason I think we should stand.'

'We?'

'Yes, David. We. I mean you and I.'

'What in the world has put this idea into your head? You hardly know me from Adam and in any case I've only just arrived. I've hardly got to grips with the language lab. let alone anything else.'

'It doesn't matter. I already have you taped, marked out, or whatever you like to call it these days. We are the best two people for those jobs, like it or not, whether you like the idea of working with me or not. Someone has to do it. It needs doing.'

'OK, but why me? You may have your own reasons for wanting to do it; for all I know you'll do a good job. But don't go including me in your plans. Why not ask one of the others? I plucked two names at random from among the colleagues I'd already met. What about George, or Huck?' I was regretting my choice of a *panaché* rather than something stronger.

'George is an oaf, as you must have noticed already,' she answered, 'and Huck isn't as strong as we'd all like him to be; you must know that too. But I think you may have a gift, Peter, as a builder of bridges, an ironer-out of creases. I see it in your face, in the way you talk. As the French say, *tu sais mettre les choses à plat.* '

'Good God,' I said. I wondered if perhaps Sarah really was a witch, or in some way clairvoyant. 'OK, but compliments apart, I don't know anything about French employment legislation, company law or anything like that. I'd be quite useless.'

'Ah yes, but in that respect I would not be,' Sarah said. 'I worked once in a French law firm. It was a long time ago, I must admit – fifteen years or more. But I still know where to get my hands on the bits of paper. That's where I come in. Also, I have a portable typewriter. We'd complement each other. You're good at handling people, which I'm not.'

'You're asking me to put my head on a block, you realize that.'

'Someone has to.'

'And get it chopped off?'

'The clever ones don't.'

'Supposing I'm not clever.'

'Supposing you are. Just say yes. Go on.'

'I'll think about it.'

'Bloody hell!' Sarah exploded. Other people turned to look. She lowered her voice to a hiss. 'People who say they'll think about things always find an excuse not to do them. Just say yes. Say it.' She took off her dark glasses and pushed the hair back from her eyes. They were the same beady brown ones I remembered but now they seemed to indicate that they might be ready to smile if certain conditions were met. 'Also, I suspect,' she said, 'there's someone in your life you'd like to try and impress.'

'Dear God!' I said. 'Where did you get that idea from?'

She shrugged and smiled. 'Just a hunch,' she said. 'Woman's intuition, if you like.'

'*Merde,*' I said. 'I'll do it. You're on. All right?'

'I didn't really doubt that you'd say yes,' said Sarah. 'I feel I know you quite well, though we've scarcely met.'

Wait till I tell Ian this! I thought. How uncannily Sarah had hit that last nail on the head. That I wanted to impress Ian. Of course I did.

Our *tête-à-tête* ended then. The door opened and Malcolm came in. His eyebrows rose in surprise as he saw the two of us.

Chapter 22

'That was a shock,' Malcolm said, after Sarah had finished her glass of Côtes du Rhone and left. Though she'd stayed long enough for the new development to be discussed between the three of us. 'But it'll probably do you good. Stop you moping over Ian for a bit.'

'I'm not moping over Ian,' I said. 'You forget, he's coming here in less than three weeks.'

'I hadn't forgotten,' Malcolm said. 'But you're still moping over him. And after he's spent a weekend here with you and has gone back to London again, you'll be moping even worse.'

'We'll cross that bridge when we come to it,' I said.

'Anyway,' said Malcolm, evidently deciding to lighten things a bit, 'it'll give you something to brag to him about. Even if, in the end, it costs you your job.'

'Thanks a bunch,' I said.

During my first week as a *délégué du personnel* the burden of my new responsibility felt ominously light. I was first congratulated on my appointment, along with Sarah, in Madame Suger's office over a glass of Institute champagne. (Institute champagne was indefinably different from other champagnes. There was always a quid pro quo suspended invisibly among the bubbles.) Madame Suger, raising her glass, said she hoped we could all work happily together in pursuit of the general good. As far as the first week went, and apart from the fact that Sarah dusted down her old portable typewriter and bought a new ribbon for it, that was that. I couldn't help seeing it as a symbol of something: the fact that we had an ancient portable typewriter at our disposal, while Madame Suger could avail herself of the Institute's computer Behemoth. Like David and Goliath, perhaps.

In the second week things began to hot up. The typewriter was put through its paces. It produced a dignified letter requesting clarification of the Institute's precise attitude to adult students who wanted to smoke in class.

'I'm sorry,' said Sarah, handing me the letter in draft. 'The typewriter's an English make. You have to put the accents in by hand. Will you check I haven't missed any?' Madame Suger spoke perfect English. Nevertheless it was *de rigueur* that all communication with her took place in French. It was her country after all. As Sarah's written French was vastly more polished than mine was it had been decided that she would actually compose the letters. Besides, though neither of us mentioned this, her typing was better too.

Madame Suger responded graciously on three sides of paper, managing to take three separate positions on the issue which overlapped without exactly contradicting each other. As a preliminary exercise in getting the measure of the other side this exchange was not without value. But it was in the third week that things began to get interesting.

'It's just got to be a strike. It's the only way.' This was the opinion of George, delivered through the cloud of cigarette smoke that had been generated by a fair number of teachers during an impassioned half hour in the *salle des profs*. George was one of the more ebullient personalities among the staff. Presumably ebullience had come in handy the day he had rediscovered, in this very room, the wife he had left America to get away from. ('He that loseth his wife shall find her,' as Malcolm had biblically put it.)

'Do you really think a strike's the best solution?' asked Sarah.

'The Métro and the SNCF do it often enough and to good effect,' said someone else, backing George. 'You know, just one day at a time. A brief inconvenience but one that shows muscle.'

'But we're not the Métro or the railway.' I piped up for the first time. 'Just look at us. This organisation has thirty competitors in Paris alone. If we start getting strike-happy the clients will go elsewhere and the institute will cut down on...'

'Then we'll go to the other ones,' George intercepted the argument. 'They'll be needing more staff to deal with the upturn. What's wrong with that?' He inhaled slowly on the cigar he had been gesturing with during the discussion and blew a new cloud of smoke across the table.

'It's not so simple,' said Sarah, 'as you well know. Employers aren't necessarily going to favour staff from a place with a record of strikes.' There were a few supportive nods from around the table and more smoke was exhaled into the thickening atmosphere.

'And also,' I followed up, 'how could we ever get unanimity? It's not like the Métro. Everyone knows everyone else for one thing. Individual people may have special reasons not to join. Families to worry about.' I was taking a gentle swipe at George. 'That kind of thing. A partially supported strike would be a disaster. It'd play right into their hands, split the staff down the middle for ages to come.'

George looked round the table and took his cue from the number of heads that were almost imperceptibly nodding agreement with me.

'Well, all right, David,' he said. 'Have it your way. But you've given yourself a tough job to do. Getting a deal out of Suger over the coffee cups won't be child's play. But there you are. It's up to you. You're our representatives. Get in there and do something. But let's keep the strike option open – for if you fail. OK?'

Sarah and I promised to do what we could and then the meeting broke up. But it was hard to know how to crystalise a miasma of discontent into precise demands for improvements. In the end Sarah typed a letter, to which I added the accents, which informed the management ... that the staff were unhappy with the irregularity of their lunch breaks.

Two days later Madame Suger, Rebecca, Sarah and I were seated in a perfect square at Madame Suger's round table. I felt decidedly nervous and even Rebecca seemed a little less assured than usual. But Madame Suger, in a shoulder-padded suit that managed to look both chic and sensible, with gold pendant earrings and with her honey-coloured hair coiled high on her head, was a picture of serene confidence. 'Well now,' she began with a gentle smile, 'what can we do to help?'

With exaggerated civility, and speaking in French, I outlined the cause of complaint, laying equal stress on the diminished efficiency of staff who did not have proper breaks and on the human discomfort caused to them. Madame Suger reiterated with equal civility her sympathy in principle and her inability to do anything about the situation in practice. Rebecca pointed out the dire consequences to the Institute of not being able to offer its services at certain hours in the middle of the day: lost contracts, redundancies, that sort of thing. 'Even the Métro, which has little competition, does not shut down for lunch.'

'They do have rather more than thirty staff,' Sarah pointed out.

'Well then,' I said, 'let's come to another point. The staff have asked me to put it to you that time spent travelling to work should be regarded as part of the working week and paid accordingly.'

Sarah flashed me a quick look of surprise mingled with anxiety. This was certainly not on the agenda: nobody had ever put forward such a bizarre proposal. A faint look of horror crossed Madame Suger's composed features, but momentarily, as a wind ripples a cornfield. Then she regained control of them. 'All travelling time?' she asked incredulously.

'All travelling time,' I said.

Rebecca intervened. 'That just isn't possible, David. No organization in the world pays its employees to travel in to work. Surely you must know that. You might decide to commute from London – or Vancouver.' She laughed. A little nervously, I thought.

'It's just not on,' said Madame Suger. 'You don't need to be an accountant to imagine the cost. You must learn to be a little realistic in your demands.'

'I suppose,' I said, 'I might be able to persuade them to moderate their claim for travel payments if they felt some progress had been made on the lunch front.'

Madame Suger swallowed, setting her earrings aquiver, and was silent for a moment before she replied, 'Perhaps we could make a token gesture. But then I'd need to ask in return for some extension of *disponibilité*.' Disponibilité meant the number of hours each week during which each staff member was available for work.

I drew in a deep breath, wished myself luck, and said, 'I think that if you could guarantee an hour's minimum lunch break, to include a maximum of twenty minutes travelling, they might drop the travel money claim altogether.'

Madame Suger's neatly plucked eyebrows moved expressively upward. 'Guarantee, no,' she said. 'That would be impossible. But perhaps we could undertake to make every effort to ensure that the condition were met.'

I came back. 'That would only be acceptable if you were prepared to back it up with a penalty payment – say one hour's pay – on the rare occasions when the condition could not be met.'

'Then could you guarantee five additional hours' *disponibilité*?' Madame Suger asked.

'Five?' I said.

Madame's head shook, and her earrings swung a bit. 'Too much. Two.'

'Not enough.'

I thought of Ian. I wanted him to be proud of me. I took another deep breath, crossed my fingers under the table, and went on. 'Remember,' I warned, 'I'm going to have a hard time getting them to drop the travel question.'

Madame Suger and Rebecca exchanged glances. 'Two and a half, then,' said Madame Suger, probably not enjoying, in her own office, a sensation she might previously only have experienced when shopping on holiday in Morocco. Sarah and I nodded to each other and the meeting was over, the deal done.

Sarah and I walked out into the corridor together. I had the feeling she was torn between feeling angry with me and being impressed. I sensed her trying to steer between the two. 'You might have told me what you were going to do,' she said once we were outside. 'We're supposed to be a team. How can anyone work with you when you go off at a tangent like that?'

'I didn't know,' I said, 'until the moment came, and then it was too late to check with you. Anyway, it worked, didn't it?'

Sarah had to admit that it had.

I said, 'Anyway, I've always suspected you had psychic powers. Thought perhaps you'd know what was going to happen in advance anyway.'

Sarah shot me a sideways glance. 'Whatever gave you that idea?'

'Only joking,' I said.

Sarah decided to be emollient. Perhaps she was beginning to like me. 'Anyway, I'm pleased with the result. You seem quite clever after all. But for God's sake don't tell any of the others what you did. Otherwise they really will ask for travel money and who knows what else besides. You'll have made a bed of nails for us both.'

I looked at her. The idea of a shared bed of nails did not appeal. We went for a coffee instead.

When we'd sat down with an espresso in front of each of us Sarah fired her bolt. She peered at me narrowly and said, 'I do know what that little exhibition of bravado was all about. We're lucky there's a young man in your life you're trying to impress.'

'Bloody hell!' I said, extremely startled. 'How do you know it's a man and not a woman?'

'I just know,' she said. 'Are we likely to meet him any time soon?'

'He's coming over from London at the weekend,' I said, and I heard my voice go bashful and quiet.

Sarah gave me a wonderful smile at that point. 'I think that's just great,' she said.

Chapter 23

A letter arrived from Jean-Charles. I'd written to him as soon as I'd arrived in Paris, to give him my new address. His reply, written in an astonishing copper-plate hand, filled, though on one side of the paper only, six sheets. I was touched and flattered by its length.

He told me that the weather was still holding up in Provence. Though we were in late September now it was still hot down in the south. It wasn't that cold in Paris actually, but I still envied him that extra bit of heat. Then he got down to the important part.

After I had left his house that Sunday Raoul had stayed with him. Jean-Charles hadn't felt able to turn him out, although Raoul had insisted, in writing, that he was more than prepared to leave, as he didn't want to cause any problems between Jean-Charles and his parents.

I was bolstered by Raoul's presence in the house, Jean-Charles wrote. *He gave me strength. Though as the day wore on I became so frightened about what was going to happen I thought I was going to be sick. I felt as ill and as near to dying as you do when you've eaten a bad oyster.* That was a very French comparison, I thought. I who had never eaten an oyster, not even a good one.

Then my parents arrived in the evening. I was suddenly calm and in control. I said I had a friend over, and could he stay the night? I presented Raoul to my parents, explaining that he couldn't speak. I told them he was a talented painter, and got him to show my parents his sketch book. They said, of course he could stay the night. They talked about getting a room ready. That was when I knew I had to do it. I took a deep breath, then told them that he had stayed with me the previous night, and that he'd shared my room. (I didn't say 'my bed'. They knew there was only one bed in the room. I didn't

536

need to spell it out.) I said I wanted to do the same tonight.

My parents looked as shocked as if I'd hit them both with a hammer. My mother recovered first. If that's what you both want, she said – and she looked very closely at Raoul's face as she said the word 'both' – it's all right by us.

Jean-Charles's letter went on a bit after that. The main thing was that Raoul was now a fixture in the house. His parents were a bit uncomfortable about telling friends and family about the new arrangement and what it clearly implied about the sexual orientation of their only son, but, as he said, one things at a time. *Une chose à la fois.*

I wrote a long letter back to Jean-Charles, getting a lot off my chest about Ian and the way I felt. I told him Ian was coming to Paris at the weekend. I could feel my own excitement in my chest as I wrote that.

I travelled out to Roissy Charles de Gaulle on the RER. I actually saw the British Airways flight come in. It was just a speck in the sky at first. It seemed a very fragile, small thing. It made my mind boggle to think that this dot could contain something as solid and real, something so massively important, as the idea and physicality of Ian.

I saw him before he saw me. The door out from the customs control area was constantly opening and shutting, and gave a blinking view of the stream of people making their way out of the nowhere land of airport-airside and onto the solid territory of France. Ian was in the middle of that stream when I glimpsed him, backpack on shoulders and – the thought nearly made me cry – making his way towards … me.

We hugged. That is, he hugged me and I hugged his backpack. Our cheeks brushed but we didn't kiss. We talked about his flight, and about our imminent journey into the centre of Paris.

I showed him how to buy Métro tickets from the machine. He insisted on paying for them himself. I let him do that. I'd paid for his flight. He needed to reassert his independence, at least a little bit.

The RER took us to the Gare du Nord, from where we'd take the slow, stopping Métro line to Place Blanche. At least in principle. Our RER stopped at a signal in the tunnel, though, and we waited half an hour. At last the driver opened the doors and announced that we were within easy walking distance of the Gare du Nord. Though if we took the opportunity to jump down onto the trackside and make our way along it, it would be at our own risk. Ian and I looked at each other, exchanged a smile, and jumped. So did nearly everyone else.

This wouldn't have been possible on the regular Métro or the London Underground: the tunnels are too narrow and the sides of the trains nearly brush the walls. But the tunnel we were in was a wide one. There was a two-metre width of ballast to walk on between the tunnel wall and the train. Once we were in front of our halted train the Gare du Nord appeared in front of us just a couple of hundred metres ahead. It appeared as a brilliantly lit archway towards which we made our way, a hundred or more silhouetted figures, in the dark.

I took the risk of putting my hand on the back of Ian's neck for a moment. 'I'm glad you've come,' I said.

His voice came back to me from his own little bit of darkness. 'I'm glad I'm here,' it said. Together we progressed through the darkness and into the light.

I took Ian to a restaurant I knew in the Marais. It was a favourite of Malcolm's friends Peter and Fabrice. They weren't there that evening. On balance I was glad of that. For the moment I needed some time with Ian alone.

Opposite me at a small wooden table, his face looked bewitching in the candle-light. I even liked watching him eat, which is probably a sign of being in love. The French language calls jaws *machoires*, which means mashers, and is pretty exact and blunt. In general, watching other people using them is not a pretty sight. We had steak that evening, and I even enjoyed the sight of him munching that.

I asked him what he'd like to see the next day, thinking he might say Notre Dame, the Eiffel Tower, or Montmartre. His answer surprised me. 'I'd like to go to Auvers,' he said. 'I've been reading up about Van Gogh.' Auvers, a little way outside Paris, was where Van Gogh ended his days, living first at Doctor Gachet's house, then at the Auberge Ravoux. Auvers was where his last canvasses were painted and where, in the wheat-field that was the subject of his final painting, he took his own life.

'Then that's where we'll go,' I said.

Bedtime came. I only had the one room, with one single bed in it. I made up a sleeping place for Ian. Cushions on the floor. A sheet and blankets. He gave no indication, either in speech or in body language, that he'd prefer to join me in the single bed, and I didn't suggest it. But I did do one thing. I asked him, 'Can I kiss you goodnight?'

'Of course,' he said, and smiled. Then he leant towards me, put an arm around my shoulder, I put one of mine around his shoulder, and we very briefly kissed. He gave me his lips though, for that brief moment, not his cheek. Even that was more than I'd dared to hope. We got into our separate beds, I put the light out, and we said goodnight.

In the morning it was raining. We didn't care. We had coffee and croissants on the pavement opposite the Moulin Rouge's stage door. We were sheltered under the café's awning, and watched the rain dripping off the edge of it, while we stayed in the dry. 'We're like birds sheltering from the rain under the big leaves of a tree,' Ian said. It was the first time he'd referred to us by using the word *we*.

We took the bus to the Gare du Nord. Ian would only be in Paris for a couple of days, and it seemed wasteful of that time to spend too much of it looking at the tunnel walls of the Métro. The bus took us through the colourful street markets of Barbès-Rochechouart – a place I'd only recently learnt how to pronounce. It was an immigrant area. It looked more like Tangier than Paris. Ian had been to Paris before, but he'd never seen this side of it.

Then we were on the train, nosing out of the city, through suburbs and into the countryside. Ian looked around the carriage at one point and, I think, took a guess that no-one near us would understand English. Then he popped his big question. 'How did you find out you were gay?' he asked.

I said, 'It's all tied up with Van Gogh, curiously enough.' Ian smiled at that. 'I didn't think, when I went down to Provence, following in Vincent's footsteps with Malcolm, that I'd gone to find myself. But apparently I had.' I looked sideways at Ian. A bit cautiously I added, 'It also had something to do with you, I think.' He made a little movement beside me, but he didn't speak. 'I met Jean-Charles, as you know. He showed me the photograph of you that he'd taken. A week later I left London again and went back. Jean-Charles was surprised to see me again so soon, but pleased. We talked about you, inevitably. Then one thing led to another. We spent an evening together. We went back to his place. We had sex...'

'I rather guessed that was how it was,' Ian said, deadpan. Then, still deadpan, 'I had sex with Jean-Charles too.'

'Somehow I'm not surprised to hear that either,' I said. Neither of us probed for details about the sex we'd had with Jean-Charles: the where and how and what of it. If we wanted to discuss that at some future date, all well and good. If not, well, that was fine too. For now we let the matter drop.

We arrived at Auvers, and it was still raining.

We walked the streets of the little town under the rain. We had no umbrella with us. There hadn't been much rain since I'd arrived in Paris and I hadn't thought of getting one yet. Nor had Ian thought to bring one with him from London. He was a nineteen-year-old, and, thank God, nineteen-year-olds don't do things like that.

Again I had the spooky sense of walking into one Van Gogh canvas after another. Here was that familiar row of cottages, there was that unique church. Opposite the church was the small walled cemetery in which Vincent's simple grave and that of his brother Theo lay side by side. A neatly trimmed growth of ivy covered them both, uniting the two brothers as they slept. There was another thing about the ivy. It had been planted as a cutting from the garden of Doctor Gachet. Doctor Gachet who had befriended Vincent. Doctor Gachet whom Vincent had painted – he'd painted his garden too. Doctor Gachet who had dressed his wounds after he had shot himself.

We went into the Auberge Ravoux, where Vincent had lived out his final months. Here he had breathed his last in his room upstairs on July 29th in 1890. Ian did a quick calculation. 'Ninety-nine years and two months ago to the day,' he said. It was not the most exact of anniversaries.

It was barely noon but we drank a toast to Vincent's memory. In Pastis. Which Ian had never tried before. We watched the clear liquid turn milky as the ice and water were added to it. Vincent would have sat here drinking Absinthe, but you couldn't get that now. Pastis tastes much the same as Absinthe anyway. We chinked our glasses, said, 'Here's to Vincent,' and made do with the drink we'd got.

One beer and one French hot-dog later we climbed the lane out of the village, past the church again and onto the lonely plateau where in summer, wheat-fields waved. There was no wheat now but fields of maize that whimpered under the rain's assault. It rains cords, they say in France but up on that desolate hill that day it rained like ropes that slanted from a predatory sky. Below us the village lay, a blur of blue, while the yellow-grey maize fields stretched towards Paris, not far off but unseen. Crows, unaware of the fame of their forbears, started out of the crop at our approach and it was then, there, that I caught hold of Ian's head, his soaked hair, and pulled him towards me. He didn't resist. I felt his rain-sopped face against mine and kissed it. He kissed me back. Then, in that place of portent, among the waving corn, the rain, the crows, we embraced tightly, fiercely, and kissed each other properly for the first time, realising in that moment what we had both wanted, without always knowing it, all along.

Chapter 24

We didn't talk much on the journey back down the hill, or even on the train back into Paris. We both had too much going on inside us, and although wonderful, it was all too complicated to be put into words so soon. The rain had just about stopped by the time we got to Paris, but we were still wet through and through. Our clothes, our hair...

As soon as we got back to my studio we took a shower. We took a shower. A Tardis of a phrase, that, with an awful lot going on inside it.

The shower in my small studio was in a recess in the kitchen, which was screened by a semi-opaque plastic curtain like the famous one in the Bates Motel in Psycho. It didn't do a fantastic job of keeping the water in its place. If I was at all energetic in my showering there would be water all across the kitchen floor. But there wasn't a bath-tub, or even a proper wash-basin. I'd got used to taking showers daily, and every day then mopping up the floor.

We undressed together. Last night we'd done this before going to bed, but done it back to back, the way straight friends usually do. This afternoon – as St Paul said in another context – we saw face to face. I'd seen Ian naked once before, when he'd jumped into the River Wear that time when we'd been out for a walk three or four years ago. And I'd seen that picture of him in the basement gallery in Arles. But this was Ian's first glance at the naked me.

What do you look at first when presented with a naked man? It makes no difference whether you're gay or straight. The answer's obvious. And so it was with us. Ian's dick was so shrunk by the rain that it looked as if it belonged to a much younger boy. It was nothing like it had looked in that magical photograph. I laughed and told him so. He grinned back at me. 'Then take a look at yours,' he said. 'Yours has shrunk to nothing too.' He paused and added mischievously, 'Unless it's always like that, of course.'

'Be off with you,' I said. 'Get in that shower.'

'And leave you shivering and wet while you wait?' he said. 'No way. You're coming in with me too.'

And so I did.

It was a tiny, cramped and inconvenient space. All the better for that, perhaps. We soaped each other down, of course. And watched each other's dick grow from strength to length.

Watching was not enough for us, it turned out. I took Ian's water-lashed cock in my hand, thinking how incredible this was, remembering I'd known him since he was an obstreperous school-kid, and slid his foreskin back and began to jack the shaft. He did the same with mine. I mentioned energetic showering. But that shower cubicle, at least since I'd been in the apartment, had seen nothing like this. The kitchen floor, invisible beyond the Psycho curtain, must, I thought, by now be inches deep.

We came quickly, almost simultaneously. Our semen joined with the warm rain of the shower that poured over us and turned it milky for an instant and then another and another one, until we'd emptied out. Some of the mixture ended on the kitchen floor, no doubt.

We turned the water off, then kissed and cuddled briefly – though for no longer than a second – and then got out. We towelled each other and put clean dry clothes on. I lent Ian a pair of jeans. They were ever so slightly short on him, but not so much that anyone would notice. He still looked all right.

Ian volunteered to mop the kitchen floor. I let him do it while I watched. 'Things I hadn't envisaged this time yesterday,' he said. 'Me in your kitchen, mopping up a load of water along with our combined spunk.'

Ian had always had a way with words. I may not have mentioned that.

We'd been invited to dinner with Malcolm and Henri. We climbed the steep incline of the rue Lepic. It wasn't till we were all together, the four of us, that I realised what a symmetrical pair of couples we were, though now it hit all of us. There were Malcolm and I, both twenty-eight, and Henri and Ian, both nineteen. The two youngsters took to each other at once, and I was pleased – and I could see that Malcolm was also pleased – about that.

Ian was as startled and delighted by the walls of Van Gogh pictures as I'd been on my first visit. He was quickly in earnest conversation about them with Henri in a mixture of English and French. Halting French in Ian's case. While they were engrossed in that, Malcolm said to me, 'I get the impression there have been developments since yesterday. Am I right?'

'We went to Auvers together,' I said. 'On the Van Gogh trail, of course. We got very wet in the rain, so when we came back we had to take a shower together...'

'Got you,' said Malcolm, and grinned at me impishly. 'Enough said.'

There was smoked mackerel pâté with a fresh baguette. Then a casserole of guinea-fowl with mushrooms, onions and grapes. Brie and reblochon cheeses followed that. There were fresh peaches for those who still had room for them. To our surprise we found we all did. We sat up drinking in the salon till it was quite late. None of us were drunk, though a feeling of well-being suffused us all, for which the alcohol we were imbibing was at least a little bit to thank.

Ian and I took our leave around midnight and strolled back down the hill in the surprisingly warm dark. The cafés were closed now, except for the one or two big brash brasseries on Place Blanche. I toyed with the idea of taking Ian into one for a post-nightcap nightcap but in the end I did not. It would only have delayed the inevitable: delayed the moment when we found ourselves together in my bedroom. That paradoxically difficult moment for every new couple that have walked the earth. I imagine that even for Adam and Eve there must have been a moment like this. As I let us into the immeuble's big courtyard and then through the inner door and up the stairs I found I felt shy and nervous. Like a teenager. I guessed that Ian, who still was a teenager, must have been feeling the same thing but even worse.

Inside the studio I put the light on. It glared at us. Very gently we drew close to each other and, standing, started to kiss.

After a minute we slid apart again. 'Would you like a nightcap of any sort?' I asked.

'A glass of water would be nice,' Ian said.

'For me too,' I said. I was actually relieved by Ian's choice. Glad that I hadn't hit on – or been hit on by – a drunk.

We drank our water unceremoniously, standing by the kitchen sink. Then we went and sank together onto the bed. We started to fumble with each other's clothes.

'Thank you so much for coming to Paris,' I mumbled.

'Thank you for taking me to Auvers,' Ian said.

'And for everything that happened there,' I said.

'And everything that's happened since.'

'The shower was nice,' I said.

'And your friends are nice,' Ian said.

'I know,' I said. What else did one say at times like this? Then suddenly I found it coming out. 'Oh God,' I said. 'I'd better say this, and on my own head be the consequences. I think… No, not I think. Ian, I love you. It's as simple as… Oh shit!' I said. 'I didn't mean to say that.' I heard my voice buckle, then break, as those last words came out.

'Didn't mean to say it, or didn't mean it?' Ian asked. For a moment he was nine years my senior, not the other way round. 'Remember, I once said that to you...?'

'I'd hardly forget it...' I said.

'And I've been asking myself that question for the last two years,' Ian said, as much to himself as to me. 'What did I say? What did I mean? What part of it do I regret?'

I could hear his voice also now grow fragile. I realised he was starting to get upset. I said, 'Don't regret anything, Ian. Something started then, two years ago, that neither of us was ready for. No regrets. Maybe we're ready for something now. Maybe still not yet. Let things take their course. We've all the time in the world ahead of us. There's no rush.'

He didn't answer. Not in words at least. He nuzzled his head in between my chin and collar-bone as if had become a violin suddenly, and needed me to coax the music out. I stroked his hair. My hand the bow, his scalp the strings and fingerboard. 'OK,' I said. 'Let me be brave and stupid. I'll say it now and mean it. You don't have to say it back. I love you, Ian. I love you with all my heart.'

He started crying then. I felt his hot tears fall and run between my shirt collar and my chest. His whole body heaved and shook. He made no effort to change his position but just slumped on top of me. I stroked him, rocked him, held him till the tears and heaving stopped. Then my collar-bone picked up the vibration of his whisper. It came to me through the bones that were his bones and my bones, not through the air between us. *'I love you, David.'* And it was my turn to weep.

Sunday. Bloody Sunday. The day that shows you the seeds of its own destruction the moment you wake up.

I woke up in a single bed with Ian. His sleeping head was on the pillow beside me. I knew that I wanted to wake up and find it there every morning for the rest of my bloody life. Not just his head, though. I wanted his warm soft nakedness against mine. I wanted that smell of him I'd hardly known before last night. I wanted that proximity. I wanted that cock. Wanted those bollocks. I reached for them now. The bollocks were small and tight, the cock hard, hot and stiff. I had all those things now. Had them now but not tomorrow. Tonight Ian would fly back to England, the little tail-light of his aeroplane disappearing over the northern outskirts of Paris into the dark.

I had to wake him up. 'What are we going to do today?' I said.

He looked at me the way a puppy looks at you when it has just woken up. 'I don't know,' he said. 'But I know what we're going to do first.' I felt his hand come round my morning-sized dick. And so we tussled playfully beneath the duvet, and stroked each other's penis until, as we'd done in the same way twice before going to sleep last night, we brought each other off.

The sun shone from a canopy of unblemished blue. Paris sparkled clean after its yesterday's rain wash. We took the bus down to the river. We explored the Ile de St Louis and the Quartier Latin. We examined the water-colours that hung along the Pont des Arts. The day sparkled too, unblemished like the streets and sky. Yet it was an unexploded time-bomb. With Ian's departure a few hours from now my new world would end. The knowledge that we'd someday soon be able to construct it anew did not help at all.

We lunched expensively beside the Seine on a corner of the Place St Michel, watching the water running past, between us and the towers of Notre Dame. The water running past… We might as well have had an hour-glass on the table in front of us! We stroked each other's knees under the table. It was the best, in the circumstances, that we could do.

We had to change those circumstances. Short of my kidnapping Ian and keeping him here in Paris, not letting him return to university, there was only one thing we could do, and so we did that. We took the bus back to Place Blanche, went up to my studio, then took our clothes off and got into bed for two hours. We stroked each other to orgasm once during that time, but we both knew that wasn't the main thing.

'Don't come with me to the airport,' Ian said. 'I don't think I could cope with that.'

'I won't be able to cope with it either,' I said. 'But I'm coming anyway. I can't not do. Sorry but there it is. Not to come would mean parting with you a whole hour earlier than I need.' It was going to be bad enough whatever we decided to do.

We hardly spoke on the RER. Whatever was there to say? We parted at the departure gate. We kissed modestly. We were in a public space, after all. We stood tall and looked each other in the eye. 'I love you, David,' Ian said.

I said, 'I love you, Ian.' I added, 'Come again very soon. You have to. I can't survive without you for very long.'

His eyes dropped away from mine. I saw only his long lashes as he said, 'Nor can I.' Then he beamed back up at me again. We smiled courageously. Neither of us was crying. He turned smartly away, and so did I.

I lingered in the terminal. I know I shouldn't have. I toyed with a coffee, then I had a beer. I watched the board. Saw his flight called. Go to gate. Boarding. *Dernier appel:* last call. When the time came I walked out of the building. I went to the place where the buses pull up and walked from there across some waste ground towards a distant fence. From here, through a gap between buildings, closed only by the high security mesh fence, I could see the runway.

After a few minutes I saw the British Airways 757 taxi out from the floodlit apron area and away across the dark field. Eventually it was just a pattern of lights among other patterns of lights, a mile away. It slowed, then turned and stopped. It seemed to wait an age, but at last it moved. The lights began to gather speed. Detached themselves from the other lights and rose into the air. The lights flashed in a complicated sequence that was impossible to fathom. They grew closer together, fainter, till they merged. At last the plane was a mere pinprick in the sky. I strained my eyes to follow it. Eventually the night's giant hand snuffed the light out – snuffed Ian out as if he'd been a candle flame.

I broke up then. I banged the palms of both hands against the mesh of the security fence till it rang with the noise of a dozen cash-registers. Grief and rage coursed through my veins and my whole being shook. There was no-one near enough to see me. But even people hundreds of yards away would have heard me. They would have wondered what pain on earth was causing a grown man to bang on an airport perimeter fence, howling like a wolf against the night, raging against the dark.

Chapter 25

My success in extracting Madame Suger's reluctant concession over lunch breaks proved a mixed blessing. As far as I was concerned the most important thing to come out of it was the wide-eyed admiration of Ian when I told him about my unexpected success as a negotiator during that weekend. It was vain and foolish of me, I suppose, but I had put myself into that gladiatorial situation principally because – as Sarah had rightly surmised – I wanted Ian to be impressed, and to have some reason to look up to me. It was inevitable, I suppose, given that I was the older one. The trump cards of youth and beauty were in his hand, after all.

And also I had won much respect from my colleagues and found I'd considerably enhanced my standing in their eyes. The problem was that their expectations of me and the office of *délégué du personnel* were growing in proportion. Every other day now I found it necessary to work with Sarah on some carefully formulated letter or other, either to ask for clarification of management policies or else to make the inevitable demands for improved conditions. Mostly these skirmishes were no more than volleys of paper exchanged by Sarah's portable typewriter and Madame Suger's Goliath of a computer. But from time to time matters needed to be thrashed out at Madame's round table and these sessions involved careful thought and preparation: so much so that Sarah and I found ourselves spending almost as much time preparing negotiations for which we were not paid as the classes for which we were.

Malcolm thought that was a good thing, though. 'Keeps you busy,' he said in a spirit of tough love. 'Doesn't give you time to pine and mope.' He had seen how distraught I'd been following Ian's departure that Sunday night. Even though, with regular phone-calls in the days that followed, my pain – and Ian's – had been assuaged somewhat.

And in the end the results of my efforts and Sarah's seemed to make them worthwhile. I learned to be more disciplined in planning my strategies, going through all the probable moves and counter-moves with Sarah in advance. We successfully persuaded Madame Suger and Rebecca to institute a stand-by system of replacement for absentee teachers; this meant the end of the 'dawn raid' telephone calls from Rebecca from which we'd all suffered in the past. We also managed to elicit extra payments for preparation for classes with specialised needs. 'They want a lesson on the vocabulary of hedge funds,' one agonized teacher had complained the week before. 'You might spend a week looking for a book that dealt with that in English here in Paris.'

Madame Suger had seen the point in the course of an energetic discussion.

Another argument was over cancelled classes. Normally, if a teacher turned up for a class but the student did not, the teacher was paid and the school sent out its usual bill. But if notice to cancel was received forty-eight hours ahead the lesson was not billed and the teacher, who had not had to prepare or turn up, went unpaid. Occasionally though, the system failed and a teacher did not hear of a cancellation before arriving for a non-existent lesson.

'Teachers are always informed of cancellations by phone,' Madame Suger pointed out.

'Huck doesn't have a phone,' said Sarah. 'He came in twice last week for nothing.'

'If he doesn't think it worth his while to have one installed that isn't our problem,' said Rebecca. 'He could always get one of those mobile things.'

I pointed out that if all the teachers stopped answering their phones during the daytime for an indefinite period then Rebecca and Madame Suger would have a problem. It took only a few more minutes to come to a more satisfactory arrangement.

'What do you think's happened, David?' George greeted me on my arrival at work one day during the second week after Ian's visit. My heart sank. George only ever purveyed bad news.

'I've no idea, George,' I said wearily. 'They're selling Notre Dame to the States?'

'Very funny. This is serious. They've sacked Huck.'

I had to agree with George. That was serious. 'But why?'

'He didn't show yesterday.' Yesterday there had been a strike on the Métro.

'Lots of people didn't turn up yesterday. People who live out in the sticks. *Banlieusards* ... They're not going to sack everyone, are they?'

'Huck lives in the centre, less than an hour's walk.'

'Cecile lives less than half an hour's walk away. Are they sacking her too?'

'Course not. She's five months pregnant. You don't sack people for being pregnant. Not these days.'

'You're telling me they've sacked Huck because he has Aids?'

'Point of information. He's HIV positive; he does not have Aids. But you're about right. They say he's not physically fit for work. Because he can't walk four miles morning and evening?! Bullshit! It's a pretext, that's all. He's employed as a language teacher, not a goddam football coach. Fact is, they just don't want him around.'

'So what now, George? A worldwide strike of language teachers?' Two weeks before, I wouldn't have dared to speak to him like that.

'OK, OK. But somebody ought to do something. Or do you not agree?'

'Of course I agree. Only I don't happen to have any suggestions just at present. On the other hand I have got a stack of photocopying to do before eight thirty. That gives me ... seven minutes exactly. Can we talk about it at lunchtime? Where is Huck, by the way? Is he in?'

'No. They told him not to bother coming back. He phoned and told me. He only had the phone put in last week. Damn all good it's done him. And there's no rush for the photocopier, by the way. There's a notice on it: *Encore en panne.*' (Out of order again.)

'Merde,' I said. No translation required, I think.

Malcolm collared me during the coffee break. 'Have you heard?'

'About Huck? Yes.'

'What are you thinking of doing?'

'Me? What are you thinking of doing?'

'I've no ideas, David. It's you who's the *délégué du personnel*, ace negotiator, tribune of the proles....'

'Plebs,' I said.

'Suit yourself. Look, I'm not trying to tell you your job. It's just that not only do you come up with the bright ideas but you manage to get things done around here which is somewhat rarer. I'm sure you'll come up with something effective.'

'Well, if flattery can be a spur to creative thinking, I'm sure I will.'

'Or even shall,' suggested Malcolm. I punched his shoulder in reply.

Owing to the indisposition of the photocopier, my class spent more time than usual that morning engaged in listening and writing tasks. It was during one of the latter that an idea came to me as I walked round the class, peering over my students' shoulders, suggesting here, correcting there. The students had been asked to compose a letter to a shop complaining about faulty goods. One of them had included the following: 'If you do not do nothing I would contact the press.'

'Belt and braces,' I said gently, pointing to the not and the nothing. 'One is enough. And use shall or will, not would. It's a real possibility so you want Conditional One, not Two.' But in my mind an idea was forming.

At lunchtime I made an appointment with Madame Suger's secretary to see the lady herself at three o'clock when, on this occasion, I would have finished teaching for the day. Until three weeks ago it had been possible to walk straight into Madame's office and beard her directly, but now the office space was so rearranged that I entered an outer office and was confronted immediately by the secretarial desk and the secretary behind it. Then there was a partition wall in which a closed door, exactly behind the secretary's back, led into the inner sanctum. This exercise in creative carpentry had been carried out at about the same time as Sarah and I became *délégués du personnel*. Whether there was any connection between the two developments I didn't presume to guess; the practical result was that, short of employing the most nakedly aggressive tactics, no-one could confront the President Director General without an appointment.

'And what can I do for you today, David?' Madame Suger motioned to me to sit down.

'I'm here on behalf of the staff,' I began.

'I didn't doubt it.'

'Sarah's working in company today. Otherwise she would be here too.'

'I didn't doubt that either.' She beamed and clasped her hands on the table in front of her. Gold bangles chimed like a tiny clock. 'Now tell me what is making you unhappy.'

I had rehearsed my part carefully, even trying over some of the phrases with a French colleague in the lunch break and polishing up on the use of the French subjunctive. I began, in brittle French, 'We are asking ourselves if the dismissal of Huck was not, perhaps, just a little hasty. We wondered if, in certain circumstances, it could not be reconsidered.'

Madame Suger leaned across the table. 'In what circumstances, for instance?'

'Perhaps it is for you, Madame, to suggest the circumstances.'

I was pretty sure that Madame Suger felt like kicking herself then. It showed in a slight hardening of her smile. She said: 'Unfortunately it is out of the question. We do not take the decision to dismiss a member of staff lightly or without long consideration.'

'I'm sure that's true,' I said. 'And that's why we beg you to make an exception in this case. Because, after all, you could not have considered for very long the fact that Huck was going to be absent from work yesterday. Not without a crystal ball at least.'

Madame Suger's smile was by now glacial. I thought of Ian, and the admiration I wanted to win from him. That gave me courage. I pressed my advantage home. 'Cecile hasn't been dismissed. Nor have Mike, Joanna, Clive, Richard or Duncan.'

'Huck was not dismissed for one day's absence from work. You know that very well.'

'Then you dismissed him because he has a non-notifiable medical condition. Is that it? Something which does not impair his teaching and which, as far as my experience goes, can not be transmitted in the course of normal classroom activities.'

Madame Suger was not amused. 'I consider his health renders him unfit for the stresses to which his work subjects him. Teaching is an arduous activity as you well know, David.'

'Have you had complaints about his classroom performance from the students?'

'Such matters are confidential; I'm not prepared to discuss them with you.'

I delivered the last of the grand, subjunctive-laden speeches I had rehearsed with my French colleague in the lunch break. 'We beg you, quite simply, to change your mind, that is all. For the sake of good staff relations and good morale. If you decided to reconsider it would not be judged a sign of infirm purpose but a gesture of humanity.'

Madame Suger got up from her chair and walked slowly over to the window in silence. The Eiffel Tower obtruded inappropriately on her reflection.

'No,' she said at last. 'I can't take him back. The situation would arise again one day. And if the clients became aware of his condition .... then that might create problems for all of us.'

I took a deep breath, thought of Ian, and reverted to English. 'In Britain there have been some similar cases recently that have reached the newspapers. The press has had a field day. It hasn't always been good publicity for the employers concerned.'

Madame Suger turned slowly round from the window and said, also in English: 'Are you threatening me, David?'

I paused for a moment before replying thoughtfully, 'Yes, I do believe I am.'

Madame Suger turned again and gazed at the Eiffel Tower as if to draw strength from its example of resistance to the pressure of the wind.

She said, 'For a cautious man like you, David, that would be an extraordinary tactic to adopt. Quite out of character.' She thought for a second. 'Though maybe not. I sometimes wonder about the nature of the men I employ here. And I wonder if you would all react in such an extreme way if Huck had been found to have cancer or multiple sclerosis. However, as your story about the British press goes to show, the Aids question provokes exceptional reactions in many quarters. I can not deny that. David, I will consider very carefully what you have told me. Very carefully indeed.' She turned and faced me once more, her features again composed in a smile, though this time the effort of it showed around the eyes. 'And now I am sorry but I have another appointment.'

A few minutes later I had to call on Rebecca to collect the file on a new group of students. 'I'm glad it's you who's teaching them,' Rebecca said as she handed over the information sheets. 'It's a new contract and I want to feel they're in safe hands.' Then her voice changed key, a habit it had; the effect was as startling as anything in Schubert. 'Remember that no-one is indispensable, David. Not even our best teachers. Not even me. It's just as well you're such an asset in the classroom.' Then she flashed me a smile that unexpectedly twinkled. I couldn't decide what was behind it: a feeling of having scored a point or one of covert admiration. Certainly Madame Suger had been quick off the mark with the internal phone.

'You're coming to dinner with us this evening,' Malcolm said when I met him in the café an hour later. We've got to call by the café' – he meant his local one in rue Lepic – 'to borrow some more cutlery. Huck's coming as well and we don't have enough knives and forks.'

'Huck coming to dinner? That's a bit of a first, isn't it?' Huck socialised little as far as I knew. Certainly I'd never found myself at the same dinner table as him. Meeting him today would be especially awkward. 'What's the occasion?'

Malcolm didn't answer that directly. 'It's a casserole of wild boar. Henri's in charge of the preparations, thank God. Listen, do you know they've reinstated him?'

'Henri?'

'Huck, dingbat. They rang him and told him it had all been a misunderstanding. He'll be back at work tomorrow. Don't know how you swung it but whatever you did it worked a treat. They're frothing mad with you down at the fun factory – so George said, anyway. Anyway, have a beer…'

Chapter 26

'That's brilliant,' Ian said, down the phone-line that evening, when I told him about my triumph. 'You're a star. And, hey, listen, there's another thing. I've got a few days clear at the end of next week. I could come over, if you liked.'

Yes, I liked. I more than liked. In my eagerness my thoughts jumped ahead. 'That's wonderful. Maybe ... just maybe, I could wangle a few days off myself and we could go somewhere. Provence, perhaps...'

'That would be fantastic...' Words like fantastic, wonderful and brilliant, plus a few exuberant swear-words made up the greater part of the rest of that conversation. I promised to see if I could get some time off, and we'd talk again next day.

'We all owe you,' Malcolm said, when I discussed the new possibility with him. 'If we all offer to do an extra couple of hours – I mean there's thirty of us – that'll have you more than covered, and they can't possibly say no. I'll have a word with everyone.'

And he did. Dear old Malcolm. And everybody said yes most willingly. Dear old everybody else. I got Rebecca's clearance to take four days' unpaid leave, two on either side of the following weekend.

It was like watching video on rewind. A star appeared in the east. It was dusk and the landing plane's light looked grand and bright. The light strengthened, wings and fuselage materialised behind it. They were the things that bore up, enwrapped, cocooned and held safe the most precious cargo on the planet. I found I could barely breathe until I'd seen the fragile container of my heart kiss the earth with a tiny magic puff of smoke.

I couldn't keep my hands off him when we met. And he couldn't keep his hands off me. We hugged and kissed so needily, so energetically, so fulsomely in the arrivals hall that people turned and looked. Even on the RER and the Métro we sat thigh pressed close against thigh, and stroked each other's leg-top for a second or two every time the people sitting opposite us looked away at anything else.

In bed that night we burrowed with our cocks between each other's legs. We didn't try to fuck each other. I hadn't found out yet if Ian wanted to do that. It didn't matter either way. Certainly not tonight.

In the morning we took the train to Avignon. I'd phoned Jean-Charles and told him of our plans. We wouldn't be asking for accommodation in his parents' house, I'd said. We'd find hotels on our travels. But we would want to meet up.

It was lovely to travel from the tepid autumn weather of Paris, as the minutes and hours passed, into the warmth and brightness of the south. Along the valley of the Rhone the grape harvest was still in progress. Bright-coloured tractors and harvesters roamed the vineyards, unscrewing – that's what it looked like – the black bunches from the vine-stocks and piling them into carts, where they glistened like caviar.

We had dinner that evening inside the antique shop where I'd first gone with Malcolm. Again there was just one dish on the menu. A rich stew of wild duck in red wine this time.

We walked back from there along the side of the stream that ran in a channel by the road. We could see the *lavoirs,* the stone slabs in the water on which, until not so long ago the inhabitants of Avignon had pounded their washing clothes with poles. I put an arm around Ian's shoulder. It was dark now, though still warm, and there were few people about. 'We've never fucked each other,' I said, bringing the subject up a bit abruptly. I'd let our beautiful surroundings do the soft talk.

'No,' Ian said. 'I have fucked boys in the past, though. And been fucked.' Then he wriggled slightly under my arm. 'Boys is an exaggeration. Just one boy in each case. The same boy in fact.'

'Much the same as me,' I said. I told him about the threesome I'd had with Jean-Charles and Raoul. I gave him all the details. I'd got the feeling that he wanted that, and it turned out that he did.

'That sounds good,' he said. 'Do you think, when we get there, we'll end up in a foursome at some point?'

I felt a frown pinching my face. 'Do we really want that? Now that we're a couple, and they're a couple...'

'No, perhaps not,' Ian said. Though he said it a bit reluctantly, I thought. As though I'd shamed him into saying it.

'Anyway, you've had sex with Jean-Charles.' And now I couldn't resist asking, 'Was he the guy who fucked you and who you fucked?'

'No,' Ian said. 'That was someone else. Tell you another time.'

'So with Jean-Charles...?' I prompted. We were both getting excited, I realised. Another minute and we'd want to get each other's dick out.

'I was larking about by the river with the two other guys I was on holiday with. We were all naked...' I told him I knew that bit.

'The others didn't want their photos taken. But they sat on a rock and watched while I posed for Jean-Charles. To make me laugh they started playing with their cocks. Seeing that made me get half hard, as you saw in the photo. They saw that, and it spurred them on a bit. The thing is...' He paused for a second as we continued to walk along the streamside. 'The thing is, even if you start playing with your dick as a joke, it pretty soon becomes more than that. Mine got fully hard after that and, not to be outdone by the others, I started playing with it.

'At that point Jean-Charles, the only one with shorts on, undid them and dropped them, showing us his own hard prick. By now we knew we were all going to go for it. Jean-Charles took his shorts right off, and stood there in just his socks and boots. We others had bare feet. We came close to one another, then standing in a circle by the edge of the river, all wanked – some of the time doing ourselves, sometimes reaching across and, well, you know…'

'Wow,' I said. I found myself picturing the scene only too easily. 'That's the bit J-C did *not* tell me.'

'The post-script to that,' Ian said, 'was that, although the three of us boys had never touched each other before or even thought about it, after that we all wanked each other when we went to bed – every night for the rest of the holiday. Not that the others were really gay. In their case it was just high spirits.'

'And was either of them the boy you first fucked with?' I couldn't resist that.

Ian giggled. 'No. I hadn't done that yet. That was much more recent.'

I decided to let it go at that. I wanted him there and then. In a doorway perhaps… We were passing a bar at that moment. It was brightly lit. There were no dark doorways in sight. I decided to be prudent. 'Why don't we go in and have a drink?'

It was a nice bar. Full of bare stone walls, a log fire, and atmosphere. We only stayed for one quick beer, though. We had other things to preoccupy our minds and hearts.

Back at our hotel we could hardly wait. All the way upstairs we were fondling and groping each other. Yes, we had been together in bed as recently as last night. But before last night it had been a fortnight, and we hadn't really caught up yet. We took our clothes off in a frenzy. I knelt at Ian's feet and started dementedly to pull on his cock with my mouth. He stopped me – pulled me off him by the hair on my head, almost. 'Shit, I'll come too soon,' he said.

I laid him on the bed, on his back, noticing approvingly the stiffness of his six-inch cock. And then I remembered something. My heart sank into my boots. 'I didn't bring condoms,' I said.

'I did,' said Ian, a little shyly. 'They're in my backpack.'

I laughed my relief. 'You little fox,' I said.

He wasn't as easy to enter as Raoul or Jean-Charles had been. He was less practised, of course. He'd only been done the once (same as me!) and I had to go slowly and gently, even with my modest-sized dick. (Though Ian was an inch or two taller than me, when it came to our dicks we were pretty much of a muchness, both as to girth and length.)

My patience was rewarded. He relaxed, and I massaged the inside of him gently with my penis, while his soft inner tubing slid my foreskin back and forth.

He came almost at once. I'd barely had time to feel for his penis before he clutched at it himself and tugged it briefly, immediately squirting white plumes of semen up his chest.

But that was all the stimulus I needed, apparently. I felt my own fountain rise within me and found myself starting to pound away at him in the manner of a much rougher-behaved chap. I only just had time to say, 'Are you all right with this?' before the time came when it made no difference whether he was or not. I felt myself empty out inside him in spurt after spurt.

I didn't pull out of him. Neither of us wanted that. We pulled the duvet up over us – a bit of a contortionist's trick, that was, in the circumstances – and dozed a little, while still plugged together by my slowly dwindling cock. We unplugged eventually in the small hours, and I took the condom off. Then we had to get up and piss, which we hadn't done before going to bed. We watched each other doing that with mild enjoyment and then, like good boys, cleaned our teeth. We slept cuddled closely together, then. Tummy pressed against tummy, and spent cock against spent cock. Throughout the night they both incontinently dripped.

In the morning we toured the Palace of the Popes. We saw the hall where Antipope Benedict XIII had held court, sitting between two roaring fires to ward off the ague that was spread by mosquito bites. I told Ian the story of the bites that Malcolm and I had suffered in Avignon back in the summer. 'Pope or Antipope,' I said. 'he has my sympathy on the mosquito front.'

We walked out to the garage on the ring-road, where Malcolm and I had got the clapped-out hire-car. 'I wondered,' I said when we go there, 'if you still have...'

They had. We rented it.

On the road to Arles I took advantage of that driving situation – the one in which you can't eyeball the other person, or be eyeballed back – to ask Ian a question. 'It's very easy to see why I'm crazy about you,' I said. 'You're nineteen and I'm twenty-eight. What I can't get my head round ... is that the reverse also seems to be the case. I mean I'm humbled by that and gobsmacked. But...'

Ian took his time about replying. At last he said, 'Complicated, that one. But isn't everything in life? You weren't gay when I first knew you. Now you are. I'm having a bit of difficulty getting my head round that one. Although it's very nice, of course... Me and you, though...'

I took one hand off the steering-wheel and rubbed his thigh with it. 'You and I,' I said. I'd been his English teacher once.

'I just looked up to you. Don't know why. I had lots of teachers. All facing up to us lot every morning. We were a rowdy lot. It must have been a brave thing for all of you to do, now I look back on it.'

'It was just a job,' I said.

'But you stuck me as the bravest of the lot of you. Funny... Don't know why I thought that.'

I said, 'Did you fancy other men in their early twenties when you were just fourteen?'

'A few, perhaps,' said Ian. 'Not many. None more than you.'

The rear-view mirror, which was anchored to the windscreen by a not very efficient suction pad, now took the opportunity to slide snail-wise down the glass. Ian captured it with a hand and stuck it back up.

'You were clever, brave and handsome,' Ian said. I was shocked, knocked for six, by that. I'd never thought of applying any of those adjectives to myself. Neither, until this moment, had anybody else.

'I'm duly humbled,' I said, and I meant it. 'From this moment on I'll try and live up to that.'

'Until forever?' Ian queried.

'Is forever what you'd like?' I asked.

'Yes,' he said.

I don't know why but I felt suddenly angry with him. I tried not to show it, but failed in the attempt 'You don't know that,' I said. 'You're just a kid.' I tried to soften it, but it was another failed attempt. 'King Lear, remember. *He's mad that trusts in the tameness of a wolf, a horse's health, a boy's love*...I'm twenty-eight. I can't help thinking that.'

He lost it and suddenly bawled his eyes out. I had to stop the car and sort him out. Sorting him out meant a kiss and cuddle and my saying sorry about a hundred times, with tears streaming down my cheeks as well as his. I hadn't expected this morning to be like this.

Jean-Charles had found us a cheap hotel neat the Place du Forum, and after we'd checked into it we met, the four of us, in the café there. The one that was painted by Van Gogh. 'It heightens the atmosphere a bit, doesn't it?' said Ian, looking about him as we sat on the terrace in the spilling yellow light. 'I mean, knowing that this was the very place.'

It also heightened the atmosphere to know that the last time Ian and Jean-Charles had said *au revoir* to each other they had just had sex. And that the same went for me and Jean-Charles, and Raoul as well. None of us mentioned any of that. In Raoul's case, of course, in order to comment he would have had to write a note on a piece of paper. He did not. He gave me a beautiful smile, which spoke volumes, instead.

We spent much of the weekend together. Ian and I, Raoul and Jean-Charles. I learnt that Raoul's paintings and sketches were beginning to sell. It helped that he now had an address and a phone number, even if he couldn't actually speak on the phone himself. It also helped that, with a roof over his head, he could keep his finished and unfinished canvasses dry. There was talk of his having an exhibition at the gallery within the next six months.

There were moments – I could feel them coming on, then feel us surfing through them – when the idea that the four of us might all get it together in bed seemed wonderful to all of us. Yet we didn't go down that road in the end. What happened in bed between Ian and me – yes, that is correct; trust me; I'm an English teacher – was in the end so much better than anything that might have happened among the four of us. I've no doubt the same went also for Jean-Charles and Raoul. And for Ian and me, at any rate, it seemed to get better every night.

We drove out along the flat roads of Provence, and across the hills. To Cavaillon, where the melons grow so quickly it's as if they're being inflated with bicycle pumps. We bought pink-fleshed juicy garlic from roadside stalls. We made love in the yellowing, brilliant fields, among vineyards where the leaves were turning to sunset-red.

In Arles itself we went into the Roman theatre, a rising ring of stone slabs. The acoustics here were fabulous. Ian sat in the stalls while I declaimed a part of *To be or not to be* under the vaulting blue sky. Then we changed places and Ian did...

I couldn't believe what I was hearing when he began it. King Lear's last speech. The speech that he hadn't been able to get through when he was a schoolboy. When I'd had to rescue him. That had begun our friendship... Broken my marriage. Brought us to where we were now...

'And my poor fool is hanged! No, no, no life!
Why should a dog, a horse, a rat, have life,
And thou no breath at all? Thou'lt come no more,
Never, never, never, never, never...'

I ran to him. He was so alone, standing on that vast stone stage beneath the infinite sky, an imaginary Cordelia dead and weighty in his arms. I wrapped him in my arms. 'Let it go,' I said. 'You've got me now. You always will.'

We stood there and held each other a long time. On that spot where Roman actors had said their pieces and brought tears to men's and women's eyes two millennia ago. We didn't cry noisily. Just as well, that was. I shudder to think what that amazing acoustic would have made of that.

The next day we retraced our steps to Paris. When you're a tourist the first sight of the Eiffel Tower from the train window, across the featureless suburbs, gladdens your expectant heart. When you live in Paris, though, it has the opposite effect. The first sight of the Eiffel Tower makes your stomach sink, as you think – Shit. Back to work.

Only it wasn't back to work this time in my case. When we got back into my studio and opened all those post-holiday envelopes that are mainly bills … I found there was one from Madame Suger. It told me in very elegant French, in a style that dripped with subjunctives, that I'd been sacked.

Chapter 27

Ian wanted to talk about Happy in bed that night. Perhaps that was simply because he'd talked about everything else. He'd exhausted the subject of the disappearance of my job in two short sentences. 'Good. That means you can come and live with me in London.'

'Believe it or not,' I said, 'that's what I wanted to hear you say before I came to work in Paris in the first place.'

'Sorry,' Ian said. 'I didn't know my own mind back then. I do now.'

'The tameness of a wolf,' I reminded him gently, *'a horse's health…'*

'A boy's love,' he finished. 'Mine's the exception. You can count on that.'

At that moment I began to believe he meant it.

'I may not be able to come to London at once,' I cautioned. 'A few things to sort out here first.' I felt him stir uneasily in my arms. We were well wrapped in the bed-clothes. It was a cold night in Paris. I relented. 'But we'll be together soon,' I said. 'You can count on that.'

He rewarded me with a squeeze in the dark. It was then that he brought up the subject of Happy. 'I'm sure he knew the boy who went to prison,' he said. 'The one who was being blackmailed. I'm sure they'd met.'

'You have a lively imagination,' I said. It wasn't the first time I'd told him that.

'That was what he was going to talk to you about that night…'

'That doesn't make me feel good,' I said. 'I didn't let him talk, remember. I had an essay to write.'

'That's hindsight,' Ian said. 'Nothing that happened, or may have happened, was any of your fault.'

'It's always nice to be told that nothing is one's own fault,' I said. 'But some things have to be. That's what growing up is about.' I pressed him to me then, and rocked him gently. 'Growing up is hard to do, my precious.'

He said, 'If I can do it with you I'll be all right.'

I kissed him. I said, 'It's time you went to sleep.'

Madame Suger's letter had told me that because of a downturn in the Institute's fortunes it would be necessary to make some redundancies. Last in first out... That meant me, evidently. I would be paid a month's salary in lieu of notice. I would only need to return to the Institute to empty my *casier*. Ian's flight wasn't till the evening. I went to the Institute in the morning, taking Ian with me. I had nothing to lose by that. It would be nice to show him off to my fellow staff.

They loved him, of course. Especially Sarah. 'I knew he'd be handsome,' she said. 'It was a feeling I kind of got.' She smiled at Ian approvingly. 'You must cherish David, Ian. He's good.' She turned back to me. 'There's something I ought to tell you. Huck's gone back home to America. He feels his condition's getting worse. He asked me to say goodbye from him – and a big thank you for what you did.'

Malcolm walked into the *salle des profs* at that moment with a thunder cloud of a face. 'I've just heard,' he said. 'I'm going to walk in to Madame Suger's office right away. There's going to be fireworks. We'll walk out, sit in, act up, you name it. You're going to be reinstated or there's going to be no more school left. Do you realise? After all you did for these guys they're not going to let you go under now.' He looked around the room and was rewarded by the sight of nodding heads. 'Madame Suger ought to be strung up!'

'Thank you,' I said. 'I wouldn't go overboard about the good I did for anybody. Huck's going back to America for one thing. So don't you go putting yourself out on a limb. I don't actually want to be reinstated as it happens. I'm going to join Ian in London.'

Ian, standing beside me, and momentarily tongue-tied, gave a little start. 'Really?' he asked. 'You mean that?'

'In a day or two,' I said. 'As soon as I've had time to pack my things and make arrangements about the flat.'

Malcolm looked astonished, though Sarah simply nodded. She seemed to know somehow that I'd want to do that.

Parting at the airport wasn't quite such a hardship this time, though it was still painful enough. I would be joining Ian in London two days from now. What I was going to do for a living I had no idea. But I would be living with Ian, sharing his bedroom, at his shared flat. That was the important bit.

I had dinner with Malcolm and Henri that night. They'd also invited their friends Peter and Fabrice.

Henri had done a starter of Puy lentils dressed with sweet peppers in olive oil, anchovies, lime zest and juice, which was followed by roast quail. I enjoyed it, but with a reservation. The reservation was that Ian wasn't there to enjoy it too. I knew I wouldn't enjoy anything properly until I was with him again. Our first meal together might be baked beans on toast or bread and cheese, but I looked forward to it already, as if it would be the greatest feast on earth.

Without Ian to share it with me I doubted if I would ever completely enjoy anything again.

But tonight's company was good. Fabrice and Peter were a couple in their late twenties, I guessed, and thought Fabrice was the older of the pair by a year or two. They'd been together about two years. In their company and that of Malcolm and Henri I was relaxed enough to wear my heart on my sleeve. 'I love Ian more than I've loved anyone before. And that includes my ex-wife. But in going back to London, jobless and penniless, throwing myself on him ... especially with the nine year age gap ... well, I just hope I'm doing the right thing.'

'There's nothing wrong with a nine-year age gap,' Malcolm said, and he and Henri exchanged a grin. 'You just have to remember that you'll have to make it up as you go along.'

'Every couple has to make it up as they go along,' Fabrice said, and Peter nodded his agreement. 'You won't be alone.'

Peter changed the subject suddenly. 'Have you ever heard Messien play?'

I had trouble with this. Mentally I tried to change gear. 'The composer? The one who transcribed all those bird songs?'

'I wouldn't say transcribed,' said Fabrice. 'It was more like he built great musical structure on the foundations their songs laid.'

'I see,' I said. 'But, heard him play...? No. Play what?'

Peter answered. 'He plays the organ in the church of La Trinité. Just behind where you live. You ought, before you leave.'

'We're going to hear him tomorrow,' said Fabrice. 'Want to come along?'

It was an extraordinary thing to find myself doing, on my last evening in Paris, my last evening before joining Ian in London - for good, I hoped, and certainly for better or worse. Attending an organ recital. It was a thing I'd never done before. And this one was being given by the greatest living French composer of classical music. Not just Petere and Fabrice were with me. Malcolm and Henri came too.

The sounds were beyond my comprehending. I knew nothing of musical structure or style. Ian, or maybe

Happy, might have understood. But the grandeur of the music, its yearning and its passion, engraved themselves on my heart. I thought of my uncertain future and the muddle of my past, and found them echoed in the harmonies the great composer - who sat playing just a little way from us - had found. I felt then, safe among my four friends, that Messien was unwittingly giving me a glimpse of my own soul. And deep inside I saw something else there: I saw the future of Ian, and I knew then beyond any doubt that it was my job to help him shape that. I had the awesome responsibility of helping my beautiful boy grow into the man he would become.

Tomorrow life would begin for Ian and me. The challenge of that thought was as big and awesome as the music that echoed around the lofty vaults of La Trinité. But so was the confidence that suddenly filled me now. I felt stronger than I'd ever done. And yet with all of that I felt my chest begin to heave quietly and my tears silently run. I wasn't the only person to feel that, apparently. From either side of me a hand came, one Fabrice's, the other Henri's, and at the same moment each of them quietly grasped mine.

Chapter 28

St-Rémy. Summer. 1999

The blackbird ceased his singing and dived into the darkness of the oleander bush in the corner of the garden

As a garden it was small but as a piece of luck it was considerable. It would have been impossible but for the shop-cum-gallery, of whose ground floor premises it formed a part. The flat upstairs would have entitled u only to the view of it: of the red brick wall along which fig trees sprawled and lizards lazed, of the improbably tall and scrawny yucca that skewered its way skyward and of the cypresses that shed shade and bred blackbirds.

An item in the newspaper I was scanning caught my attention. 'Messien has died,' I said.

'I never got to hear him,' Ian said. 'Pity. But you did.'

'Yes. With Peter and Fabrice. The day I stayed behind in Paris to pack my things after you'd flown back. The day before I joined you for keeps. It was … well, you know I'm not clever about twentieth century music. It was impressive.'

Ian was drafting a newspaper *annonce* for a new exhibition; it involved much crossing out, the knitting of his brow and the studious protrusion of his tongue from the corner of his mouth. He looked down again at his draft. 'Shall we say drinks are available, or is that asking for trouble?'

'I think people will assume that's the case anyway. No need to spell it out in neon letters.' I flicked a beetle from the newspaper. 'It says here they've found another gene.'

'Oh great!' said Ian. 'Like the gene that makes you gay. And the one that makes some people depressive. Soon they'll be able to have us all aborted before we can see the light of day. Think of all the adolescent angst that'll save. Down with diversity. *A mort la différence!* Though while they're at it, are they any nearer finding the gene that makes some people deny the truth of their own natures for up to twenty-eight years?'

'Ha-ha,' I said. That had been one of Ian's more irritating jibes at first. Now, after eight years, I hardly noticed when it was trotted out again from time to time. 'What time did they say they were arriving?'

'Malcolm and Henri? Between five and six, I imagine. They said they'd leave Monpelier after lunch.'

They lived in Monpelier now. Malcolm lectured at the university. Henri was marketing officer for the Hérault tourist board. 'They've come a long way,' I said.

'While we slog away selling artists' materials in the smallest specialist shop in Provence,' Ian said.

'You still don't mind?' I checked.

'Mind? In a place like St-Rémy?' Ian stopped. 'You always ask me that. I always give you the same answer. Pathetic, really.'

I smiled, mainly to myself. 'Hardly.'

'And tomorrow, what happens?' Ian asked.

'You're staying in to take a delivery in the morning,' I said firmly.

'Leaving you free to flirt with Henri.'

'No such luck with Malcolm about. And anyway, would I?'

Ian, who knew that I would, screwed up the sheet of paper he had been writing on and flung it at me by way of reply.

'Seriously,' I said, 'there are things to take care of. Noëlle isn't in tomorrow. And Malcolm and Henri will go off in the car, I guess. It's their holiday, not ours.'

Ian remembered something. 'There is another thing on tomorrow. Dinner with Jean-Charles and Raoul. The six of us.'

The blackbird reappeared from the bush and flew up into a cypress where he began a new, more solemn song, a lament perhaps for the dead composer who had once transcribed his wild music.

'You know,' said Ian, 'it didn't actually need Messiaen to write the blackbird's song down for the piano. Beethoven did it all in his third piano sonata.'

'You would say that, of course.'

'Of course,' said Ian. 'Did Happy never play it to you? The one in C.'

'Probably. You should know, anyway. You claim to know him better than I did.'

'Not literally. Mind you, we did live in the same town. Our paths may have crossed.'

'You were only eleven when he died. I didn't think even you were chasing older men at that age.'

'Don't be too sure. It has been known. But seriously, I do feel as though I knew him. We're so much a part of the same scheme of things. He had his picture of the night sky at St-Rémy; I have the real thing. He had a half-woken feeling for you while I... Well, there you go.' Ian broke off and gazed around the garden. 'I wish he could have come to St-Rémy and seen it for himself. He might have rediscovered himself – as a painter, I mean.' He looked straight at me, his head a little on one side. It was a look that I found irresistible; both of us knew it. 'Do you suppose,' he said, 'that we owe all this to him?'

'How do you mean?'

'That somehow we got here on his coat tails – because of his death?'

'That's morbid,' I said. 'Forget it.'

'I hope he's happy for us anyway.'

'And that's sentimental too, as well as being an unforgiveable *jeu de mots*.'

'Don't be so bloody English.'

'Then don't you go on maintaining the stupid fantasy that Happy was in love with me. You're as daft as Malcolm.'

'Just as well then isn't it? It took someone that daft to wait around long enough for you to make your mind up about who you were.'

'Waited around?' I objected. 'You were hardly unexplored territory by the time...'

'You know what I mean. Don't lower the tone.' Ian leaned back in his chair until it tipped right over. It was a party trick of his. He broke his fall with his hands at the last, precisely judged, moment and lay where he landed, draped across his fallen chair and moulded to its new contours as compliantly as if he had been a bundle of washing.

'You know,' he said, gazing up at the sky, 'I still sometimes try to imagine those last few minutes of Happy's. The ice still just thick enough in a few places. He steps onto it. Above his head the sky is a vortex of stars – like in Vincent's paintings, only this time it's for real. Everything is suddenly *en jeu*. You. The boy in the county court. (I'm still sure they'd met – to say the least; you'll say it's my tidy imagination.) Anyway, he looks down, and there is no ice any more, just a second infinity of stars, infinity multiplied by two. That is the last thing he sees. Then he takes his own place in the picture for ever.'

'You've too much imagination,' I said.

'And you've too little. You don't change.' Ian smiled at the sky. 'Mind you, I'm glad. Hey!' He got to his feet suddenly. 'I must go and get the baguettes before they run out. Do we need anything else?'

I said I thought not.

'By the way, Raoul sold another picture yesterday. One of his wheat-fields.'

'Good for him,' I said. 'Though I still can't see why people get so excited about his splodges. If he didn't label them wheat-fields nobody would guess. I liked his work better when he was doing his naturalistic stuff. When we first knew him. Still, I'm pleased he's making some money.'

'Maybe he's another fragment of whatever energy Happy left behind – the creative bit.'

'Oh cut it out. And anyway, Happy was a good draughtsman, not a splodger.' A memory stirred: Happy's history lecture notes, all composed of sketches of seals...

'So?' said Ian. 'You can never tell what people will turn into, given time and opportunity. Anyway, I'm off.' Ian went into the house. Seconds later I heard him leaving it by the other door into the street. I was left alone with the blackbird in the garden.

Five years in the south had tanned me deeply and any elfin quality I might have had was gone for ever. Ian, who boasted of what he called his 'nine years' juniority', still remained boyish in face and figure but we both knew that this could not last much longer; Provence's climate was hard on the complexion while its cuisine, though healthy, was not noted for its slimming properties. We both knew, and neither of us cared.

It had taken us a while to get to where we were. All those years ago, when I'd left Paris to join Ian in London, I'd found a job working in a pub. And there I'd stayed. We'd had a hard winter. Ian suffered some illness that left him barely able to walk for two months. He decided it was Aids, a legacy of an incautious university first year, but investigation proved it to be no more than an acute case of homesickness. He cured it by never returning home. For while Peter's parents had been discreetly tolerant of their son's surprising change of life style, Ian's were the kind that love too much, desiring all possible good for their son except that he might have a different way of being happy.

We'd stayed together. We'd stuck it out. Ian completed that second year of his at university and then his third. I continued to wait at restaurant tables and work in pubs. Then we'd migrated south. And things had gradually fallen into place. The gallery inside St Rémy's charmed plane tree circle, where Raoul could show his work. With Jean-Charles to manage it. The art shop in the same building... We'd pooled our resources, Jean-Charles and I, and bought the place. We made a living, the four of us. Just. Unlike Raoul or Van Gogh, Ian and I would have nothing in the way of art to leave behind us – for all the beauty of our dreams. All that we had, all our experience, all our past, was invested in the brief present: a time and place that history might prove would be no more than a small window in the weather. Still, it was ours, never to be torn from us: our own vision, like Vincent's, of the sun.

THE END

****

There are three more three-book collections of Gay Romance novels by Anthony McDonald. They are **Gay Travel Package, Gay Romance Christmas Hamper Vol 1**, and **Gay Romance Christmas Hamper Vol 2.**

About the Author

Anthony McDonald is the author of thirty-one books. He studied modern history at Durham University, then worked briefly as a musical instrument maker and as a farmhand before moving into the theatre, where he has worked in every capacity except director and electrician. He has also spent several years teaching English in Paris and London. He now lives in rural East Sussex.

Novels by Anthony McDonald

Gay Romance Series:

Sweet Nineteen
Gay Romance on Garda
Gay Romance in Majorca
Gay Tartan
Cocker and I
Cam Cox
The Paris Novel
The Van Gogh Window
Tibidabo
Spring Sonata
Touching Fifty
Romance on the Orient Express

———

And, writing as 'Adam Wye'

Boy Next Door
Love in Venice
Gay in Moscow

———

Other novels

TENERIFE
THE DOG IN THE CHAPEL
TOM & CHRISTOPHER AND THEIR KIND
DOG ROSES
THE RAVEN AND THE JACKDAW
SILVER CITY
IVOR'S GHOSTS
ADAM
BLUE SKY ADAM
GETTING ORLANDO
ORANGE BITTER, ORANGE SWEET
ALONG THE STARS
WOODCOCK FLIGHT

Short stories

MATCHES IN THE DARK:
13 Tales of Gay Men

———

Diary

RALPH: DIARY OF A GAY TEEN

Comedy

THE GULLIVER MOB

All titles are available as Kindle ebooks and as paperbacks from Amazon.

www.anthonymcdonald.co.uk

Printed in Great Britain
by Amazon